I0599844

The
Trouble
With
Trauma

A novel by JSR

It's September 11th, 2001. A gorgeous day in Manhattan.

FBI Agent Rebecca Taylor's grateful to be in the
field today; she's had it rough.
Long ago, she fumbled a kidnapping case…
she's been stuck behind a desk ever since.

But yesterday, another child went missing.
Witnesses spotted something—a connection to that same botched job.

Becca is tasked to track down this ghost from her past,
facing her fears and anxiety in the scariest place imaginable.
This is her chance to prove she's still the best in the Big Apple.

So why is she so afraid? Perhaps it's the way he murdered his victims…

Get going, Becca! It's a little after eight, and it's a *big* place to search.
…you wouldn't want to get trapped in there.
…not with a serial killer on the loose.

From the author:

Hello! I apologize for the delay. I know some of you want to jump right in. For those still here, I propose a question that I'm sure many of you might wish to ask me: "Why 9/11?" Well, there are a few reasons, but the most significant to me was this—9/11 scares the *shit* out of me.

I was seventeen that day. And, like so many others, it changed my life—but not in the way you'd expect. The day *of,* it felt so far away from me (I lived in Las Vegas at the time). I felt *awful* for them, but I was isolated from it... it didn't affect me *directly,* so it didn't hit me as hard. That is, until the next day, when I learned that my teacher was killed in Washington.

And ever since, it has *haunted* me.

The fragility of life hit me like a ton of bricks, and it changed me forever. I needed to exercise my *own* trauma, and create a gripping, yet *fictional,* story around it. Living vicariously through my own characters, I can experience the horror—and appease the curiosity—that has crippled me for twenty-four years. Truly powerful stuff.

But even more so, the survivors that witnessed it, the victims who had to make those extremely morbid choices, the strength they showed... the first responders that came from wherever they could to help, knowing full well what they were *willingly* running into... That was *non-fiction.* And the strength those men and women showed on that day is something you would describe as unbelievable, if it were a fictional story. Hollywood couldn't write drama that captivating.

Now *that*... that is truly powerful stuff.

I did my *best* to ensure that all characters directly based on (or representative of folks who were a part of) these events in real life are represented respectfully and accurately. Again, the events involving fictional characters in this story never actually happened, but I wanted this in the preface just to cover my bases. One thing I refused to do while researching this novel was to contact any survivors or first responders for their accounts. This *does* mean there might be minor inaccuracies in the condition of the North Tower on 9/11. However, I *did* research and read many survivors' firsthand recollections and accounts of the events. I have read much about the PTSD and trauma these brave men and women *suffered* through.

Because of the nature of the attacks, I was forced to take some liberties in how events might've occurred. I took great pains to ensure accuracy, but even with sources and survivor accounts, much information was still lost that day. Therefore, I want to state that the events in this novel are not intended to be historically accurate. This is a fictional retelling of how an escape *might* have played out.

To those that were not old enough to fully understand that day's horrors —*or* those that simply have a morbid curiosity, I invite you to come along with me, to experience *my* interpretation of what it might've been like... and not simply to *scare* or *thrill.* Rather, to appreciate how horrible it would've been for the many people who *were* there, and to live that experience vicariously, through Rebecca Taylor's eyes.

I dedicate this story to the thousands of innocent victims. The poor folks in New York City, the passengers and crew of the four hijacked flights, and those inside the Pentagon in Washington, D.C., who *never* got to go home that day. Their courage to face their fear in the shadow of Death's door inspires us to *never* forget.

I dedicate this story to the survivors and the families of survivors of September 11, 2001. For their strength to recover, move on with their lives, take care of their families, and persevere. That kind of resiliency is what *actually* makes Americans great and inspires us to *never* forget.

I dedicate this story to the firefighters, police officers, paramedics, search-and-rescue teams, engineers, tradesmen, first responders, and each and every person who selflessly and willingly went to battle for those who couldn't fight for themselves that day. All sacrificed some; some sacrificed it all. We will *NEVER* forget.

I dedicate this story to anybody that got sick, or had injuries or complications, due to their exposure to elements present at Ground Zero. The survivors had no choice but to face the risks that first responders *chose* to face... but *all* of whom did so with bravery and integrity, and they did the work they needed to do, and we will never forget.

Last—and *certainly* not least—I dedicate this story to Frau Barbara Edwards. You taught me German in high school. You were extraordinarily kind, and you cared deeply about all your students. I remember the lesson you taught me, the day you caught me cheating on that final in my freshman year, and the stern, yet compassionate and empathetic way you handled it changed me to the *core*. You didn't deserve your fate on American Flight 77, but I know you were brave that day. *Ich vermisse dich, und ich werde nie vergessen.*

(Sorry, I had to look that up. It's been twenty-four years, alright?)

At least as of today, the sun has never failed to rise.
No matter how dark it gets at times, remember
that light will never falter.
The sun will rise tomorrow, you can bank on it.

I

"A White Dodge Van"

"We are less than ten minutes away from the dawn of a new millennium, and here in Times Square, you can feel it in the air... there's a *buzz*, you—"

Shut up, Dick.

As Mr. Clark vanished into a narrowing beam of light, the relief of switching off the television gave way to anxiety as the room was enveloped in complete darkness. Becca felt exposed. The muted scream of silence embraced her eardrums with the gentle caress of a *bulldozer*. Swallowing the lump in her throat, she gripped her pistol tightly, thumbing the safety off.

It wasn't the *mansion* that frightened her, no. She'd dealt with the dankest hell-holes and roughest punks this side of Queens—compared to those places, this was the Ritz!

So why was Becca afraid? Perhaps it was the gruesome condition in which they found his victims? The press was having a field day with it, and the pressure continued to mount. Their investigation into this kidnapping had taken weeks, but a lucky break had finally led them to this house—a decrepit old mansion in suburban New Jersey.

Tonight, if all went well, they'd save the kid and have this clown behind bars before Corn Flakes.

Maybe it was because she was now alone? There was no sign of the suspect or the victim on the first floor, so her partner had broken away to investigate the guesthouse... She got stuck with the upstairs. *I didn't even get a chance to draw the short straw...*

She'd teamed with FBI Special Agent Jim Serrano after she graduated from Quantico in '93; ever since, the pair of them had the best track record in Manhattan. The pair had won scores of awards, including an Excellence in Investigation award they'd received for their efforts in 1998, during a robbery attempt at the World Trade Center.

Of course, if you asked Jim, they were 'doing the job'.

Probably because he's way better at the job than I am.

Yet, despite her experience, she was battling an insatiable urge to dash madly up the stairs and kick down every door, her gun at the ready. Of course, she knew this was a terrible idea; if not for her own sake, then certainly for the kid's.

No... she wasn't afraid for her safety; every agent knew the risks. Instead, she was worried she couldn't stop him. That was fear talking... *that* was foreign to her.

Her footsteps *tip-tapped* as they echoed off the marble of the 2nd floor landing. Despite the frigid weather that enveloped the mansion, her Smith & Wesson felt slippery in her palms; a sweat-soaked lock of her bangs drooped in front of her eyes. Becca shook her head in a vain effort to move it. She usually kept her brunette hair tied neatly in a ponytail, but while undercover, she had to wear it down. She liked the feminine way it framed her relatively plain face, but it was bothersome.

I'm such a tomboy; of course I forgot a damned hair tie.

As she crept further across the second floor, the details of their case played back in her mind in a sickening loop. Jeremey Young was a seven-year-old boy from Brooklyn who'd been trick-or-treating with his friends when a white Dodge van pulled up, and someone snatched him off the sidewalk, driving away from the scene within seconds. All witnesses reported seeing was the van.

The kidnapping wasn't reported until that evening; the FBI wasn't even aware of the incident until the next day. The way he was taken lined up with the *modus operandi* of two previous kidnappings.

Both victims in those kidnappings were children. And both had been murdered.

As soon as the press began to talk about New York's newest serial killer, the FBI got involved. She'd *expected* they'd be assigned to this case, and they'd been hard at work for weeks trying to track this man down... before he killed again.

And so far, Becca's hard work was paying off! If only they'd been tipped off sooner, they might've had him weeks ago. But at least they were here now, with a chance to stop him; it was happening *exactly* as Jim and Becca had predicted—

SLAM! CRUNCH!

Becca froze. Her heart leaped into her throat.

"It tends to bury you, doesn't it?"

*　　　　*　　　　*

"Wha—?" was all Becca had time to mutter as her eyes fluttered open. A stack of folders smashed the only food on her desk—a bag of Ruffles potato chips, now crushed under an anxiety-inducing stack of file folders.

"You *alright*, Agent Taylor?"

Last January 1st... a familiar nightmare. Becca relived it almost every night. She rubbed the short-lived nap from her eyes, as if the memory had burned them. "Oh yeah, Jenny, I'm fine... what did you say?"

"I said, 'All this extra work... it tends to *bury* you.'"

Her aide patted the pile of files she'd just dropped on her desk, the sound of crushed chips making her angrier. Now she had *nothing* to eat. Rubbing the sleep from her eyes, she peeked at the label on the file folder atop the stack; written in black Sharpie was the name 'M. HERNANDEZ'.

Another missing persons case. Which means it has nothing to do with me...

Her aide, Jennifer, silently stood there, waiting for a reply from her colleague. Poorly hiding her irritation with her, Becca rolled her eyes and fingered through the papers in the folder, reading them as if she had any intention of doing more work before break.

The silence stretched like a rubber band, ready to snap—

"Uh-*huh.*"

Her aide's snooty tone nearly brought Becca's blood to a boil as she *clacked* away. The hammering sound of each of Jennifer's heels, rising above the chatter of phone calls and the constant tapping of keyboard strokes... each step seemed to drive another nail into the coffin of her lunch plans.

Clack clack clack clack....

With a groan that started somewhere near her shoes, Becca slammed the folder shut, sending a tremor through her entire desk and knocking over a picture frame. Her tummy mocked her, sending its own rumble through her body.

It wasn't that she didn't appreciate the work... but it was *boring.* There was zero excitement in the office. For a while, she'd yearned for the safety of it, but after a year of sitting in this chair, suffering in this office, she'd had enough.

She was a special agent, damn it! She needed to be in the *field.*

The scars from last January healed differently for both of them. Jim bounced back with his usual resilience, returning to fieldwork as soon as his wounds healed. If the incident haunted him, Becca hadn't noticed; he'd buried it effectively, losing himself in the job as he'd always done.

Meanwhile, I can't even handcuff a junkie anymore without

feeling like I've messed up.

Her superiors referred to what happened to Becca on January 1st, 2000, as a 'traumatic incident' in their sterile, bureaucratic way (she was later diagnosed with PTSD), and they confined her to desk duty while mandating twelve months of therapy.

And, if she was honest with herself, those sessions had done her good; she realized she'd shouldered all the blame, which wasn't fair... *but that won't stop me, will it?*

That hadn't helped much at work, however. When she finally returned to the field, she'd become dependent on Jim's leadership, since it took the liability of making mistakes out of her hands. And of course, that meant she had no reason to worry... *right?*

Her boss certainly didn't think so; her performance had slipped so badly that her superiors put her right back into desk work... all because she was afraid to make a decision without Jim's approval.

It wasn't a 'healthy' way of dealing with trauma, but hey—at least she still had a job.

Yeah... for now.

There was an unexpected positive outcome that came out of it, specifically when she joined the group therapy sessions—*CeCe.*

She met Cecilia Chapman at therapy, a plain-faced and athletic woman with a go-getter attitude. She was a firefighter, stationed on Staten Island whilst living in Belleville, New Jersey, and had been dealing with the pressures of being an out lesbian in the firehouse.

As if being a woman in a male-dominated environment wasn't difficult enough already...

They had become quick friends... and not long after that, *more* than friends. Becca hadn't realized she was bisexual until she'd met CeCe. They'd been dating about a year now, but Becca was confident Cecilia was the one. She'd never met anyone before —man *or* woman—who made her feel so comfortable with sharing anything about herself.

Well, that, and the way her muscles look when she works out...

CeCe was the biggest catalyst towards Becca's recovery. Before long, she was telling Cecilia things she wouldn't even tell Dr. Mitzel. She'd made remarkable progress and felt more confident than she had in years.

And yet, I'm still on desk duty...

Her desktop clock (a Mother's Day gift that Becca treasured more than she'd *ever* admit) cast a red glow across her desk. She fondly thought of her only child as it caught her eye:

9 10 2001 MON
11:46 AM

It sat beside the framed photograph she'd knocked over moments earlier, and she set it back in its place. The snapshot captured a moment of perfect bliss: herself, Cecilia, and Chad at the Boardwalk weeks prior, dressed in their bathing suits, with sun-kissed smiles as they laughed to the camera.

The painful *growl* of her tummy brought her mind back to the crisis at hand. Selection anxiety crippled Becca as she couldn't decide; she figured Jim would be fine with one of their usual spots.

In New York City, you're never short on choices...

She shot Jim a text message. His birthday yesterday had been a subdued affair; *that* was typical of Jim, keeping things quiet. Becca thought it would be nice to treat him to lunch, just the two of them, so she texted her old partner.

I need to get out... of here, Jim... Let's hit... the Odeon, I'm... buyin'... and send. His reply came quickly... but was not what she expected:

"Oh, really?" Becca had to re-read the message. Meeting with William Bushnall, the Assistant Director in Charge—and their boss—in the middle of a shift usually meant a development in a case... or something *worse*. Jimbo was still working on priority cases, unlike Becca... who was sure he'd tell her all about it at lunch.

Bill's office had become a source of negative experiences for her lately, particularly since last January. Hoping she could slip away during whatever crisis currently occupied Bill's attention, she left the message hanging. However, as she stood to make her exit, her gaze fell on the photo once more, causing her to pause.

Wow, CeCe looks so fit in that bathing suit. She fought the urge to fan herself.

Becca loved this picture. It was the first one she'd printed on her new fancy photo printer at home, and she'd made many copies; she had this picture in her wallet, on her keys... even in her gym locker. The frame's faux brass finish caught the overhead lights, and the reflection shone brightly in the glass, creating a halo effect around their faces. It gave her the courage to smile again.

Once the moment passed, she gathered her things. Now, she only needed to reach the elevators before—

"Taylor!"

The bellowing roar ricocheted off the acoustic ceiling tiles like a gunshot. Becca retreated in a flinch, as if she had fallen. *"Where do you think you're going?"*

She froze, her wallet still clutched in her hand. Fear gripped her as she peeked over her shoulder to find Bill and Jim framed in the doorway of the assistant director's office.

With a sheepish smile crossing her face, she shuffled out of her cubicle and crept through the aisle. Her fellow agents pretended to be absorbed in their work, but she could *feel* their eyes following her progress.

Bill held the door for her. Her boss's office always smelled of coffee and old papers, but today there was an undercurrent of tension that made the air thicker than motor oil. She sank into one of the chairs facing his desk, the leather *creaking* under her back.

Jim took the seat beside her, his presence reassuring despite the circumstances. Bill, meanwhile, circled his desk like a shark.

"We need to talk. Your lunch can wait."

She caught Jim's slight head shake, the way his eyes darted toward their boss. She thought she knew what he was about to say, and her mouth grew dry as her hands found her face.

It's finally happened. I'm being fired.

"You're back in the field, Rebecca."

The words hit her like a physical blow, punching her squarely in the gut.

"I *am*, sir?"

"Yes, you'll be working with Jim Serrano again. Effective, immediately. Your other duties are no longer your duties, understood?"

Her eyes flicked between the two men. "You mean the case I just got on my desk? 'M. Hernandez'?"

"No, I mean Derek Jeter," her boss scoffed as he finally settled into his plush executive chair, lifting his coffee mug from his polished mahogany desk. Before he drank, his eyes grew weary.

"Sorry, Becca... I have a migraine." Her snide smirk didn't

validate his apology.

"Yes, I'm putting you on this case. You and Serrano. And I know..." he raised his hands, palms out towards them, "I know it's been almost two years since then, but I want—no, I *need* my best on this. I've already lost one kid to this son of a bitch, and I won't lose another one. Especially not some little kid on her way to school."

Becca nodded. A knot formed in her gut, but she couldn't afford to be timid. She had to nail it... If not to prove it to Jim, Bill, or CeCe, then to *herself* above all.

She was ready... *right?*

"It's the same MO? How'd they make *that* connection?" Becca observed an unusual pile of files on his desk. "I assume there's a new lead?"

What could he possibly know that would lead to giving me this case? In the Bureau's eyes, Rebecca Taylor was old news... although she was realizing that wasn't necessarily true anymore. She worked out at their gym nearly every morning (usually with her best friend, Special Agent Kelly Willis,.. although Kelly had been too busy lately). They lifted weights, did fitness training—even sparred with Jim and the other agents. And she was getting *good*.

On top of that, she was taking driving and shooting courses, *and* in addition to her continued therapy, she'd begun taking psychology classes at CUNY.

Truth be told, Becca was in the best shape of her life, mentally *and* physically.

Her boss took a sip of his coffee, grimacing at how bitter and cold it tasted, before digging into the stack of folders. Eventually, he found the manila file he was looking for and dropped it in front of Becca with a *plop*.

"We didn't get wind of this until about an hour ago, so this is hot. Same MO, but this time a witness spotted the vehicle." He hesitated a moment, leering at his agent, and Becca's eyes met his for a split second before he finally opened the file.

"White Dodge van, stopped at a school bus stop this morning, and he was gone within ten seconds. The kid never knew what hit her."

A white Dodge van—

Becca drew a deep breath. "Who is the victim?"

"Marissa Hernandez. Seven years old, a second grader. Lives in Flushing, goes to PS 166. Bus stop was on 46th and 21st. Last seen at the bus stop this morning around 0700, but she never made it to school. Our witness said the van stopped next to her, an arm reached out of the door, and they were gone."

Bill methodically separated the sections until he found what they were looking for, producing a Polaroid photograph of Marissa and another photo of a similarly aged little girl.

"His first victim. Isabel Esquivel, seven years old; *also* from Queens. Both kids were taken in the same way, but we never got the intel about the van till today."

He removed the paper clip from the photo, revealing a morbid picture underneath. "Her body was found in a vacant apartment downtown a week later, which is why *we're* getting the case instead of Brooklyn-Queens."

Kelly's not gonna be happy about that. She worked out of that agency.

Her boss seemed apprehensive as he thumbed through the files, until it appeared—a photo of a late model 1990s Dodge van, and Becca's mouth grew dry.

No license plate... missing side mirror... rusty chrome bumper...

Her heart skipped a beat, and sweat formed on her brow, like condensation on a cold glass. Alarm bells rang out in her mind. Bill noticed her face growing flushed, and he threw his hands up preemptively as if to shield himself from her.

"Wait—now *wait* a second, Taylor..."

"It's him!" she cut him off, the words practically exploding from her. *"Bill, goddammit, it's him, I know it!"*

"Calm down!" Bill's open palms slammed against his desk, the *bang* ringing like a gunshot in the confined space. "We haven't even seen this—"

"It's the same van, I *know* it!"

Before she could grab the photo of the Dodge, her boss caught her hand in mid-air and gently placed it back upon the desktop, underneath his own.

"Look, Taylor," he began, the tone of his voice much softer and controlled, "I know you haven't worked on missing kids since Y2K, but you both are the best we've got in these sorts of cases. I *know* you're ready. We need to keep an open mind about this, but... you know the Y2K case more than anyone. Even Serrano. If you smell a rat, I want you to snuff it out."

He placed his other hand on his desk, the tone of his words gaining bass and volume as he seemed to grow larger. "And at some point, you have to let go and do your fuckin' *job*, you know?"

Becca's face was fighting an array of emotions. Her eyebrows were furrowed, her hazel eyes wide, and her lips were pursed together as tightly as a vice.

The Y2Killer case had gone completely cold. After January 1st, 2000, the suspect seemed to vanish. Even Isabel Esquivel's case was considered isolated until now; at least, as far as Becca could tell.

But now, they have the van. That's why he wants me on this.

The old Becca would make excuses; she would tell Bill to get someone else to do it. But she was wiser now. Passing the buck did no good for anyone. Instead, she sat, burning holes into the back of her boss's weathered hand with her gaze. The awkward silence stretched until Bill *finally* released her.

He had a sense of empathy in his eyes. It was a side of Bill she'd never have guessed existed.

Twenty-one months. That's how long Becca had lived with the guilt of January 1st. Sleepless nights bracketing days filled with regret over tentative actions and timid decisions. If not for CeCe, she might've spiraled out of control... *but that never happened!*

Gently, she again withdrew her hand from Bill's desktop. Jim's steady gaze never left her.

"We all know that it wasn't your fault. We're in this together. We got this, Taylor... you and me."

It felt awkward fist-bumping Jim in front of her boss, but she was too emotionally exhausted to give a damn. Bill had even *less* of a damn to give as he reached into his desk drawer, and removed an unassuming, small black box.

"This is a GPS tracking bug. If you get close to the Dodge, stick this under the rear bumper or the tailpipe. It's magnetic, and it has a sticky back." He opened the box and showed it to Becca, holding two wire harnesses.

"You connect it to a battery pack, and then connect the other wire to an RF transmitter. Each piece has a magnet on it. Takes about, oh, thirty seconds to attach and activate."

Becca's eyes went wide; she'd never used one of these. *"Ooh!* This is really neat!" She toyed around with the tiny device for a moment, twirling the little wires around her finger.

"Is this new? I've never seen these. Do we need a device to track with this?"

"No," Jim scoffed. "We've had these for about a year now. They work with our Garmins."

"This is so cool, dude; I feel like James Bond!"

"Well, come along, now, double-o-seven," Jim said in a terrible British accent. "Let's get lunch. I'm buyin', and we can talk more about it."

"You are *not* buying! Yesterday was your 'seventieth' birthday, and... and I *refuse to...*"

Her words trailed off into laughter as she bowled over; her antics only earning a roll of Jim's eyes.

"Jesus, Taylor. I'm fifty—I'm not *dead!*" He tapped her boot with his own. "You do this case with me, 'pal', and I'll let you buy every time from now on!"

"She is doing this case, Serrano, whether she likes it or not. You two can go play patty cake at The Odeon or you two can go jump off the Brooklyn Bridge, for all I give a damn. As long as you both are on this, and we get this piece of crap before this little girl gets hurt, then the *both* of you can keep your jobs!"

His face was stern, but he lifted his eyebrows and smiled at them.

"You get this guy, you might get a fat Christmas bonus. Now, how does *that* strike you?"

*   *   *

"For twenty minutes and twenty bucks," Jim grumbled through a mouthful of burger, "this had *better* be worth it."

Becca glanced at her watch; it was 12:29. It was an old Pulsar watch with a gorgeous red LED display belonging to her late husband, Ken; it was a *gorgeous* stainless steel piece from the '70s. After he'd passed away, she began wearing it. It was her most cherished item.

But it eats batteries like crazy...

As they discussed their recent lives, Becca sipped some of her French onion soup. The Odeon was a nice place for her to grab a quick lunch, mostly because it was so close to the FBI office.

It was relatively busy for a Monday afternoon; a few folks at the bar were watching highlights of last night's Yankees-Red Sox game, and Becca overheard one of them saying something about "...boom! Tino fuckin' Martinez, three-run home run!"

The tables were mostly empty, which meant the ambiance was perfect for catching up with a friend... or having a conversation that shouldn't leave these walls.

Becca wasn't sure *which* this was.

"C'mon, at least you get fries and a pop."

"Pop?" he mused, as he sipped his straw, smirking mischievously. He poured his Bronx accent on extra-thick. "No... it's soda 'ere in the City. C'mon, are ya *kiddin'* me, Taylor? You Midwesterners, whaddaya gonna do, huh?"

Taking a chomp out of a large, crinkle-cut fry, he let out a scoff. Despite spending most of her life in New York after moving from Stillwater (a tiny little town on the border between Minnesota and Wisconsin) with her father as a kid, Becca had never quite shaken her heartland roots.

"You gonna tell CeCe 'bout this?" he asked, a fry still half-chewed in his mouth.

"Of course. She's gonna want to hear about it. She knows all about this case."

Jim's face hardened as he swallowed. "You know, this might not even be the same guy? In fact, I'd bet lunch on it."

"Oh, so if I'm wrong, I can buy you lunch twice?" She winked at Jim, but his expression remained stone-cold. She could see the concern, but wasn't sure what was on his mind.

"You don't think Bill would fire us if we...?"

Jim shrugged subtly. "I mean, he is the director, Taylor, he can fire us if he wants to." He chomped down on a fry, smeared in ketchup.

"I'm not kidding, *Serrano,*" Becca whined, earning Jim's gaze at her use of his last name. "That van *is* the same Dodge from last year. We both know it."

14

"We don't, though. That's what Bill was saying. We still don't even know his name, and—"

"Oh, *bullshit*, Jim!" She kept her volume low despite her whispered scream at her partner. "Why would he put me on this case with you, knowing about my history with Y2K, *and* he knows that's the same Dodge?"

Jim kept his cool, sipping on a gulp of Coca-Cola as she ranted at him, and finally speaking up when she finished. "'Cause you're the *best*, Taylor."

Becca's face went red, and she dropped her spoon in shock. In all the years she'd worked with Jim, he had always been supportive, and he had taught her everything she knew... but he had never once admitted that he thought she was a better agent than he was.

For him to admit that was a Hail Mary—and it might've worked.

"We're the best, Serrano, and don't you fuckin' forget it, wise guy."* She angrily chomped a chunk of soggy bread she'd had soaking in her soup.

"I'm serious. *You're* the best and *I* know it." He drank a gulp of cola as she watched, knowing the gears in his head were whirring away, before he put the burger he was about to chomp into back on the plate.

Oh, shit; if he's putting his food down, then this is serious.

"At least, you *were*... before you became a fuckin' chickenshit."

The *clang* of her spoon overpowered her gasp as she dropped it into her bowl again. This time, the handle disappeared into her soup.

"Wow. Tell me how you really feel, asshole."

His grin was reassuring, not taking any offense at her tone. "I'm sorry, Taylor; I *had* to say it." Becca growled as she looked away, her arms folded tightly against her chest.

"I've been on priority cases ever since I healed. What, you don't think *I* had some fuckin' trauma from that, too? I drank myself into a coma every night for, like, three *months* after January 1st!"

Even as her blood began to boil, she could see empathy in his eyes. Jim didn't open up to her often, so Becca refrained from interrupting. Instead of a comeback, she grabbed her sinking spoon and stirred her soup aimlessly.

"Look, I know it hit you way harder than it hit me, and I'm sorry for makin' this seem like it's about myself, 'cause I'm not. This is about *you*, Taylor.

"Like I was sayin', I've been in priority cases with so many other fuckin' agents that my head is startin' to hurt. I miss workin' with *you*. You're the smartest agent I ever worked with, and I've been in this shit since you were still in high school. And I don't give a damn if you're a lady: you got some fuckin' balls."

Funny, I was thinking the same thing about you, ya jerk.

"You wanna know why I want you with me on this? Because *Bill* wants you on this. Bill's been asking me to get you back in the field for months now, and I kept puttin' it off because I didn't think you were ready."

She *gasped* in shock. "Wait-wait-wait... lemme get this straight. *You* were the one keeping me chained to the desk?" Her face drained of its color, replaced by a shade of red.

"You can get pissed at me if you want, but you damned well know I ain't lyin'! We've worked together what... eight years, now? You changed after Y2K. Started gettin' lazy and makin' all sorts of excuses, showin' up late and shit. I didn't want you to get fired— and you *were* gonna get fired, let me just make that clear as fuckin' day!"

His face softened as he took a breath. "But now, you're *you* again. I see it every day. And I dunno if it's because of CeCe, or therapy, or whatever; I just know that right now, you're holdin' yourself back, Taylor, because otherwise..."

His eyes scanned her body, making her squirm in her seat.

"I mean, look at you. When we spar, I can't hang with you anymore—*especially* when you don't hold back, you kick my ass! You're already the best driver in the whole damn Bureau, and you're smart as a fuckin' tack. You *are* ready.

"And yeah, that's chickenshit; I'm sorry if you don't wanna hear it, but you know I don't hold anything back. I love you like a daughter, Taylor, and I want you back in the field. And it's not only because we wanna save this girl...

"No, it's because we need to save *you*, too. "

That's odd... for a moment, his eyes sparkled in the overhead lights. Except Becca knew better. *Monkeys might fly out of my ass before I see Jim Serrano cry.*

"So let's go—but I need you to keep a clear head on this. If you are gonna shoot someone first before you know the deal, I can have Bill put you on a different assignment..."

"No, no, no..."

She dropped the bread into her soup, forming a little doughy iceberg. "I can handle this—you *know* that. It's just..." She picked up the spoon and slowly stirred her lunch, gathering her thoughts.

"I don't fail often. When I *do,* I learn and grow; I don't fail twice."

"But you *didn't* fail, Taylor. Shit happens."

"Well, I blamed myself for a long time. Regardless if it were my fault or not, I failed to do my job that night. And I wouldn't expect *you* to sacrifice the job for my sake, even if you wanted to. We both took this job to be the best at it. I get that, now.

"I've learned a lot about myself since Y2K. That night, I saw one of my best friends in the world—my *partner*—in serious trouble, for the very first time, and I panicked. I wasn't confident in myself, for whatever reason." She took a deep breath, as if to will her tears back into their ducts, before smiling up at him.

"But I am, now." Her tone impressed him as reassuring. "You can trust me, Jim. I won't react more than is necessary. I promise."

Those are bold words, Becca. I hope you know what you're saying...

He held her gaze for a long moment, making Rebecca anxious about what she should say next, before Jim attacked his burger with an exaggerated bite, lettuce clinging to his gray handlebar mustache like Velcro.

"Gooh uh-noof foh meh!" he mumbled through his mouthful, *"leh's eah!"*

Becca hadn't noticed the waiter strolling by their table, placing the leather folder on the table, which contained their check. Before she could react, Jim had already produced a fifty-dollar bill and slapped it onto the tablecloth triumphantly, strutting out of the restaurant before Becca could protest.

II

"I Love It When You Do"

"Why can't *you* cook this good, Mom?" The words hurt Becca more than her teenager intended, as Chad wolfed down another bite of CeCe's famous lasagna. His fork clinked against his plate as he shoveled bite after monstrous bite into his mouth, strings of melted mozzarella stretching between the plate and his fork.

Becca was seated in front of her plate, which she'd barely touched.

"You alright?"

CeCe's words floated across the dining room. Becca withdrew, absently pushing pasta around her plate instead. The red sauce created tasteful Rorschach-like patterns that telegraphed her troubled thoughts.

Jim's right; I was tired. I guess I dozed off for a bit.

It had been a roller coaster of emotions for Becca today, and she was ready to get off this ride. After lunch, they'd done some investigating, including stopping by the Hernandez residence, interviewing witnesses, and checking security cameras around the bus stop. Still, they didn't dig up a *single* lead.

Frustrated, Becca went home at the end of her shift, despite her incessant pleas to stay with Jim in the field. But he'd made a good point—what good were *they* gonna do by themselves? Besides, Bill had already put out an APB with the NYPD; if they spotted the van, he'd call her.

"I know what it's like to not spend enough quality time with the ones you love, and that bit me in the ass, Taylor. It bit me

19

hard. You staying out all night ain't gonna help."

She didn't like it, but if anyone knew what he was talking about, it was Jim Serrano. Not a month after his youngest daughter Jessie graduated from high school, his estranged wife Stacey decided to leave him. The years that had passed since hadn't changed how Jim operated in the field, but they changed how he felt about work-life balance—*especially* Becca's.

"The job's important, but so's your life. Just keep your phone on, and if I call you, get out here. Otherwise, go have a nice night with your family."

The lonely drive home had been a quiet one; Becca had zoned out listening to the radio, trying to beat the brewing storm home (the weather today was disappointing... what good was driving a convertible if you can't drop the top?). She'd fully intended on thinking about the case, or about how this conversation would go down... a*nd instead, I just rapped about getting high with Afroman.*

"What happened at work, Babe?" CeCe demanded, catching Becca's daydreaming in its tracks. A heavy bass in her chest accompanied her question—this was not a request for info, it was a *demand*. Rebecca continued her artistic endeavors with the marinara, eyes fixed downward.

"I'm back in the field."

"So?"

CeCe's mouth was full of garlic bread as she reached for her glass of orange juice and swigged it to wash the dough down. Her casual response drew Becca's startled gaze upward, incredulous in response.

I'm not sure how I thought you'd react to that news, Babe, but I wasn't prepared for that.

Cecilia shrugged innocently at Becca's angry scowl. "What? You sayin' you're not ready for this?" She swigged a quick sip of juice. "We *both* know you're gonna crack the case, am I right?"

"I dunno," she replied with a bitter tone she couldn't hide behind her trembling voice. "It's not just that, though. It's the kidnapper. They're connected to a case I once worked."

"And...?"

"The kidnapper who struck today drove a white Dodge van..."

The room fell silent.

Chad stopped chewing. Cecilia froze with her mouth agape before her glass slipped from her fingers, shattering the silence as it clattered off the tabletop. Juice spread across the tablecloth like oil on the surface of the sea.

"You're saying...?"

"Yes, I think so."

CeCe clapped her hands together and craned her head up. "Thank you, God, *I knew it!* I knew you were gonna find that son of a bitch and—"

Her eyes darted to Chad and back to Becca, her mouth forming a silent *"Sorry!"*

"I'm sixteen now, you can say 'bitch', CeCe—"

"Watch your mouth, young man!" Rebecca snapped sternly, and Chad's laughter snapped off like a dry twig. Even at his age, he still respected his Mama.

"Sorry, Mom..." He went back to his lasagna, a smirk still plastered on his face.

"And now," CeCe continued as she stood, "you can prove yourself to all those squares at work that doubted you. Nothin' to it!"

As CeCe shuffled dishes around the table, preparing to clean the mess she'd made, Becca remained still, her fork hovering above her cooling lasagna. The moment stretched until she finally dropped it with a loud *clink*, causing CeCe to flinch.

"I'm grateful for having met you, Cecilia. If it weren't for that bastard, we wouldn't have met. But January 1st was the worst day of my life... and if I can just move the hell on, I might die the happiest woman on the *planet!*"

Her voice had risen with each word, emotions breaking through her voice like flames through a roof. CeCe raised her hands in surrender.

"I get it, I get it... and look, Babe, Becca, *baby*... you know I love you more than anything."

"Even the Jets?"

Chad's attempt at levity cut through the tension like butter, and Becca nearly spat her water across the room. CeCe's mouth pursed as he broke out in laughter.

"Okay, mister, you're grounded," CeCe joked, scrambling into the kitchen hoping to find weapons to fight the spreading juice menace. Despite Becca's sulking, she managed to toss a crumpled napkin at her girlfriend (Becca was a Vikings fan).

"What? Vinny's the *only* man on the planet that could compete with you, Babe; you know that."

"They just lost," Becca retorted, trying to play along, but not quite ready to match her banter. Her words couldn't hide the darkness in her eyes, something Chad caught with teenage perception. He exchanged a helpless glance into the kitchen with CeCe, both recognizing the weight settling over Becca's shoulders.

"Look, Babe," CeCe began, "you can kick yourself and stress out over things you can't control. Or you can, uh... what did your father always say, Chad?"

He rolled his eyes loudly. "C'mon, *that* stupid motto again?"

Chad was a great kid, despite his angsty teenage wit. He loved skateboarding, video games, and loud music—typical teenage faire — and had plenty of friends in his junior class. "As long as he keeps his grades up and stays out of trouble, he can do whatever he wants," she had told CeCe a long time ago.

Her late husband, Ken Taylor, had been an aspiring author, murdered by a drunk driver just days after Christmas, 1994. He had an abstractness to his personality that Becca always found attractive. He often spoke to his family in idioms and riddles—one in particular, he would always say before a stressful situation arose.

It was his tried-and-true motto. He uttered it when he needed to compose himself. She *used* to think it was cheesy, but when she heard him whisper it just before asking her to marry him, she fell in love with the silly sentence. After he passed away, she fully adopted it as the family motto.

As Chad stood with a smirk and a roll of his eyes, CeCe shot a stern glance back at the teenager, who cleared his throat theatrically as he saluted.

"Clear your mind, write your story, and then breathe!"

"But he's right, you know," CeCe continued, a paper towel roll tucked under her arm. She hesitated before cleaning the spill, her free hand landing gently on Becca's shoulder.

"Your Dad was a smart man. And Becca... I love you so much. If you loved that man as much as you love me now, then I *know* you picked a good one. I ever tell you that before? I *know* I have."

Becca struggled against the familiar welling of tears. She hated crying more than anything. *No, Babe... you haven't.*

"Look, I just think that saying is a good one, 'cause it's okay to be afraid as long as you did *everything* you could to prepare. 'Cause you got a job to do. And no matter what, ya gotta do it, right? So rewrite the narrative. Get rid of your doubts. Relax, take a deep breath, and do it. You breathe."

Becca's lips were quivering. "Sure." Her voice was barely above a whisper.

"When you got a job to do that scares you, ya don't think about anything once you're ready. You just do it. C'mon, you think I like going into burning buildings, what, for my *health?* No... I do it because it's my job. And that's gotta take precedence over all else."

Becca's voice cracked as she spoke. "I know. I *try* to do my job; what if I make a mistake again?"

"Well, if you make a mistake, *whoopdie fuckin' doo,* am I right? We all do! I was grillin' hamburgers the other day while we were watching the game, up on the rooftop? And I forgot about 'em and damn near burned the firehouse down!"

"Burgers aren't the same thing, Babe," she muttered. She wasn't certain CeCe even *heard* her retort... but she regretted saying it in the first place. CeCe's heart was in the right place, a place of love... and it reminded Becca that she really was the one. Every time Becca found herself dwelling on the past, struggling to move a foot forward, CeCe was always there to give her a gentle push, helping her to move on.

Thinking about her did help take things off Becca's mind; she smiled meekly. *She's trying to make me feel better, and even if it's not working, she's not wrong.* The effort wasn't lost on her, and she took a deep breath, smiling more naturally, now.

As CeCe wiped the OJ from the tablecloth, some of the juice dripped onto Becca's plate. She could hear CeCe mutter *"Shit!"* as she stopped just short of sticking the juice-soaked towels directly into her food... before freezing with an awkward expression pasted upon her face.

Becca's glossy eyes went from CeCe's... down to the plate... and back up to hers. This broke Becca's trance, and she closed her eyes, lowering her voice to a low growl.

"*Orange* you gonna apologize for this *juicy* intrusion? No? You're an im-*pasta,* then!"

Before her very eyes, Becca's hands transformed into makeshift claws, a terrifying tickle monster hellbent on attacking

CeCe. The couple laughed uncontrollably as they tore exuberant wads of paper towels off the roll and began wrapping each other up like giggling mummies.

This is nice, they both thought, at the exact same time.

After a few silly moments, they went back to mopping up the mess together with the towels they'd played with.

"You're off tomorrow, CeCe?"

"No... not till Thursday," she replied, carrying a wad of soaking-wet paper towels back to the kitchen. Their puppy, a 4-month-old black Labrador named Pepper, was watching from his bed in the den and taking note of every drip landing on the linoleum floor.

"Probably gon' be a quiet week, the weather is gonna be helpful. Supposed to be *gorgeous* tomorrow."

"It almost rained just now, driving home." Becca followed her into the kitchen as Chad retreated to the living room, Pepper padding after him. "I didn't *dare* drop the top on the Eclipse."

"Yeah," Cecilia nodded. "Hurricane Erin."

"I thought that was gonna miss us...?" Becca tossed the used towels into the wastebasket with the ease of a free throw. "So as I was saying, Jim said there's an APB out for a white Dodge van, mid-90s model. Same one we saw last year, I think. So I'm on call tonight. If they find it, I'll have to go—"

CeCe cut her words off with a soft kiss, lips planted directly on Becca's lips, hands planted directly on Becca's hips. Her knees nearly buckled.

"If you have to go, you'll have *that* waiting for you when you get back."

Heat bloomed in Becca's belly, and blood rushed to all the right places. "We have to *wait...?*"

"Mom? CeCe?" came a cry from the living room. "Can Pepper have garlic bread? I still have some of mine, and I'm *full!*"

CeCe took the lead on this one. "No, Chad, it'll hurt his tummy; give him a biscuit instead, okay?" Turning back to Becca, she delivered a wink that promised more.

"Maybe tonight, you sexy thing, you."

As Becca turned back to the garbage can, CeCe's juice-dampened hand found her posterior, leaving an impromptu handprint on her slacks. The playful slug she received in return carried no real force.

"I suppose I should try and get some rest," she thought out loud, as CeCe opened the refrigerator and grabbed two ice-cold Miller Lite cans from the door of the fridge.

"You read my mind, Babe."

Hand-in-hand, the two of them walked into the living room, joining Chad for a nice evening at home, blissfully unaware of what the future held. While it was a peaceful evening for CeCe and Chad, Becca lost herself in the moment as she blankly watched TV.

A story on the evening news made her stomach churn. The headlines were mundane, for the most part—there had been a fire at Newark Liberty International Airport, President Bush was facing economic pressure, and Bill Gates was still under scrutiny by the government. Becca barely noticed *any* of it, her mind instead racing with details about last January.

When the local news stories picked up, the kidnapping of Marissa Hernandez was mentioned—*it was only a matter of time before the press got wind of it.* Suddenly, Becca was very interested in the news.

"Turn that up," she cried, pointing at the screen.

"...witnesses claim she was taken at her bus stop this morning by a man in a white Dodge Ram van. Some local residents are claiming this might be the same suspect from a *different* kidnapping a few months ago, when seven-year-old Isabel

Esquivel was later found dead in a Manhattan apartment. Residents are referring to him as "The Manhattan Mauler". News 7 sat down for an exclusive interview with her desperate parents, who wanted to share *this* message with the—"

"I changed my mind," Becca grumbled. "Can we watch something else?"

CeCe didn't complain; she happily switched the channel to the 'Monday Night Football' game between the New York Giants and the Denver Broncos. The 'G-Men' were already losing 14-7 in the second quarter.

Becca wasn't in the mood for football... but forgetting all her worries was *worth* it. Instead of stressing over the case, she laughed with her son, cuddled with her girlfriend, and the family spent the evening together while she waited for her cell phone to ruin *everything.*

But it wouldn't ring until she was long past falling asleep.

*   *   *

After love, Becca lay there in the dark, resting her head on her beloved CeCe, both of them breathing heavily. A sheen of sweat covered their naked bodies, and the bed was *completely* disheveled. The ceiling fan cooled their bodies as they snuggled in the dark, enjoying the evening together.

"I'm *so* happy, Rebecca," Cecilia whispered to her girlfriend as she mindlessly observed the blades of the ceiling fan, rotating faster and faster. CeCe was hypnotized by them, seduced by them, as she had seduced Becca moments prior.

"I'm gonna have to work until Thursday, probably through all weekend, Babe," CeCe said. "I'm getting close to lieutenant, so I gotta help out when they need someone, ya know?"

"It's fine; I'll try to stop by tomorrow then. Gotta get one of those famous firehouse frankfurters."

CeCe let out a guffaw and plugged her nose, making her voice nasal-sounding. "I always *knew* you was a wienie!"

"I just like free food, that's the only reason I'm gonna visit you."

CeCe poked her in the rib, before her hand playfully explored a bit. "The *only* reason, eh?"

"*Okay,* okay..." Becca giggled, looking her in the eyes and doing her best to ignore the teasing. "I love the way you look in a firefighter's getup, what can I say?"

"Oh, yeah?"

"I want you to come save me from a burning... *a burning in my loins!*"

Becca puffed her cheeks out and sat up on her elbows, looking over at CeCe with a playful expression on her face, before she crossed her eyes as much as she could. Her girlfriend laughed as Becca buried her face into CeCe's breast, giving her a raspberry, which made them both laugh at her sick bedroom moves. A goofy grin crossed her face as she rested her chin on CeCe's collar.

"If that's the case, I'm retiring, Babe."

CeCe playfully pushed her head off her chest as she sat up, reaching for her lip gloss. As she did so, Becca glanced at her watch; it was 10:28.

"I gotta get some sleep, CeCe. If they find that van, I'm gonna be out all day."

She didn't reply, instead reaching for the lukewarm can of Miller Lite she'd been babysitting ever since dinnertime. Unwisely, she took a swig of the regretful beer.

"Oh, *God...* " The bitter brew was spewed back to the place from whence it came, replaced quickly by a drink of water.

Becca laughed as she sat on her side of the bed. "I love the way your eyes light up when someone talks about the Jets."

"You know the Vikings ain't winnin' the Super Bowl before my Jets do, Babe; c'mon. Get real."

CeCe poked her in the armpit, making her giggle; she was a bit ticklish, and CeCe loved to tease her.

"I love the way you snort when I tickle you."

"Don't tickle me, Babe, *please!*" Becca pleaded, snorting with laughter even though CeCe hadn't moved a muscle.

"Gotcha," she whispered smugly, lightly pinching her lip between her teeth.

"Cecilia, I love the way you bite your lip when you concentrate." Becca raised an eyebrow. "At least, when *I'm* paying attention."

"Well, *I* love the way you always check your watch every five minutes when you're nervous."

"I do *not!*" Becca's jaw dropped.

She started cracking up. "I'm *serious!* Yes, you do!"

"I do not!" *She's right, I do it all the time.*

"You *totally* do! And it's fuckin' cute, I mean it!"

Becca disagreed with CeCe's assessment. She was embarrassed by her obsession with order and being neat constantly. It was a nervous tic she'd always had, but her therapist suggested it was her way to keep her life organized. A way to keep tabs on things; to control her impulses.

Lost in thought, she glanced towards the nightstand to check the time again, before catching herself in the act, hoping Cecilia didn't notice.

"I told you!"

While CeCe cracked herself up, Becca blushed profusely. She pouted and rolled into a ball, turning away from her. Rolling over in pursuit, she poked her head around Becca's, kissing her lips softly. CeCe pulled back, hovering her lips just above her ear.

"I love you *so* much, Rebecca Taylor."

Becca feigned anger, but her clandestine reply gave her away.

"I love you, too, Cecilia Chapman."

"I love how you sound when you whisper, Babe." Her soft lips brushed Becca's earlobe. *Every* hair on her arm was at attention as Cecilia's breath tickled against her skin. Her lips explored Becca's neckline, slowly inching their way down her back.

She needed to make a decision quickly, because if Becca didn't act fast... things *were* going to happen again. Her words were meant as a stark, stern warning, but they were spoken slowly... *seductively.*

"You know, eventually, I do have to get some sleep, Babe."

She shivered as CeCe's hands brushed her breasts. She knew the hard truth already—sleep was *not* going to happen at this rate. *The fact that I don't mind says it all...*

"I *love* the way you turn me on, just by being this sexy."

Becca practically *squealed* her sigh as her body admitted defeat. The time for pillow talk was over. She was already free-falling; between CeCe's skilled hands and her silvery words, no force on Earth could stop what was about to come.

"I love the way your body trembles when I kiss you."

Cecilia's lips lightly glided along Becca's hipbone, giving her goosebumps from head to toe as her head disappeared beneath the bed sheets. Becca wanted to pout badly, but it was becoming impossible to resist when—

"I love the sounds you make when I do *this...* "

Becca let out a soft *moan.*

*　　　　*　　　　*

Becca's throat was a barber pole as she flinched at the *crunch* sound under her boot. It was only now she remembered her flashlight hanging on her belt; she clicked it on, providing a tiny bit of relief. When she finally gathered the courage to lift her boot, she saw the remnants of a small porcelain figurine. It was a white Boeing jet, shattered into dozens of pieces.

Fighting the urge to run for her life, she instead ducked behind a curio cabinet next to the fireplace, not realizing until the tense moment passed that the little knick-knack she'd stepped on probably fell from the *same* cabinet. Nervous, she swept her flashlight back and forth, revealing a few other decorative objects, scattered around the floor like pervasive debris.

"I *need* to focus," she reminded herself, leaving the safety of the curio. Her flashlight sliced through the blackness as she took a deep breath—

BEEP BEEP BEEP. BEEP BEEP BEEP.

Becca nearly had a heart attack at this second intrusion on her concentration. Quickly, she silenced the Pulsar's alarm; the time was now 12:00.

Midnight. January 1st, 2000.

Happy New Year, Rebecca. Now get your ass in gear.

The second-floor hallway's rotten wooden frame beckoned to her like the entrance to some ancient labyrinth. Step by step, she crept, gently allowing the soles of her boots to sink into the carpet, her calves burning by the time she reached the hall. She peeked around the corner and beheld a single light illuminating the very end; it might as well have been the *sun* in Becca's eyes.

With a *gasp*, she pulled back, raising her weapon and fighting adrenaline.

Calm down! What is the matter with you, girl?

The lamp at the end cast a yellow glow, creating ghastly, long shadows. They stretched the length of the hall uncannily, plucking every nerve in Becca's spine. When she reached the first door, she exhaled almost as much out of *relief* as from holding her breath.

"Clear your mind, write your story, breathe."

Becca nudged the door open, causing it to swing with a soft *creak...* and revealing a laundry closet. The small window in the room was open. Her breath condensed in the frigid air as she retreated from the room, not bothering to close the door despite the ringing music playing loudly—

BANG! BANG BANG!

"Someone had *better* be dead!"

The gunshots caused Becca to scream, and she pressed herself flat against the wallpaper in the hallway.

H...ello?

"Taylor! I got the bastard! Get your ass down here!"

III

"We Should Be Barbecuing Today"

"Someone had *better* be dead!" CeCe's voice was thick with frustration as she rolled over, burying her face between two pillows. Her girlfriend rolled over, blindly reaching for her cellular phone. She didn't even realize she'd answered it; it had vibrated so hard, it was knocking against the wall with a *bang! Bang bang!*

The word was cotton in her mouth, her tongue heavy with sleep. Her eyelids fought against gravity, achieving only half-mast.

"H...ello?"

"Taylor! They found the bastard. Get your ass down here." The voice on the other end was businesslike. "Are you in bed?"

Becca's hand fumbled for her eyes, knuckles rubbing against sleep-crusted eyelids as if she could physically push consciousness back into her brain. Each eye screamed in protest as the darkened bedroom swam into view; the alarm clock read *3:38 AM* in large, digital numbers.

"Yes, sir. I'm awake now."

"Good." If Bill himself were on the line at this hour, she knew it was important.

"You said you got him?"

"Well... no," his tone softened; Becca grew annoyed. "They *found* the van. Serrano's already on his way."

The mention of her partner's name sent an electric current through Becca's spine, instantly clearing the fog from her mind. She rocketed to a seated position, causing her partner to moan. "I'm on my way."

Becca rocketed out of bed, oblivious to how much she was disturbing CeCe—who was fully awake and lying with her head on top of a mountain of pillows. She watched through half-closed eyes as her girlfriend transformed from sleepy civilian to federal agent in record time; she was fully dressed and brushing her teeth within a *minute*.

"Babe," CeCe protested as Becca spat her toothpaste into the sink with careless precision. She tossed her hair back in her signature ponytail, rushed back to grab her phone, and turned to sprint out the door before CeCe yanked the back of her white dress shirt.

"Hold up there, Babe," she demanded. CeCe's voice was thick with sleep, but tinged with love. "I don't care if it's *Oprah* out there, you give me a kiss before—"

Becca interrupted Cecilia with a firm kiss on the lips. For a reason she couldn't comprehend in the moment, Becca burned the image into her memory: CeCe's tousled curly brown hair, her worried hazel eyes, the faded New York Jets T-shirt hanging off one of her muscular shoulders...

"I gotta go." The words came out softer than intended, Becca hoping she'd fall asleep as soon as she left. "I love you *so* much, Cecilia Chapman."

CeCe fought a tear in her morning daze, knowing full well she'd immediately fall back to sleep when she left, but she was enjoying the moment.

"I believe in you, Rebecca Taylor. And I love you too. Good luck, Babe."

As Becca turned to run out the door, she snagged her car keys, which caught CeCe's eye.

"You're not gonna take the train?"

"Not on your life. It's gonna be *gorgeous* today!" Becca fully intended on dropping the top on her car and cruising later.

She kissed CeCe again and bolted out the door, a trailing cry of "Bye-bye; I love you!" following her as she jumped into her Mitsubishi Eclipse. She was finally going to come face-to-face with the person who'd haunted her dreams for *years*.

Today was gonna be the greatest day of her career—what could *possibly* go wrong?

She turned the radio dial to 97.1. A commercial about life insurance was wrapping up, and then the familiar jingle for Hot 97 blasted through her speakers.

"Yooooo New York! Welcome *back,* to Hot 97, hot jams coming your way. Ten 'til the hour; gonna be a *gorgeous* day out there, too bad it's only Tuesday. Isn't that a damned shame? We should be barbequing today! Well, if you're lucky enough to get the chance to get outside, I say 'Do it.' Hit the beach, go shoppin'— *maaaan*... live your best life!

"And for those of you out there that are suckers, like me... yeah, we gotta *work* today. Gotta make that cheese... am I *right?* Well, don't worry, hustlas; I *got* you! I'm 'bout to ensure your mid-week has a nice, soft landing. Alicia Keys *might* need one. She's "Fallin'"; it's Hot 97.1 FM..."

*   *   *

The morning zipped by in a blur as Becca sped through Hoboken heading into the city. She admired how different the Big Apple was before sunrise; seeing her all dressed up like this felt forbidden, like seeing your parents dressed up for date night as a child. The starry, cloudless sky cast a silvery glow over the many illuminated skyscrapers of New York's iconic skyline, ablaze with headlights and taxicabs weaving in and out of the maze-like roads far below.

She arrived at the Jacob B. Javits Federal Building in record time. Traffic was so light that even with her long commute from

Belleville, she beat Jim to the office... even though he lived in the Bronx! When she pulled into the parking garage opposite their building, her dashboard clock glowed 4:16 when she killed the motor. A shadowy silhouette stood not far from her chosen spot.

To Becca, Bill looked as tired as *she* was. He was leaning against the wall, appearing fuzzy in the shadows. Before she could begin voicing the questions swirling in her mind, a black 2001 Cadillac DeVille pulled into the garage, pulling smoothly into the spot beside Becca's car. A burly middle-aged man with bloodshot eyes joined them soon after.

"Tough night?" Becca quipped, unable to resist.

"I got home at one. I *barely* fell asleep." Jim grumbled as he sipped his gas station coffee, the steam curling through his mustache.

"Guys, we found the Dodge," Bill interrupted their banter, his voice steady and authoritative. Becca and Jim both turned to face their boss—this *wasn't* the time to fool around.

"Here's the situation. NYPD picked up the van driving past them in Brooklyn forty-five minutes ago. They followed it into Manhattan. They've been tailing them since in an unmarked cruiser, and as of right now, they're still driving. They haven't stopped.

"PD says they are staying far back because he's a flight risk. At some point, he's either gonna run, or he's *gotta* stop. And that's where you two come in.

"I put SWAT on standby, but we *must* find this kid first. So I'm not gonna call them till you find her. Your job is to follow this psychopath wherever they stop the van, and then investigate. Do *not* engage unless you find out where she is; Marissa Hernandez is the priority, got that?"

"Yes, sir," they said in unison. Bill's gaze met Becca's, and she heard every word his eyes demanded of her.

"Is the kid with him?" Jim's brow furrowed.

"We don't know," Bill shrugged, producing a small manila folder and handing it to Becca. "Inside are some surveillance photos of the van taken by the PD."

Becca peeked in the folder; the timestamp on the images was 0331. "That wasn't an *hour* ago! Why haven't they stopped yet?"

"We're not sure. Possible he saw the trail car and is trying to lose 'em? This might just be his MO. But yes, we confirmed the van is the same one eyewitnesses saw."

She was digging through the stack of photos, when Bill closed the folder on Becca's hand, a scowl etched on his face. "We don't have time. Look it over on the way."

"*I'll* drive, Taylor," Jim nodded. "Where are they?"

"I'll put you in contact with the NYPD, Jim. Have Becca call them on the road."

They turned and ran toward Jim's G-Ride. Before Becca could buckle her seatbelt, Jim had already thrown the car into drive and was pulling out of the garage.

"Here," Jim offered, passing his partner the steaming cup of coffee. Her eyes were bloodshot and crusty with exhaustion. "I've already had too much coffee tonight."

"Are you sure?" she asked, happily accepting the balmy cup of joe. Normally, she'd have been upset with Jim for taking the keys, but she was too tired to argue—the coffee was Jim's olive branch, she supposed.

"Heh, I've had about *six* cups since I dropped you off yesterday."

She giggled lamely and sipped the awful coffee. Despite it tasting like battery acid with too much sugar, the caffeine hit her bloodstream like a freight train smashing into a concrete wall. She was wired within *minutes*.

"Double-shot." Jim snickered.

Becca took a larger gulp of the wretched coffee. As she drank, she grabbed her phone, dialing the number Bill had scrawled on the front of the manila folder. After a few rings, it picked up.

"NYPD, this is Officer Rumph speaking."

"This is Special Agent Rebecca Taylor, FBI. Director Bushnall said you were our contact."

Before she could continue, Jim interjected. "Where do you want us to meet you, Officer? We're comin' from Worth and Broadway."

Some static crackled over the line before he responded. "Are we on Madison? We *are?* Okay... We're west-bound on Madison Street, just turned off of Grand. He's been circling around here for a while. He's done something like three laps, but hasn't stopped outside of red lights and stop signs."

"You haven't been seen...?"

"We don't *think* so; he hasn't driven recklessly or nothin'. We're staying pretty far back; he's two cars ahead right now."

Oh yeah, Bill did say they were in an unmarked car, didn't he?

Jim stomped the gas pedal, revving the Cadillac onto Worth Street. "Okay, Officer, I'm only a couple minutes away. We're headin' to your location."

"Wait, don't hang up!" the officer exclaimed. "He's doing a U-turn. Looks like he's parking facing east."

Jim drove rapidly as Becca's heart pounded, more so from adrenaline than caffeine at this point.

"We're stopped. He's parking the van on the street, looks like... 110 Madison. We're... a block from PS 001. We're heading westbound, pulling over now."

"We should approach from the east, Jim," she said aside, Becca's face twisting into a scowl. "Copy that, Officer Rumph. We're en route. Keep an eye on where he goes. If he moves, call me back. ETA... two minutes."

She hung the phone up, turning to Jim, who was concentrating heavily on the road ahead. "Why on Earth would this jerk-off use the same van as the Y2Killer? I mean... even if it *isn't* the same van, it's such a conspicuous choice..."

Jim muttered a half-hearted "Uh-huh" as he drove down East Broadway, dodging taxicabs and a few leftover nighttime pedestrians.

"He's obviously stupid, but ya know what, Taylor? I think this guy forgot about us."

He's right. This guy is getting cocky.

Becca smirked at her partner's words; it was the first time he had sounded like the Jim Serrano she remembered riding with. She removed her Smith & Wesson from its holster; this was the first time she had drawn her weapon in the field since last January—and this *wasn't* the shooting range. She checked the clip; it was fully loaded. As she reloaded her weapon, she held it up like she was Martin Riggs, looking over at Murtaugh with a cocky smirk creeping across his face.

"Well, then, shall we remind him, Jim?"

She grabbed two pairs of binoculars from the glove compartment, placing one in Jim's lap as he drove. She threw the other pair around her neck, where it rested against her chest. She adjusted her tie under her lightweight jacket, which had 'FBI' boldly emblazoned on the back of it. She had extra ammo clips on her belt, her phone was fully charged...

Then why do I feel like I'm not ready? I'm not that sleepy... perhaps I'm just not able to—

No... that's the old 'me' talking. I need to be ready to act.

As Jim turned the Cadillac onto Market Street, they slowed to a crawl before he killed the motor, across the street from an old Chinese restaurant. Becca grew nervous with anticipation in the newfound silence, something she hadn't felt since she was a *rookie*. Her gun was heavy against her breast, a reminder of the potential lethality it represented. But it was also an admonition of her responsibilities, one that she told herself she was ready for. All of her self-doubt was behind her now, and she was ready to save this girl... *right?*

Did she trust herself to make a split-second decision when the benefit of time was absent? Ready or not, she was going to find out... and *soon*.

Clear your mind, write your story... and breathe.

It might've been the coffee, but Becca was antsy. "Sit tight... or go in?"

Jim wasn't discussing it. He'd unbuckled his seatbelt and exited the car as soon as they stopped. She finished the coffee, tossed the empty paper cup in the Cadillac's cup holder, and followed Jim's lead. Becca took a moment to absorb the ambiance of the city, bustling with life even though her trusty Pulsar watch claimed it was only 4:58.

"We don't want 'em to see us. We need to hang back until we hear from Rumph, Taylor."

She nodded in agreement, scanning the area for a place they could use for surveillance. Diagonally across the intersection of Madison and Market Street, Becca spotted an old, decrepit laundromat—with a fire escape on the side. *Perfect.* Her excitement bubbled below the surface as she waved at Jim to look... except, he was distracted, spying through his binoculars.

"We're *so* close to downtown," Jim whispered. "Does this guy have a death wish or somethin'?" He stared intently, but the van was cloaked behind a sea of parked cars and traffic. "See anything?"

She tapped Jim's shoulder, pointing at the fire escape. "Why not *there?* We'll blend into the dark, and we can see *them.*"

Jim nodded. Quickly, the two of them ran across the

intersection. Becca was stunned that traffic was as light as it was, even at this hour.

When they reached the fire escape, she smiled at her good fortune. The ladder was unlocked. Jim knelt and boosted Becca up by her boot; she strained to grab the latches of the ladder, and it swung down, protesting with a metallic *groan*. When they reached the first landing, fifteen feet in the air, they were enveloped in pitch darkness. The glow of the street lamps didn't quite reach this high, and they found themselves cloaked in darkness.

This is perfect!

A block or two down Madison, the white Dodge van sat facing in their direction on the opposite side of the street. It was in front of some ancient restaurant, which appeared closed for the evening with its shutter locked down, decorated in New York's finest graffiti. A burgundy Crown Victoria was parked on the opposite side, about a block closer to them, next to an old red-brick church.

That must be Rumph. Becca pulled her Nokia out, tapping another text message quickly, and talking out loud as she typed: "Agent... Taylor... here. We're above you. We see... the van. Tap your... brakes once... so we can... confirm... your location."

After a moment, the phone vibrated, and she read the reply:

Becca noticed the brake lights flash briefly on the Crown Vic, confirming her suspicion from earlier. *"Jim,"* she whispered, showing Jim their conversation.

"Tell Rumph he can take off... we don't want this guy to *see* 'em." Becca's fingers flew as she *tap-tapped* a reply to Officer Rumph.

Becca's phone vibrated; she glanced down at the screen. "Nice. They're gonna drive around the corner to get breakfast. They're standing by." A few moments later, the Ford's engine turned, and the car pulled out and rolled slowly past the white van.

Becca swallowed hard. The last thing they wanted was a chase. She involuntarily held her breath for moments, until her heart began pounding. The Dodge sat silently where it remained parked.

She exhaled with a *phew*. *If the guy was gonna jet, he'd already be gone.*

"We might be here a while," Jim grumbled as he looked back at Becca, the binoculars creating an abstract impression of a raccoon on his weathered face. If the situation weren't so serious, she might've laughed at this. "We can take turns, if you wanna?"

She nodded, and 'Jim the Raccoon' went back to his binoculars. She *barely* held back a giggle, struggling to restrain her juvenile sense of humor for the sake of remaining professional.

Not the time, Becca. Focus.

"Is that building empty?" Jim hissed, staring intently at the apartments beside the van. "Can you watch it for me?" He could sense his partner's immaturity, and he was on edge.

"Sure, Jimmy."

Becca couldn't stay silent; her mind was racing. "If this is the same guy as January 1st, he's getting what's coming to him. I can't believe someone this *stupid* got away from me..." She trailed off, realizing her yapping would only distract them both.

"Sorry, I'm just cold."

The dampness and chill that had hovered around earlier had

started to vanish, but the final hour before dawn remained brisk; her fit-yet-feminine frame fought a shiver as she retreated into her jacket. Her sleeves dangled from her sides like nylon elephant trunks.

As her thoughts drifted towards fighting a chill, she had forgotten her words to Jim by the time he finally replied in a nonchalant manner.

"Uh-huh."

Jim was paying her little attention as he surveyed the Dodge. Becca moaned softly in defeat, leaning back against the rail of the fire escape. "This is gonna be a *long* day."

IV

"High Stakes"

The gunshots caused Becca to scream reflexively, and she pressed herself flat against the wallpaper in the hallway.

BANG! BANG BANG!

"Taylor! I got the bastard! Get your ass *down* here!"

Jim's voice triggered something primal in Becca. She flew down the stairs with the grace of a gazelle, descending in seconds what had taken an *eternity* to climb.

As Becca retraced her steps through the mansion, the living room's silent CRT stood as Becca left it. Besides her flashlight beam, the only light came from the VCR's green glowing display, which read ¦2:02 as she burst through, weapon ready.

"Jim! Where *are* you?"

Her rhetorical question was answered when she burst through the mansion's front door. Her partner was lying on the snow-covered driveway, bleeding from what appeared to be a stab wound on his upper arm.

"Are you okay?" she gasped, rushing towards Jim. Ripping her tie from her neck, she tied a tourniquet around his bicep. With a *grunt*, he rolled over on his side, covering his barrel-sized chest with his hand.

"Hold still, you're *hurt,*" she demanded, as she finished her knot. As she worked, Jim clutched his chest.

"I got 'em good," Jim bragged, a smile crossing his weathered face as she assisted him in sitting up. "I popped her in the ass as she ran away."

"You shot him?"

Jim let out a groan as he rolled onto his rear end, trying to stand without much success. "She... she fucking *stabbed* me, whaddaya *want* me to do, huh?"

With Becca's assistance, he managed to stand, supporting himself against a snow-dusted cherry tree beside the driveway. Becca shivered against the bitter cold, anxiously glancing around the yard, scanning for any sign of the suspect. Her partner was still clutching his chest, which raised red flags in Becca's mind.

I need to find this guy; I can't get distracted!

"Which way did he go?"

Jim released the death grip on his chest as he swayed unsteadily in pain. His finger waved in the direction of the white Dodge van, its tires half-buried in a white blanket of fresh snow. Leading around the corner in the fresh snowfall were a set of brand new footprints, and dripped along the trail was a successive line of crimson dots.

Blood. *Lots* of blood.

"The guesthouse, Taylor," Jim groaned. "I flushed them out." His hand, released from clutching his chest, was now dripping with blood. *Jim's* blood. Becca felt like throwing up.

"You're bleeding like a stuck pig—*Jesus.*"

Realizing his mistake, Jim's hand clutched onto his jacket again. When she tried to pull his hand away, he held it tightly. Her second effort was too much for her injured partner, and with horror, she unzipped his shredded jacket.

"Oh, no..."

Her eyes widened as she beheld it—a gash, diagonally through his chest, and almost a foot long. As she inspected the wound, Jim *moaned* weakly.

How could anyone get Jim like this? She'd witnessed him take down men *twice* his size! And he was armed, to boot; how could this guy get the drop on Jim Serrano?

If Jim had stayed in the house, that would've been me...

It froze Becca in place. She wasn't afraid of dying, right? Every agent knew the risks. Whatever the reasoning, and despite every bone in her body screaming at her to follow the bloody footprints... her partner's painful moans, combined with the spreading crimson stain on his chest, caused her to freeze in the wintry driveway.

She felt conflicted. She wasn't denying to herself that she was afraid; *every* agent knows the risks that come with the job... no, this wasn't fear—

I-I can't leave him like this!

Jim pushed her hands away, as if his wound were a hot stove and she was an ignorant child reaching for a burner.

"No, I *need* to call this in."

"Forget about me, Taylor, *save the kid!*"

*　　　　*　　　　*

Something nudged hard into Becca's ribs. The blinding darkness of a snowy, moonlit evening dissolved into the dingy, dimly-lit domicile beside them. Her eyes flew back open like curtains, and she shook the cobwebs off.

"Don't fall asleep on me, Taylor. It's *your* turn, now."

Becca gasped as she jolted awake, her heart racing. "I'm not asleep!"

Jim shook his head in mock disappointment. The city below was still dark and quiet, but the darkened hue of the sky above slowly transformed into shades of pink and orange as the sun prepared to rise.

She squatted against the rail, her right knee popping as she did so. She let out a subtle *yelp*, earning only a slight glance from

Jim, who didn't complain aloud as they swapped places, his knees cracking like gunshots as he stood.

Her tummy, full of half-digested coffee and not much else, growled in protest as she stared into her binoculars. The white Dodge van appeared pale-yellow under the incandescent glow of the street lights, even as the sky above the distant building began to transform into a shade of purple, the stars disappearing into what promised to be a picturesque day.

The plan was simple—if they see both the Mauler and the kid, either he surrenders, or they're gonna pop him. End of story. No hesitation, get the kid to safety.

Of course, they had little reason to believe Marissa was *inside* the van. If they only saw their suspect, they were *not* to engage. They needed intel more than anything... but the Dodge was their only lead. If they arrested him too early, he might refuse to talk— and besides, he wasn't *guilty* of anything yet. He might simply be a man driving a white Dodge van—

Yeah... with a dented side, a missing mirror, and no license plate? C'mon, Becca! Don't kid yourself!

Jim was already breathing heavily in the corner; Becca figured he might drift off to sleep, considering how tired he was, and she didn't blame him one bit. It had been a long night, and she knew he'd be ready to rumble when the time came.

For now, she tried her best to keep still and quiet; if it became necessary, she'd wake him.

As the seconds passed, the night gradually succumbed to the approaching sunrise. New York City sprang to life with the morning traffic's hustle and bustle, heightening her concern with each taxi that passed.

With all these people here, he won't have the balls to do anything... right?

The sun welcomed Becca as it rose behind her, casting a

blinding golden glow over the street. It reflected off the distant Twin Towers, looming over the skyline to the east, not far from their location. She glanced at her watch once again; it was 6:35.

Jim was asleep within seconds. *I forgot how awful his snoring is... sounds like someone trying to drown a walrus!* It wasn't loud enough to blow their cover... *but I might blow my top.*

Rebecca *sighed*, about to start talking to herself out of boredom, when she happened to glance at the Dodge van, casually observing it as its headlights flashed on and—

The headlights are on!

"Jim!"

Becca kicked his boot. She was now staring intently through her binoculars as smog flowed from the vehicle's exhaust pipe, sneaking around the van in a vapor cloud. After a few moments passed without Jim acknowledging her, she kicked him harder, sending his boot flying back into the metal handrails of the fire escape with a soft *clang*.

"*Wha—?*" he mumbled. Becca stood, unwilling to look away.

"The van just started!"

At that moment, Becca flinched as the sun's reflection off the Twin Towers smacked her in the irises, filling her lens with blinding sunlight. She squinted helplessly against the onslaught, trying to determine if anyone was in the van, or if they might try to drive away.

I'm not risking it.

"We have to go!" she cried urgently, already making her way back towards the fire escape ladder. But Jim was still frozen in place. Frustrated, Becca turned back to him, ready to protest, but then she realized what he was staring at.

"*Look!*" Jim pointed at the van. The Dodge was still parked and idling, its headlights struggling to overcome the brightening sunshine that outmatched them in every way. But what caught

48

her eye was a hand sticking out of the driver's side window, holding a cigarette.

It was the arm of a black man in a black business suit, but that was the only discernible detail from this distance. The tinted windows made it impossible to see anything else inside; the bright sunlight in her eyes only frustrated her further. He flicked the cigarette away from the van, and the window rolled back up, obscuring the man in darkness once again.

"I'll watch the van," Jim instructed, as Becca scampered down the ladder. "Once you're in position, I'll get the car. Sneak over there, but don't let them *see* you, Taylor. Stay on this side of the street."

She undid the clasp on her leather holster, freeing her Smith & Wesson as she ran, crouching low to the asphalt, alongside the right-hand side of Madison Street. Becca slipped behind each parked car, like a panther stalking her prey. She deftly ducked, dipping directly behind a derelict Dodge Durango, moving car by car down the road.

A minute later, Becca reached the van, now a few car lengths away, on the other side of the street. She would need to risk getting closer if she wanted to observe anything further, but without the cover of night to protect her, Becca knew that she had to be careful.

There was another problem: a *lot* of people were around now. The morning rush had arrived. A rush of school buses, taxicabs, and delivery trucks clogged the road, and pedestrians joined the rush, starting their Tuesday routines. Becca was suddenly aware that a woman dressed in black, wielding a pistol and ducking behind cars, might arouse suspicion—and they couldn't afford to be discovered.

She glanced around, hoping for a stroke of inspiration—*I have an idea.*

The building she was near had an entrance below street level, and she scampered down the steps before turning to scout the Dodge, which hadn't budged an inch. A work truck sat obtrusively parked in front of her, with a large, painted lobster on the side of its camper shell, and she couldn't see above it...

But, as she'd intended, it also blocked their view of *her*. She could see underneath the lobster truck... and that's *all* she needed. She pulled her phone out; it was a Nextel phone issued to all the agents in Becca's office. The 'PTT' feature was *extremely* handy.

BEEP BEEP! "I'm in position. I can't see him, but if he runs, I'm ready." A few tense moments of silence passed before Jim's reply beeped through, barely loud enough to hear.

BEEP! "Stand by. Someone's movin' inside the van."

Becca was growing warm in her jacket, especially with her suit underneath; the sun was fully over the horizon of buildings now. She retrieved the small, black box before removing her jacket and tossing it over the handrail, swiping a thin bead of sweat away from her brow. She then turned towards the street and returned to her post.

That was when the Dodge killed its motor.

Here we go.

Anxiety clawed at Becca's scalp. As the driver's door of the van swung open with a *groan*, she craned her eyes over the lip of the cement stairs, ignoring the coming-and-going of New Yorkers walking on the sidewalk—they paid her little attention in kind—as their man stepped out of the vehicle.

He was dressed in very fancy, executive-style leather shoes, which were polished black and flawlessly glistening in the rising sun, along with black slacks and socks. Becca's efforts to see his *face*, however, were thwarted by pedestrians and the lobster truck obstructing her view.

Frustrated, she slumped back onto the staircase.

BEEP BEEP! "I can't see his face, Serrano. Can you see him? I'm obstructed."

"Hard to tell. Black male. He's very tall, thin... dark hair. Possibly forty years old, maybe older. Dressed in an all-black suit. Wearing glasses. Can't make out much more."

"Copy."

She replaced her phone and watched the man's feet carefully. Fighting a surge of worry, she observed the man shuffling towards the back of the van, unable to see what he was doing. He disappeared beyond her view, now blocked by the lobster truck.

Panic was setting in when Jim spoke again. "Suspect is moving towards an apartment, looks like 98 Madison. I'm moving the car towards you, Taylor."

She stared over the stoop as the suspect's shiny shoes stepped into the street, as he shuffled slowly across. The red-brick apartments were a six-story mixed-use building, with a street-level entrance for residents, and the grated-shut entrance to the Ma-and-Pa hardware store below them.

Without hesitation, the man entered the apartments.

The moment the door closed, Becca climbed the steps to street level, spotting the Cadillac driving towards her. Jim parked it a few spots behind the lobster truck and killed it quickly, dashing over to Becca's side with his Glock in hand.

A few passersby noticed the pair of agents conspicuously holding guns, and Jim flashed his badge at them. Exasperated, they turned to flee, a worried expression etched on their faces.

"We're runnin' out of time."

Becca's heart raced as she looked at Jim with excitement. "Do we run inside?"

"No, *I'll* go in." Becca's shoulders slumped.

"I want you to stay with the Dodge, Taylor." He handed his partner the car keys and gave a firm nod towards their Cadillac, parked a few yards away. "If this van moves, you stay on 'em like flies on shit. You still have the box?"

Becca nodded, understanding her role. She holstered her pistol and gave Jim one last glance before he stepped toward the red-bricked apartment building in front of them.

"You call me if you need backup," she called after him.

"You worry 'bout *yourself*, Taylor," Jim snapped, stopping in his tracks. "We have a job to do. You do *not* let this van out of your sight, I don't give a damn if the fuckin' building *explodes*."

Becca's furrowed brow matched her glaring eyes, which gave him pause for a moment. He wanted to reassure her, and his voluminous voice wasn't working. He smiled with a sigh.

"Look, if you ain't heard from me in ten minutes, then call for backup, okay?"

Becca began to ask why they weren't calling for backup *now*, but thought better of it as she observed their surroundings—a bustling street packed with people and cars going about their morning routines. The *last* thing they wanted was a fleet of SWAT vehicles surrounding the joint.

Until we find the girl. Then we light this place up like Times Square.

Jim jogged towards the red-brick building, pistol in hand, yet hardly earning a glance from the New Yorkers crowding the sidewalk. He rushed up to the small perron leading to the front door of the apartment building; when he reached the door, he tried and failed to peer through the painted window. Exasperated, he tried the front door; it opened without complaint.

Jim's casual gait suggested he owned the joint. He removed his FBI jacket, stuffing it into a nearby trash can, not wanting to be noticed. Next, he shuffled past the mailboxes, pulling a pack of cigarettes out of his shirt pocket in an effort to appear natural. In this case, he didn't want the suspect to realize who he was until—

SLAM!

The sound from upstairs pervaded the silence of the lobby. Quickly up the dimly-lit stairs he tiptoed, the old wood quietly *creaking* under each step.

When he reached the third-floor landing, he could hear a voice inside the apartment. Hopeful to catch any hint of what was being said, Jim placed his ear to the door. The muffled voices carried through the thin wood, fragments of a one-sided conversation he struggled to make out.

"...moving out now... I know, I'm doing my best, but they won't go *away!*"

"I'm *trying,* this place is almost ready. I'm—"

"No, Mama! I'm not doing this for money, that was all *your* idea!"

"I-I think it's too risky."

"This isn't about *you*, Mama. Can it be about me for once?"

"Once I shake these clowns, I'll be back out there this afternoon."

Jim's heart raced as he steadied himself, quelling his instinct to burst through the door. With nearly twenty-three years' experience in the Bureau, he was well-versed in how these situations turned out. He knew how quickly things might turn, both in favor of his luck—

"How *dare* you, sir!"

...and in *spite* of it.

A commanding voice rang out, bellowing over him as he crouched there, causing Jim to jump in startled surprise.

"I don't think that's very *polite!*"

Jim turned to face an elderly woman, at least seventy years old, with a scowl on her face, a cane in one hand, and a leash in her other. The tiny Maltese dog on the other end *yipped* at Jim as she tried to squeeze by.

"Shh, I'm with the FBI!" Jim whispered frantically as he holstered his gun, holding his index finger to his lips, hoping to calm them down. "Please be quiet! You're—"

"...yes, I got keys made, but—*what was that?*"

Too late.

Jim's guts twisted up like a pretzel; he gulped air as he tensed his body—

With surprising strength, the old lady pushed Jim aside, impatiently squeezing between him and the door; this old lady was *not* having it. Caught off guard, he nearly fell to the floor.

"Hmph. I'm going to call the police—"

The door to the apartment flew open with a loud *bang,* and the man dashed out, running past the woman and Jim in a blur of black polyester. He scrambled down the stairs without stopping for a moment; he was gone before Jim could even react.

The woman let out a terrific scream as Jim scrambled back to his feet.

"FBI! Stop right there!"

V

"The Slowest Police Chase in New York History"

The moment Jim disappeared into the apartment building, Becca sprang into action. She sprinted towards the rear doors of the white Dodge van, hopeful she might check inside while Jim was investigating the driver.

"Damn... locked."

Her head whipped around wildly, wondering if anyone was watching her, before creeping to the side door. Her heart raced with anticipation as she hoped for a window she might peek through, but finding no such luck, the van was locked tight, and the rear windows were painted over. With a resolving *groan,* she shuffled back to the rear of the van, sitting cross-legged on the road behind it.

She dumped the black box's contents onto the asphalt, beside her butt. As she'd practiced, she attached the magnets of the tracking bug to the inside brackets of the rusty chrome bumper, connecting the wires to their respective harnesses. With a flick of her finger, the device's LED light began glowing red, and she pumped her fist.

Okay, we have a safety net. But what's taking Jim so long? She hadn't heard anything from him, and it had almost been five minutes; her Pulsar told her it was ⅂:◲⅁.

For whatever reason, her inner voice *screamed* at her that she needed to go upstairs. It distracted her so much that she'd forgotten the empty black box behind the van. Embarrassed, she scampered back over to retrieve it. She felt like everyone was staring at her, judging her; in reality, not a *single* stranger strolling by even noticed.

What's next? We end up in a snow-covered mansion on New Year's Eve? She punched the lid of the box in frustration, caving it inward. *I can't even do something this simple! Maybe I'm not cut out for field work anymore.* Rubbing her temples, she shook her head slowly.

The dented black box still in her hand, she crossed back towards the stoop. Stretching her legs and cracking her neck, she prepared herself in case of a foot chase. She knew she needed to get back into cover and monitor the van, but she was worried about Jimbo.

"We have a job to do. You do not let this van out of your sight!"

He was right, and she knew it. It was *vital* to prioritize the job.

If Marissa wasn't in the apartment, the plan was to let the man walk, so she had to be ready to trail the Dodge. The tracking device was a great backup plan, but that was all it was. If he escaped on foot, Becca was swift of foot (and Jim was a fifty-year-old with bad knees); if he got in the van, Becca was the superior driver. *She* was the true backup plan; her role was the *most* important.

Besides, Jim was one of the most experienced agents in the Bureau; as skilled as Becca was, she wouldn't be much help upstairs—

The door to the apartment building crashed open with a loud *smack,* and a man bolted out, his face covered by some sort of blue cloth, like a bandana or a balaclava. Becca froze, unable to act.

The man towered over her—he was much taller than Jim was —as she watched him dash down the stoop. Pressing buttons on his keyfob, he unlocked the van and threw the passenger door open in a panic.

Jim emerged from the apartment a few moments later. Upon his exit, Becca's paralysis broke; she dashed towards the Cadillac. The man began to panic, desperately fumbling the keys into the ignition as Jim reached the passenger side door, flinging it open.

"C'mere, you little *bastard!*"

He dove into the van, desperately reaching for the steering wheel. As the Dodge's motor roared to life, the driver threw the transmission lever into gear before turning his attention back to the FBI agent. Jim desperately tried to stop the van, reaching for the ignition as it accelerated away.

With a mighty *grunt*, the tall man brought his elbow down hard, smashing it towards Jim's eye. He ducked, deftly dodging the blow. The man's elbow rebounded off the cloth backrest of the bench seat. Jim reflexively grabbed it, slamming the man's forearm as hard as he could into the steering wheel.

The man *howled* in agony; the van's horn gave a *honk* as if it also felt his pain. The van veered to the right, bounding onto the curb and smacking through a road sign. It scraped over it with an awful *grind,* tossing both men around as the cab bounced and jolted.

Becca scrambled behind the wheel of Jim's Cadillac, revving the motor to life and peeling out as she revved after them. Her eyes dilated as she gripped the wheel; her breath came out in short bursts.

I've always wanted to find out what this Caddy could do.

"*Let's go, bitch!*" Becca exclaimed in glee as she floored the Cadillac, but immediately upon pulling onto Madison, she was forced to brake; the van was heading *directly* for her!

"Oh, *hell* no!" she screamed, throwing the DeVille into reverse. She turned the car sideways, blocking traffic on Madison Street, and slammed it back into park.

Her eyes were wide and white, a facsimile of the van. Becca

couldn't tell what was going on through the tinted windows, but judging by how much the van was rocking out of control, *some* mighty struggle was happening inside. Hoping to block his way east, she stopped in the middle of the road.

The driver was not a small man, and recovered quickly. He took control of their brawl as the Dodge slowed to a crawl. Reaching across the bench seat, he landed a solid blow to Jim's cheek with a closed-fist right hook. It knocked Jim back into the passenger door, bouncing off the seat. Dazed, he fumbled frantically for his firearm, which was still strapped in his shoulder holster.

With a grunt, the man jerked the van left and slammed the pedal to the floor. Protesting with an underhood *growl*, the van revved up, rebounding off the side of the parked lobster truck with a *crunch* as he attempted an overly optimistic U-turn. It jolted the men out of their brawl.

"Jesus!" Becca screamed, tossing the DeVille's gear selector back into drive.

The impact was pretty severe, forcing the man's balaclava to fall from his nose. At long last, Jim was able to get a good look at the face of the tall man they'd been searching for—

His eyes...

But his eyes weren't the most crucial detail he noticed. When his suspect realized his face was exposed, he turned towards Jim with a Cheshire Cat smile. Upon seeing the man's snarling grin, the grizzled agent felt his heart drop into his bowels.

It was his voice that threw Jim off. He had a heavy accent, with an unnatural pitch about it.

"Mornin', clown!" His sneer evolved into a growl as he clenched his teeth.

He's fuckin' crazy! Jim's mind screamed. *He's like that clown from "It". Except... his tooth... is it made of...?*

As the Cadillac easily caught up, the Dodge jolted with each impact, repeatedly kissing the van's rusty chrome bumper, a *thud* punctuating each hit. They weren't hard (Becca didn't want to risk knocking the tracking device off the bumper), but it was enough to throw Jim off balance.

"Where is the girl?" Jim demanded over the screaming engine. The punch Jim had taken had only done superficial damage, despite his daziness as he drew his Glock, haphazardly aiming it in the man's direction.

The van bounded recklessly from the sidewalk onto Madison Street. The Cadillac grew larger in the van's single mirror, as Becca *easily* closed the small gap between the two vehicles. The desperate driver sped the van up, unwilling to stop, and each bump forced Jim's hands *wildly* around the cab, disrupting his aim; he might as well be planting a flagpole in a tornado.

And now, they were moving too fast for Jim to force them to stop safely.

"Shut the van off, *now!*"

He glanced toward the Dodge's backseat and noticed the seats were replaced by a gurney, secured to the van's floor with a white sheet on top. There appeared to be a figure underneath, a lump of some kind. It was too difficult to make it out while the van was swerving and bouncing... but it appeared to be a... *person?*

Jim's eyes widened, and his face turned pale.

"What in the *hell?*"

This time, his Glock pointed at the man with purpose, but Jim's imagination was running wild. He knew it was *stupid* to look away, but as he struggled to process this horrifying realization...

His suspect was no fool. He watched Jim's eyes in the rearview mirror. The *moment* they glanced away, the man jerked the wheel left, blocking Becca's attempts to pull alongside them. However, he overcorrected; the van began to slide, drifting into the intersection with Catherine Street, narrowly missing a city bus as the tall man struggled to straighten back out.

Becca let out a *sigh* of relief, but it was short-lived; almost immediately after the bus cleared her view, the van jumped onto the opposite curb, causing its right front tire to burst loudly with a *bang* she swore she could feel, even inside the car.

Jim went airborne. His head smashed into the roof of the van so hard that it dented the metal, before falling to the seat in a lump and rolling onto the floorboard. He temporarily blacked out, his Glock tumbling beside him.

Now limping along with a *thump-thump-thump*, the van was bouncing down Madison. The Cadillac was growing larger in the crippled van's mirror—unable to gain any speed at all. The man couldn't reach Jim's gun without slowing down; he knew he couldn't stop, either.

Instead, he buckled his seat belt with a sinister smile. He had a plan.

Becca floored the DeVille. It easily kept pace with the disabled vehicle. With how erratically the van was swerving around the road, she knew they were still brawling inside. For a moment, she entertained the thought of shooting the back tires out, but didn't want to risk crashing the van, *especially* with morning traffic getting thicker.

Instead, she pulled her phone out, opting to call the office to keep them informed on the status of their chase. She struggled to steer while fishing through her pocket, and she fumbled the phone, watching it tumble from her hand and onto the floor with a *thud*.

"*Shit!*" She bent to grab the phone, and precisely when she looked away to unbuckle her seatbelt, the man slammed on his brakes; Becca never even glanced up.

The Cadillac smashed into the back of the Dodge with a

terrific *slam!*

On the bright side, Becca hadn't *yet* unbuckled her seat belt... but on the other hand, she was caught off-guard, never touching the brake pedal once. The sedan smashed into the van, doing nearly twenty as a tremendous force tore through the car. The impact was so violent that the rear of the Cadillac went airborne temporarily.

As Becca's head whipped forward, the first thing she noticed was that time seemed to slow momentarily. A blur of white airbags floated towards her as the car came to an abrupt halt. Things seemed to float in the cab like she was in orbit; the coffee cup she'd finished earlier came barreling forward. The other thing she recalled later was the sounds and smells—burning rubber and brakes, squealing tires, and an awful *grinding* she thought she'd remember for the rest of her life...

It wasn't until the car completely stopped, that time seemed to return to normal. Her first action upon realizing she was still alive was to punch the steering wheel three times in frustration.

"Awesome. Superb. Fuckin' *stupendous!*" The Cadillac's horn *honked* pathetically with every strike. Her head started to pound—likely from all the smoke now filling the cab—and she shook off a ringing in her ears.

"I'm *alright;* I'm okay," she mumbled, her hands busy checking over her body for injuries. She was breathing very hard as she glanced up, seeing the Dodge thumping west down Madison.

Her bearings were slow to return to her; fortunately, the van could barely move at *all* at this point. She rubbed her eyes, trying to force her vision back to normal. The engine was still running; the impact had been so forceful that the transmission shifted itself into neutral. When she selected 'D' with the lever, she was stunned when the Cadillac resumed the chase (albeit with a hard pull to the right now, and a lot of protest under the hood).

She struggled to steer the car with the deflated airbag in her way, but she managed to continue her pursuit of the Dodge as the DeVille limped forward again. The impact from Becca's car had been *significant;* the bumper of the Dodge was completely mangled, pushed into the rear door, and Becca let out a sigh with her realization that their tracking device was probably broken.

Unbeknownst to Becca, the crash broke much more than *that.* The impact from the Cadillac tossed Jim like a ragdoll from the floorboard, slamming him against the dashboard. He rebounded *hard,* landing awkwardly on the floor of the van, trapping his leg at an unfortunate angle.

When Jim's shinbone shattered, he screamed so hard his voice went hoarse.

Now, as the chase resumed, he was trapped on the floor of the passenger side, unable to move and barely conscious. He held his Glock tightly, whimpering in pain.

The Dodge bounded down Madison heading west, nearly running over an elderly man as they careened down the road. It seemed unwilling to drive in *anything* resembling a straight line.

I need to call Bill. We need backup!

Becca reached for her phone, but it was lost on the floor somewhere. She dared to glance down, but the deflated airbag covered her view of the floorboard. Her hand fumbled through the airbag, but she couldn't find it, and when she looked back up, *she* was the one that nearly hit an innocent bystander. Jerking the wheel left, she avoided the disaster, giving up on her phone with a *groan.*

"Well... *crap.* Maybe PD will call it in..." Still blinking the stars away, she followed the Dodge as it slid wildly onto St. James Street, now heading southwest onto Pearl.

As it struggled to turn at speed, the Dodge bounced off of a limousine and back into traffic as Becca strained to keep up in her crippled Cadillac. The car tried its best to test her driving skills, but she gripped the wheel like Jeff Gordon, doing *all* she could to keep straight. She tried to coax the car's V8 motor, but it seethed and groaned with every depression of the gas pedal.

The Cadillac's cabin continued to fill with smoke and exhaust fumes, so Becca cracked the windows, letting the morning breeze blow the smoke out. Her ponytail whipped behind her as she gripped the leather wheel, her knuckles white, her palms sweaty. In the moment, there was something about the chase that struck her... perhaps because she was still unaware of Jim's condition? Despite the danger involved with this suspect, this chase was... *exhilarating* to Becca. She felt sinister in realizing she was enjoying this.

The rusty Ram swerved and swayed as it bounced beneath the Brooklyn Bridge, leading the slowest police chase in New York history. Sparks flew from the now-exposed rim as the van struggled to get up to speed.

Her check engine light flickered on, and the engine began billowing various gases into the air at an alarming rate as it struggled to stay in gear. As much as she felt *alive,* time was running out. When a park approached on the left, she decided to end this chase now.

They crept up to a relatively fast pace, and Becca recognized this as her best opportunity—possibly her *last.* She saw the Dodge swerve to the right, and despite her hesitation to cause a crash, she had no choice—the time was right to try a PIT maneuver.

She floored the Cadillac, and it surged forward, protesting as she struggled to keep the disabled sedan heading true. The PIT maneuver was risky, *especially* with Jim still in the van... but she saw no other choice.

"C'mon, you hunk of junk!" Becca gripped the wheel with all of her strength, the hamstrings and veins on her forearms popping

out of her skin as she clenched onto the steering wheel. She pointed the beaten nose of the sedan at the rear arch fender of the van, and metal met metal in a grinding *crunch*. The Dodge drifted to the left with a *screech* as Becca jammed her wheel right, and the van spun in front of her in a cloud of white smoke.

The tall man let out a *yelp* as the top-heavy vehicle spun, threatening to roll over, spinning one half turn before smashing into the curb. It bounced backwards over the sidewalk in a shower of sparks, taking out a USPS mailbox and sending mail flying like confetti into the morning air, before smacking into a tree in the middle of the park. It came to rest beside an antiquated lighthouse, stopping *just* before smashing into it.

After hitting the van, the Cadillac crawled to a stop on the side of Pearl Street. She reached for her missing phone, which was buried under the massive deflated airbag on the passenger side. The smell of gasoline and ozone filled the Cadillac's cabin as she mule kicked the mangled door, using both legs to force it open with an effort as she escaped the mangled sedan.

The passenger door of the van flew open the moment she stepped out, stopping Becca in her tracks. She watched, frozen, her hand resting on her sidearm, as the tall man fell out of the Dodge first.

He rolled around in the mail-covered grass, moaning in pain and appearing bewildered, though Becca still couldn't get a good look at his face. As Becca attempted to approach, she nearly fell forward onto the asphalt. With terror, she realized she *too* was disoriented, and she shook her head, attempting to regain her composure as she prepared to draw her weapon and—

This time, she fell to her hands and knees, unable to make her legs work. As she struggled to stand, she heard a guttural scream, before a warning shot thundered from inside the wrecked vehicle.

This was all the cue the man needed. He rolled over,

scrambling to his hands and knees in a panic. Jim spilled out of the van, crumpling to the grass as his suspect made a break for it.

As he landed, he screamed a bloodcurdling roar of pain, and Becca saw that his left leg was absolutely mangled. Her face grew pale in horror, and she was going to be sick.

"Taylor! I can't get up. You gotta get the bastard!"

VI

"I'm Just Gettin' Warmed Up!"

With an effort akin to an Olympic powerlifter, Becca forced herself to her feet, waves of vertigo punching her in the head as she rose. Now back on his feet, the tall man was frantic to get away as he scrambled out of the park, rushing towards Fulton Street. Becca strained her eyes to see his face, but as he ran, the man had replaced his fallen balaclava.

Frustrated, she stumbled towards the wrecked Dodge van, where her partner was rolling on the grass, writhing in pain.

"Jim," she called out as she wobbled towards him, her hand on her forehead in a vain effort to recover. But she was also battling the shock of the sight of Jim's broken, twisted leg, which he was gingerly holding. "Are you alright?"

Jim rolled over with a *groan*, ready to scream at her when she joined him... except she wasn't there. She'd run right past him towards the rear doors of the Dodge... and her jaw hit the floor when she swung them open. An old, rusted gurney was strapped in the back of the vehicle, with a white sheet covering some lumpy form.

Her breath caught in her lungs. Terrified, she peeked under the cover, expecting to discover some macabre sight... but found a wad of dirty clothing, a portable television set, and a bundle of rope. There was *no* sign of Marissa Hernandez anywhere in the Dodge.

"What are you *doing?*" Jim screamed to Becca after a few seconds; his cry was half out of urgency, and half out of agony. A familiar surge of fear turned her bowels into Jell-O.

"He's our only lead, Taylor! Do the job!"

For a split second, she was standing in the snow again. *"There's two of them, Rebecca..."*

*　　　　*　　　　*

"You're bleeding like a stuck pig, Jim—*Jesus.*" Jim pushed Becca's hands away, as if his wound were a hot stove and she was an ignorant child reaching for a burner.

"No, I need to call this in." She reached for her phone to contact her office using the PTT feature.

"Forget about me, Taylor, *save the kid!*"

BEEP! BEEP! "Agent Taylor here." Becca ignored her partner, his blood-soaked shirt causing her great concern. "Agent Serrano is down—laceration to his chest and arm. Get help out here *right* away!"

After a moment, the response cracked through: "Copy, Agent Taylor. We're getting help out there. Do you want backup?"

Her face went pale as she watched her injured partner, swaying in the snow. Jim's hand held onto the tree, his other holding his wound.

"Yes!" she screamed, "I'm going into the guesthouse. Send backup!" She glanced at her partner, returning her phone to its holster.

"Are you gonna be okay?" she asked timidly. "They're on their way."

She bunched up her freed windbreaker, desperate to stop the blood oozing from Jim's wound. However, when she applied it to the laceration, he shrugged with a *yelp* so hard it knocked her backwards, causing her to fall with a wet splat in the slushy snow piled beside the driveway.

67

BANG!

Was that a gunshot? That came from the guesthouse!

Horrified, Becca was in fight-or-flight mode, and her gaze found Jim's, still barely standing.

"*Go,* Taylor," Jim screamed with surprising volume, causing Becca to flinch.

"Jim, let me help you!" Becca's maternal instincts overrode her sense of duty. She looked back up at Jim with horror, and he let out a series of heavy coughs as she stood, quickly brushing snow off her wet jeans. "You're really hurt!"

"But the *kid...*" Jim muttered, letting out a second set of coughs. "He's still in the house..."

"You got him, right?" Becca had assumed the suspect was wounded, so it shouldn't *matter* if he got to the house... unless—

At that moment, a scream unlike anything either of them had heard came roaring from the guesthouse, piercing the winter night. It was primal, guttural, and utterly terrifying; it struck Becca's core with ancestral terror, every instinct screaming to flee even as duty anchored her in place. It reminded her of the sound of a caged animal being tortured, a ghastly howl which would haunt Becca the rest of her days.

Becca was shaking, but she couldn't tell if it was from nerves... or from *fear.* She was nauseous as she grabbed Jim, glancing again towards the foreboding structure. "I'm not gonna let you die out here, not *alone!*"

"I told you to forget about me; you have a *job* to do!"

"*Dammit,* you said you got him... *Right?* I'm not gonna leave —"

"I didn't get *him,*" Jim said starkly, cutting Becca off. Her eyes went wide in horror as realization slowly dawned on her. Her eyes flicked back to the spattered blood drops which led around the corner, and her face went white.

"But... you said you got *him*? Didn't you—"

"I said, 'I shot *her.* '"

Becca's world swooned as she swayed on her feet.

"There's *two* of them, Rebecca."

*   *   *

A scream of "Hey!" floated into the back of the van, breaking her short-lived trance. Becca wasn't waiting for Jim to devise a plan; she already had one. She wasn't looking for guidance; she was looking for *Marissa*... and once Becca cleared the van, she started pursuit.

"He's getting away," Jim called, unaware she was already pursuing the suspect, her words barely audible as she blurred by him.

"I got 'em. *Call an ambulance, Jim!*"

Clear your mind, write your story... and breathe!

She took off toward Fulton Street, expending *every* bit of her strength. Although she knew little about him, two things were apparent: he appeared older than her, and he was *tall*... suggesting he was *quick,* even as Becca noticed him limping while dashing down the street.

She smirked. He might be fast, but Becca and Kelly jogged through Manhattan *all* the time. *Running on a gorgeous morning, like today in New York City... I would kill to work out like this.*

Sprinting as fast as she could down Fulton, she spotted the tall man heading down the street a block ahead, breezing past various shops and restaurants beginning to stir with life. Becca glanced at her Pulsar as she ran; it was 7:25. She shook her sweat-soaked sleeve as she sprinted along the street, straining to stay stuck to the seemingly serpentine suspect as he struggled to slip and slither to safety.

The tall man favored his left leg over his right, but he was still *fast*. Despite Becca's physical conditioning, she wasn't closing on him quickly enough. In this forest of skyscrapers, the baby blue sky overhead cast a strange, serene sensation over the city. But Becca recognized the actual stakes—if she lost her quarry for even a second, he could *easily* escape into any of the dozens of buildings that blurred by them as they dashed past.

Full of innocent people, no doubt. I can't risk that.

As Fulton Street dog-legged slightly west, the tops of the World Trade Center appeared over the buildings closer to her, slowly rising above her in a stereoscopic display of depth. She marveled, as she always did, at the sheer scope of the city and how everything seemed so important and monumental compared to her humble hometown of Stillwater, Minnesota.

She couldn't put her finger on it in the moment, with all that was happening, but at that exact moment in time, and place in her life... she felt alive. It was similar to the sensation she felt while pursuing the Dodge... she was *liberated*. Becca told herself to remember this for the rest of her life.

The funny thing was, she had no idea at the time how *seared* into her memory this run would become.

Dodging between taxicabs and cars crossing Fulton on William Street, the man dog-legged left, running against the one-way traffic flow. He came to a stop as he squeezed between the lanes, *narrowly* missing being clipped by a box truck, and crossed over to the right side of the street and onto the sidewalk, stumbling as he accelerated.

The flow of vehicles trickled to a stop by the time Becca reached William Street. As she turned left to follow, she *easily* crossed over to his side of the road without slowing. She closed the gap significantly, now within screaming distance of the man.

"FBI!" she hollered, a warning peppered by breathlessness.

"Stop now or I'll shoot!"

The man continued down the sidewalk, pushing past pedestrians and newspaper posts, until he reached another one-way road: John Street. He turned right, sprinting against the flow of traffic.

As Becca reached the corner a dozen seconds later, the Twin Towers invaded her field of view. They *dominated* the skyline as she sprinted to the northwest. A heavenly, yellowish-tinted glow reflected off the steel-and-glass superstructures as they welcomed their early-morning sunbath. The light glistened in Becca's eyes, and she momentarily lost herself in their beauty.

The man darted right, onto yet a *third* one-way street—a narrow alley called Dutch Street. Her lips pursed as he squirted around a Chevy Impala clad in NYPD livery, clipping the bumper and *nearly* falling. As the man fled past him, the stunned officer's jaw went agape as he watched from behind the wheel; Becca was soon to follow.

The officer stepped out of his car, his hand held high. Becca kept sprinting, her head turned towards him as she passed the Impala, her badge awkwardly dangling from her hand.

"I'm FBI," she breathlessly exclaimed. *"Call for backup!"*

The officer nodded as he climbed back into the Impala, flicking his lights on as Becca pushed herself even *faster,* barely noticing how out of breath she'd been until she'd spoken. The gap between them was shrinking, and as he hung a left back onto Fulton, she made the same turn about ten seconds later.

The man turned to check on his pursuer. His blue balaclava prevented her from identifying *anything* besides the man's bottle-green eyes, which filled with terror behind his steel-rimmed eyeglasses as he turned to focus on where he was running.

His eyes...

He dashed through Nassau Street until he reached Broadway.

For a short moment, he halted in the middle of the intersection, giving Becca time to consider tackling him. As she prepared to pounce, he juked quickly right, sprinting towards St. Paul's Chapel—*just* out of reach of Becca, who lost her balance and tumbled onto the asphalt, leaving her rolling on the ground.

With a *yelp*, she scrambled to her hands and knees. As she attempted to get up, her knees wobbled like broken toothpicks, her head still groggy from the earlier crash.

Shake it off, Becca! Get up and—

It dawned on her that many New Yorkers were now watching her, eyes fixated as she lay there like a clown in a suit. Her cheeks became glowing-hot embers as she stood in the street, forgetting the past ten minutes for a few short moments.

"Where did he *go?*" she thought out loud, recovering from her trance before beelining towards St. Paul's. Already sprinting at full speed, the man disappeared around the right corner of the church.

Becca faced a choice: follow him around the blind turn, or *guess* and try to cut him off. She chose the latter.

Sprinting along Fulton Street, she vaulted over the wrought-iron fence and ran beside the southwest side of the ancient brick chapel. Upon reaching the end, she pressed herself against the wall as she neared the corner, hoping to sneak—

The tall man walked right by Becca's corner with a casual gait, surprising her into an involuntary *gasp*. His walk was that of an innocent person on a morning stroll... his covered face the only giveaway. His eyes grew wide as they made eye contact, neither sure how to react.

Is this guy gonna attack me? If he does, he's got me dead-to-rights...

Instead, he shoved her to the side, bouncing her off the wall of the chapel and to the ground, before taking off across the church's courtyard, towards the fence Becca had leaped.

"That's assault, you *bastard!*"

Rolling to her feet, Becca resumed the pursuit, closing the gap with a more aggressive angle. He was about fifteen yards ahead as he leaped the iron fence and wheeled to the west, running down Fulton again. Becca reached the fence a moment too late, her hand grasping only air, *barely* grazing his clothing. His unbuttoned suit jacket fluttered behind him like a cape as he fled.

"Are you serious? *Stop running!*" Becca screamed after the man, who refused to oblige as he accelerated to a full sprint, only a few yards ahead. She'd catch him eventually; he was beginning to limp and grunt with every step.

And he's slowing down, too. I feel like I'm just gettin' warmed up!

Once they passed the churchyard, he sidestepped to the left, catching her off guard once again. She tried to keep up, but she stumbled—fortunately staying on her feet this time—allowing him to widen the gap. The tall man broke away from her, reaching the sidewalk on the southwest side of Fulton.

As they approached Church Street, he crossed under the porte cochère of the Millennium Hotel, zipping past an unsuspecting family unpacking bags from a taxicab. Becca heard them yell "Hey!" as they passed in a *blur*.

Her heart pounded so violently; her vision throbbed with *every* heartbeat. But she pushed through the pain as the man, running for his life, kept his pace up. The buildings to the east of Church cast a shadowy darkness over the entire area. The only skyscrapers illuminated by natural sunlight were the Twin Towers, which now loomed ominously above Becca.

She paid them no mind, however. He cut to his right, sacrificing some space between himself and Becca, before crossing Church and scampering onto the opposite sidewalk.

As the man pushed forward, a large throng of tourists was

emptying from a tour bus, parked in front of a long line of buses and taxicabs. A wave of stress rippled through her body as he desperately dove into the pool of pedestrians, obliviously craning their heads up to gawk at the massive Twin Towers.

When she entered the massive crowd, she identified the path he'd taken easily enough. A few people were knocked over, angrily yelling back at him from the sidewalk. She screamed "Sorry!" as she scurried through the crowd, trying not to lose sight of the tall man squeezing between unsuspecting tourists.

Like Barry Sanders, he kept bobbing and weaving through pedestrians like they were the opposing team's defense. As they approached Liberty Street, the entrance to the Concourse level of the World Trade Center rose into view as the crowd of people standing between him and the mall's entrance shrank in size.

He took one last quick peek over his shoulder and saw the trailing agent not far behind him, and made his mind up. Wheeling around, he disappeared into 4 World Trade Center.

"Oh, no," she muttered breathlessly. Her heart sank into her boots.

As the man disappeared inside, Becca's *own* glance shot upwards. The South Tower of the World Trade Center now rose high above her, a proud symbol of commerce standing starkly against the powder-blue morning sky.

Yeah... and there's tens of thousands of innocent workers in there. She *had* to stop him!

And so, Becca ran inside. As she entered, she had little reason to consider that she might not see that beautiful sky ever again.

VII

"She's Always a Woman"

Racing down the escalators and into the artificially lit entrance of the Mall under the World Trade Center, Becca squinted through the overhead halogen spotlights, trying to spot her suspect. Her futile attempts to rub the sunspots in her eyes away paid little dividends. She recognized two things immediately: the welcoming scent of freshly baked cookies and the hustle and bustle of shoppers. A contemporary version of Billy Joel's 'She's Always A Woman' played throughout the mall's speakers, and the gentle notes of flutes and guitars floated in harmony.

Sure sets an eerie ambiance for a foot chase.

It was still quite early. Becca glanced at her watch; it read ⅂:ϾϞ. Throbbing sensations behind her eyes seemed to harmonize with her rapid, breathless gasps, and Becca unsuccessfully blinked her headache away as she scanned for her man. Most of the shops in the mall weren't open, but that didn't stop the place from being packed.

Yeah, I'm not opening fire in here... She replaced her pistol in its holster.

It wasn't the pursuit that made her heart race; rather, it was the *pulse* of New York City, *throbbing* behind Becca's eyes. Despite most shops remaining closed, hundreds of people were already passing through the shopping area, starting their morning by grabbing a bite to eat, or relaxing in a café with a warm cup of coffee and a book.

This place is a zoo! She groaned out of frustration. In this vast sea of commuters, even this tall man could drown beneath a wave of anonymity.

"Son of a..." She seethed, her hands balled into fists. Becca stopped, scanning the crowd, her eyes *finally* adjusted. Passing by the cookie bakery she had smelled upon entering awoke her hunger, rising in intensity as she fought the urge to drool. She hadn't had a bite to eat yet, and she was *starving*.

Focus! Do the job!

Her suspect had vanished... and *panic* began setting in. She was about to pull her phone out and call Bill before a tall man walked casually across the concourse. Cautiously, Becca pushed her way through passersby as she approached the man—

"Oh?" An elderly, tall black man greeted her with a friendly, yet apprehensive, smile. "Did you need something, young lady?"

"N-no, sir..." she stammered, blushing. "I'm so sorry."

She turned around, continuing north down the hallway, passing a shoe store and reaching a four-way intersection. As she anxiously scanned the crowd, Becca stood on her tiptoes, resisting the urge to hyperventilate.

The tall man was nowhere to be seen.

"I'm too *short,"* she muttered, disheartened and panicking, before she had an idea. She surveyed the intersection's plaza until she discovered what she needed—a nearby bench.

Now, she *could* see over the mass of shoppers, some of whom stared curiously at the suited woman standing and panting on a bench. She searched all four directions, carefully scanning the crowd. Near the Borders bookstore and the Fine & Schapiro deli at the termination of one row of storefronts, she spotted a tall, dark-skinned man pacing ahead of the crowd.

He's heading for the subway! She leaped off the bench, flying through the air like a superhero in a suit, hoping the man hadn't spotted her yet. If she could reach him before he saw her, the chase was over before—

BEEP! "Taylor, are you there? Answer me!"

It was Becca's boss. Her phone was *not* on silent.

She ducked right, near a shuttered Sunglass Hut. Becca knew she had to answer. Jim *must've* been picked up by an ambulance by now, and nobody had heard from her since the accident... ergo, she understood Bill's concern.

As she delayed responding, she observed the man walking into the Borders at the end of the hall, filled with folks sipping coffee and reading newspapers. He snatched a page of the *New York Times* off a table and slid into a vacant chair, using the newspaper to shield his face. She sighed with relief; he likely thought this would help him hide. Ironically, this was the respite she *needed.*

BEEP BEEP! "Do you... copy, Bill? We're in the Trade Center... down in... the concourse."

"Good. I was wondering—*why* are NYPD cops calling me about you? I want a status report—*now!*"

She was still gasping for air, and her throat was sandpaper. "I-I have an eye on the guy, but I've been running all through Manhattan. I'm... waiting for backup to engage with the suspect. Copy?"

The silence was *deafening.* Watching her suspect—possibly the man she'd been chasing for *years*—casually reading the funny pages had her frothing at the mouth. Becca considered charging *right* at the man before her boss finally replied.

"Can he hear you?"

"Negative. He's in a coffee shop, hiding."

"Copy. We just picked Jim up... and he's *not* in great shape, Becca. He's on the way to Presbyterian right now." Becca's brow furrowed at the news. *Shit... I'm on my own.*

"Backup is on the way to the Trade Center. Can you secure

the suspect?"

Shaking the cobwebs off, she glanced towards the Borders. "I can engage him now if they're gonna be..."

Her speech trailed off, and her phone nearly fell from her fingers. The man stood up behind his table, staring past his balaclava into Becca's eyes. They locked gazes for what felt like *forever,* one anticipating the other's move.

His eyes...

She wasn't far from him—*maybe* forty meters—but the chase was *over* if he reached a subway station. Keeping track of him would be impossible.

Bill's response vanished into the ether. Becca was a diver deep underwater, now trapped in this muffled, ethereal world. The only sound was the bassline of her pounding heart; her vision in these murky depths was a wormhole linking directly into his eyes.

The tall man broke the stalemate first, side-stepping towards the subway station to his left. Becca's senses swam back to her, as a rush of color and sounds invaded her consciousness like a heavy dose of drugs.

She cut to the right, reaching the corner before him and cutting off his escape route. Aborting his plan, he pivoted back towards the deli, his shoes marking a scuff on the floor with an accompanying *squeak.*

As she turned, Becca *also* slipped on the slick shopping surface, straining to catch up. Running through crowds as if they weren't there, he took off at full speed towards the PATH station escalators, but—unbeknownst to either of them—that way was impassable. The rush hour in Manhattan had *truly* begun.

The man pushed through the throngs of fresh-faced New Yorkers climbing up from the station. Initially, this worked in his favor as Becca struggled to make up ground, but the crowd was too thick, *even* for a desperate criminal. He eventually gave up on the PATH plan, scrambling around the escalators. She tore through the crowd after him.

"Will you just *stop* already?"

He broke out of the crowd first, almost ten seconds before Becca did. The break in the coffee shop reinvigorated him, and the gap was significant when she resumed pursuit. A shocking revelation came alongside his newfound stamina: looming just ahead of the man was an enormous bank of elevators. The meager bits of saliva she had left dried up instantly as it dawned on her—they were underneath the North Tower.

If he's planning on going up... Their gap was too significant; she *knew* she wouldn't catch him in time. She assumed this guy wouldn't attempt going through the security checkpoint without a badge; he had a different scheme in mind.

The tall man approached the checkpoint and deftly vaulted over a stanchion-and-velvet rope barrier—the guard *barely* glanced up. An express elevator occupied by a group of commuters in suits was about to depart, and he turned towards it.

"*Hold the door,*" the man exclaimed with his hand up, gaining Becca's attention as well. She desperately tried to push through the passersby... but the doors slid shut moments before she arrived.

"*Shit!* You've gotta be *kidding* me!"

As the elevator began its arduous journey up the North Tower of the World Trade Center, Becca glared at the door, as if she could stop it with her eyes. Frustrated, Becca hammered her fists into the stainless steel surface of the doors, leaving tiny imprints as reminders of his escape.

She stepped back, gasping for breath and holding her dizzy head, before kneeling in front of the lift. She needed to calm down; she was teetering on the edge of an anxiety attack.

What would Jim do in this situation?

Becca considered her options. The 'obvious' choice was to pursue him, but if he was able to get back down before she could catch him, she *never* would. She also thought of calling Bill and asking him to set a perimeter in front of every single elevator bank. However, when she pulled her phone out of her pocket and pressed the PTT button, it gave her an error sound; there was no signal under the tower.

I can't even tell Bill where he went...

Left with little choice, she had to go up the tower... *now.*

VIII

"Becca Ate Here, Once..."

Becca stared at the digital display beside the express elevator doors, unwilling to look away for *anything* as she watched the numbers increase. The wait was killing her, and she was pissed—mostly at herself, for not taking him down when she had the chance. This was her penance; stewing in her own self-diagnosed failure while waiting for an elevator, seemingly taking forever before finally stopping on the 107th floor. The tall man could hide upstairs as long as he needed to; the Twin Towers were *massive*, encompassing millions of square feet of offices and mechanical floors.

Yeah... and 50,000 people.

Shuddering, she pressed the call button, knowing it would take a while. Becca couldn't stay here and watch all these elevators by herself—not to mention the stairwells—and she didn't want to risk leaving to find a phone.

Think, Becca—think! What would Jimbo do?

Becca was struck with an idea, and knew it would take luck.

Still breathlessly panting, she turned to scan the crowd. A few people who'd witnessed her chase were now staring at *her*... and that included the turnstile's security officer, whose attention was entirely on Becca. Proactively sensing he would talk to her anyway, she cleared her throat loudly, signaling the man with her index finger.

"Come here. I need your help!"

Dressed in a sharp Summit Security uniform, the officer

glanced around as if she were addressing someone else before timidly approaching her. After Becca explained what had occurred, the officer made some calls on his radio before confirming he would call the NYPD. She asked him to watch the elevators the best he could until they arrived; she requested he contact Bill as well.

Nearly *five* minutes elapsed before the express elevator returned to the concourse. As expected, the man wasn't part of the sparse crowd leaving the car. Becca stepped alone into the stainless steel lift, hitting the button labeled 'Restaurant' for the 107th floor.

Windows on the World. She had no idea where to start her search, but she figured that was as good a place as any. *I can work my way down, floor by floor, if necessary.* She counted herself fortunate he'd gone all the way up here; he could've started on the 50th Floor, and she would've had to guess.

The ride up was uneventful. The car zipped up the tower at an impressive pace, yet still took long enough that Becca grew impatient. Her ears popped twice as she counted the numbers increasing.

BEEP BEEP BEEP! Becca silenced her watch; the time was 8:00.

Finally, the doors opened with a *ding,* and Becca stepped into the most prominent restaurant in the world. Sunlight flooded the floor through the restaurant's massive east-facing windows, thin slats of glass which made you feel like you were standing on the doorstep of heaven when you looked outside. The view surrounding them was breathtaking; *you could practically see Boston from here!*

At the same time, the view from the balcony Becca now stood at was equally as impressive. The two-story venue was relatively empty, but there were *still* over a hundred people at *Windows* this morning. Most of them were folks who worked in the tower, enjoying their breakfast; however, the servers and bussers were also preparing for a busy day of diners. The smells of freshly-fried bacon and other morning foods wafted into her nostrils, making her tummy rumble once again.

Empty tables were already set with brilliant white cloths and bright yellow dahlias in crystal vases. Soft classical jazz played in the overhead speakers. She could hear the hustle and bustle of a conference downstairs, in the banquet area.

It would be so easy to blend into the crowd down there.

Staff prepared to serve the conference downstairs, and some glanced at Becca as they worked. Regardless, they didn't seem concerned about the FBI agent standing over them, staring out over the crowd like some Roman emperor, assessing *everyone* there. After a few minutes of fruitless searching, she gave up, returning to the center lobby.

Becca's boots stepped onto the plush carpet, her legs wobbling with exhaustion. Overwhelmed and overheated, she stopped to slump against the marble façade of the elevator lobby. The cool stone surface felt refreshing after her long run, and her sweat-soaked shirt absorbed the cold, sending a shiver throughout her body. She found herself not wanting to move, *finally* experiencing a shred of relief.

Despite the respite, however, a visceral ripple tore through Becca. It could be that familiar lump in her throat, but she needed to get moving. She approached a pretty young woman preparing the reception desk nearby, and she smiled in greeting.

"Hello! I'm Special Agent Rebecca Taylor; I'm with the FBI. Did any suspicious men get off the elevator a few minutes ago? *Right* before me?"

The woman stopped organizing menus, and her baby blue eyes met Becca's. She was *maybe* twenty, with blonde hair cut to shoulder length and a bright red headband holding her bangs. She wore a big pearl necklace around her neck, accented by a low-cut white dress. The intoxicating scent of cucumber-melon body spray floated around her like an aura.

The cherry on top—she came with a million-dollar smile. Becca caught her eyes flicking downwards, before scolding herself.

"*Oh!* Yes, a group came up a few moments ago, and this *really* tall guy walked out of the elevator, and he took the stairs down." She paused a moment before continuing, making finger quotes as she spoke. "Like, I dunno if I'd call him '*suspicious*' or not, but he seemed nice."

Her finger shot past the lobby, towards one of the stairwells.

"Was he acting weird?" Becca was struggling to remain calm. "Was his face covered by a cloth? Can you remember what he looked like?"

"Um... I didn't see much, except he was black, and, uh—*oh!* I think he was wearing a suit." The young lady cooed. "Oh, he was, *super* cute, though. He was really tall... had the most *dreamy* eyes —oh, and his face was *totally* not covered, and he had a great smile..."

"*Thank you!*"

She didn't wait for the receptionist to finish; Becca was already turning to sprint back across the lavishly luxurious carpet. She caught herself feeling guilty—how could she continue ignoring the opulent restaurant, with its plush rugs and marble walls emanating a sense of stature and class... being ultimately desecrated by her filthy work boots. Her brain felt like it was overheating—almost *cooking*—in her skull, prompting her to pause and scan the venue again... when her eyes landed on their old table.

Well... the area where it was... The place had changed a *lot* since then. Becca ate here once...

It was their seventh anniversary. December 27, 1994. She recalled his soft, wavy hair... his little goatee he always kept trimmed. The smell of his Ralph Lauren aftershave... the way he winked at her when he told a joke—yes, Becca *was* distracted. Becca swooned simply by imagining him.

That day belonged to the Taylor family, fully dressed to the nines. *He always looked so damned handsome in a suit.* Ken insisted on taking her somewhere fancy to celebrate. It wasn't only their anniversary they were celebrating that year; he'd finally published his first novel: a sci-fi fantasy thriller titled *Bernhardt.*

Before their anniversary meal at *Windows,* the Taylors enjoyed a family outing into the city. First, they went to the observation deck of the South Tower. Next, the Statue of Liberty, followed by various other touristy locations around Manhattan. Chad got the genuine New York experience for the first time with his birth parents.

It was, tragically, his *only* time...

She missed Ken so much right now. She missed how he would always make their lunches for them every morning and tell her how appreciative he was of everything she did for the family. She loved his witty sense of humor. Memories she had repressed for so long now poured back into her mind as she longingly stared at that table... wishing impossibly hard to see them still sitting together and madly in love on a snowy evening in 1994.

And that, in turn, reminded her of CeCe. She loved her as much as she'd ever loved Ken; they were the only two people in Becca's entire life who treated her with the respect she believed she deserved, and she cherished them both for it.

"Snap *out* of it, Becca!" she scolded herself, skipping across the plush carpet towards Stairwell A.

Well, if he's not on 107, I might as well descend, floor-by-floor...

The narrow void beckoned to her like a forbidden cavern, a hollow and empty tomb. It was dimly lit and unnervingly quiet, with bright reflective tape covering the concrete steps, guiding her down in the dingy fluorescent lighting.

Becca did not want to go in; her body was *screaming* at her to get out of here. But she had no time to be nervous. Ignoring her instincts, she hesitated, listening for the man in the silence.

A few tense moments passed before she heard the echoing *clang* of a door, one or two floors below them. It rang out in the hollow, empty stairwell—Becca could feel the door closing from the air pressure alone.

"No place to go 'cept down, I suppose," she whispered nervously.

The only sounds that pervaded the silence of the narrow stairwell were the echoing of her boots pounding on each stair. Dread caressed her nervous system like an old puppet on catgut strings as she anxiously descended.

Becca desperately wanted to turn tail and leave, and exit back to the street. The urge was *overwhelming,* and she had no idea why. Something in her subconscious was screaming at her, and she tried her best to ignore it. It was likely some leftover kernel of doubt, finally germinating into a stalk of insecurity... nothing she would listen to, anyway.

Skipping 106, Becca stopped at the next floor heading down. The placard beside the door announced:

STAIRWAY A
FLOOR
105

Uncertain what awaited her, she freed her holster's clasp and slowly opened the door to the office area. It was unoccupied, with only a few overhead lights illuminating the elevator lobby as she stepped out of the stairwell.

You could hear a pin drop, it's so silent! It reminded Becca of a church. *Heh—the Church of Commerce. Free absolution with every short sale!*

This floor was a pristine, sterile atmosphere she'd contaminated; even more so than in *Windows,* Becca felt she didn't belong here. *This place gives me the creeps... I would hate to be lost in here.* As she crept through the lobby, she could hear elevators zipping through the tower behind her, reminding her of the situation's urgency. If the suspect escaped to the ground floor, her goose was cooked. *I sure hope Bill got some people down there... because if he escapes, Marissa is a goner.*

"She won't be the only one—get back to work, girl."

This snapped her out of it. She glanced down at her Nokia... still no signal. *Shit.* With a *sigh,* she walked through the door to the offices, searching for a landline to call Bill.

"FBI! Anyone here?"

There was no response. Eventually, she rounded a corner, revealing another open-floor office space, complete with cubicles and desks aplenty. Becca was familiar with the general layout of each floor; this was similar to most of the tower's other floors. The grand windows of the North Tower, both impressively tall and remarkably *skinny,* filtered the sunlight in from the east, giving the office a heavenly glow which made Becca feel even worse for invading it. Nevertheless, she spotted a phone and sprinted over to it.

Looking up Bill's phone number in her Nokia, Becca wrote it on the back of her arm using a pen before dialing it into the conference phone. It rang twice before her boss answered, his voice more 'friendly' than it typically was when she called.

"FBI, this is William Bushnall."

"Bill, it's Becca."

"Becca!" He grumbled, obviously caught unaware. His tone changed to its more familiar, 'authoritative' pitch. "Where are you?"

"I'm on the 105th floor of the North Tower. My suspect ran up here. I'm in pursuit." She rubbed her eyes, desperate to rid herself of her migraine. "Didn't those rent-a-cops downstairs call you?"

The silent office floor made her uncomfortable as she spoke. It might be quiet, but that meant he could be hiding *anywhere.*

He might be watching me right now. She shuddered. *That's so creepy...*

The thought that she would have to sweep every floor caused her to *groan.* How was she supposed to find him alone? And instead of searching for the tall man, she was on the phone... again.

"Yeah... I've already got the exits covered. NYPD is heading down there with our boys; if he comes downstairs, we'll catch him."

"Elevators *and* stairs, Bill. If he gets out before I catch him, you're the last line." Becca scribbled notes on her arm as they spoke.

"Jim was unconscious when we picked him up, so if you have anything on this guy, it'll help."

She cleared her throat. "He's about six feet five, a black male. Approximately forty years old. He hurt his leg in the crash, but he's still fast. Wearing a blue face covering. Dressed in a suit. Has green eyes and dark brown hair. That's all I got."

Bill groaned on the other end. "Tall black man in a suit? That's not a lot to go on, Taylor."

"I know. Maybe ask Jim when he comes to?"

"Becca..." her boss trailed off. She *knew* it was bad, but wasn't prepared to hear it.

"He's in surgery. Worst goddamned broken leg I've ever seen."

Jim... I wish you'd have let me go up there with you... "Well, he's jumpy, Bill. If he runs, he's probably your man." She pulled her Nokia out, groaning when the useless thing still refused to connect to the network. "My phone has no signal up here, so I won't check in for a while..."

"Stay on him. I'll text your phone if we get him. When you get down, call me, but keep looking for him!" Bill paused for effect. *"You* know what it means if he gets away..."

She hung the phone up with a *sigh.* With no reason to stay on 105 any longer, Becca returned to Stairwell A and dropped to the 104th floor. This time, when she opened the doorway, the lobby was *alive* with activity. There were likely only a few people... maybe a *dozen,* but it was still a shock to the senses after the emptiness of 105.

As she had previously, she scanned the floor, searching through an endless sea of cream-colored cubicles and offices. Convinced her suspect wasn't hiding here, Becca returned to the lobby. A quick peek behind the bathroom door led to an unpleasant smell, and she decided it was a crappy place to check, so she returned to the lobby, holding her hands up high.

"Your attention, folks, *please!"* The folks in the elevator lobby looked up at the agent who had gained their attention. "I'm Rebecca Taylor, I'm with the FBI. I'm searching for a tall man in a suit with dark brown skin and a face covering. Has anyone seen him?"

The employees looked around at each other, some shaking their heads no or shrugging helplessly. After a few moments had passed, Becca cleared her throat.

"He's armed and dangerous. He's a wanted man. If you see him, call 911 *immediately!*" The others glanced at one another with nervous expressions. Oblivious, Becca shot them all a salute.

"Have a good day, everybody!"

Her next target was the 103rd floor. She turned left out of Stairwell A, running out of the elevator lobby and into the office area. The floor that spread around Becca shocked her senses; this space was *massive* compared to the other floor.

This floor was *abuzz* with early life on this Tuesday morning. She could smell fresh coffee brewing as she walked on a pattern of drab tiled carpet, lit by sunshine filtering through the east-facing windows, which rendered the overhead fluorescent lights useless.

Becca disliked the office environment, but at least it was quiet here. She listened carefully for the tall man, but she heard no commotion. Before turning the corner back towards the elevators, she peeked around it carefully, not wanting to startle anyone, but also giving her the element of surprise. The area was silent, and Becca was about to enter the stairwell when, from behind, a elevator's chime announced its return.

Turning, she stared in stunned silence as the occupants of the lift exited onto the 103rd floor. The first person in a conga line of employees to exit the elevator was the tall man, who stepped out nonchalantly.

She was already moving towards him before he even noticed her.

"Stop! FBI!"

For the first time, the dark-skinned man's expression was visible, as the balaclava was no longer covering his face. He was a lot younger than she expected.

The man's gaze locked with hers, adjusting his tie as he smiled at her invitingly.

His eyes...

"Can I help you?"

Becca didn't waste a breath, sprinting across the lobby at full speed. She drew her pistol, her brisk walk turning in to a jog... then a full-out *sprint*. His fight-or-flight instincts kicked into gear, and he wheeled around, fleeing through the door to Stairwell C.

With a *sigh*, Becca resumed the pursuit.

IX

"An Angry Tea Kettle"

"I'm *going* to catch you eventually," Becca declared triumphantly, gaining on her suspect as they raced down the stairs of the North Tower. The numbers indicating their floor, labeled by a placard above each door, decreased alarmingly as they descended past the 100th floor.

The man whimpered as he fled, scampering down each stairway, nearly slipping and falling multiple times. It struck her as odd. He seemed more terrified of her *now* than before; in the mall, his eyes seemed filled with anger and hatred. But Becca knew better.

He's afraid now, because he's guilty, and I'm so close to catching him. He knows his time is running out—and once she caught him, at least they'd buy Marissa some time. With each passing landing, Becca fought the urge to leap onto him from above.

If he stops to open a door, I'll make my move.

Upon reaching the 99th floor, the door into the lobby was slightly ajar, and the suspect took this opportunity to escape. He slung the door against the wall with a *smack* and ran into the elevator lobby, barely evading Becca's grasp.

The suspect, demonstrating *incredible* agility, leapt like an Olympic hurdler over a young man bending down outside the stairwell door, tying his shoes. A glance back confirmed she was still hot on his heels, so the tall man pushed into the eastern offices.

Surprisingly, the man was able to stay a few steps ahead—in

fact, he seemed to have *gained* ground on her.

Becca could not say the same. She was starting to fatigue; her muscles were filled to the brim with lactic acid, and every breath she inhaled burned her lungs as she desperately needed to rest. *Not to mention the pounding headache I have.*

But she kept pushing with everything she had, staying hot on his heels as he wheeled around the corner, heading south towards the opposite side of the office floor, before turning right. A hallway led back to the elevator lobby, and the man entered it, throwing open the door leading to Stairwell B.

If he really thinks I'm going to chase him down ninety fucking floors...

Becca stumbled into the stairwell, her calves now threatening to cramp. She was running out of time, but she couldn't just *shoot* the man.

She needed him to make a mistake, and once she saw an opening, she'd nail him.

They crossed back and forth down the stairs before he reached the 93rd floor, and bolted out into yet another office area. As she followed him in, the office space here was even busier than the others, with a cluster of people preparing to start their work days.

"What do you *want?*" the tall man cried, the gap between them still growing ever so slightly larger.

She didn't respond; she was too busy gasping for air as she pursued him. Out of curiosity, Becca glanced at her watch; the time was 8:22.

I've been chasing this guy for over an hour? The realization made her desperate to end this, but no force on Earth could stop her before she caught him.

As he led her through the offices, they reached a dead end. She nearly collapsed as the man stopped in a corner of the office, between the windows of the tower and a large conference table, and he and Becca began a standoff.

She couldn't quite reach him—but he couldn't *escape,* either.

"What do you want?" the man repeated, breathless and exasperated.

Becca leaned onto the table, breathing so hard she couldn't even reply, and she held her pistol up with one hand in a pathetic threat. She was dangerously close to passing out.

"I... I just... wait a second..."

A crowd of onlookers began to gather behind the stalemate.

"What do you *want* from me?" He was barely breathing hard as he held his hands out passively, suggesting he wasn't a threat, but she continued to wave the pistol around.

Is this guy on drugs? How is he still standing like that? I run marathons, and I'm about to faint!

"Excuse me, ma'am," a deep voice emitted from behind her. "What is going on here?"

"F... FBI... I'm Special Agent... Rebecca Taylor..."

The suspect began to shift towards her left, where an aisle led through the cubicles back towards the elevator lobby. The man with the deep voice approached Becca, who was still brandishing her gun.

"You need to put that away," the man stated, pointing at the weapon. "We don't need anyone to get shot."

"You need to mind... your own damn *business...*"

She could barely stand up straight. The stranger who was intervening had been joined by a small crowd, gathering to see what the fuss was about. As the tall man began to squirm away, she wobbled in his direction.

"Stop right there—*you're under arrest!"*

Unwilling to acquiesce to her demands, the tall man was (at least for the moment) *not* under arrest, despite Becca's claim. She held the gun up in protest; it was all she could muster.

"Hey, *wait a second—*"

He turned towards the hallway, sprinting through the pack that now jammed the hallway. It was fortunate for Becca, though; it slowed his progress.

That's good, because I don't know how much longer I can do this.

With a *groan* that emanated through her entire body, she lumbered forward, the already-parted sea of workers allowing her through. She made it to the lobby right as the doorway to Stairwell B closed, and she breathed a sigh of relief—a moment later, and he might've *escaped*.

The chase resumed once she reached the stairwell, and the man nearly slipped and fell on a landing between floors. Becca took her chance; she leaped from the third step and snagged his collar as she stuck the landing. Despite being exhausted in comparison, she was still strong enough to drag him down hard onto the concrete landing with a *thud*.

"Hey!" the man cried, her fingernails digging into his neck.

He reached up, grabbing the handrail and using it to vault himself upright, his silk tie slipping from her sweaty palm. He scrambled down the last flight of stairs and ducked into the 91st floor doorway.

Becca followed right behind him, close enough to reach his tie again, as it flailed behind the fleeing man. She glanced at the placard on the wall, hanging beside the door on the landing:

95

* * *

They entered the quiet, early morning serenity of a vacant elevator lobby. The tall man ran past another stairwell and into an office to the east, sprinting into an open office cubicle ahead of Becca... which had *no* way out.

I got you, now.

The man turned, trapped, and raised his hands. Struck with a second wind, she leaped forward. Using her body weight as a battering ram, she speared the man hard in his chest as he fell backwards through a cubicle wall. The structure buckled and cracked into a pile of plastic and composite wood as they landed on the other side in a crumpled mess, the man still struggling in vain to escape his captor.

Becca scrambled to get up, her suspect buried beneath the rubble—she had to act *fast*. Pushing into his neck with her knee, she grabbed his left wrist in an attempt to pull it behind his back... but this man was strong! Becca had surprising strength for her size, but she needed to restrain him... and *quickly*.

"Stop moving... or I'll... *shoot* your ass!"

Becca gasped for air as she fished a pair of handcuffs from her slacks. As she placed the cuffs on his left wrist—the man *whimpered* as she did so—a few of the floor's employees wandered over towards them, curious what the ruckus was about.

"Ow! You are hurting my arm! *Why* are you doing this?"

He complained in a heavy accent of exotic origin, his voice muffled by the pile of debris he was buried in. She rolled over, throwing her hands over his back as she strained to cuff his other wrist; he was as sweaty as she was, and her exhausted body barely had the strength to grip his hand.

"I did not *do* anything!"

"Stop resisting!" she screamed with a cough as she tried to twist the man's free arm behind his back, the man screaming about

it hurting as she completed the task. Her mouth sticky and dry, Becca turned her head, hawked up a thick wad of spit, and ejected it into a nearby trash can.

Nice shot. But that's fuckin' nasty.

With a final *moan*, Becca rolled off the tall man's back, lying on the broken piece of cubicle wall as she stared at the ceiling, breathing so hard that she lost her eyesight for a moment. The seductive caress of sleep teased her eyelids briefly, forcing her to slap herself awake.

"Isn't it a little early for all this commotion?"

A tall, thin, redheaded man with eyeglasses wandered over, slurping a mug of coffee as he stood over Becca's lying body.

Sluuuurp!

"I... give me a second... I can't *breathe...*"

The red-headed man walked into the destroyed cubicle as Becca lay on her back, breathing heavily to the point where she couldn't even lift her head.

"Are you going to explain what the hell just happened here?"

"FBI," she stammered, fishing her wallet out of her slacks as she squirmed onto her butt. "This man is under arrest. He's wanted for multiple crimes."

The tall man, still buried in rubble, rolled himself to his left, finally freeing his face from underneath the cubicle's remnants.

"I have never seen you before in my *life!*"

Becca dusted the sleeves of her suit jacket off, only noticing the small hole in it as she did so, and she *moaned* as she took it off to inspect it. She glanced down at the man as he rolled around in the debris. "I've been chasing you for an hour, you son of a bitch. You're done."

"I do not even *know* you—I was just trying to get a *job!*" the man complained as Becca and the redheaded man picked him up and sat him in a mesh office chair. "You are *crazy!*"

Sluuuurp!

Becca turned to the red-headed man, finally recovering an ounce of strength in her voice as she caught her breath. "Jeez, dude, you *think* you could do that any louder?"

The red-headed man lifted his mug for another slow slurp; the sound was seemingly sprinkled with sarcasm, and she struggled to suppress the urge to cuff him next.

Sluuuurp!

"Hi, there. I'm Tim Atwood. I work for Lower Manhattan International. And I don't have one of *those.* "

He snapped his fingers, pointing at her Smith and Wesson, which was now clearly visible since she'd removed her suit jacket. She shrugged and set the ripped suit jacket on the desk. The cool air in this office was nice against her sweat-soaked dress shirt, and she *instantly* felt relief.

"Nice to meet you," she grumbled, finally sitting atop the desktop, next to her jacket.

She fought her desire to risk closing her eyes, remembering how easily she nearly slipped away moments ago. Despite his annoying slurping, the smell of Tim's coffee was making her drool. She was probably going home after this was finished; she needed to recover *badly*.

But she had to admit, she *was* thirsty.

"Hey Tim, can I get a couple bottles of water, please?"

Tim set his coffee down and walked past them, over towards a kitchenette near the elevator lobby doors, before making a pathetic noise that struck her as mock disappointment. "*Oooooooh*, we're out—but I might have some in my office, I'll be back in a jif."

Becca sat there for what seemed like forever, enjoying the air conditioning of the 91st Floor. Still seated in the mesh chair, the tall man was gasping for air...

But compared to how hard *she* was breathing, it was

nothing...

His bottle-green eyes were as wide as the towers were tall, and burning with fear. After an uncomfortable amount of time had elapsed, he looked away, staring down at his own dirty suit.

"And what's *your* story?" Her breathing finally returning to a manageable level, she shifted to face the tall man. "I need to know how you stay in shape, kid. I've never had a foot chase that intense in my entire career!"

Her attempt at levity in her questioning didn't entice the man to respond; he wouldn't even look at her. She tapped his polished dress shoe with her old, dirty work boot.

"I'm talking to *you*, sir. You got your ID on you?"

It had been nearly *two* hours since she had tapped Jim's boots to wake him up the same way. And, in all that time, this was the first time Becca had a decent chance to get a good look at her suspect—*at least, when I'm not about to faint...*

He wore a silver polyester dress shirt, with a blue polyester tie and black slacks. He wore polished dress shoes and steel-rimmed eyeglasses, which had somehow stayed on the man's face during the arrest... but were now twisted badly. His black, wavy hair was slicked back, and was very clean and well-maintained—even after he'd gone through a *wall.*

He looks like a green-eyed Tyson Beckford. I can see why that hostess thought he was handsome; he's quite attractive.

However, what stood out to Becca the most was his age. They'd thought he was middle-aged, but she would've bet dinner he wasn't even old enough to *drink!*

Jim... I hope you're alright... Her eyes instinctively flicked up at the man's own, glaring at him with spite. The man stared at her, his eyes as wide as dinner plates, though Becca noticed they were *also* glossy and teary.

He wasn't like this before... is he trembling?

"Why were you running from me?" she demanded.

"Why are you *chasing* me? You frightened me!"

"Because that's my job. I chase bad guys. And *you* are a bad, bad guy."

"What? I do not even *know* you!" Tears finally broke their surface tension with his eyelids. As the streaks coursed down his face, he sniffled hard to fight his runny nose. "I did not *do* anything!"

"You ran downstairs as soon as you got off that elevator on 107, didn't you?"

"I got scared, I am sorry!" His eyes pleaded with Becca to hear him out. "I was not running, I was just trying to find..." he trailed off, processing what she had said.

"Wait, what do you *mean*, 107? I never—"

"What's your name?" Becca demanded, cutting him off. He remained silent, so she grabbed his right arm and yanked him out of the office chair.

"You got an ID on you, champ?"

"Hey!" he exclaimed angrily as she reached into his slacks, retrieving a navy blue vinyl wallet from his right rear pocket, with a picture of 'Mega Man' adorning the front of it.

"Classy." She rolled her eyes audibly at the man.

With a *rip*, the velcro clasp tore open to reveal the man's driver's license. Her face twisted, and she tried not to laugh at the man. It claimed his name was Quarren Michaels, and he was from Los Angeles:

"Quarren Michaels, eh?" She looked at 'Quarren' with skeptical enthusiasm, shaking her head dramatically. "Born in... October 1947? Holy shit... when we start chatting about your workouts, you've *gotta* tell me about your meal plan too, because... wow! You look *good* for almost being fifty-four!"

Her counterfeit smile melted into genuine exasperation. She scoffed as she put the fake ID back into the wallet, before replacing it in her jacket on the desk. "That's not your *real* name, is it?"

The man refused to look at her. "My name is Quarren Cambanda. There, are you happy?" He turned away from Rebecca, pouting like a toddler in a business suit.

"Quarren, I've lived in the Tri-State area since I was a little girl. So I've heard a lot of accents. You're not originally from California, are you?"

"No, I am from a village, far away from here."

She repeated her question. "Quarren, why'd you run from me?"

"Why did you chase me?" he replied bitterly, his glare demanding an answer. "*You* are the one who pulled a gun on *me;* I am only trying to find a job!"

"Bullshit; you just caused a lot of damage." Images of the scene at the park flashed through Becca's mind; she saw Jim falling onto his twisted leg, which had practically liquefied under his body weight, and she grew angry again.

"You assaulted *two* Federal Agents, Quarren. Not to mention, you hit a bunch of cars, you nearly killed me..."

"What are you *talking* about, you mad woman?"

"And now you're resisting arrest and running from me?"

She took a breath; her tone had been growing more and more irritated with 'Quarren' as she spoke, and anger was taking over. She needed this burst, this release, more than she realized, and the breath she drew afterwards brought her much-needed relief.

"We're not even *talking* about the kidnappings yet, and you're already looking at some jail time; I hope you have a good lawyer, Mr. 'Michaels'."

"You are crazy! I have never met you before in my *life.*" Quarren strained his voice, heavy with what Becca described later as an African accent. "What would you do in *my* shoes?"

"I wouldn't run, Quarren."

"Why did you chase me, then?"

"You fit the description of a suspect in a missing person's case. That's why I chased you."

Upon hearing this, Quarren's body tensed up. His lips curled into a snarl, and his nostrils flared. "N-no... I did not *do* it!" Becca didn't anticipate *this* reaction to her accusation—his eyes were practically popping out of his skull and pressing against the lenses of his eyeglasses. "I have *never* seen you before!"

Sluuuurp!

The sound hit her in the head like a brick. Flinching, Becca disregarded Quarren and turned back towards Tim, who had returned with two tiny water bottles.

And a fresh mug of coffee, I see...

"I need a phone. Can I use a landline?"

"Sure," he replied, snapping and pointing to her left. Her gaze followed his finger, falling on an old conference phone, yellowed with age, a few inches from her bottom.

"Thanks," she nodded with a subtle roll of her eyes.

Sluuuurp!

Tim's insistence on annoying Becca had her at a boiling point. She nearly screamed as he returned to his cubicle. With a *growl*, Becca yanked the receiver away from the cradle, punching in the number she'd scrawled on her arm earlier... to no answer.

Odd... okay, I'll try the SIOC. After a few rings, the line connected.

"Special Agent Rebecca Taylor here," Becca began, cutting off the receptionist. "I need to be transferred to Bill's—er, William Bushnall's office, in Manhattan, please."

"You mean *Director* Bushnall?" The lady on the other line gasped before going silent for a moment. Becca cleared her throat in an attempt to get her attention.

"OK, Agent Taylor, transferring you now, have a great day!"

The line clicked as the call was transferred, and Becca could hear the familiar, dreamlike notes and bassline of "Opus No. 1" playing as she waited on hold for her boss to pick up. She was rather concerned when it wasn't *his* voice that came back on the line.

"Agent Taylor? You there?"

"Yes."

"Director Bushnall left the office. I'm sorry. I didn't know. I *can* tell you he's heading down to New York Presbyterian Hospital."

She let out a *sigh.* "Thank you. Can you message him that I have the suspect in custody?"

The *clunk* of the phone hanging up drowned out her sigh. The news that he was heading to the hospital made Becca curious; even after she'd told him she needed backup, he prioritized checking on Jim over supervising her.

The irony was not lost on her.

Perks of the job, girl. He gets to do that. You have your own job to do.

When she finally looked up, Quarren was gazing directly into her eyes, insistently demanding her attention and making her uncomfortable. When he spoke, his voice trembled with nervousness.

"Do *I* get a chance to speak?"

Becca shook her head 'no' overdramatically. "Don't bother talking to me about anything unless I ask you a question first."

"But I cannot be arrested, I have a job interview!" His voice growled with rage. "This is *unjust!*"

He stood up defiantly with a booming, deep voice, earning attention from some employees who were still watching the scene. "Listen. I have done *nothing* wrong. I am being *oppressed!*"

Becca casually lifted her foot and pressed his chest with it, practically kicking the man back into the chair. He flopped back into the chair, tears streaking down his face, and he moaned pathetically as his body fell limp.

"If you're innocent, then you have nothin' to worry about!"

She glanced at her watch; the time was 8:41. If she was fast enough, she could get lunch and then visit Jimbo once she was finished processing this guy.

She kicked Quarren's shoe again. "You ready to go?"

When Quarren shook his head to say 'no', she laughed.

"Well, tough breaks, 'old timer'." She picked the young man out of the chair; as she turned towards the elevators, her captive seemed to be stuck to the floor. She opened the door to the lobby, but Quarren refused to come closer.

"*Please* let me talk to you. Then you can arrest me. We can talk right now if you want."

Frustrated, she scowled at the man she'd been chasing all morning. She grabbed his suit jacket forcefully with both hands, causing it to fall off his shoulders and bunch up around his handcuffs, behind his back.

"You know, my partner is in surgery right now. When you wrecked into that tree back there, you nearly *killed* him."

She motioned towards the door to the elevator lobby, holding the door open for her suspect, but when she turned to beckon Quarren, he stayed glued to the spot.

"Lady," Quarren begged, "I need to tell you, *please*. Just let me talk!"

"Fine!" Rebecca snapped. "Once we're done, you shut up and come with me. No more complaining. Deal?"

He nodded, and she slammed the door shut again. "You wanna talk? Fine. You have the right to remain silent; anything you say can and will be held against you in a court of law..."

*   *   *

With a *groan*, Becca dragged Quarren back to the chair he had just vacated. By this time, the onlookers had dispersed, getting their day started; she could hear the faint sounds of *The Howard Stern Show* coming from a distant radio. She spotted another chair and wheeled it over to her cubicle. With an irritated scowl, she sat beside Quarren, putting her torn suit jacket back on the desk as she did.

"...do you understand these rights?"

"Yes," he stated sullenly.

"Alright, Quarren, tell me: what's your *real* name? Your *real* age?"

"My name is Quarren Cambanda. I am from Senegal; I was born in a small village called Baïla, and moved to the USA a few weeks ago. I am twenty-one years old and came here hoping to find a job."

"You speak pretty fluent English to be from that part of the world."

He nodded, his eyes closed. "I studied hard in school."

"I see," Becca said, writing notes in a spiral notebook she produced from her jacket pocket. "What's with the fake ID, Quarren?"

"You can call me Q," he replied.

"What's with the fake ID, *Quarren?*" Becca repeated, a spit of vitriol in her voice that she didn't like. She winced at her tone; Quarren looked like he might cry again.

"I do not have my driver's license yet."

"You're an illegal immigrant?"

He shook his head. "Check my wallet. I have my green card."

She obliged him, glancing at the issue date; it read August 20th, 2001. His story collaborated, she replaced the vinyl atrocity in her jacket pocket. It now battled for position with her cell, bunched up on the desk.

Interesting... perhaps he's telling the truth; if that green card is real, he can't be the Manhattan Mauler. Isabel was taken a few days before he even arrived in the States...

"So you deny I just chased you on foot through New York?"

Quarren nodded vigorously. "I swear it. I *just* got here!"

Butterflies began flapping madly in Becca's stomach. In part, it was the intense effort she'd expended to catch him, her brain struggling to fire on all cylinders after their ordeal; on the other hand, there was something about his body language, the tone of his voice... as much as she hated to admit it, she might've made a mistake.

But if I did... why would he run in the first place? She shook her head—if she *was* wrong, it was far too late to do anything about it, now. Either he was telling the truth, or he was one *hell* of a liar. Regardless, she had to press him further; she had to know for certain.

"So if I were to mention a name to you, you wouldn't react?"

"But I am inno—"

"Where is Marissa Hernandez?" Becca demanded, cutting him off and getting in the man's face again. Quarren's breathing sped up rapidly, and he was beginning to sweat.

"I swear to Allah, I do not know who that *is!*" He began bouncing in the chair, which squeaked with every rebound.

"Do you remember the name Isabel Esquivel? What about *her?*"

His eyes stayed true as he screamed at her. "What are you *talking* about?"

"Where did you get the Dodge?" she screamed aggressively, her lips now inches from Quarren's face. "The white van. Where did you get it?"

"What van?" He screamed back at Becca, showing some fight, forcing Becca to flinch. In her experience, if someone was lying, you could read it in their body language, or they would back off in interrogation. However, the aggressive way Quarren was responding to her made her uneasy... she was beginning to suspect she'd made a serious error in judgment.

"The white Dodge van I *just* saw you squirm out of."

"I don't *know* about that! I rode the... um... I forget what it is called... subway."

She barely heard him; she was distracted by something. Over the digital ringing of a phone and the electronic *whirr* of an office printer... There was something else. A sound. And it was getting louder... and closer. Her expression softened, the anger and aggression melting into horror.

"Do you hear that, Quarren?"

An omnipresent sound, like white noise.

Her facial expression also frightened Quarren, and he rose

from the chair. Becca remained frozen, hypnotized by a terrifying, encroaching beast, with a roar like an angry tea kettle. She was trying to look past the windows... and it wouldn't take long for her to identify the source.

I know that sound, could it really be—?

Quarren's gaze shot past her towards the row of windows to the north, and fear filled his eyes.

"*Subhanallah!*" He turned, running towards the row of cubicles.

Becca stood in the hallway, staring towards the northern windows, unable to look away. She was a statue chiseled from marble, her limbs as heavy as stone, and destined to stand in this very spot to bear witness to this invader, whose deafening *roar* was getting louder each second.

This can't be real. This must be a dream... or some sick night—

It hit around the corner from where Becca was, before she could react. An enormous fireball engulfed the entirety of the north side of the floor; the tower tossed her aside like a rag doll as it swayed violently from the impact.

The explosion knocked her into next Friday.

And Rebecca's world went black.

X

"I Died For Nothing"

"Mom! Dad!" The young child screamed excitedly as he tightly held onto his mother's hand, pulling his parents towards the glass. "Do you think we can see our house from here?" Chad was pointing excitedly towards the streets far below, almost a quarter mile away.

"Look, Mom! Everyone looks like ants!"

Rebecca let out a bellowing laugh as they reached the World Trade Center's observation deck windows; today was December 27, 1994, a frigid afternoon in New York. It was Ken and Rebecca Taylor's seventh anniversary today, and Ken had made reservations for dinner with his wife later tonight—but for the *day,* they were having themselves a family day in the city.

And why not? Ken had reason to celebrate. He'd just inked his first publishing deal a few days before Christmas, and was receiving a large advance for his new sci-fi thriller, *Bernhardt.* He'd been trying for *years,* and along with his wife's new career with the FBI starting wonderfully, the family had *every* reason to celebrate.

Rebecca was donning a maroon faux fur gown, with an ivory knit scarf and matching mittens. Her son looked quite warm in his crocheted sweater and mismatched beanie.

And my husband... God, he looks so good in that suit...

The skies were overcast, their gray canopy sprinkling snow from what seemed like right above their heads in the tower.

Ken put his hand upon the pillar between the panes of glass, the cold steel radiating outward like a block of ice. When his bare skin touched it, Rebecca could hear a *sizzle* as it seemed to sear his flesh.

Despite this, he didn't pull his hand away.

"I don't know if I can see the *sky*, Son. Wow, it's so *white* outside!"

He stood there, alongside his son, staring out over a blanket of snow that now buried the Big Apple. The Hudson River was beginning to freeze, and the world appeared to be covered in a layer of powdery dust.

Rebecca couldn't tell if the falling flakes were snow or ash.

"Hey, Dad," Chad said, giggling at his father. "You think your tongue would stick to that?"

"Why don't *you* try it first, and let me know?"

Ken swooped his son into his arms and swung him towards the window, playfully tossing him into the air as if pretending to throw his son through. The motion of their bodies seemed to rock the tower back and forth like a rubber band.

Rebecca grew dizzy, losing her balance. The world spun around Becca, a cavalcade of images surrounding her, a replay of her entire life.

As a little girl, Becca used to ride the carousel at the park, and she remembered that she would get sick if she rode for too long... but there was *no* escape this time. She couldn't move; she sat on that cold steel and spun. The world was a series of blurry streaks flowing behind her as it rotated. Faster and faster still... she was thrilled, her adrenaline pumping.

The air grew warmer, *choking* her lungs.

It was searingly, *devilishly* hot.

She closed her eyes.

"Clear your mind, write your story, and breathe."

When she finally opened them up, she was hanging from Dad's arms.

"One, two, *three!*" Little Becky's father cried as she swung backward, feeling like she was going to fall from the top of the building.

It was April 15th, 1973. Little Becky was seven, going on eight, and she'd recently moved to the city with her father. The World Trade Center was brand new—and what *better* way to celebrate their move than to experience the tallest buildings in the world for themselves?

It was a gorgeous spring day, and the newly finished Twin Towers painted an utter masterpiece only viewable from the South Tower's rooftop deck. The sun shone brilliantly on Becca and her father, welcoming them to her own little paradise.

Exhausted from the constant swinging, her Dad boosted her atop his shoulders, and all of New York City was visible from her new perch. The blooming trees far below provided a refreshing splash of color in a sea of yellow cabs and gray concrete.

She was a visitor in heaven... without the heavy price one might pay to get there.

"Daddy," she whispered in his ear. "Do you think Mommy can see us up here, since we're so close to heaven?"

"I think that as long as she stays *here,*" he whispered back, guarding his true emotions carefully as he gently poked Becky in her chest, "then she will *always* be able to see you, Kitten."

Touched by her father's words, she clutched her chest and smiled to herself, bathing pleasantly in the brilliant spring sunshine. Tony Fazzone died in 1992, while she was still enrolled at Quantico, and if not for Ken's (and *Kelly's*) support, Becca might've lost her focus. Her father had been the light of her world, and he was *gone*... as if the sunshine *itself* was extinguishing around her...

No, that's not a metaphor... it's darkening outside...

Becky's world went dark... she swooned... her body growing

lighter, the world taking on an inky darkness as she lifted off, floating into the ebony void. She was falling, spinning, on an ethereal journey between realities...

No... she was Dorothy Gale, and this was a tornado ripping Kansas *apart*.

She closed her eyes.

"Clear your mind, write your story, and breathe."

When she finally opened them up, Ken was putting the needle down on their phonograph, and the house was filled with the silky voice of Perry Como singing "Silent Night" as Ken disappeared into the kitchen.

It was December 27, 1986. Rebecca's twenty-year-old *boyfriend* was fixing her a cup of coffee. The smells of fresh pine and smoky flames filled the living room as she sat beside their two-year-old toddler. Little Chaddy bounced excitedly on his bottom —with a freshly-soiled diaper, no doubt.

I'm certain I'm the one who'll get the pleasure of unwrapping that present later.

As he returned, Ken was donning a green-and-red wool robe, carrying two steaming mugs. They celebrated Christmas two days late this year because Rebecca's childhood best friend, Stacy, had been kidnapped. She had been missing for nearly a *month*.

On Christmas Eve, they'd found her body.

She was taken from outside a store, it was Black Friday, and she was a grown adult standing in public when she was taken. Why don't I seem to remember this? That's why I joined the FBI in the first place!

As her world warped and wobbled, the fireplace became blazingly warm, a furnace of *hell,* as its flames kissed the nearby Christmas tree. Rebecca didn't flinch as the top of the tree ignited, even as the intense heat radiated onto her skin. Perry Como's voice warbled and slowed until "Silent Night" sounded more like a warning. She was surprised to hear the fire alarm annunciate its ear-piercing warning as quickly as it had.

The room morphed around her, changing into a distorted, deformed madhouse. The burning wallpaper curled up as it shrank from the intense heat.

Rebecca retrieved two tiny gifts under their Christmas tree, fully ablaze in her hands. She tossed one of them to Ken before picking up their baby and slamming him down into her lap, causing him to vomit as he turned his head up, grinning up at her with a giggle.

"Merry Christmas, Chaddy," Rebecca exclaimed in terror as her son began ripping into the wrapping paper with his teeth.

"I can't *believe* we did this, Ken. It's... amazing."

"If we're amazing, all *three* of us deserve the credit."

Ken sipped his coffee—Rebecca could hear his tongue sizzling with each sip—and she loved him *so* much right now, the light from the windows reflecting colors of translucent ornaments and sparkly tinsel all over the room, slowly wafting into the clouds of smoke that were now darkening everything.

This was a surreal sensation, and Rebecca did not want to leave—

Rebecca was *beyond* terrified. *I have to get out of here!*

As she took the other box over to Ken, she smiled.

"Until he finishes, shall we open *ours?*"

Maybe as if to hint at what's to come, he winked at her.

"Absolutely, Darling—but don't think *you're* getting out of this scot-free!" He reached between the sofa cushions and retrieved a tiny jewelry box, gently wiggling it as he showed Becca her gift.

Her heart skipped a beat. *Isn't this where he proposed to me? Didn't I say yes?*

"I'm terrified..."

Rebecca's mouth was bone dry in the literal inferno of their living room before she focused back on Chad, who was still ripping madly at the wrapping paper on his bow. Seemingly frustrated, the boy tossed the box across the living room. It *smacked* into the fireplace mantle; a white Boeing jet made of porcelain fell from the mantle, lifting off and flying through the smoky air like a miniature apparition of a jetliner, engulfed in flames as it soared through the living room before shattering into thousands of fragments which floated into the air, transforming into ash as they fluttered around the smoky living room, the smell of holiday gasoline bringing yule-tide joy.

"Clear your mind, write your story, and *breathe,*" Ken told himself as he turned to throw the little box, which was now *engulfed* in flames, and it smacked her directly in the forehead, branding itself into her flesh. Her head rang, a mockery of the fire alarm wailing around her.

"I love you, Rebecca Fazzone." The fire surrounded him now, and his skin melted from his bones before her eyes. *It reminds me of that Nazi guy from Indiana Jones.* "Will you marry me?"

She started laughing maniacally, cackling in her reply.

Is this what it feels like to lose your mind? She reached for the box and opened it carefully; she already knew what was inside it, so she flinched when she saw what was inside.

What is this?

It was a key... to a Dodge van.

I love you too, Kenneth Taylor is what she began to say, but she choked to death.

I love you too, Kenneth Taylor is what she began to say, but she burned alive.

I love you too, Kenneth Taylor is what she began to say, but she plummeted from a great height.

I love you too, Kenneth Taylor is what she began to say *did a fucking passenger jet just hit the tower?* but her windpipe was crushed.

I love you too, Kenneth Taylor is what she began to say, *and yes, I'll marry you* she so desperately yearned to tell him; despite her inevitable awakening encroaching on her dream-like fantasy, Rebecca stood to return to the couch, walking through a curtain of flame, and as she sat down, a furry monster's humongous claw appeared from within, reaching out of the cushions, and latching onto Rebecca's newly-singed right foot, and the monster began to drag her into the void by her ankle *but haha I know this is just a nightmare so you're powerless here, Cookie Monster* and she felt her foot being devoured by his rusty metal teeth, razor-sharp, ripping through her ankle no matter how hard she fought it, a mouse trapped in a garbage disposal, as the world began to tumble once more, her vision became a tunnel, such as a kaleidoscope might appear to be the entrance to a portal into a void, a deadly place— the worst hell *imaginable*—and *how* could Rebecca truly find happiness in this world when she always felt like she was going to be sick, and she *desperately* wanted Ken to hold her—she remembered *all* the good things that happened right after this, after the terrifying screams finally died back down—but it was far too late to go back now because "HELP! I'M BEING EATEN ALIVE!" and she screamed a terrible scream, *how did I even make that sound* she said to herself as the monster devoured her entire leg, and it *hurt*, but there was nobody to listen to her cries, her pleas; they were hate-fueled, selfish rants; *who* did she *think* she was, taking on this case when she knew she was going to fail, if it wasn't for Jim she wouldn't have solved a single case in her *life*, but of course Jim lied to her all the time, telling her she was a good agent when she was never going to be the agent that could've saved Stacy's life because she *always* failed, even as a kid, even with good grades, even with attention from boys because she still *liked* boys—at least, until *Ken* died—and her first job at Cold Stone ice cream, which was a great summer job but she hated working there in the winter, especially *this* year when the snow kept on coming, and coming, like ash falling, she made an ash angel on a grave, she was destined to burn alive but if Cecilia was here she could stop the fire, but even CeCe could not help Becca, because she was at her core, a failure; the kid still died and it was Becca's fault—the blood that spilled was on her hands even if the knife that drew it was not her own, she couldn't breathe; it was too hot, *much* too hot to live here, and despite the darkness, it was so goddamned *bright*—she really *was* losing her fucking mind—Becca's world was a giant hamster wheel in a cage, and she was powerless to step off of it; she was a prisoner of her own mind, and she'd seen this dream before; she had it often, a familiar nightmare yet *different* this time; the carousel was spinning faster and faster and Becca wanted to throw up but she hated throwing up more than almost *anything*, yet she was too dizzy to stay on the ride and she was flung away—didn't she *just* fall down?—it felt like she had gone through a wall, her ribs were as tender as her self-image, knowing that she was being carried by Jim in all these cases because she was so goddamned useless, she couldn't even catch the Y2Killer and now she was supposed to get the Mauler *How long have I been out, wasn't there an explosion*—Bill was gonna have her ass so she *can't* go back without the guy or else the fire would take what's left of her dignity and burn it up, like the fireball sweeping her office floor nope that's not gonna happen that's not gonna happen that's not gonna happen that's not gonna happen *I need to wake up or I'm as good as dead* nope that's not gonna happen that's not gonna happen that's not gonna happen so you might as well give up—

She closed her eyes.

"Clear your mind, write your story, and breathe."

When she finally opened them up, it was late evening on December 27th, 1994, and she had the phone in her hands. She stared at the handset with incredible lucidity.

I'm still asleep. But this feels more... real.

Rebecca was sobbing, little bubbles of snot bursting out of her nostrils. She hadn't cried this intensely since childhood, and she was close to *hyperventilating.*

Oh... no. Not this...

It was already dark. She'd arrived home just after nine, expecting her husband to be home, waiting for her. When she arrived, the house was dark.

After their anniversary dinner, Rebecca had to go to the office —*I was still a rookie... I wonder if Jim still called me 'sport'*—so she left the World Trade Center earlier than Ken had.

"I have to go, Ken. I'm so sorry, I don't want to—"

Her husband simply smiled, giving her a pat on her back. "Go, Rebecca. It's fine. I'll grab another drink. then I'll catch a cab." Her husband checked his Pulsar watch; the time was ٦:٥٦.

"I'll see you when you get home. I love you, Rebecca."

"Okay; I love you so much, Ken." Rebecca kissed her husband for the final time, before she left. He'd had a charming smile on his face as she'd folded her soiled napkin and set it next to her salad plate. The salmon had been *delicious,* and the Big Apple was illuminated brilliantly in this snow-crusted December evening.

It was a magical way to spend her final moments with her husband... except for *one* regret. *Because I was oblivious that I'd never see him again... of course, I forgot to look back.*

She arrived home later to a message on her brand-new answering machine: his cab had been pulverized by a large truck.

"He just *left!*" she screamed in denial upon returning the call. "I just *saw* him!"

The police officer on the other side gave her a moment to let the histrionics pass.

"We've got the suspect," the police officer informed her. "He's on the way to the station for a blood draw." *No, that is my case, not yours. I will be the one who brings Quarren down to the office. Thank you very much, officer.*

Her ten-year-old son was standing in the doorway to the kitchen as Rebecca spoke. She let the receiver fall to the floor as she ran over to their child, picked him up, and cradled him closely. Chad cried into her bosom, and she into his hair. They held each other for days, for centuries, for as long as they needed each other.

The chronic nightmares she suffered from stemmed from these past traumas—at least, according to Dr. Mitzel, her therapist. Becca's issues were rooted in every corner of her mind, now symbiotic with her sanity. She'd reached the point where she *needed* that trauma to balance herself out. Without it, she couldn't function, breathe, or cry. She needed it to love, hate, and live.

You even need it to die—

Bullshit... my trauma doesn't define me. I won't demean myself by taking the blame for others' mistakes.

Her thoughts were mashed potatoes. Again, her world began to rotate around her, the dizzying momentum feeling like she would be flung from this macabre ride at any moment.

I need to snap out of this!

She closed her eyes.

"Clear your mind, write your story, and breathe."

When she finally opened them up, she was standing in a snowy driveway, over Jim's bleeding body. It didn't take her long to remember; it was January 1st, 2000.

"But... you said you got *him*? Didn't you—"

"I said, 'I shot *her*.'"

Becca's world swooned as she swayed on her feet.

"There's *two* of them, Rebecca."

She stared blankly at him, as if she knew what his words had likely meant... *"She fucking stabbed me, whaddya want me to do?"*

echoed in her head as she realized what he had been saying.

And, as she realized the massive *mistake* she had just made.

There's two of them.

Fear and despair crawled all over her body. They paralyzed Becca. *There's two of them—there's two of them—*

"*Go!*" Jim repeated with surprising strength, causing Becca to flinch. "Save the kid!"

With a deep breath, Becca's paralysis broke, and she took off, high-stepping through the packed snow like Randy Moss, running full speed until she reached the corner of the house nearest the white Dodge van.

The guesthouse loomed before her, its darkened windows watching like the hollow eye sockets of a long-dead skull. She slowed momentarily to unholster her gun before continuing through the snow. As she trekked towards the guesthouse, she passed the white Dodge van.

It wasn't *that* old, yet she saw rust on the chrome bumper. A *massive* dent on the sliding door and a missing side mirror were telltale signs someone had hit *something.* Most amusing to her, at least in the moment, was that the van had no license plates.

What a careless choice. It's almost as if he wants to get caught.

The front door was wide open. A trail of blood spots led through the entranceway, as if the tracks of heavy footsteps that compacted the snow all around the walkway *weren't* a dead giveaway. She followed the blood into the house, her Smith & Wesson held at the ready, as she kicked the door open, sending it slamming into the wall of the entranceway.

"*FBI,*" she screamed, scanning the entrance with her flashlight. "We've got backup on the way. Let the boy go, and we can *all* leave here alive!"

Becca's demands were met with a lingering silence. The decor here drastically varied with the elaborate, ornate layout of the mansion, whereas this was much more *humble*. The trail of blood she was following went around the corner, into a bedroom. Feeling like she was back in that hallway from mere moments prior, she fought déjà vu and peeked around the corner.

"FBI. We're coming in!"

She took a deep breath, using the tip of her pistol to nudge the door open. It protested with a soft *creak* that Becca paid no mind to; at this point, she was too afraid to *care* anymore. The moonlight spilled across the bedroom; as her pupils adjusted to the low light levels, she was *stunned* at what she was seeing.

The scene revealed itself to her in fragments. A still form lay prone on the floor; it appeared to be a woman. She was caught in a shaft of light from the doorway, reflecting off a spreading pool of fresh blood. A bloody knife, glinting dimly against the darkened floor, hinted that it played a role in her death... that is, until Becca rolled her over to check her pulse.

The entry wound in the middle of her forehead quickly rendered that pointless.

A mercy kill, most likely. That wasn't from *Jim's* gun.

The window was open, its curtains flapping gently in the chilly evening breeze. There didn't seem to be anybody else in the room. Almost on cue, she could hear the white van outside as the engine started, and she heard the Dodge's exhaust getting quieter as it drove away. Becca started to reach for her phone, knowing she needed to tell them the van was—

When Becca saw the small figure convulsing on the bed, she stopped in her tracks. It appeared to be that of a *child*.

Her throat closed tightly. She rushed into the room. Forgetting about calling for backup, she turned back towards the door, and flicked the switch on, unleashing a rush of light into the room that overwhelmed Becca; she shut her eyes tightly.

Clear your mind, write your story, and then breathe.

When she opened them up, the scene which would unfold in all its vividness and clarity burned itself into Becca's mind so brightly, so vividly... that she would never forget what she saw that night.

Except this time, the boy was *not* dead. *Well, not yet, anyway...*

Jeremey sat up, his throat bleeding out, as Becca stared at him in terror. His mouth moved, but at first, the only sounds were of gargling blood. He smiled at her, innocently holding a hand out to her.

When the blood finally finished gushing out, the boy spoke.

"It's not *your* fault, Agent Taylor. I don't blame *you.*"

He smiled, running over towards her, before he fell over on top of the dead woman. Despite his body lying still, the boy kept speaking.

"If you doubt yourself, then I died for *nothing...*"

Becca couldn't move. She was frozen, unable to believe she was too late, once again. Even with the benefit of hindsight, she couldn't save the boy, even in her *dreams.*

Don't let doubt win, Becca. This is just a nightmare.

Or is this what it's like when you die? *When will I die?*

Undoubtedly, when we *all* die.

Becca—snap out of this. You need to live.

This is all a dream, I need to wake up—I don't wanna die!

When will YOU die?

In my mind, I see a life of forgery. What a pathetic woman I am!

No! It wasn't my fault.

Sadly, it was, and you know it, you pitiful loser—"No! Don't *listen* to yourself, Becca! That is not me anymore!" She struggled to silence the voice, still prominent and bold in her mind.

Lose your mind, die in your story, I can't breathe!

"I need to wake up now!"

Lose your mind, lose your suspect, lose your kid. You lose. Lose-lose-lose.

She focused on waking up, slowing everything down.

"Clear your mind, write your story, and breathe!"

Fighting the urge to cry, Becca opened her eyes.

XI

"A Red Headband"

When she opened them up, she couldn't see, even though Becca *could* open her eyes—although it took a great effort to do so. Desperate for sensory input, she rubbed the dust from them and opened her mouth to gasp for air, but she couldn't breathe, either.

The air was thick with a choking layer of smoke and ash. The smell of fuel, the taste of metal and ozone were pervasive in the air. Trapped in her own personal hell, deep down in the darkness of despair, she screamed for help, but could only hear the ringing in her ears. And it was scathingly hot, so hellishly balmy, she thought her very own skin was *searing* into her clothing.

She hated admitting it, but if she wasn't still asleep, Rebecca Taylor really *was* dead.

She attempted to roll over, but her legs wouldn't obey; they were dead stumps, *useless* to her. She wanted to scream, but she couldn't breathe; she was helpless to do anything. So instead, she curled into the fetal position, wishing the torture would end so she could move on... or else, wake up in bed next to CeCe, and they could laugh together at another one of her silly nightmares.

CeCe... Chad... my family. What I would give to be home with them right now...

Gasping for air, she cried silent, dry tears as reality swam back to her. She shook her head quickly, whipping her ponytail, and a cloud of dust fell out of her brunette hair in large clumps.

For the first time since she had come to, she tried to sit up. Her back screamed in agony, but nothing *seemed* broken or severely injured. Someone was wailing in the dusty darkness, but she couldn't make out who it was until she stopped *screaming*—

Oh... I see...

She lifted her hand and brought it to her face, slowly rubbing her caked eyes free of whatever this... dust was. It caked every surface of her body and pervaded every orifice. Involuntarily, she coughed up a cloud of it, after which she could *finally* reopen her eyes.

"I caught the blast wave? A *bomb?*"

As she regained her composure, the room around her began to focus, and a cacophony of sounds invaded her ears... not the *least* of which was the deafeningly intrusive fire alarm annunciators. She thought she heard liquid trickling, as if it were *raining* inside the—

Wait... I'm in the World Trade Center! What on Earth just happened?

She realized now why she couldn't breathe. The *entire* office was thick with a fog of smoke and dust. Becca blinked her eyes rapidly, wishing she could make this hellscape vanish.

It was very dark, and as she attempted to stand up again, she realized her foot was caught under something heavy. Becca groaned in frustration; the monster from her dream was, in fact, the *desk*, which had tipped over on her leg. Right beside it, flames licked the remnants of her cubicle.

Water was flowing down the walls near the center core; thick and viscous, with a rusty, maroon color. The way it oozed along, it looked like the walls were *bleeding* to death.

Becca reached over from where she was lying on her back, stretching and hoping she could grab her jacket, which held her Nokia in its pocket. Unfortunately, as hard as she strained, she wasn't able to snag it, mere *inches* outside her reach.

She did the only sensible thing she knew how to do.

"Help!" Becca could barely hear her voice over the tinnitus ringing in her ears.

She tried to press the desk off of her right leg, pushing and squirming until she finally gave up. Rubbing her temples, she now had an awful headache that was only intensifying. Perhaps it was the ear-splitting whine of the fire alarm, combined with *many* other factors. *Let's see: dehydration, lack of sleep, no food, stress, a car accident...* and now, this...

The sound of her own howl set her off. *This* scream came out involuntarily before crossfading into a plea. *"Anybody! Help, please!"* Surely her pleas would reach someone—

"Hold still. I will help you push on three."

She recognized the accent immediately. A large figure appeared from over Becca's shoulder, stepping over her legs to the other side, where the tabletop had fallen on her foot.

"Q?" Becca was filled with hope, as well as very real terror. She watched him carefully, thinking that if she had been wrong about his innocence, *this* was his best chance to prove it. She reached for her pistol and received relief in return when she felt its familiar weight pressing against her breast.

"Aren't you still cuffed?"

Quarren didn't reply, instead squatting and facing her, straddling both sides of Becca's leg, his hands resting against the desk. He placed both hands under the lip of the desktop and prepared to stand up.

He gave Becca a confirmation nod, and she nodded back.

"Okay—on three. One... two... and *three!*"

Becca strained to push with her loose leg, using every ounce of strength she had left, as the two of them worked in tandem; with one final effort, her right ankle was finally freed from its trap. She quickly pulled it away before Q let it fall to the office floor with a final *crunch*.

Gingerly, she rolled her foot in circles. Other than a bad gash in her shin and some minor cuts and scrapes, her leg seemed fine; she was able to put her bodyweight on it, at least.

"Thank you!" she beamed. "But why did *you* help me?"

Q looked at her with a solemn expression; she knew full well that it was in his best interest to leave her here, in this office of ruins, probably to die a slow death... *alone.*

But he also had compassion in his blood; he knew the truth would set him free.

"Madam, I do not know what you want from me, but I will cooperate with you if that will help to prove my innocence."

She sighed in relief. She felt so genuinely terrible for misjudging the man, wrapping him in a big hug.

"I'm looking for a kidnapper," she stated upon pulling away. "You fit his description. That's why I came after you."

"But *I* am not a kidnapper." He held his hands out. "I am *not* a kid—I do not even *have* kids, and if I *did* have kids, I would not allow them to take naps unless they were *sleepy!*"

She couldn't tell if Q was joking, but the levity was undeniable; she cracked up laughing.

"I do not see what is funny. We need to get out of here." He motioned his still-cuffed hands towards the elevator lobby. *"Quickly!"*

Becca's laughter turned into painful hiccups—*to be fair, I totally deserve it*—as she dusted her clothing off. It was ruined. Her white dress shirt was now gray, covered in concrete dust and ashes, and her slacks were torn down the side. Her jacket was somewhere in the debris pile, and was already ripped, so she left it for now.

At least I still have this. Becca checked her wristwatch, wondering how much time had passed since she'd been out; it was 8:49.

That's it? Her nightmare seemed to last for *hours.* Still searching for her bearings, she glanced at Q; he was searching for something *else.*

Something about the way he's acting... if he were truly guilty, why would he help me?

"Wait," she put a hand on Q's shoulder. "Will you come to the FBI office with us after we get out of here? I'll buy you lunch. I just want to talk with you."

"I will agree, on one condition: would you consider releasing me, Boss?"

He turned his back to Becca so his cuffs were visible, but she never reached for her cuff keys. An *inconceivable* sight captured her attention, and she stepped around Quarren, her mouth agape at the level of destruction she bore witness to. Her world became a tunnel of ringing tinnitus and terrific smoke once again; she slowly shuffled over from the destroyed cubicle, continuing towards the row of blown-out windows on the north side of the room.

"Mother of Christ," she mumbled, stepping onto a broken picture frame with a *crunch,* trembling so hard from terror that she nearly fell again. Her knees almost buckled as she stepped over a body, looking down out of morbid curiosity.

Tim Atwood was dead. His body lay mere *feet* from the kitchenette where he'd been standing, a few moments before everything exploded. She checked his pulse, but it was futile; he had been nearly decapitated by a chunk of steel trussing, which had collapsed from the ceiling above. She tried not to look at his crushed head any longer, taking a wide berth to avoid the pool of gore that now gathered around him.

Everyday objects were strewn all over the office. The air in the large room was completely molested with floating ash, bits of paper, and dust... so *much dust.* The overhead lights were dangling by an electrical MC cable, along with some pipes and a few wires, all knocked out of the T-grid ceiling and barely hanging onto the trusses overhead. It was hard to tell, but it looked like the floor above was *collapsing*.

This is a war zone! What happened here? One moment, we were sitting there talking, then...?

The view from the windows on the north side of the North Tower was completely obscured because smoke blotted out the sun like a morbid umbrella. Countless papers, folders, office supplies, and computers, burning all at once, their toxic gases stirred into a sickening conglomeration with ash, concrete dust, glass, and steel.

And bodies. Becca knew bodies were burning in this inferno. She pretended not to remember that as she moved forward.

What happened? We were sitting there talking, and next thing I know, I'm waking up on the floor. She was trying to remember what was happening, but couldn't quite fit the pieces back together. There had been a noise and—

"The plane!" Becca's face lit up as she remembered. "It hit the tower?"

"Yes, the entire *building* moved. Perhaps two meters... possibly three."

Her brow furrowed sceptically. "You mean two or three *feet*, right?"

"No, I mean *meters*. I thought the building was going to fall over."

Becca pursed her lips in disbelief as she continued forward, slowly making progress towards the northeast corner of the building.

As she looked north, flying office papers and ash blotted out any light remaining on the shady side of the North Tower. They littered the air, thousands of cover sheets, printed spreadsheets, contracts, newspapers, and files. Entire floors of documents now emptied outside, all flying around in the space around the inferno, many of which gathered towards the south, swirling around in the air space between the buildings.

A strange sound caught her attention, like the soft tinkling of wind chimes in a gentle breeze. Becca's attention was stolen by something she saw on the few windowpanes that weren't broken yet. The window glass was splintering down, freshly cracking like ice on a warming lake, and she was mesmerized by it. The air from outside rushed through the broken windows; a fresh breeze churned into a stoichiometric gale-force wind as it mixed with the pervasive air, feeding the inferno above them.

She noticed something else... a liquid, slowly cascading down the panes. Where the windows were already destroyed, the liquid instead dripped past her floor, and this broke her hypnosis. She held a hand through the broken glass; the liquid was warm and slippery, almost *oily*. She sniffed it, and flung her fingers away, repulsed, trying to clear them of the offensive fluid.

Quarren had followed her over to the windows, stepping over Tim's body. His eyes met hers as she realized what the fluid was.

"Jet fuel?" they both said in unison.

"It's over there, too. The plane must've been *full* of fuel."

"We are in danger," Q cried. "If that ignites, we could be *trapped!*"

"That wasn't a private plane," Becca warned him. "That was, like, a 747... 767 or, like, some *other* big jet..." Her voice trailed off as they watched the fuel trickle down the windows like straw-colored rain, turning the powder-blue sky in the distance green.

A commercial jet full of fuel... Something wasn't adding up. She spun with a scowl, her hands animating her words as she spoke.

"But how did they not *see* us? This can't be an accident! I mean, this is one of the tallest buildings in the *world!*"

She walked to one of the broken windows and stood timidly at the threshold; her heart skipped a beat. Craning her head out as far as she dared to, she looked at the city below, observing a curious crowd of ants and fire trucks which was growing thicker around the buildings. Despite several firetrucks already lining the plaza below, she heard *none* of the sirens or commotion over a thousand feet below them.

Becca thought better of encroaching on the window any closer. It wasn't that she was afraid of heights, and she didn't believe Quarren would try to push her out, but... *I don't think I'm willing to take that chance.*

Fortunately, *this* part of the building was stable... for now. Most of the fires were burning on the north side of the building, but closer to the center core, it was nearly as hellish.

That's where all the stairwells are. If we don't hurry, we might get trapped here.

If they didn't need another reason to hustle, they still got one; the air was growing saturated with smoke. It bellowed out of every gap in the ceiling above, and from the center core. Thicker than a Bay Area fog... and *exponentially* deadlier.

"Q," she coughed. "We gotta get *out* of here!"

She scrambled behind Quarren, unfastening his handcuffs and replacing them on her belt. Upon being freed, Quarren gently rubbed the little imprints the cuffs had left in his wrists.

"We have to work *together*. You want to live, right?"

Q nodded. She patted him on his massive arm and turned towards the door to the lobby, which had a river of smoke flowing into the office from underneath it.

"We need to find a fire extinguisher." Becca walked over to the door, staring at the smoke with trepidation. "Stay on this side of the floor. We don't want to get—"

Becca's heart leapt into her throat. *"...trapped."*

The door was jammed shut. She couldn't budge it, no matter how hard she pulled *or* pushed. She looked around in desperation; the steel beams of the trusses were falling around her at an alarming rate, crushing desks with a loud *bang*. The office space was rapidly becoming buried.

The smell was growing overwhelming, the air was choking, and the annunciating alarm added to an already anxious atmosphere.

"Quickly! Check the break area, under the cabinet!"

Q ripped through the cupboards, while Becca scrambled into a nearby office for any object she might pry the barrier open with. She found a metal ruler in the ruined cubicle she had been in, as well as various paper clips... nothing that would help. The walls were likely all sheetrock, so if she absolutely *had* to, she could dig through.

Yeah, with a fucking ruler? Get real.

Fortunately, Q returned with his hands weighed down... by a large, silver fire extinguisher.

"*Q,*" she screamed. "Hit the door *here* with the bottle!"

She pointed to a spot right near the doorknob. Q waved at her to step aside and used his foot as a battering ram. He drove his right leg into the door, and it shuddered hard in its frame.

"The frame is twisted, Boss."

He kicked a second time, and the door didn't budge. Q's foot bounced off the door so hard he nearly fell over.

"The *bottle*, Q!" Becca dropped the ruler and pointed to the side of the door's handle. "Hit it right here, and it should give."

Looking at the relatively heavy tank, he shrugged and held it out in front of his chest. With a mighty grip, he yelled and drove the bottle into the door using his bodyweight.

It didn't budge.

"Give me a moment," he wheezed in the smoky atmosphere.

Fear started to caress her temples, gently at first, but she knew... *the longer they were stuck here, the harder panic will be to resist.*

He stood up, about to try kicking the door again, when suddenly the door violently opened... *inward.*

Q stumbled backwards, nearly falling into Becca as the door hit the wall with a *bang.* They stared at each other, dumbfounded, their ears growing redder than they already had been. The situation might've been hilarious if it weren't for the terror that gripped Becca's heart.

I thought I tried pulling the door... maybe the frame's more twisted than I thought.

"Wow! I didn't think I'd find *anyone* alive over here."

Becca stopped beside Q, patting him on the back. The new guy stepped forward through the doorway, with his hand extended towards them. He was dripping wet, and she couldn't tell if it was from sweat or one of the other strange fluids dripping from every corner of the tower.

"You came from above?"

Becca looked past both men, staring out the recently opened door leading to the elevator lobby... and what she beheld was *dreadful.* The elevators were engulfed in flames. The lobby was thick with heat and smoke. Massive piles of debris from both the ceiling and the walls surrounded them. She struggled to keep her eyes open in this inferno.

"No. We all work on the south side of the building. I just got to the office, I noticed you arresting *this* bozo when the plane hit."

The man thumbed towards Q, and a surge of guilt rippled through Becca's body. "I haven't seen anyone else... except for *one* other man, but he's..."

"Our side looks bad... but *this* side, man..." he trailed off. "You two sure are lucky."

As the man spoke, her eyes flicked towards the wall beside the bathrooms. An injured man lay in the corner of the scorching elevator lobby, breathing very shallowly as he lay there moaning.

"We're sweeping the floor," the man explained. "We split up. Everyone is *supposed* to meet in the lobby, b-but I..." The man looked at the scalded man, and he seemed to struggle with the reality of seeing dying people. Even Becca—who saw dead people with routine regularity—was still shocked by it.

"You found everyone?"

"Almost. I didn't even know you two were here till we came out here to help *that* guy... that's when we heard you guys bangin' on the door."

Her eyes again shot towards the man on the ground. He was an older man; his white hair was streaked with soot and singed to his scalp. Becca could barely stand the heat in here, and yet this man was lying there, *broiling* to death; his skin was mostly burned away, the remaining bits hanging off his bones like a macabre curtain.

She wanted to go to this man, to drag him to safety... but the heat was unbearable. Becca's eyeballs were searing in their sockets. She recoiled from the lobby, back towards the stairwell.

"It's too *hot!*" She turned to Quarren, still holding the extinguisher. "Q, give me that!"

"There's nothing you can *do* for him, lady," the man said solemnly, stopping Q from passing the extinguisher. "I'm sorry. I don't mean to sound insensitive or nothin' but ya know... he's a *goner,* so..."

What a dickhead.

Becca looked back into the lobby to see a group rushing from the opposite side. The heat was so intense that many were shouting in pain as they hurried past the infernal elevators, which were makeshift furnaces amid the chaos. They crossed the lobby towards the east, heading into the relative safety near Becca.

When they arrived, they too were covered in soaking-wet concrete dust. Each of them was dressed in suits and was petrified with fear.

Yup, they look like lawyers, all right. She held her right hand out. "Rebecca Taylor, I'm with the FBI."

"Wow, you got up here quick as hell!" the man said in response, bellowing a sarcasm-laced guffaw. "I'm Nick, Nicky Rice. I work for Cutler, Puzzel, and Ryu."

He reached for a business card, which was dripping wet, before he realized the futility of it all. Becca took the card reflexively, shoving it into her pocket.

Nick Rice

Associate Attorney at Law
Business: (212) 555-2121
Cell: (332) 555-9229
Fax: (212) 555-1298

Cutler, Puzzel, & Ryu: Attorneys at Law
1 World Trade Center
New York, NY 11048

"You guys okay?"

"I'm fine," she lied, looking down at her ankle with concern. "I'm good to go if we want to get out of here."

As if they didn't need any more encouragement to abandon this Dutch oven, a loud *bang* erupted from the east offices, followed by a rush of smoke and dust; Becca looked back towards the area where she'd been pinned under the desk. The ceiling above had collapsed, and the cubicle they had been in was entirely buried under rubble and steel.

Becca's eyes went wide. *If Q hadn't rescued me, that would have crushed me!* Just then, a *new* realization dawned on her as she swiped sweat from her brow. She remembered where they were, and realizing their predicament... she was suddenly stricken with *fear*.

"Oh my God, this is the 91st floor... what if this building collapses?"

Nicky belly-laughed at her question. "C'mon, lady! Get *real*. No skyscraper has ever fallen down from a fire, period."

Becca took a deep breath, waving her hands as if to waft the scent into her nostrils. "You smell that? That's jet fuel. Jet-A, to be specific. If it ignites..."

She trailed off, fighting a gag; the jet fuel and concrete weren't the only things she smelled. She was afraid to even *think* about it, let alone say it, but she was convinced she could smell burning flesh and hair, as well.

Becca ran towards the kitchenette, grabbed some rags, and dumped the water bottle Tim had retrieved over them. The smoke was growing ever thicker, and they were quickly running out of time.

The man crouched low to the floor, coughing. "You know what, though, Detective—"

Becca placed a wet rag over his mouth, muffling his words. *"Agent* Taylor, to you, please, Mister Rice."

Nick cleared his throat overdramatically, waving his hands and bowing toward her. "My apologies, *Agent."* He held his hands out in submission. Becca ignored his teasing, wrapping the awful gash in her ankle with another wet rag, tying it in a knot. "For what it's worth—I agree with you. We oughta get outta here..."

Nick's speech trailed off, as if he faded away from the room they were in. The smoky air no longer concerned him.

He started stumbling past Becca, and she began to follow, his expression changing before her very eyes. Her mind was racing as she followed Nick's face, his walking resembling a zombie-like stumble as he walked back towards the east face of the building.

He went as white as the paper fluttering outside. "I just saw a person." Nick's voice was extremely monotone and low. The vitriol in his voice vanished as it cracked, and his breath came tumbling out in a sob. "I swear to God, I just saw a *person!*"

"I saw it too, Nick," one of the others said, "but I mean, we've already seen bodies—"

"No-no-no, that is different—I just saw someone *falling!*"

Nick's voice was as broken as his resolve. "I mean, why would you jump? Idiot. You survive the explosion, what—just to *jump?* It can't be that terrible up there, right? *Right?*" Becca's rag fell from her face as the grown man turned and buried himself in her arms, crying like a baby. "The firemen are already coming, don't you see the trucks down there? You *idiots!* C'mon. All they needed to do was hold on! Dumb fucks. *Why would they jump? Why?*"

His voice reached a histrionic pitch as he wailed into her chest. Though Becca felt annoyed with Nick, she embraced him, turning slowly to shield him from the view of the windows. However, this came with a caveat; now the same windows were in front of *her* as she glanced eastward.

She couldn't resist the urge, and her timing was impeccable because... as her gaze shifted, she saw her first jumper. Time slowed to a crawl. *Everything* was in slow motion, and in fine detail. Becca imagined hearing music playing in her mind, a melancholy melody matching the moment.

Her eyes dilated as she witnessed a young girl falling face up from floors above, a look of terror and shock etching years into her youth with *every* millisecond. The entire thing occurred to her as slowly as the moon rises at night. The girl's eyes locked with her own as Becca yelled a primal cry, an involuntary, painful moan that started from her womb and rose in both terror *and* volume.

Now, it was *Becca* clutching onto Nick, powerless to do anything but stand there and scream. So she screamed again. But no sound came out this time, because she had no *air* left in her lungs.

The falling girl was in a flowing, low-cut white dress which billowed in a small cloud behind her as she fell. Her shoulder-length haircut streaked in front of her face as she plunged past their floor, her blonde bangs blowing away from her face as she plummeted.

The scream painfully escaped her as a *moan* upon noticing her pearl necklace... confirming what she *refused* to believe.

"No! No, no-no-no..."

As the girl fell past their floor, Becca couldn't look away. Frozen in place, destined to witness this girl's final moments, a witness to her powerful—yet *final*—choice. She tried desperately to talk to her through her eyes; to *comfort* her.

I owe it to her. I must honor her.

A red headband followed, billowing and wobbling... practically *floating* in mid-air. It was some sort of time-traveling talisman which could possibly prevent—maybe even reverse—the woman's horrible, yet inevitable, fate... before finally releasing its apparent hold on time, accelerating faster and faster as it fell past her view.

"It's already bad in here!" Nick collapsed his face into Becca's shoulder. "How could it be so much worse up there? What if we can't escape, either? I don't want to jump! *I don't want to die!*"

Another person fell, a man in a chef's tunic. Then another, plummeting past the 91st Floor.

It is so bad up there that they would rather take a chance on freedom, but at the ultimate price. Because the alternative was agonizing and torturous, the temptation to escape to the relatively cool September air outside was irresistible. *Or maybe it was their way to give themselves their freedom of choice back.*

In a way, it was a little poetic, even as it *was* disturbing; poetic because these people were exercising the right to choose their own fate, taking it from the hateful bastards that had decided to fly a passenger jet into their building in the first place.

Becca tried to blink it away, but she couldn't do so; it was a branding she could not conceal, and she saw it every time she closed her eyes. As rapidly as Becca blinked, trying to forget what she'd just seen, she couldn't change it. It was permanent, tattooed into her retinas.

Because every time she blinked, she saw a floating red headband.

She broke their embrace and collapsed into a dusty office chair, moaning as tears trickled through her eyes despite her damnedest efforts to stop herself. She hated to cry, more than anything.

"Allah has *abandoned* us," Q moaned. When a pair of people plummeted past their positions, their screams fading in and out as they fell past, he didn't look up. Instead, he grabbed the fire extinguisher, and as he returned to the lobby, he lowered his hand, turning Becca's face up to his. Her tear-streaked and forlorn expression looked at his own, their eyes locking with a grimace.

"Tell me we will be alright, Boss. *Tell me we are not damned!*"

Becca couldn't reply, instead shutting her eyes. She simply saw a red headband.

*　　　*　　　*

The fires in the lobby were no match for Q's extinguisher, and the flames licking their way between the elevator's blown-out doors were beginning to subside anyhow. Most of the fires had burned themselves out long before Q had arrived. Becca figured it out pretty quickly; the plane's fuel had poured down the shafts after the aircraft was destroyed. It then ignited, exploding out into the lobby with *tremendous* force.

The smoke was still getting worse—it was nearly unbreathable on the 91st floor by now—but at least, the intense heat had stabilized. *For now.*

"Good job, Q," she patted the mule of a man on his broad shoulders. "Now we might be able to get out of here."

She snuck a glance at whom she had once believed was the kidnapper—that seemed like a lifetime ago now, although it had only been about five or ten minutes since the explosion.

But time was merely a suggestion at this point.

Nicky and the rest of his party followed them into the smoky junction, where the staircase doors were. "I'm not taking the elevators, lady. I'm taking the steps."

I don't know if you have much of a choice, bro.

"You gonna take A, B, or C?" Her Pulsar's alarm broke the conversation up with a *BEEP BEEP BEEP!* which Becca quickly silenced. A press of the nubbin revealed the time: 9:00.

As she spoke, a crew of construction workers in hard hats and reflective vests rounded the corner, running towards them. The foreman had his *own* fire extinguisher in his hand, hanging down by his tool belt.

"Those are blocked," the foreman announced. "Bunch of drywall and concrete. We haven't checked C yet, though."

She opened a door to her right with a sign declaring it as 'Stairway C'. The stairwell was *utterly* dark, with lingering swirls of smoke casting a terrifying cloak over the chasm leading down. Her head craned to look up the stairwell, and she gasped in horror —the stairs were completely impassable above them. The stairways had folded on themselves like warm taffy, and the entire stairwell was filled with smoke and debris.

Becca shuddered, imagining how close they were to being trapped, and how fortunate *they* were that they were still alive—

Oh, my God... she realized with terror. *If those other stairwells are blocked as well, the people above us...*

She'd been holding her breath, and it finally exploded out of her in a *whoosh*. There was a convenient doorstop just inside the stairway (she supposed the office workers snuck their cigarette breaks in here), and she pinned the door against the wall.

"C looks good, everyone." She gestured for the others to follow. Nick was coughing loudly; to Becca's ears, it sounded *painful*. He wasn't alone; the huddle of people was vanishing behind a black veil of smoke, which was clouding the lobby to the point of choking them.

"Yeah, it's getting bad. We need to go down, now. If we stay, we're *history!*"

"Agreed, Nicky. Hey, Q—"

Where the hell...? She wheeled around in a panicked circle, not realizing her mistake until now. "Q! Where'd you go?"

Damn! I was distracted; if he's trying to escape... so help me, God...

She took a peek into the stairwell, hearing Q's footsteps echoing in the tomblike chamber, and she looked back at Nick.

"You guys coming?" she asked, frantic to follow Quarren down the stairs. Nicky turned to the throng of people standing where Becca's ruined cubicle lay; it grew even larger as the electricians joined the fray.

"I'm right behind you. We're gonna check the floor one last time first... ya know, make *sure* we have everybody."

She nodded confirmingly. "Good luck, you guys."

She rushed into the stairwell to see Quarren on the next staircase heading down from hers, crawling over large chunks of concrete and pieces of drywall that had fallen all over the staircase.

As she struggled to catch up, her sore ankle barked at her, and her head pounded with pain as she fought her sore back, she noticed Q climbing up the debris like a mountain climber descending a dastardly, dangerous drop-off. She'd thought he was trying to escape *her*, but the tone of terror in his voice suggested otherwise.

"*Q!* Be careful!"

"I am getting out of here!" He was *not* being careful.

"Wait!" She could see it in the way he moved—it was exactly how he was moving when she was chasing him. He was in full panic mode.

"I cannot stay here anymore!"

"*Stop*, Q. We've gotta stick together."

The pile was extremely loose and jagged; she had no clue how Q was able to scramble over this hill. There was a gap between the rail with just enough space, but it was a tight squeeze. Becca compressed her body as flat as a pancake, squeaking between a plank of gypsum and the handrail, her body hanging *far* over the rail and over the next set of steps.

Once through, she had no time to rest; she could hear Q flying down the stairs. She felt fortunate that she was wearing her boots today; the debris was very loose, and she was struggling not to roll her injured ankle. Her legs already felt like jelly from the long, stressful chase through Manhattan, and she knew that getting out of bed tomorrow was going to be a *chore*.

As she descended, Quarren was on the lower flight of stairs, climbing over another mountain of crumbling debris, and he was leaning over as if he was trying to walk down the other side. He was standing on a large piece of drywall, reaching out to regain his balance.

When the loose top layer of drywall began slipping down, Q started glissading forward on it, awkwardly surfing the pile.

"Q! Get off that—"

He didn't have time to react. As the gypsum began to slide, Q leaped off the board, grabbing onto the handrail as the debris collapsed all around him, threatening to take him down the stairs with it. It was only a matter of time; after the pile gave way and overwhelmed him, his grip failed, and he slid down the stairs with the landslide.

Becca rolled off her own rubble and scrambled to the bottom of the next landing, where Quarren was now buried alive in a pile of drywall chunks.

"Q!" she screamed, practically leaping down the stairs. "Are you *alright?"*

She removed a large chunk to reveal Q's buried body. Fortunately, the rubble was mostly drywall. He was coughing up dust clouds as she pulled pieces off his body. Once Becca freed the man, Q stood slowly, checking his arms and legs for injuries before he remembered that he was panicking.

"Thanks, Boss. I am getting out of here!"

He took off immediately, seemingly uninjured from his slide, and Becca reluctantly took off after him. Her legs felt like Jell-O, but luck was on her side—the stairwell cleared up *drastically* after that.

"Q... I'm *coming!* Wait up!"

The panic was threatening to take hold as she wanted to run, faster and faster through the darkness, not stopping until she was back down to the ground level—

A sudden shift in the tower tossed Becca from her feet, flinging her into the handrail and threatening to flip her over the side. She felt a tremendous wave of pressure that forced her ears to pop, followed by a solid, muffled *bang.* The building again swayed, and she gripped the handrail tightly, waiting for the tower to collapse around her.

"Jeez!" Holding both her breath, and onto the rail with white knuckles, she regained her footing. The building rocked for a few seconds, and once again, the perverse taste of metal filled the air—as did the scent of jet fuel. Once the swaying stabilized, she released her breath.

"I'm alright," she sighed in relief. Finally letting go of the railing, she called out into the blackened stairwell. "Q? What was that?"

No response. Becca froze, her eyes straining to see down the darkened stairs. A chill shot down her spine as she realized she was completely alone. She'd been unable to catch up to Quarren. Her breath grew short as she gasped for air, on the teetering edge of a panic attack; her heart threatened to *explode* from her chest. Waving her flashlight desperately down the stairs, she listened carefully; the sound of a nearby door opening freed her from her paralysis.

"Q? Where are you?"

Becca pressed forward, her legs threatening to collapse under her weight with each painful step, before mercifully reaching a door which was ajar, an invitation to escape her madness. What had felt like a dream moments ago now seemed almost like a self-diagnosis of an exotic mental illness; this entire experience was nothing more than a glimpse into *hell* itself.

Either Becca was losing her mind... or she really *was* dead.

I can't lose him; I don't want to be alone in this place! I don't want to go crazy.

Some evil creature was threatening to consume Becca's consciousness. Perhaps the monster from her nightmare? Whatever it was, she fought it off with all her might as she rounded another corner. The door was ajar with a ray of welcoming light squeezing through... *seducing* her. It had to be Q, because she was going through regardless:

* * *

STAIRWAY C
FLOOR
78
SKY LOBBY

He must think the elevators are still working. I hope he didn't ditch me. Becca ran through the door, entering the lobby just as a door to the south closed with a *thunk*.

"Q!" She sprinted down the hallway after him, throwing the door open and nearly smashing into his stationary body.

Q stood there, frozen and lifeless, as if he were a statue guarding the hallway, which lined a row of low-walled cubicles up to his waist. Becca could see the entire row of windows facing south.

He was perfectly still, staring out the windows, his mouth agape.

"Jeez, you're cut *bad*," she exclaimed, noticing a bleeding gash on the back of Q's head. The blood was oozing down his neck, soaking his shirt. The injury was probably bad enough to require stitches, and yet... he wasn't concerned at all.

She yanked his arm back towards the lobby, but Q didn't budge.

"We have to stop the *bleeding*; what are you...?"

Her speech trailed off to a whisper. He was thoroughly mesmerized by *something*, and she walked beside him, unable to spot what he was transfixed on. Whatever he was looking at was obscured by obscene amounts of smoke and flame outside.

Except... that was thirteen floors above us...

"Do you see it yet, Boss?"

She indeed *saw* it, but she didn't *believe* it. The South Tower of the World Trade Center filled the view out of the windows of the floor, and what she beheld was chaos.

Utter chaos...

Becca forgot about Q's injuries as she stumbled towards the South Tower, drawn to the destruction like a moth to flame. That explosion must've been what rocked the building moments ago. Her sea of thought evaporated into fumes, mixing into the smoky air swirling from the wound in the building.

Clear your mind, Becca. Clear your mind!

She pleaded with herself to clear the apprehension that was clouding her judgment and shattering her self-confidence. But she simply couldn't. Her resolve... it was *gone.*

Her eyes, unblinking, were fixed on the flames. After a few moments, her paralysis broke, but she was no longer herself. She descended further into madness, even if only temporarily... overwhelmed by the horror of what they were experiencing.

I can't do this... there's no way. Marissa is as good as dead.

Becca fought the urge to cry, to descend into histrionics, and she emitted a guttural *scream* as she dared to close her eyes. As soon as they shut, her mind's eye opened.

She could *only* see a floating red headband.

XII

"The Screwdriver Police"

"Ouch!" Quarren cried as Becca put a damp towel over the laceration on his head, with the 'medical precision' of an FBI Agent. Her hamstrings on her forearms bulged as she pressed into Q's bleeding wound. Every other muscle in her body was screaming at her to get out of there, but he was losing a *lot* of blood.

"Shh!" Becca hushed as she worked diligently. "Just relax; once the bleeding stops, we can get out of here."

"I think that was another plane?"

She nearly dropped the rag. "It... it *couldn't* be... could it?" That would mean...

"We are under attack, Boss?"

Her response was *never* going to be spoken. Her throat was twisted into a barber pole; she could barely *breathe.* With a final gasp of air, she turned back to her newfound ally's injury.

The wound on Q's head was still bleeding enough to worry her... and, fortunate for her sake, it took most of her attention. The *last* thing she needed was to dwell on what was happening. If they *were* under attack, they needed to evacuate the tower. *Now.*

Unless they drop a nuke on the Statue of Liberty, next. The chill that went down Becca's spine forced her to shiver.

"Thank you for tending to my wounds," he offered, keeping his head still. "You are a very compassionate person."

She scoffed slightly at his language, which struck her as uniquely proper; he was very articulate for a man whose second

146

language was English. *Despite his ignorance, he's quite intelligent. He's like a gifted child, wise beyond his years.* She might've giggled, had the mood been less somber.

His accent still sounds funny to me, though...

"You're quite welcome. You might need stitches once we get outta here, but as long as you keep this wound covered until it stops bleeding, you should be fine." She removed the rag and inspected the gash on his head; the flow of blood had slowed to an oozing. "Just... no more going off on your own, okay? We're a team."

"I understand, Rebecca. I did not mean to frighten you, I could not help it."

A smug grin crossed Becca's face as she watched Q, himself oblivious as to what she was doing. Her eyebrow raised mischievously.

"Well, *I* thought you were trying to run from me again."

His eyes widened in fear. "But, you *freed* me, did you not? I thought—"

Becca burst into laughter, a feeling of levity relieving the tension as she did so. "I'm just *fuckin'* with you, Q." Despite her amusement, his eyes filled with hurt; he found *no* humor in her jokes. "But seriously, what made you take *off* like that?"

He stared back at the South Tower as he contemplated his words. "I suppose I was afraid. There was a lot of smoke, and it was so *hot*. I did not *wish* to be on that floor any longer, so I decided to leave."

He stopped and glared into Becca's eyes, and for the first time, she wasn't afraid or anxious at his gaze. Instead, she was sympathetic; he was *clearly* offended.

"Hey, I'm sorry, Q. I make jokes when I'm scared; it's a defense mechanism, I guess." She grabbed his chin and wiped dried blood from his cheek with a damp rag. "I'm scared, *too*.

Those pilots couldn't have hit these buildings by mistake..."

"You think this was *intentional?*"

His eyes were a porthole into his soul, and his anxiety rubbed off on Becca. She not only understood why he'd run away—she felt the *same* way.

"I'm not sure, but I know that we have a big problem, and we need to get moving—and *now*." She stood, dusting herself off, as she offered Q her hand.

"If we want to get out of this building alive, we need to work together. Do you trust me?"

Quarren's eyes flicked up to hers, before they met her right hand extending out towards him. For a moment, it appeared he might take it, but his hand hovered in midair as he hesitated.

"You *did* treat my wounds..."

Her heart melted a bit as he bit his lip, looking back up at her. *He really is like a big ol' kid. I feel like this is all my fault, but we need to get out of here quickly...*

"Q... I'm sorry about earlier. I *promise* I believe you, now. But we can talk about it while we move; we have to get out of here before we get *killed*. We need to work together... and if you can trust me, I'll trust you, too."

Her hand remained extended in faith, hoping he would accept her olive branch. After a few awkward moments of silence, he took it.

"What choice do I have? I feel like I am stronger paired with a police officer than on my own."

Becca scoffed playfully, feigning to be offended. "I can't believe you just called an FBI Special Agent a *police* officer..." She trailed off as she glanced at Q, whose eyes were full of confusion and misunderstanding. Before she could explain further, she burst into laughter again.

"What should I call you then, Boss?"

Realization dawned over her like a weighted blanket; she hadn't properly introduced herself to him yet. She cleared her throat, her snickering cut off at the source.

"For starters, don't call me 'Boss'. You can call me Rebecca Taylor, or Becca for short. And I apologize for not introducing myself earlier. I'm a Special Agent with the FBI."

Until this point, Becca had been trying to make herself casual with her approach; she'd felt he would trust her more if he felt comfortable around her. *Now, I kinda like the guy, myself...* She didn't mean to smile, but her grin went ear-to-ear.

"And all things considered, it's nice to meet you, Quarren."

She was still holding the bloody rags, and she offered a clean one to her newfound colleague.

"You'd better tie this rag around your head. Once we get out of here, I'll get you a doctor; you'll be fine. How do you feel?"

He tied the towel around his head like a bandana and stood up slowly. Blinking rapidly, she thought he was having trouble seeing clearly—it was then she realized his eyeglasses were gone. *Were they on earlier?* She couldn't remember; the last hour was a *blur* to her at this point. As he gained his balance, she smiled to herself.

He looks badass with that towel on his head.

"I think I am alright, Rebecca."

After she gave him a moment to gain his balance, Becca stood up, wiping dried blood from her arms with the rags.

"Shall we, then?" Q took her hand and they walked back towards the elevator lobby, *together*. With the worst behind them, they could *finally* get out of this tower.

*   *   *

And yet, the worst was yet to come. Neither of them knew what awaited them upon their return to the lobby. Becca suggested that, since this floor happened to be the Sky Lobby, the elevators going down might still be operational. However, she was mistaken; the lifts in this lobby went *up*... and what welcomed them there was the acrid stench of smoke, jet fuel... and death.

Her *gasp* sounded foreign to her. Every single local elevator's doors were blown out from the inside, resembling a row of spent cocoons, long since abandoned by their moths. The lobby was charred, still smoldering in places. The occasional flame would lick its way through the doors—it seemed like a *bomb* had gone off in each elevator shaft.

The marble that had previously decorated the walls had mostly fallen, peppering the floor with chunks of soaking-wet rubble. Every step she took over the debris made a sickeningly wet *crunch* sound, and the carpet was singed from the fire that had since burned out.

And then there were the bodies: three victims, charred and likely deceased. Waiting for the elevators when the plane hit, they were probably dead before they knew what hit them. The terror dried her mouth out like mothballs as she imagined their final moments... she couldn't bring herself to look at them for long, and she didn't *dare* sniff the air in the room.

I can't believe this is really happening... these poor people...

The 78th Floor was nothing but death and despair. Becca nearly threw up.

She turned to find Quarren kneeling beside a body, still smoldering and pinned under a chunk of marble. Gingerly, he placed his fingers to the man's throat, pulling them back as if the man was still burning.

"They are all dead," he mumbled. His eyes were glossy as he looked back at Becca.

"It's alright, Q," she sighed. "There's nothing we can do for them."

"I just feel so guilty..."

His hands found his face, rubbing his temples firmly in a vain attempt to reject this new reality and replace it with his own. She put a hand on Q's broad shoulder, rubbing it gently.

"Don't. This *isn't* our fault." She swallowed hard, trying to steady her voice. "There's nothing we can do. We're helpless."

Just like Marissa is.

The sudden remembrance of the missing child shook her to the core. The relief of catching Quarren had driven her job from the forefront of her mind; the events since effectively *buried* it. If he attempted an escape now, there was no *way* her backup downstairs would see him. She imagined the lobby in her head—it was likely *pandemonium* down there.

However, there was the other possibility... he might still be in the tower. And the building was still *full* of innocent people. The circumstances made Becca feel *tiny* in the massive burning structure. She was one of thousands, perhaps *tens* of thousands, of people in mortal danger—it wasn't only Marissa in trouble anymore...

It was all of us, now.

"Rebecca, are you alright?" Q was no longer looking at the victims in the lobby, instead approaching slowly with a hand extended. "You seem distressed."

Becca choked a lame-sounding laugh. "I-I'm fine, Q."

Without asking again, Q approached her slowly, and she felt a twinge of nerves she couldn't explain as he reached out with both arms... and hugged her.

"I said I'm *fine*, Q—"

"We are gonna be *alright*, Boss. We are *gonna* be alright."

She wasn't sure if he was telling *her* that... or *himself*. She was annoyed, sure... but she still had empathy for the man—*especially* since she still felt guilty. As the embrace went on, she decided it would be better for him if she returned his hug, and was surprised that it felt so nice.

So... *safe*.

"You will get home to your family, and you will find your napper of kids."

She couldn't help it. She broke the embrace and spun away laughing, doubling over as she cackled.

Oh, Q... you're an adorable man.

The laughter trailed off as their situation came back into focus. She hadn't touched base with Bill, who incorrectly believed that Becca already had the suspect in custody. *He doesn't even know if I'm alive...*

"I wonder if I have any signal yet—"

Her face went pale, and her hands came up to her chest. *"My phone!"*

Becca *growled*. It was *far* too late to go back for it now. She'd left her suit jacket on the ninety-first floor. Once she remembered the cubicle had been buried under six feet of rubble, she realized her phone (as well as Quarren's wallet) were stuck up there.

Face it—if it even still works, you won't get that back until they put the fires out... Her eyebrows furrowed as she considered the difficulty of that task—how on *Earth* were they even going to *accomplish* that?

"I'll have to find a working landline at some point," she said, banging her palms against the blackened door.

With horror, she realized that without backup or a partner to help her... Becca was completely on her own. She *also* had to assume the possibility he might escape, and if so, Becca was Marissa's only hope.

And that's why Becca *had* to survive.

Because if I die, so does Marissa.

"I think it is time we get out of here, Rebecca," he said with a simpered grin plastered on his face.

He reminds me of a shamed dog, but one that doesn't realize what's happening. Q's grin was contagious; she smiled back. *He's so polite and innocent; he really is like a big child.*

The people in New York lived a frantic, non-stop lifestyle, so those sorts of pleasantries were usually reserved for friends and family, and *nobody* could love as fiercely as a New Yorker could... but that also came with the caveat that strangers were typically treated—

Well, like *strangers.*

And yet, this man had saved her life, moments after he'd nearly been arrested by the very woman who had accosted her.

Most people I know probably would've left me there to die if they were in his shoes. Instead, he continued to show selfless generosity, and it was utterly refreshing.

With a manufactured smile, Becca tugged on Q's silver dress shirt, which was now covered in dirty sweat streaks, and a long, streaking bloodstain on the back now stained the fabric.

Becca didn't want to know how *she* looked, but she was certain it was worse than she felt.

"C'mon, Quarren. Let's go home."

*   *   *

Stairwell C felt like a smoky sauna full of debris and flooding mystery fluids, a jungle gym they didn't want to play on anymore. The damp chamber echoed like a tomb with each footstep. The smell of jet fuel was *suffocating,* and the smoke was chokingly thick. As Becca struggled to keep her composure, she figured that small talk might help to lighten the mood and distract them from the carnage.

"You said you're from a small village, Q?"

"Yes, Rebecca, in the country of Senegal. It is called Baïla. I was born there." He grinned proudly. "My entire *family* lives there."

"So why come to New York? Did you want the big city life?"

"No," he shook his head. "I wanted to find a job; I am good with numbers."

"You mean like *arithmetic?* You're good with math?"

"Yes. We do not have good universities where I hail from, so I decided I would start from the beginning and work my way up the company."

Becca grinned at Q as he spoke; his face lit up with childlike innocence that melted her heart. She was *thrilled* that he wasn't the 'Mauler'; he was such a sweet man. She didn't think he even had it in him to hurt someone.

"It is so different in America, Rebecca. Everything moves so fast." They climbed quickly over a small pile of drywall that had come off the wall on their landing. "But the food... although it is strange, it is *very* tasty."

"*Hah!* I've heard New York food called a lot of things, but I've never heard 'strange' and 'tasty' in the same description of it." They stepped over a fallen electrical conduit, cautious not to touch it. "What kind of food did you eat in your home, Q?"

"All sorts of things! My favorite is yassa; there is nothing quite like it."

"*Yassa?* I've never heard of it?"

"Are you *joking?*" Q exclaimed incredulously. "My Mammy prepares it with chicken. She soaks it with orange juice, cut onions and peppers... then she puts it on rice with a sauce she makes."

"Man! That's makin' me *drool*, Q!"

Her tummy reminded her with *another* tremor that she hadn't eaten since last night. She was scolding herself for not finishing her plate. Despite her anxiety and moodiness at dinner, she flashed back to that meal, which seemed so nice, so *cozy*...

Yet so far away, now.

She cleared her throat loudly. "Are you close with your family?"

"Most of them, yes." He ducked under a piece of conduit whose straps had popped off the wall, jetting out like a metallic limbo stick. "My oldest brother is in the army; I have not seen him in many years. The rest of my family live in my village, helping with farming and chores."

Becca let out a sigh. "It honestly sounds wonderful."

"Yes, but we are very, very poor. This is why I come to America; I need to make money for my family." He let out a light cough. "*You* have a family, Rebecca Taylor?"

"Yes," she sighed, reminding her again how much she missed Chad and CeCe. "I have a girlfriend and a teenage son."

"You... have a *girlfriend?*"

She nearly collapsed in shock at the *gasp* preceding his question. Q's eyes had *doubled* in size.

"I... *do*. Why?"

"Do people *know* about this?"

Becca guffawed at that one, and Q's puzzled expression only made her laugh harder. "I... I—yes, Q. In America, it's not illegal to be gay."

Q's stunned demeanor melted into relief, his tensed shoulders slumping with a loud *sigh,* simultaneously forcing her to exhale, as well. He smiled widely.

"I think I might like it here. It seems nicer than my home country."

"Yeah, when we're not under attack by *lunatics,* it ain't so bad." Becca's smirk hid her relief; she couldn't *imagine* living somewhere where she wasn't allowed to be with Cecilia. She stopped a moment to tie her boots, and Quarren dusted his clothing off as she did so.

"Rebecca... when we get out of here, I could meet your family?"

Becca's face lit up. "I would *love* that! We can have a barbecue."

Q was enamored with their conversation as they kept descending the steps. Feeling better about their partnership with every step, she quickly ducked through the doorway to the 77th Floor... but when she saw a large horde of people queued in front of Stairwell B, she withdrew back through the doorway.

"We need to stay in C, Q. Don't want to compete with a crowd."

"So... So what is the d-difference in which staircase we take?" Q's voice trembled with nerves as he spoke; his stuttering reminded her of Morse Code.

"It's not only the crowd..." Still in the stairway door, Becca watched the people who had come out of the other stairwell disappear back into B, before she started walking down Stairwell C. She knew this tower well enough.

"I was assigned to investigate a robbery here, a few years back. Big armored truck heist, back in '98.

"Anyways, even though the robbery took place on the street, we had to do a lot of investigating and looking for any clues or... you know, like, evidence they might've left behind. Long story short, when I looked at the layout of the stairs in this place, I *distinctly* remember my partner, Jim, saying how much of a pain-in-the-ass it would be to evacuate this whole tower, like they had to in '93."

But why? Becca searched her memory to no avail; *why* did she remember that? Something was missing...

"Wait," Q said, stopping mid-stair to rub his forehead, "this was not the *same* robbery?" Becca shook her head no. "What happened? There was a fire here?"

"I mean, technically, yes, but it wasn't a *robbery*... it was a truck bomb. It was a big deal. I think... *six?* People died?"

He looked at his hands, as if his brain couldn't process the story. "It is surreal to me how badly people want to terrorize the World Trade Center—"

"Aww, *shit,*" she interrupted, "I can't believe I *forgot!*"

When they reached the 76th floor, Becca threw her arms up in frustration. The stairs terminated here, and she *slapped* her forehead with her palm. "I was distracted... I'm such an *idiot*..."

Yeah, you sure do know your way around here, jackass...

Q was breathing heavily, as if he was experiencing the start of an anxiety-induced panic attack. Instead of another stairway leading down, the floor snaked around the corner to another door, which led to a hallway that connected to another stairwell. *If my memory serves me correctly, that is...*

"Rebecca!" Q exclaimed shakily. "A-are we *trapped?*"

She didn't reply, instead holding her breath and grabbing the door handle; it opened with a *creak* and no other issues.

"Yeah, just as I thought..." Becca pondered aloud. "There's switchbacks." The heavy fire door revealed a pitch-black void, stretching into a smoky abyss. Becca couldn't see the end of it. She took her flashlight out of her belt and glanced back.

"This way, Q. If I'm right, the stairs continue on down this hallway."

The foreboding, cavernous hallway greeted her with the familiar caress of anxiety. A knot quickly formed in her gut. The passageway reminded her of a hallway she once went through... in a dark mansion on a snowy evening—one which Becca did *not* look forward to entering...

Instead, she grabbed Q's hand, and they entered together.

She concentrated hard as they walked, the beam of light illuminating the smoke in the hallway, giving the passage a haunted ambiance. It danced all over the place, reflecting off of glossy surfaces that Becca realized were wet.

The red, rusty river she'd seen in the stairway was leaking from above here as well; it ran down the walls, telltale signs that the building was indeed *bleeding* to death.

"Back in '98, did you *find* them? Did the robbers get away, Rebecca?" Q didn't seem fazed at all by the creepy hallway. Becca smiled proudly.

"Nope. The FBI caught every last one of them!"

He laughed out loud, a bellowing belly laugh, and he slapped Becca on the back hard enough to cause her to stumble.

"Alright! Good job, agent!"

He held his hand out to her until she gave him five, making Becca blush profusely out of embarrassment. She patted his back reassuringly as they pushed through the passage.

They continued to travel further into the tomb-like chamber. It was *hellishly* hot and humid in this hallway; Becca hadn't paid much attention to it until now. Her lungs were filled with cotton balls as she struggled to breathe in the sweltering air.

Becca could hear voices at the end of the corridor beyond the final corner, and she was convinced her thirst and exhaustion were causing her to hallucinate. She pressed on further, terrified to continue despite her weapon sitting heavy at her side; as they rounded the final corner, the small cone of light revealed a surprise that caused her to scream.

Shining eyes and grimacing faces full of *teeth* greeted the two of them. Her flashlight clattered to the ground, as a bright beam of light blinded her anyway.

"What in the—"

Bending quickly, she snagged her light, reaching for her pistol at the same time. Some incredulous monster; some fire-dwelling *creature* with teeth and claws was waiting to devour her *alive,* and the only thing Becca could do was see what it was before it was too late—

Her beam flooded the corridor, revealing a group of people, six in total, who were staring back at Becca with equal levels of fright; one was aiming their light back at *them.* A couple of men were trying to open the door into the next section of Stairwell C. One of the two was jabbing a flathead screwdriver into the jam, hoping to flick the latch so they could pull it open.

Q approached the party. "Is it locked?"

A bald man, the one with the screwdriver, turned with an annoyed frown on his growling face. He resembled a taller version of Danny DeVito, wearing a plaid collared shirt that was drenched in sweat. His body language portrayed an intimidating vibe.

This guy's used to being the center of attention, I bet...

A woman next to him swung her own beam from a little plastic flashlight right in their faces, causing them both to flinch.

"The fuckin' door is *jammed* shut."

He wheeled around, chucking the screwdriver as hard as he could into the drywall, where it penetrated the gypsum and hovered parallel to the floor, its blade stuck in the wall.

Oh! That's why seventy-seven was full of people... I suppose we'll be joining them shortly.

Q removed the screwdriver and inspected it. "Where did this come from?"

"Get a load of *this* guy, eh? Nice bandana, *Captain Hook."* With a fake belly-laugh, the man shrugged. Perspiration pouring down his face, Q removed his makeshift bandana to mop sweat from his brow. His face was blushing as he did so.

"I was simply asking—"

"What *about* it? Are you the *screwdriver* police now?" He

coughed dryly; the smoky environment made it a chore to breathe. "I borrowed it from some utility cart we saw a few floors back. We've been tryin' for a while, now."

The lady with the flashlight spoke up next. "It's locked, but that ain't the issue. The door jam got *twisted,* can you *believe* that?"

"We had the same problem on ninety-one," Becca noted.

The bald man's jaw dropped. "You came from *ninety-one?*"

"Yeah. We saw the plane hit the building."

"Yeah, *right!*" The man started cracking up as he looked back at the door, wiping the sweat from his forehead. "You 'saw the plane?' Must've been one *helluva* Cessna, lady!" Turning his back on her, the man let out another bellowing laugh, and Becca wanted to slug him in the face.

"This ain't no plane, sweetheart. This was a *bomb.* Ain't no *way* a commercial pilot wouldn't see the Trade Center. *Impossible!*"

Becca rolled her eyes at the man. "Well, I'm telling you, *buddy,* it *was* a plane. I saw it myself. And it wasn't a Cessna, it was a jetliner, two of 'em." He craned his head to look at her again. Her hands were busy trying to portray the size to 'Danny DeVito' properly.

"Big ones. Like a Boeing. The other tower got hit as well."

Shaking his head, 'Danny' grumbled as he went back to picking the latch. Becca rubbed her temples; she was extremely dehydrated after all the running and the fires. Her awful headache from earlier was back, fueled by sounds of fire alarms and stress as much as heat and humidity.

And, lest we forget, I probably suffered a concussion in the crash this morning.

Q was watching their attempts to pick the lock with curious interest and folded arms. "It feels like this was not an accident," he said. "This was intentional."

Once again, he glanced back—this time, at Quarren. It was dawning on 'Danny DeVito' that this dusty duo, dressed in shredded suits, might be telling the truth... and he didn't want to *believe* it.

"What, you're tellin' me that this was all caused by a *single* plane?"

"*Two* planes," Becca corrected, two fingers held up. "Well, only one hit *our* building... but yeah—that's what I'm telling you. This was a terrorist attack."

"Yeah, okay, sure thing, lady. *Whatever* you say."

As he worked, Becca observed each of the people waiting as patiently as they could stand for him to finally free the jammed lock. An average-framed young man with short red hair and glasses, wearing a white dress shirt and tan slacks, approached Becca with his hand held out; he impressed her as friendlier than the bald man.

"I'm Jason Palmer," the man exclaimed. "Nice to meet you both."

As she shook his hand, the others stood to introduce themselves. The lady in a red dress with high heels introduced herself as Moira Desmarais. A short, muscular black man, dressed in a white chef's tunic with the word *Skydive* embroidered into it, greeted them both; his name was Mike Manfred.

The group was antsy, but half of them were friendly and cooperative. Jason and Moira both worked at Toei Bank, up on eighty-three. The other two didn't bother to introduce themselves —a tall black man in a dirty dress shirt wearing sunglasses, and a full-figured, olive-skinned woman in an emerald green suit, holding the flashlight.

"I'm Rebecca Taylor, I'm a Special Agent with the FBI. Does anyone here have a working cell?"

"It was a plane! Two of 'em!" she could hear 'Danny DeVito' mocking her under his breath. "Gimme a break..."

Jason shrugged. "I have a phone, but no signal; none of us has had reception since the explosion."

Oh, well... "I know there's another way out, but we'll have to work *together.*" She felt that familiar anxiety brewing deep within her bowels. "You'll have to trust me. But Q and I are going back up to seventy-seven to cross over to another stairwell. You're all welcome to join us."

The bald man *finally* turned to face them, leaving the tall man with the sunglasses alone to work on the door. It was the huskier woman holding the flashlight who got him to stop. She whispered something in the bald man's ear, after which he came over, and the five of them congregated, the huddle whispering to each other insultingly loudly.

Becca knew they were talking about her, even if she couldn't make out a word of what they were saying. After a few tense moments, they stood and looked at them.

"Please, detective, if you'd like to lead the way?" The bald man waved his hand overdramatically towards the pitch-black labyrinth, growing smokier with every second.

Becca growled upon hearing him misaddress her; it was a pet peeve she could not abide.

"It's *'Agent',*" she snapped bitterly. She was too stressed, tired, hungry *and* sore to give a damn. How dare he—she was trying to help these people, and 'Danny' here was fighting her on everything she said! The bald man approached her, but now he wore a friendly grin on his face; his stressful animosity seemingly whispered away by the lanky woman's words.

Still annoyed, Becca turned away from him, nursing her migraine as best as she could.

"I'm sorry, Agent...*Taylor,* wasn't it?" He grabbed Becca's shoulder to turn her to face him, as he spoke in a heavy Bronx accent, and held his paw of a hand out to shake hers.

"I apologize for being an ass; I'm a little on edge. Name's Don Costas, Donny is fine too. I'm an engineer with the Port Authority."

Of course, his name is Donny. She barely resisted this bout of giggles, hiding her smirk as they shook hands.

"I was on the way up to work on the antenna array on the roof. I'd have gone all the way up if I hadn't stopped—first, on forty-four for a cuppa coffee, then my wife's office afterwards."

"It's a good thing you didn't, Danny—er, *Donny*. I think they're all trapped up there; that's why some people were jumping earlier."

Coughing in the smoky hallway, he wiped sweat from his brow. "This lovely lady here is my wife, Janet. She works for Toei Bank up on eighty-three. That's where we were, when..."

Donny motioned towards the larger woman in the emerald green suit, who handed the flashlight to Don as she shook Becca's hand.

"See, Honeybunch, if I didn't love you so much, I'd have got *trapped* up there!" Donny reasoned, before giving his wife a big, fat kiss. She scoffed in response.

"Oh, Muffincakes, you *know* you wasn't gonna get up there till noon, anyhow."

Becca felt a wave of relief upon breaking the ice; she was glad they were all on the same page now.

Well... all, except for *one* of them. The tall man with the shades still hadn't uttered a single word to *either* of them.

Becca glanced at her Pulsar, which was now scratched and beaten. The time was 9:11. She didn't know if they had a reason to rush... but she couldn't shake the feeling that time was running out.

Her mind was made up; they needed to backtrack.

"We have to go back a floor or two and jump into A or B," she instructed the others, still standing between Donny and Q. "Once we get past the mechanical floors, around the 74th Floor or so, we can switch back over to C if we want to."

"We just came from B, and it's doable, but... it's crowded, *lots* of debris. So I mean, ya know..." Donny trailed off, and his expression was one of guilt. Becca could read between the lines; she supposed they'd seen some of the things that she herself had witnessed.

He cleared his throat. "And there's tons of water and jet fuel pouring down the stairwell. So yeah, if A is available, we can try that. Get a little further away from all this fire and jet fuel, maybe get ahead of the pack a little."

Becca nodded in agreement. "Let's try A first. Worst case, once we pass the mechanical floors, we can try B."

She led the party, now eight people strong, back through the hallway to Stairwell C. She kept the flashlight trained on the floor ahead of her, the clouds of smoke wafting in and out of the beam of light.

Near the stairs, the water was running down the walls again, the bleeding hallway *screaming* in agony at her. She couldn't resist her curiosity any longer; she touched the liquid with her pinky and sniffed it, but it smelled like a swamp to her.

"Eww," she gagged, "that has to be from a busted sewage pipe or something." She shook it off and continued forward.

The group climbed the stairs in C, going up a single floor to the 77th. As they stepped into the elevator lobby, they entered a surprisingly undamaged area, providing a bit of reassurance. Unlike seventy-eight, there weren't any corpses in front of the doors, but the room's eerie stillness still reminded Becca of a *tomb*. On a whim, they tried the elevators, but their bad luck held.

The lobby had a small fire in one of the restrooms, sending black smoke out the door. The smoke was being sucked directly into an elevator shaft, siphoned up the tower as if the shafts were nothing more than chimneys, a snorkel of *death* delivering the choking fumes to the forlorn souls above them.

Of course it would... as if those people don't already have enough of that.

Depressed over that notion, she continued towards Stairwell A, opening the door into yet another dark, quiet tomb of a chamber. She could hear noises high above them, and the stairway was empty, so they decided to press their luck here. Her band of survivors stepped slowly into the narrow catacombs, which (as the other stairwells did) smelled strongly of smoke, but it was not nearly as thick as it had been back on seventy-six.

When the heavy stairwell door closed behind the group, the chamber was deathly silent... save for the sounds of shuffling steps and flowing fluids.

The only light in the stairwell were the group's three flashlights, flickering and bouncing off the walls and each other. The eight of them began following the stairs down; Becca and Q took point, with Donny and Janet behind them. Mike and Jason followed, with Moira and the man with the shades taking up the rear.

Their fortunes changed for the better when they returned to the mechanical floors in Stairwell A. This time, the door opened up without incident. After a few more harrowing minutes of claustrophobia, they had *finally* surpassed the seventy-sixth floor —earning a sarcastic cheer from the others.

"*Quel bonheur!*" Moira exclaimed in joy. "We are *free!*"

"I appreciate your enthusiasm, but we ain't free yet," Mike warned. "Hopefully, we don't have no more issues going down..."

Two by two, the group marched down the stairs, the

building groaning around them as if warning them to rush. Becca was on edge the entire time, the left hand of horror simultaneously massaging her temples while the right was throttling her throat tightly.

Little did she know, even with all of the death and destruction surrounding them, that as long as she kept the group moving, she had *nothing* to be afraid of.

...yet.

XIII

"Shades of the Past"

"I think he should switch it up, come out to some Jay-Z, ya know?" Jason's arms waved wildly as he emphatically presented his argument; the two friends continued their discussion as they descended. Mike's white chef tunic was the cleanest outfit anyone in the party was wearing, and it practically *glowed* in the darkness of Stairwell A; Jason's dirty white shirt paled in comparison.

"H to the Izzo, V to the Izzay, ya know? Get the Garden *poppin'."*

"Michael Jordan is *not* signing with the Knicks—get real, bro! He's not signing with Chicago, either. They're already saying he's gonna play in Washington."

"Yeah, right, like he'd play for a bad team like them," Jason countered, adjusting his steel-rimmed glasses. "Why even come back, then?"

"Because, you idiot! He *literally* owns the Wizards."

Becca ignored the irrelevant conversation as she led the group, mushing them forward like sled dogs. She allowed them to distract each other from the carnage with whatever topics they could fill the silence with. Annoying as it was, she couldn't argue with the results. They were descending the stairs at a reasonable pace.

It was slow-moving at first, with all the drywall and concrete littering their pathway. The conditions, however, improved with every landing they left behind them. Stairwell A was not as busy as B had been, but the smoke and flooding in A were a *worse* trade-off than they had been expecting, and *everyone* had been tense ever since they'd entered.

As they went, floor by floor, they chatted about where they came from. Family, work, sports, music... *anything* to ease the tension. It had only teased Becca at first; now, it fully enveloped her consciousness, causing her to withdraw.

She was holding it together, barely...

Just barely.

Clear your mind, write your story... and breathe.

Of course, she joined in from time to time, despite her anxiety. It was imperative to keep her wits and composure... *especially* if she was to lead the group. Becca told the others about herself, and they had seemed rather intrigued with her story... all, that is, except for the tall, silent man with the sunglasses, who was focused on something else. Q was the next to tell his story; the others followed suit.

Each spoke a bit about themselves. Janet Costas was a bank manager who worked on the eighty-third floor. Mike Manfred was the executive chef at *Skydive*, who'd been taking a break with his buddy Donny at the time of the explosion, and had gone up the tower to hang with him. Jason and Moira both worked under Janet and were similarly antsy to get out of the building.

Becca found herself particularly fond of Moira's charming voice. She was a *petite* woman, *maybe* five feet tall, with a strong French accent. Her red dress was covered in dirt, but the rest of her seemed rather clean—*quite the juxtaposition,* Becca thought amusingly.

"*J'ai peur...* do you think this... man will *hurt* us?"

Becca smiled her tension away. "Not if we stay together."

"I'm not good with these sorts of... um..."

"Situations?"

"*Oui,*" she replied. "I do not wish to die, Agent Taylor." She reached her hand into Becca's open palm, squeezing her hand tightly. Becca glanced down at it before squeezing back. Her eyes flicked up to Moira, and she smiled a sweet, homely smile full of crooked teeth and innocence.

"If we stick together, none of us will." She smiled back in reassurance, but it was a false smile. Becca was as anxious as *any* of them were.

Unfazed, the group marched on, making remarkable progress. They'd bumped into a few people on their way down, but none kept pace with Becca's crew. Some moved faster, eager to keep pace with them, while others took their time; those moving slower tended to hurry once they saw people coming down from the higher floors. Becca looked as if she'd been hit by a cement truck, and her appearance earned double-glances from *most* of the strangers.

Some people had no idea what had happened; quite a few had mentioned how perplexed they'd been when the elevators didn't work on their floor. The local elevators below the Sky Lobby on seventy-eight weren't affected as badly as the higher ones were, and these cars weren't blown to smithereens.

It was usually Becca who informed them that planes had struck both Twin Towers, and some outright refused to believe her.

As they passed the seventieth floor, some of them cheered.

"Don't celebrate *too* much," Becca warned, lifting chunks of drywall from the stairs as she went. "We still have another set of mechanical floors with switchbacks. We have a *long* way to go."

The stairwell was growing increasingly crowded as they descended into the sixties. Most of the people on the stairs were quiet—almost as if in a catatonic state—but others were annoyingly *chatty*. Folks of all walks of life were together in that stairwell; they even saw a pair of men carrying an injured woman down on a portable wheelchair.

Everyone around here is being so cooperative, helping each other out and being friendly...

She craned her head back to look up, observing her party. *And yet, that guy hasn't spoken once...* As they descended, Becca allowed herself to fall back in the group until she was beside the tall, quiet man at the back of the line. He was still wearing his sunglasses even in the dark, murky stairwell.

"Beg your pardon, Shades, but you haven't said a *word* since we met. What's your story?"

The man cleared his throat; Becca noticed he was sweating profusely in the furnace-like stairwell.

"I, uh, I work up on ninety," he stammered shyly, before turning to shake her hand. "My name is Alset Aholé."

In the darkness, the cone of light careened across his face as he spoke, and for the first time, Becca noticed he had a golden tooth. It reflected her flashlight's beam in a brilliant flash.

"Al-seat Uh-hole-eh?" Becca enunciated aloud, before giggling slightly. "I'll need to write that one down, later."

"I didn't choose my name, Mrs. Taylor." He spoke in a heavy accent, which sounded Middle Eastern to Becca's untrained ears.

It sounds almost fake to me... odd.

"What's with the *shades*, Alset?"

"Oh!" With an awkward laugh, he removed the glasses, revealing brilliant green eyes which reminded her of Q's. "I forgot I was wearing them."

I'm sure you did, pal...

Becca sensed something that troubled her. "Why are you so *quiet?*"

"I saw someone who is going to die," he stated solemnly, his eyes looking *through* Becca. It sent chills down her spine.

His eyes...

Becca was thrown off by his statement and struggled to figure out her response. A pervasive image once again invaded her mind; it was that red headband, as clear as day in her mind. It replayed over and over. She was going to re-experience the incident in a sickening loop until the day she *died,* a macabre video playing on repeat, rent-free in her head.

"We did, too," she muttered, the image plastered in her imagination. "Everything is gonna be—"

"I'm looking for something."

Becca raised an eyebrow. *This guy's odd... but he's only starting to open up. I don't want to press him too soon.*

"Can we help?"

"No. You're a clown," Alset scoffed bitterly as he spoke.

"I—"

She began, insulted, but she bit her tongue and increased the rate of her descent, allowing some space between them. Donny was right beside her now.

"Forget about that *knucklehead,"* he whispered in her ear. "He's a douchebag."

They continued on a *nice* pace, flying past the 69th Floor... next, the 68th... Even though the stairwell was filling with other folks evacuating as well, they were still descending at a steady pace. Focused, they pressed onward, and she seemingly drifted off in her fatigued state. The monotony of their descent was almost enough to lull her to sleep on her *feet;* by the time they passed the 60th floor, her burning quad muscles were the *only* thing keeping her awake.

That is, until she happened to see what was on the next landing ahead, because Alset was there—sunglasses back upon his face—holding the door open near a placard. It shook her awake like a jolt of electricity as *something* was triggered in her brain.

* * *

STAIRWAY A
FLOOR
59

"I'm taking a break. The smoke is hurting my lungs." He excitedly waved as if to beckon the others to take a rest. Moira didn't even wait for anyone to comment; she followed Alset's hand into the 59th floor lobby before anyone could speak.

Whafuck? He was behind me!

"We needed a break. This should be nice," Q agreed, following them in, the others filing one by one through the door Alset was holding.

Wait... what did I miss? We're stopping now? What just happened? One second, he's insulting me, and the next...

Suddenly, Becca was standing alone in the stairway with Alset, who was still holding the door. With a helpless shrug, she followed them into the Morgan Stanley office on the fifty-ninth floor.

I don't know if we should rest right now, but my legs are rubber, and my back feels like I slept on a pile of rocks. She sighed as she stepped through, welcoming the clean air of the elevator lobby as the heavy door closed behind her.

"We should switch over to Stairwell B when we start again. The smoke in A is getting bad."

The exhausted evacuees were greeted with the reprieve of a peaceful, clean office space; the first she'd observed being this *pristine* since the plane had rocked the tower. Moira checked a door, and it opened without protest. Fortunately, all the offices on this floor seemed to be unlocked—the tenants must have *rushed* out.

Becca observed the odd, random damage that ruined the illusion of an undamaged office. The lights were on, the walls and ceilings were mostly intact, and everything seemed normal... until she noticed a few of the light fixtures had fallen from the ceiling and were now illuminating the floor, hanging by the very cable that powered them. There was a bit of debris, a few ceiling tiles had collapsed here and there...

The sound of a television set nearby wafted softly to them. Becca couldn't quite make out what the broadcasters were talking about, and she wondered if they were showing anything about the World Trade Center.

As Becca's team filtered into the offices from the lobby, the smell of burning coffee completely invaded her nostrils once again. She spotted the offensive pot, steaming invitingly next to a refrigerator inside a small kitchenette. A TV set was turned on in here as well, but it was not the source of the audio she'd heard in the lobby. As they entered the room, Donny switched it on.

"I can't take it anymore," Becca grumbled as she led the group into the break area, "I'm getting some coffee."

Becca beelined to the brewing coffee maker and poured a cup of black coffee into a paper cup. As she did so, Donny and Janet investigated the fridge and found a 12-pack of Diet Coke and a dozen bottles of Dasani water.

"It is *frozen* in time," Q stated, his voice filled with wonder.

Jason was the next one in the coffee line, and Rebecca slid out of the way. Q found a large cloth shopping bag, and as Janet tossed each person in their party a bottle of water, Donny and Q loaded the sodas and extra water bottles into the bag, and handed it to Mike to carry for everybody.

"Everybody, drink some water, at least," Becca warned. The refreshing, cool water seemed to revive her. "If you can eat, grab a snack; we still have a long way to go."

When Janet finished, she had one extra bottle in her hand.

"Hey... anyone seen Alset?" The tall man had vanished.

The floors were large enough to get separated, but they weren't *that* large. She'd realized that, after she'd been the last one through the doorway, she hadn't bothered to check if he'd followed her in.

"Maybe he had to go to the bathroom?" Moira's soft voice spoke up from a plastic chair beside the table.

"Wee wee," Janet snarked at her, rolling her eyes as she spoke. "I ain't worried; I don't know that *spook.*"

Wow... woke up on the wrong side of the bed today, didn't you, Hitler?

Janet's casual racism was quickly flushed from the forefront of her mind. Alset was the one who ushered the party onto the floor... *and then he disappears?* Becca considered it to be odd behavior, but she had bigger things to worry about.

Yeah... like Bill.

It was good she was in the field today, because she was *certain* to be back behind a desk tomorrow after the ass-chewing she was gonna get...

Remembering that she hadn't checked in, she returned to the hallway, checking the offices until she found a small office beside a conference room on the other side of the hallway... with a phone. The room itself was as good a choice as any; the only distraction was a television in a nearby office; *the one I heard coming out of the stairwell.*

When she returned, the group was huddled around the pot of coffee, snacking on muffins and cookies.

"I've got some phone calls to make. Come get me if I'm gone more than five minutes."

The others nodded, mumbling through half-chewed mouthfuls. She glanced at her watch; it was 9:22 when she reached the office.

*   *   *

When Becca sat in the executive leather chair, the familiar, alluring urge to sleep began to take over; the plush cushions hugged the curves of her body seductively, and her eyes began growing heavy before she shook herself awake and sat up.

Her first phone call was to home. The lines were so busy, this call took a *dozen* tries to connect. She was close to giving up, but she *needed* to hear CeCe's voice... even if only for a moment. The phone rang for an excruciatingly long ten seconds or so before a male voice came through.

"Hello?"

"Son!" It wasn't CeCe's voice, but it was just as effective in boosting her morale.

"Honey... are you *alright?* Where are you? Are you at home?"

"Mom, I *am* at home. You just called *here.*"

"Oh, *yeah!*" Becca laughed at the absurdity of it. She hadn't allowed herself to vent or exhale, and hearing the voice of her son triggered some fight-or-flight instinct; she now wanted to run home as soon as possible and *hold* him.

Her lips quivered as she struggled not to choke on her words.

I can't break down yet. Not until we're out of this damned tower.

"You're supposed to be in school," she stammered, trying not to get emotional. "But that's okay, it's good to hear your voice, Son."

"I came home. As *soon* as we saw the Trade Center on TV. I got home—"

"Chad, sweetie," she cut him off. No time for that. "Is CeCe there?"

"No... she's at work."

I knew it. Her mouth grew dry. "She... she's coming d-down to the World Trade Center, *isn't* she?"

The line went silent; after a moment had passed in silence, she grew nervous. By the time Chad spoke, Becca was afraid the call had disconnected.

"Mom, you're not down there... *are* you?"

She froze. Should she *lie? How do you tell your son that you're trapped in a burning skyscraper?* If Chad were younger, she *might've* hidden the truth. But he was nearly a man; he was old enough to drive a car, so she figured he could handle the facts.

She took a deep breath before she spoke. *Oh, Rebecca, I hope you know what you're doing...*

"Um... we're here, yes," she admitted. "I'm fine. But I'll be down here for a while."

"Mom?"

She fought the urge to cry once more; Becca hated crying more than *anything.* "Yes, son?"

"Come home safe, okay? You and CeCe, too."

Becca's voice cracked. "I love you, son."

"I love you, too, Mom." The line went dead.

She called the number to Bill's direct line next—remarkably, the number was still legible on her left forearm—but *this* time, the call connected on the first try. It forwarded to her aide, Jennifer, who answered in his place.

"Bill's heading to the Trade Center, Rebecca."

"Really? Is it because I'm here?"

"No. You don't understand... this is, like, *worldwide* major news. Every news channel is showing the towers live. I even saw..." Becca could hear Jennifer's sobs on the other line. "It's bad, Rebecca. They're saying it's a terrorist attack. They're saying other planes might be hijacked. You need to get out of there, Rebecca.

Now."

Becca nodded silently. Usually, she was the one who would push to stay in the field, but she was running out of gas at this point—so she *wasn't* about to argue.

"Can you tell Bill I'll meet him in the lobby of the North Tower?"

"Oh! I almost forgot," the aide exclaimed. "Bill left me a message to give you."

"A *message?"* Becca wasn't sure if this was good news or bad.

"Yeah, he said he spoke with Jim at the hospital. Jim wanted you to know something about the driver of the van."

Her heart skipped a beat as she heard Jennifer unfolding a piece of paper. "Whatcha got?"

"It... well, that's not much. It just reads, 'Important: share this with Taylor. The suspect has green eyes and a gold front tooth.'"

Becca froze.

The phone fell from her hand in stunned disbelief, the receiver banging off the table with a clatter as it bounced off the hardwood tabletop. She picked the phone up, quickly stammered, "Thank you, Jenny; I gotta go," and replaced the receiver in its cradle.

The son of a bitch was right there! I had him! No wonder he wasn't saying anything about himself!

The office fell silent; she could hear the television speakers from the other room, and nothing else. Justifiably, she was *completely* on edge; Becca was vulnerable, and so were her friends... Her belly began folding on itself like a tube sock.

Her shock transformed into rage, and she ripped the conference phone's cable from the wall, before wheeling around and throwing the phone as hard as she could at the wall, where it shattered with an awesome *crash.*

"I should've known it was him... how could I be so *stupid?"*

Despite her anger, she already knew the answer—she'd lowered her guard after her chase with Quarren. Once the plane hit the tower, she'd nearly forgotten about him, ironically spending more energy being concerned with what would happen to her job, than the job *itself.*

Returning to the hallway, Becca followed the floaty sounds of the TV, which led her through the door to the next office. Paranoia replaced her anger as she peeked around the corner, her hand creeping across her chest towards her gun.

Did someone turn the TV up? Was it Alset?

Becca drew her pistol and crept into the room. Upon entering this new, sterile environment, she observed another, larger conference room with a long, wooden table. A tube television set atop a trolley, similar to the one they used in high school. The TV was tuned to NBC, which was broadcasting the Twin Towers on fire; both buildings now had gaping, burning holes in their sides where Becca could *clearly* see the entry holes left from the planes.

"Christ Almighty," she whispered, her wide eyes transfixed on the TV's display. The sight of the buildings on fire, which she was seeing for the *very* first time, drove Alset from the forefront of her mind.

"This really *was* an attack. Those planes hit dead-center. There's no *way* this was an accident..."

The picture was fuzzy and kept fading in and out in a hail of snow. Becca tried to adjust the antenna to improve the picture, but she was interrupted by a noise from outside the conference room that she hadn't heard yet. It sounded like a metal trash can, declaring its presence with a hollow metallic *clang*.

Becca found her resolve and called out with authority. *"Hello?"*

She turned the TV off. As Bob Kerr's voice faded away, the relief of turning the television off quickly morphed into anxiety as a curtain of terror fell over Becca, weighing her down.

"Q? Donny?"

Oh, God. The realization hit her like a ton of bricks. *It's him. It has to be!*

This was too much for her stress-saturated mind to process. She closed her eyes and could only imagine his golden tooth flickering in the dimly lit stairwell. With an angry *groan,* she nervously scanned the room.

I had the son of a bitch, I had him; I had him!

A sound in the hallway startled Becca, and she froze, holding her breath. It sounded like someone scraping something metallic against a rock. Becca's throat twisted into a pretzel as she pointed her Smith & Wesson back towards the door and thumbed off the safety. *Breathe, girl, you're trembling...*

She crept around the conference table. Every step was deliberate; the pistol heavy in her hands. Every urge in her body to run into the hallway, ready to shoot Alset, was carefully balanced by her cautious and experienced approach. There was no reason to panic—

"Hey!" The door began to swing closed from the hallway... faster and faster, until it slammed shut with a *bang!*

Becca ran to the doorknob, hoping it was a random draft, or maybe someone was there—

The doorknob turned, but the door wouldn't budge.

"Okay... *now* you can panic!"

XIV

"L'enlèvement"

Today was *already* the worst day of Becca's life, a wretched, never-ending cavalcade of misfortune. But until *now*, she had kept her composure throughout the ordeal, because she always had some control; there was always some audible she could call upon if things went astray. But now, trapped in this office room, she had lost her self-control, because she *had* no backup plan; she *had* no audible.

She was trapped. And Becca *knew* she was going to die. L'enlevement

The smoke billowed outside the tower windows, reminding her of the urgency of her predicament. When the sound eventually came from her mouth, it seemed distant, with a tone of suffering to it like she was drowning... as if she were under an ocean, trapped on the sinking Titanic...

"Help!"

She tried pushing on the door, then pulling the knob, but to no avail. As she holstered her pistol, she was forced to consider alternate options.

Clear your mind, write your story... and breathe, Becca—

"But this... this is too much," she mumbled aloud.

The skulking paw of a shadowy monster, some supernatural fiend from the dankest, most cabalistic corners of her subconscious, caressed Becca's temples in a firm, circular motion, drilling its claws into her skull as if it were made of styrofoam. She was slowly losing her grip on her sanity, and if she didn't escape this conference room soon, this monster might devour her alive.

Becca couldn't stand it much longer... she was trapped in this room by herself, with no escape; she hadn't eaten all day, and she was thirsty *and* exhausted—

And extremely vulnerable.

The monster grabbed Becca's head with his enormous paw, and she lost the battle with her composure. *Yep, it's time to panic now.*

"Help!" Becca screamed in terror, frozen in place despite an irresistible urge to run.

Run? Run where?

"Q, Donny, anybody... *please!"* She gave in to her urge and rammed her shoulder into the wooden door as hard as she could, driving into it with every ounce of weight she had in her thin frame.

It didn't budge. It felt as if it were barricaded by something heavy. Becca pounded on the door with the butt of her gun, barely able to abstain from her desire to fire madly at the door.

"Let me *out* of here, Alset. I'll *kill* you, you sick little *bastard!"*

She scrambled to the phone and picked up the receiver; to her dismay, the line was busy. She attempted twice more before she fumbled the receiver, trying to catch it before it skipped over the polished wood surface like a stone on a pond.

The creeping hand of the monster continued drilling into Becca's skull, teasing her with tingles of terror that truly took her to the tipping point. She pounded on the door, hoping the others could hear her across the office floor.

Becca was no engineer, but she'd witnessed the damage on ninety-one first-hand, and she could only *imagine* what the floors above (where the building had taken the brunt of the impact) looked like. The stairs going up had been completely blocked.

She couldn't help it, but she had the sneaking suspicion that the buildings' integrity was compromised, and if it began to collapse, would anyone inside the building even have a *chance?*

She wasn't sure, but she didn't want to stick around to find out.

As she scrambled around the room like a puppy left home alone for the first time, she thought about her options aloud. "Okay, take a breath, Rebecca; let's figure this out... I can keep trying the phone. I can try to break the door down. Or, I have to wait until someone realizes I'm missing."

If they even come looking for me...

She scanned the room, looking for anything that might help her break out of here. A brass statue sat on the conference table; a miniature model of *The Sphere* from the Austin J. Tobin Plaza, hundreds of feet below them. She didn't care all that much about *The Sphere*, but she knew this replica was massive enough to do some damage.

Channeling her days as a high school softball player, she lifted the little likeness, momentarily marveling at how *heavy* this tiny thing was. She stood in front of the entrance and, like a right-handed Randy Johnson, she fired a fastball, tossing the overweight orb directly at the door as *hard* as she could—

Her throw was close... not close enough. It impacted the wall to the right of the door, passing right through as if it were constructed of papier-mâché, before landing in the hallway with a very loud *thunk*.

At first, Becca was frustrated, but then she realized the hole was big enough for her to reach her arm through. It was a bit higher than she'd aimed, but if she could only reach the doorknob, perhaps it would—

"What?" she cried suddenly. Alarmed, she began sniffing the air.

Becca had simply grown accustomed to the scent and hadn't thought about it in a while. She had grown used to it. However, the atmosphere had improved with every floor they descended; the air here was the cleanest air they'd breathed since the plane hit.

So *this* smell was different enough to grab her attention. The odor she was picking up smelled like a lit match, but it was sweeter; it was a chemical scent, like a cheap vanilla candle mixed with Vaseline.

"Help!" she shrieked in alarm when the smoke began billowing through the hole in the wall. It wasn't long before the wall on her side of the room started to smolder, and within a few seconds, the fire had spread into the conference room.

She was out of time.

Becca looked around, trying to figure out another option. The walls were all made of the same material; it was flimsy, but could she break through it? She supposed she could try, but she was already extremely weak and tired from all of the physical exertion she had been using today.

Not to mention, I'm not exactly built like Chyna here... But the door is the only other option, unless...

As she turned, a realization slowly occurred to Becca, and the reality of her situation sank in. Her only escape from the flames that would likely take her life... was the window.

The horror dawned on her as she stared across the table. The fire spread across the cheap temporary walls that constructed the office's conference room.

If she couldn't get out of here...

The only way out is to jump.

For the first time in a while, the only thing that filled her thoughts was Chad and CeCe. Not Jim, or Alset... not Marissa, or Bill, or even *Q*.

No... *all* she could think about was her family. And how she would never see them again.

I don't believe this. How could this have happened?

She dared to look down from the window, and her heart crept up into her throat. Fifty-nine floors below them were masses of fire trucks, emergency vehicles, and dozens upon dozens of people scattering about the debris-riddled Austin J. Tobin Plaza, far below. The vertigo caused her head to spin, and she had to look away.

Her room filled with a toxic cloud, *much* worse than the one they'd been breathing all morning. Fighting her nausea, Becca involuntarily closed her eyes and saw a red headband falling, and she nearly fell over as her eyes shot back open.

I can't jump. No way, man. I'll use the gun if it comes to that.

The smoky room transformed into a sick time chamber, some alien place where the laws of physics were *made* to be broken. Time slowed to a crawl; her breathing intensified. As if trying to discover some hidden code needed to unlock the door, Becca's eyes flicked around the conference room, hoping to spot some secret weapon or item that might help her escape.

As she did, her thoughts drifted towards Alset.

The Y2Killer. The Manhattan Mauler. She had him in her grasp! She'd *finally* found him... and if she'd only called Bill earlier, she could've arrested him right then and there. She doubled over, coughing. "I can't just die while this son of a bitch gets away with this."

Feeling a surge of adrenaline, she rushed at the door, kicking it as hard as she could, before the smoke and heat drove her away. Her eyes welled with tears as she desperately searched the room for another option.

"I can't just give up—I have to get *out* of here!" Her cry sounded almost as if she were giving herself a pep talk. The fire was spreading faster, and she was running out of time; it was going to cut her access from the door off soon.

I need to act, and now!

Becca grabbed her pistol and dashed toward the door. With a primal yell, she shoved her arm through the hole she'd created. Quickly, she fired three shots across the hallway before the intense fire started to burn her arm.

BANG! BANG! BANG!

She couldn't stand the heat any longer; Becca yanked her arm back out of the hole, crying "Ow!" as she did so.

"If they can't hear that, they won't hear anything else..." She rubbed her singed forearm. The fire engulfed the entire wall now, forcing her to retreat behind the conference table. It spread to the T-grid tiles of the drop ceiling, as well as the carpet on the floor—

The drop ceiling! It was her only option left; if it were a standard office drop ceiling, she could simply crawl over the wall to the other side!

Becca grabbed the heavy table with both hands... but as *hard* as she pushed, it wouldn't budge. Her eyes grew as large as dinner plates. She was out of time—

The *fsss* and *whoosh* of gases scared her enough to scream. Funneling through the hole that Becca had punched came a white, powdery puff of something resembling snow. She backed up against the columns near the windows, watching hopefully as someone continued to discharge a fire extinguisher, putting the flames out on the hallway side of the wall.

A heavy, scraping sound rumbled outside the door before it finally opened. She couldn't tell who her savior was yet; she was too busy coughing, trying to get low enough to breathe.

"Rebecca! Are you alright?"

He revealed himself through the smoke as he came running into the conference room with the extinguisher still in his hand. Without hesitation, he turned and extinguished the blaze on

Becca's side of the wall, as well.

"*Q!*" She latched onto his tattered dress shirt. "Where is Alset?"

Quarren didn't reply; his focus was on putting the flames out. She grabbed his shirt as soon as a clear path out of the room emerged.

"If he's still *out* there, he could trap us both. Let's *go!*"

As they exited the conference room, Becca saw the waist-high steel file cabinet that Quarren had slid aside a moment ago. It was heavy enough that moving it by himself as silently as Alset *had* was an impressive feat, to say the least; Becca couldn't even *budge* it. The carpet had bunched up under the edge of the cabinet when Q had pushed it. Right beside the smoldering wall sat a pile of scorched, smoking cans of what appeared to be WD-40.

She shook her head in anger. *So that's what he used to start the fire...*

As Becca and Q returned to the area by the lobby, the others were all standing inside the kitchenette, preparing to get back underway, watching replays of the planes hitting the towers. When Becca returned, panting and sweaty, they were oblivious to what had occurred, having been distracted by the carnage on the break room TV. They hadn't even *noticed* her plight.

"Did you guys see Alset?" Becca asked breathlessly. "Somebody tried to kill me." Cries of "What?" and "Are you serious?" rose from the others.

"I went to the restroom, and I saw fire. What happened, Boss?" Q placed the spent extinguisher on the floor of the kitchenette as they regrouped.

Becca's skin sheened with sweat. Her hands trembling from adrenaline, she sat down, took a deep breath, and recounted everything—about the phones, the fire, and someone attempting to kill her—*but I think I'll leave the parts out where I was debating which form of suicide I'd prefer, thank you very much...*

"I am just glad you are alright, Agent Taylor." Moira handed Becca a bottle of water as she joined the others at the table. The relief was instantaneous; Becca couldn't *help* but smile at everyone; Moira returned it with her homely grin (which still struck Becca as pretty, in its own way).

"Me too. It was pretty scary." *That's putting it mildly; I would've shit myself if I'd eaten breakfast, I'm sure.*

"I bet." She took a tiny nibble from a chocolate chip muffin. *"La situation semble désespérée."*

It was Donny who spoke up next, mouth full of pretzels. "That guy has been acting weird all day, ever since we found him. But do you *really* think he'd do something like that?"

"I do." Becca took a deep breath. "Remember how I told you I was here investigating a kidnapping case? Well, Alset fits the suspect's description." She paused momentarily, hanging her head as her mistake became clear—she'd been so focused on escaping that she never even *suspected* Alset... not until it was too late.

"I just wish I'd realized it sooner."

She couldn't resist the involuntary urge; her eyes flicked over towards Q, who glanced down in shame.

Jason wiped crumbs from his goatee. "You think Alset was the kidnapper, Rebecca?"

"Alset's a sick man, if he is who I think he is. I've been chasing this man for nearly two years, and I believe Alset is the man I've been chasing. He's already killed four kids... and there is a *fifth* one out there that needs my help."

Becca smirked with confidence, cracking her knuckles. "I have to escape this tower. And I *have* to stop him."

Her eyes closed for a brief moment as she took a deep breath; in her head, she saw the red headband once again, causing her to shiver as her swagger melted back into anxiety. Her head sank as she twiddled her thumbs, unaware that the others in the group were watching her with both empathy and concern.

"I *have* to..."

The smell of muffins destroyed her willpower—her long-dormant war with her insatiable hunger decided that *now* was the best time to return to battle. Deciding to snack on something lighter for now, Becca snagged a miniature bag of pretzels from a basket next to the microwave and ravenously tore into the packaging. It only took a few salty bites to refresh her before she felt full.

Besides, watching the buildings burn on TV—the very building she was inside of, casually eating pretzels—wasn't sitting well with her. She rose to her feet, pocketing a small bottle of water, then reloaded her pistol with a fresh clip.

Mike had been watching her in a daze. "Those *were* gunshots we heard!"

"Did you shoot someone, Agent Taylor?" Moira's quiet, accented voice reminded Becca of Fabienne from *Pulp Fiction*. "Did you shoot Alset?"

"No, I shot the gun to get your attention." She glanced at Q, whose expression was one of both relief and concern. She wondered how close he was to the room when she fired her weapon.

"You really think it was Alset, Rebecca? He would be a *fool* to attack us now. Besides, would he not want to escape as well?"

"I have reasons to suspect otherwise..."

She tucked her pistol back into her holster and walked back to the door. "If he's the kidnapper, then he knows I'm the agent who chased him in here. I doubt he'll leave if he knows I'm still here. I expect him to wait until we escape..." As she trailed off, her head whipped around, staring down the hallway outside the kitchenette. Looking for something... craning around...

He's likely watching us... right now...

The thought could've unsettled her (frankly, it *did),* but now that she knew that her target was still in the building, she had an objective again. Reinvigorated and confident, she had a purpose again, other than self-preservation.

However, as she observed the different expressions the folks in her party now wore, she realized the additional stakes at play here.

Great... now I can babysit seven people while I'm searching for this asshole. Alset Aholé, the name of her long-elusive killer... it had taken two years to learn the man's name... he who had nearly broken Rebecca Taylor—

Heh... his last name is Ay-hole.

Realizing this was the levity she badly needed, she laughed to herself as she stood up. "Everyone, stay sharp, and stay on me. But keep an eye out for him; if you *see* him, tell me right away. We should take Stairwell B—"

"Let us waste *no* more time, then." Q reached across Becca and Mike's faces, switching the TV off. They'd been watching the same broadcast that Becca had seen.

"Hey, we was *watchin'* that!" Donny cried, standing up with his arms folded.

"You have seen enough. We should leave. *Now.*"

*　　　*　　　*

Stairwell B of the North Tower was the most straightforward of the three stairways—not to mention the *widest*—and since the elevators here were also inoperable, the stairwell was the only option. Unfortunately for Becca and her party, this stairway was also jam-packed. In both directions from the doorway, the stairs were filled with people, squeezing down three wide (even *four,* in some cases) and not a *soul* was making progress with their egress.

The seven survivors squeezed into the queue of people. Being in the front, Becca was in danger of being crushed if she tried to stop; the line was so tightly packed. She prayed to herself that nobody would panic and try to push.

This stairwell was a lot less smoky, but the sense of claustrophobia was potent as the conga line stretched throughout the tower, creeping along so slowly that Becca *immediately* regretted switching stairwells.

"Why is this staircase so damned *crowded?*" Donny complained.

"Because there's like ten *thousand* people that work in this building, dawg," Mike responded, his shoulders butting through the crowd like a battering ram.

"Yeah, but man, there's more people here than at an Islanders game!"

As they shuffled down the steps, a combination of heat and anxiety forced Becca's mouth to dry up faster than a snail in a salt mine. People were still having trouble believing that *any* jets had crashed into the buildings in the first place.

It was, objectively, a situation that even Hollywood couldn't recreate believably.

"On crève de chaud!" Moira exclaimed as she flapped her low-cut dress, her chest slickened with sweat. "I cannot *breathe* in here!"

You and me both, sweetie...

When they reached the 57th Floor landing, Becca had seen enough. She glanced at her watch; the time was 9:32.

"We have fifty-seven floors left to go. Perhaps we should switch stairwells?" She looked over at Donny, who nodded confirmingly.

The cool, clean air of the elevator lobby tried its best to seduce them into stopping, but Becca ignored its silky caress. This was even tougher upon stepping back into the dark and damp hellway of Stairwell C... and she *almost* regretted their decision to switch to this sauna.

A sauna... whose traffic *paled* compared to B's; it was the only reason they stuck to it. The stairwell was very hot and sticky, and the sweat dripped off her in torrents. Despite having rested a few minutes ago, she was *already* dehydrated.

In addition, the flooding was getting worse.

That wasn't the most egregious part, however. Far more terrible were the billowing, thick clouds of black smoke, which made progress slower than in clearer conditions. Climbing over bits of soaking wet drywall and concrete (it was still *leagues* better than the conditions higher in the tower), Becca led the seven survivors down the dank and dreary descent.

"Hey!" Janet cried in the darkened stairwell. "Watch where you're going, *bro!*"

She couldn't see who she was yelling at, but she could hear Q's shameful reply.

"I apologize, Janet Costas. It is difficult to *see* in here."

"Yeah, and you just touched my tushie!"

"It was a mistake!" he exclaimed; Becca couldn't see Donny's face turning back to glare at him... but Q certainly did. He held his hands up. "I *swear* it; it was an accident!"

Janet finally turned back to face forward. "Yeah, and my husband'll 'accidentally' rearrange your *face* if you don't watch yourself, ya goofy bastard."

I'm getting cranky, too. This heat is too much; we need to take a break.

Still, they were making excellent time overall, and as they reached fifty-four, the smoke was beginning to lighten up at long last. However, everyone was coughing, sweating... and *complaining*.

"Let's take five, everyone," Becca announced. "We could use a break—besides, we *need* to stay hydrated while it's hot like this."

They all collapsed onto the carpet as soon as they passed through the door to fifty-four. As Janet and Mike passed bottles of water around, they wiped sweat from their brows, poured water over their heads, and rehydrated.

Before Becca could join them, she caught Janet's worried expression, stopping her in her tracks.

"Um... why do I have one extra bottle again?"

"Where's Moira?" His arms held out helplessly, Jason took the bag back from Janet, tossing the bottle back inside. "She was *just* with us, wasn't she?"

Becca spun around in disbelief. The little lady in the red dress was not with their group anymore. Everyone seemed as confused as she felt. Nobody had realized it until now; there was no commotion, and she hadn't said anything about taking a break...

Q wheeled around, running into the stairwell and yelling behind him, "Stay right there; I will be right back!"

"No, Q," she cried, "stay with the group. If he's out there, that's what he *wants* us to do."

"Then... what shall we *do*, Rebecca?"

Where should they even start? She hadn't seen Moira since they were in... *Stairwell B? Or maybe the elevator lobby?* Becca shuddered.

We could spend hours looking for her—and we don't even know where to begin!

Standing up, she stretched her sore back high to the ceiling. "I think we need to move on without her."

This earned a *gasp* from a few of them. *"Excuse me?"* Janet cried, astonished.

Becca wasn't ready for this pushback from the others, although she wasn't surprised it was *Janet* who had to be the pain in the ass. "She could be *anywhere* up there!" she retorted, standing up and pointing back towards the staircase.

Janet was turning red, and she was pushing her way towards Becca.

"You said we need to stick together. So I'm not gonna ditch one of my own!"

"Where would we even start?" Becca *growled*, throwing her hands up in frustration. "It's not like the *building* is on fire."

"You know what—*fuck* you, lady!" Janet was so mad, she was practically venting steam. "I don't know who this 'we' business is. *We...* were doing just fine, before *you* showed up!"

"Yeah," she rolled her eyes. "L-look, that doesn't matter." She took a deep breath, trying to stay calm. "I *told* her—told *everyone,* to stick on me, so that's her fault—"

"Oh, and who died and made *you* boss, Miss *FBI?*"

Becca was growing frustrated. "Well, you need to realize that —"

"You need to realize, Miss 'secret agent'," Janet interrupted, "that doesn't work for us! You're a cop, right? Isn't that your *job,* to help people?"

Janet was now aggressively stomping her massive frame towards Becca as if she wanted to fight. Her olive skin was turning a darker, sienna shade, and her burgundy lips were pursed.

And of course, I'm beat up, exhausted, and not in the fucking mood to deal with this angry bitch right now...

"I'm *Federal.* I'm not with the PD; I'm not a cop." She placed her hands over her mouth and drew a long, drawn-out breath of the miserably hot, humid air as Janet invaded her personal space.

I can't blame her, everyone's on edge in this hellhole.

"Look," Becca began, "I get what you're saying. I have one more counter-argument to make."

"There *is* no argument, alright? We work together, we're like *sisters;* I ain't gonna ditch her!"

As she spoke, she bumped into Becca's chest with her ample bosom. Becca didn't back down, and Janet was the one who bounced backwards—despite being about *seventy* pounds heavier than Becca was.

"And if she goes, *I* go, Miss Agent." Donny shuffled over towards his wife and wrapped his meaty arm around her shoulder. "I think we need to find her—"

"Donny, man, I ain't looking for *shit!* I just want to go home."

It was Mike who interrupted the conversation this time. He held his hands up and spoke with a bellowing tone as he stepped behind Becca, crossing his massive arms. Mike's usually-friendly face was twisted into a scowl.

I haven't seen him like this; he looks like a completely different man.

"I want to be there when my wife and daughter get home tonight!"

"We have families, too!" Jason proclaimed. "But Moira, she's been with us for *years—* "

"So what? I don't work with y'all, I don't *know* that woman!"

The peace of the party was smashed to pieces. Clearing her throat didn't halt the bickering, but when she put her fingers in her mouth and whistled, it shattered the stillness of the elevator lobby. The entire group fell silent, and Becca held her hands up high.

"Hold on, everyone, hold on!" They continued bickering. *"Shut up!"* she bellowed, and this time, all arguing ceased. Everyone stared at Becca, waiting on pins and needles.

"I'll make a deal with you. We can search *one* floor. After that, I'm moving on." She paused for effect, making eye contact with every person—leaving her eyes a bit longer on Janet's—and she pointed at each of them as she spoke.

"You guys can keep looking all you want, but I'm not looking for Moira... I'm looking for Alset. I wish I could do more, but I *can't.*" Becca rubbed the anxious exhaustion from her eyes, which were stinging from tears of frustration.

"What about all the people *here* that need your help?" Jason's red eyebrow lifted inquisitively.

"What *about* them? I don't know what you expect from me. I'm not a *superhero!* I'm not a firefighter or an EMT, and... you know, I *want* to help people escape. I *really* do. But that's not my job, that's *theirs!* They're literally here for that exact reason.

"So why am *I* here? Because my suspect is here. *My* job is to catch the bad guy. That's why. And, although I respect *and* recognize the situation we're in, as *well* as the fact Moira's missing... what do you expect me to do? Drop everything and go looking for her?"

She began to leak tears from her bloodshot eyes, but she refused to allow herself to break down. "Please, *tell me!*"

"He's our only lead, Rebecca!" Jim's voice echoed in Becca's head. *"Do the job!"*

The others were all staring at her in silence, observing her like a cat sizing up an oblivious robin. Anticipating... waiting...

"I have a job to do. I *need* to find Alset. If I'm gonna search for him, I can help you search for Moira too. But I don't have time to search every floor. There's a little girl out there somewhere who needs my help. I *have* to do my job. I *will* move on, with or without you. The choice is yours."

"We lost her on the 54th floor, right, Becca?" Mike's expression had returned to normal; he was the *same* friendly guy she'd met upstairs. "We should start there?"

"If we find Moira, Alset's likely nearby," Donny offered, a hopeful expression on his face. "Maybe we can help each other, Becca?"

Becca shook her head. "It's a good idea, but think about it—if you murdered somebody, would *you* stick around? Besides, if she's still alive, she'll head down herself." The sounds of the tower creaking and groaning made her uneasy. "That said, I don't think we have a *choice*. We don't know what shape this tower is in... we might be running out of time."

"What, you *really* think it's gonna collapse?" Donny exclaimed, his voice thick with his Bronx accent, and Becca wasn't sure if he was being sarcastic or was genuinely concerned, like she was.

Becca simply nodded.

"Oh." Donny's face went as white as a hotel bed sheet. He glanced at his wife with an uneasy expression now creeping across his weathered face. "I mean, I dunno, Honeybunch, I like Moira just fine... but I kinda wanna get the hell *outta* here!"

XV

"A Strange Sense of Déjà Vu"

Unlike most of the higher levels, the door to Floor 54 led them into a lawyer's den, a labyrinth of offices and hallways. The doors at the end of each hallway led to different tenants' offices, which were separated from one another. The nearly *pristine* corridors stretched out in cardinal directions from the lobby, and the darkened corridors conjured a sense of claustrophobia for Becca's group.

The thought that Alset could be hiding on this floor—*anywhere*, for that matter—gave her the creeps. Even more so than fifty-nine, this particular office space was entirely untouched by the events high above, save for a few minor bits of office materials shifted about, and some damage to the ceilings and walls around the center core.

Janet was the first to speak, snapping the stretching sensation of silence since they'd stepped out of the stairwell. "Muffincakes, come with me. We'll check this way." Donny silently followed his wife into the south branch of the T-intersection.

"You want to split up?" Q asked, ridiculously. "I do *not* like that idea."

"*I do not like that idea!*" Janet mocked Q in an immature, child-like tone, and she could see the frustration and pain in every crease in Q's brow. He wasn't alone; Becca could barely restrain *herself* from slapping her.

"You're a *moron!* What's wrong, 'Roots'? Ya wanna stand around holding hands and singing 'Kumbaya'?"

"*That's enough!*"

Becca stepped beside Q and glared into Janet's eyes.

"You call him that again, I'll knock you on the fuckin' floor. You got that, *'Honeybunch'*?"

Janet laughed nervously, puffing her chest out... and glancing at Donny, who was too busy giggling at the two of them arguing yet again to back his wife up.

"*Look,* I'm just sayin'. If we split up, we can check each floor much faster."

Dammit, I hate that I don't disagree with this cu—

"She's right, Q," Becca agreed reluctantly, drawing her gun and loading the chamber before replacing it in her holster. "We need to keep this quick. Stay quiet unless you find them. If anyone sees *any* sign of them, whistle."

"What if I can't whistle, lady?" Donny objected.

"Then *yell* or somethin', *man!*" She'd had enough of this banter; she was tired of trying to handle their outbursts with kid gloves. "We *don't* have time to discuss this. We're in a burning skyscraper with a serial killer *hunting* us, so yeah, let's keep it fuckin' *snappy!*"

Neither offered a rebuttal; they simply walked south. Meanwhile, Jason and Mike jogged west, bumping fists and ignoring the argument.

"Where are *you* two going?"

Jason turned his head as the pair scurried away. "We'll check the west side."

"Meet back in the lobby when the floor is clear." The duo stopped in the doorway as Becca and Quarren began heading east. "Be back here in *two* minutes."

Overruled and defeated, Becca let out a *sigh*. Despite her instincts yelling at her mind that this was a bad idea—as well as her knowledge that this made each pair more *vulnerable*—Becca and Q were now standing in the lobby... alone.

"Lead the way, Rebecca," he stammered, the whites of his eyes glowing in the hallway's artificial lighting. She could feel her *own* eyes' aperture growing; her heart was beating *rapidly*.

As they walked into yet *another* office, the area was silent and still. Every cubicle in the labyrinth of walls and desks was a potential hiding spot... which only made things *worse*.

I don't like this. It feels like a trap.

"I wish I had a spare pistol to give you, Q," Becca whispered. "Can you whistle?"

His skin darkened as he blushed. "Boss... I do not know what 'wistle' means."

Her lips parted as she barely held back her giggle; the situation's seriousness stopped her silly side from surfacing. She pursed her lips together softly and performed a quiet *whistle* to him.

"That. Can you do that?" He nodded. "If you see him, whistle loudly, but stay close to me."

They crept into the silent hallway, with Becca taking the lead, and Q sweeping the rooms behind her. She kept reminding herself over and over not to fire a shot. The last thing she needed was to allow her fear to take over, because that's how mistakes get made with guns. As her hands were beginning to shake from anxiety and terror, she thumbed the safety on... *in case I get a bit jumpy.*

The office area itself was long since abandoned by its

occupants. Unlike Floor 59, the folks that worked here had shut *everything* off before they left. Becca considered the possibility that the firms that occupied this floor hadn't yet started for the day when the plane hit the building.

To her dismay, when she reached the first doorway, it was locked. She glanced back at Q, who wasn't having any better luck. He had been going in the opposite direction, back towards the south, where Donny and Janet were searching.

"Q!" she screamed in a whisper. "We need to stick together."

Quarren nodded and scrambled back over to her as she tried the next office. This time, the door opened, revealing a row of cubicles arranged in a neat grid.

"Stand watch at the door. If you see anything, whistle."

Becca snuck into the room with her Smith & Wesson held at the ready. Columns of filtered sunlight from the east-facing windows posed a stark contrast to the artificial lighting in the hallway, illuminating the room brilliantly despite the curtain of smoke filtering the sunlight above... and, of course, the omnipresent gaping hole in the side of the South Tower to her right loomed threateningly over her. It *easily* grabbed her attention.

While the situation *was* urgent, her composure was tenuous at best. Becca froze for a few seconds. Seeing the billowing, black smoke pouring out of the other building had her at a loss for words. She forgot about Alset momentarily, staring in awe at the inferno slowly consuming the South Tower. Molten metal seemed to be pouring from one of the floors, dripping in a sinister rainstorm as it fell to the plaza.

This seemed to break her trance. Returning to reality, she turned around, jogging back towards her friend. "I don't see anything, Q."

They moved on to the next office down the hallway. The

pair of them systematically checked every unlocked door until they reached the north end of the hall; a single door led to an office labeled 'William O. Therisph Law'. Becca had a strange sense of déjà vu as she turned the handle, opening the entrance to this large room.

She beckoned to Quarren to come to her, and he obliged, moving his post to this new doorway. The new room opened to reveal the entirety of the north side of Tower One. The vast room was spread out in a maze of cubicles, computers, and furniture. Becca groaned as she stepped into the silent space.

"I don't like this," she whispered. "Q, check that side, see if there's any sign of them, but stay close to the door."

She broke to the left, jogging through the rows of cubicles, hoping for any sign of Moira, yet afraid of any sign of Alset. Anxiety fueled her pace as she quickened with every row she cleared... but after a scan, she was convinced they weren't here.

Becca re-holstered her weapon as she prepared to return, a sense of tension still hanging over her, like a falcon circling an injured hare.

I smell a rat. I know you're here, you—
RING! RING!

They both screamed in surprise before she reflexively grabbed the phone. However, she didn't pick it up; her heart pounded in her chest.

"Well, it *was* quiet," she chuckled nervously.

The second ring passed, and then a third. "Should I answer it?" Becca flicked her eyes at him for confirmation. Q simply shrugged.

Becca lifted the receiver from the cradle. "Hello?" The other line was silent, save for some rustling, clicking noises. Becca wasn't amused, and her expression was growing angrier.

"Who is it, Boss?"

"Must've been a wrong number," she replied, setting the receiver back in its cradle. "Also, just 'Rebecca' is fine," she reminded her friend, softly touching his shoulder. He returned her grin with a simpered smirk—

"Oh," Becca moaned, throwing her hands up into the air where they found her dusty ponytail. *I can't believe I fell for this...* The color drained from her face as her jaw hit the floor.

"Rebecca?" Q's face appeared to mirror what hers must've looked like. "What *is* it?"

It was all Janet's fault. Both her boundless bitching and battling Becca's brainstorms brought her to the brink of *craving* a break. When she suggested they split up to search, Becca was *desperate* for a reprieve...

And that played *right* into his hands...

Q's questions hung in the air as she turned back towards the east hallway, Becca gesturing at Q to follow her. She was *frustrated*. How was this asshole constantly outsmarting her at every turn? She could feel the grip she tentatively held on her composure slipping away.

They dashed back into the east hallway, Becca wielding her Smith & Wesson as they ran. When they reached the elevator lobby, she tried the door—halfway expecting it to be blocked, but it swung inwards.

The lobby was deathly still.

"I don't think we should wait here, Q." Her eyes, filled with panic, contradicted the calm expression on the rest of her face. The T-intersection branched out heading south, followed by the other hallway heading west.

"Let's check on Donny and Janet first," she mumbled as they jogged south. *I didn't hear any noises, but I have a bad feeling...*

She tapped Q on his muscular shoulder as they reached the door that exited the hall. "Stay in the hallway, Q. If the others return, yell for me." She opened the door, her gun at the ready. "If you hear anything—"

"I will 'wistle', Becca."

She winked at him as she entered the floor's south area.

A realization hit Becca as she entered the southern hallway—they hadn't heard a fire alarm for a while, since they'd left the upper floors. It was a surreal thing to notice, and the silence was *deafening*.

The hallway branched out equally to the left and right, with an equal number of offices in each direction.

Left or right, and make it snappy...

She rolled right. The tense, still silence seemed utterly unbearable. And as she stepped, each and every soft stride and carefully crept foot forward made muffled, subtle sounds of crushed carpet. Her nerves nagged at her as she crept along.

Might as well be giant bags of Doritos I'm walking on... So what was the point of being sneaky? Hell, he's the one who knows where I am! He's probably watching me right now—

"Donny? Janet?" As Becca called out, she scanned the offices for any signs of life. She opened the first door, and this office was vacant; she swiftly moved on to door number two.

"Hello?" she cried louder this time as she entered the second office.

This office was furnished with a row of filing cabinets lined against the hallway wall. The windows looked out over the bay, but the picturesque view was spoiled by clouds of swirling papers flying out into the air...

And, in a strange, almost melancholy way... she *envied* their freedom.

Becca entered the third office and found her luck hadn't changed. There was no sign of anyone, except for the phone on top of the conference table in the room.

The receiver was off the hook. She immediately recognized the howler sound it emitted; an irritating *whamp-whamp-whamp* screaming from the phone's speaker. It was obvious to Becca that it was the *same* phone used to call her moments ago.

He used this to set me up. But how did he know we were going to check the whole floor? I-I—

"Oh... my God... he's not trying to kill me because *he* wants to escape..." Becca's whisper might as well have been a scream in the still air. "He's trying to kill *me* before *I* can escape."

The color melted away from Becca's face as she realized. *He knows he'll never be free of me. I'm no longer the hunter...*

"I'm the prey."

Her grip on the pistol pulsed in her hand. She slowly dropped the phone back into its cradle, the silence again *screaming* in her ears. Her voice came out meek and muffled, lacking any real volume or bass to it.

"Alset, are you there? Anyone?"

As she left the third office, the lack of response was alarming; there was only one more office remaining on the southwest side of the building. Her mouth grew dry, and her forehead glistened with perspiration as she crept to the fourth door. Not realizing she'd been holding her breath, it escaped her with a *gasp* as she glanced at her watch; the time was 9:33.

Clear your mind, write your story... and breathe.

When she opened the door, Becca choked a scream.

The office was destroyed. Debris littered the floor, wafted by a breeze blowing through a broken window in the corner of the office. The conference table was pushed against the wall.

Becca didn't say a word; she simply stared in *disbelief.*

In the middle of the room were two bodies lying on the carpet; they were both unresponsive and covered in blood... which was *everywhere* in the room. She checked Donny's pulse first, and then Janet's.

They were both dead; both still *warm*. Their expressions of shock and fear were permanently etched into their faces, resembling a caricature of Jack Nicholson's Joker. The entire front side of their clothing was soaked in blood; both of their throats had been slit. The carpet was crimson, as were Becca's boots after she'd been stepping in it.

So much blood so much blood so much blood—

She turned back towards the hallway, her gun now gripped tightly in her hand. As she stepped into the hallway, she held her arms up high, her heart pounding with adrenaline.

"I know you're there, you *bitch!*"

Her eyes quickly darted left and right, scanning the silent office space, her pistol slippery in her sweaty palm. The bloody footprints she was leaving on the carpet were the only set; there was no sign of her kidnapper.

And now, she had two more bodies to report.

She opened the door back to the elevator lobby, expecting Q to be standing there, but he was nowhere to be found.

"Okay, *now* I'm nervous."

Her breathing seemed to stop as she crept through the lobby towards the west doorway. It was as quiet now as it had been moments ago, when they'd been arguing here. Deducing that Q must've heard Jason and Mike, she decided to try the west side of the building, turning the corner to finally see the tall man standing alone in the open doorway to the west hall.

This is it... after all this time, we're finally face-to-face—

"Rebecca," the tall man asked, "did you see anyone?"

She nearly had a heart attack as she holstered her weapon. "Donny and Janet are dead, Q." She choked on her own words as he scanned the lobby. "Where are Mike and Jason?"

His face went pale; he shook his head. "There is nobody

here."

Becca's heart sank. She glanced at her friend, who towered over her by at least a foot. It was strange to feel *he* was in any danger, but she wasn't taking any chances...

The man she was chasing was too dangerous.

"Quarren, you need to find a weapon. *Anything.*" She motioned back towards the elevator lobby. "And then we need to get the hell out of this building."

"But... what about the others—?"

"Now."

XVI

"Quid Pro Quo"

Making his way through the dark, dampened staircase, Q held his makeshift weapon—a thick dowel of white oak he found on the 54th Floor—high overhead as they descended. He took the rear as he and Becca ran down the steps of Stairwell C of the North Tower. Becca's beam from her flashlight bobbed as it clanked atop her pistol, which she held at the ready.

As they descended, they would catch up to survivors making their way down the tower, the situation with Alset unbeknownst to them. Some asked questions; others ignored them *completely,* but it mattered not to Becca. She wanted to warn every person she saw about the crazed killer that was stalking them, but instead decided to alert them tactfully—*no reason to start a panic.*

"Don't waste time!" she would exclaim as they passed by the people in the stairwell. "Get out of here, *quickly!* This place is dangerous!" She wouldn't mention Alset; instead, she would impress them with the situation's urgency.

Their urgency led them to hurry, and their luck improved as well—as they passed the 51st Floor, the stairwell's air cleared up drastically, and the heat was bearable again. The lower they descended, the more *habitable* the escape route became. They passed a barefoot lady, limping along in a maroon dress, warning her to escape as they approached the landing on fifty.

As they approached the forty-ninth floor, the door opened *suddenly* before they reached it, interrupting their stride. Despite her annoyance at nearly being knocked down, Becca's eyes lit up upon seeing who was exiting.

"And *where* in the hell did you two go?" Becca asked, her brow furrowed.

"We thought you were *dead!*" Jason was enthusiastically waving his arms at the pair of them.

Mike lifted Becca high into the air as she hugged him, setting her back down gently, his massive arms flexing. "I'm glad you guys are alright."

"What *happened* to you two?" Becca inquired. "What did you see?"

"We were on fifty-four, right?" Jason bounced on his toes as he spoke. "And we finished checking our area, so we were waiting by the stairs like you said, but then we heard this loud sound like a *scream*, so we ran to see what it was, and Alset was running at us through the hallway, and he was, ya know, *covered* in blood, his entire front side, coming from the direction that Don and Janet had gone—"

"Did you see what happened to them?" Q asked, his face full of fear.

"Nah," Mike offered. "I just saw him covered in blood running hella scared, so we took off after him."

"And I just followed, ya know, to stay with Mike."

Becca cleared her throat. "I saw Donny and Janet. They're both dead... I'm *sorry.*"

Jason gasped. Mike stared blankly at her. *A contrast of emotions for certain.*

"*Dude...*" Mike said solemnly, slowly shaking his head. Becca could feel him struggling hard not to overreact. He paced away slowly, cracking his knuckles as he paced on the landing.

"Where did he go?" Q seemed antsy. *He's acting like he did back on ninety-one...*

"Well, he had a head start... so we was going floor-by-floor, looking for that tall son of a *bitch.*" Mike was furious, wringing his hands aggressively. "We wanted to make sure he didn't get away —"

"I saw that man," came a voice from behind them. The group spun around, stunned.

The woman in the dusty maroon dress was limping down the stairs by herself. Covered head-to-toe in concrete dust, she seemed to be in good spirits. She was a thin woman with gray streaks running through her brown hair.

She's quite attractive, even at her age. Maybe it was her lavender perfume; Becca was a *sucker* for a pleasant fragrance.

"You did?" Becca had to be sure. "He's unmistakable; he's a —"

"Tall black man in a bloody suit? Certainly *did.*"

"Let's *go,* Becca!" Mike was fired up. He shuffled to the front of the pack, now standing beside Becca. "I'll break that motherfucker's *neck,* if *I* get my hands on him—"

"*Down,* killer," Becca snarked. "When we find him, he's *mine.*" She glared into Mike's eyes, and the massive man glanced away. Pleased with her assertiveness, she turned her attention back towards the woman, and was met with a ridiculous expression of concern.

Her face... Becca couldn't help but chuckle. *She probably regrets ever talking to us now.*

"When did you see him? Was—?"

"Oh, just a minute before *they* came through that door," she said, pointing to the door on fifty. "He kept running down the steps. Whatever he *did,* you got him spooked."

Crap, he's as good as gone...

She turned back to the others. "Stay close to me. I have backup downstairs; if he escapes, they'll catch him." Mike nodded, his forehead filled with pulsing veins.

He's furious, but he's handling it well. She grinned despite Mike's emotion; she was thankful her group was thinned of the complainers, and the difficult ones were—

No... how dare you, Becca. You should be ashamed. Her grin quickly vanished, and regret washed over her in a wave of empathy. *Besides, Moira's gone, too; and lest we forget, Alset's got his eye on me, too.*

All of us are in danger, now...

Shuddering, Becca turned to look at her swollen ankle. "What happened to your—?"

"Oh!" The woman scoffed, acting as if her injury was a minor inconvenience. "I was wearing heels, and one of them snapped. Typical Versace—built for the runway, unlike *this* building."

The group collectively *gasped* at her dark sense of humor (all except for Jason; he was *cracking* up). The woman in the maroon dress shrugged gently, pointing at her bare feet. "So yes, I fell on the stairs and injured my ankle."

"Do you need help?" Mike seemed as concerned as she was. "We can help you get—"

"Oh, thank you... but I'll manage in time." She was obviously in pain, but didn't want unwarranted attention. In Becca's eyes, though, this *was* warranted.

Very warranted.

"I've only had to traverse a floor or two. I'm employed with Arakawa Motors up on seventy-two."

"Seventy-two?" Jason and Mike both cried in unison.

"Twenty-two floors already, *and* with an injury." Q's eyebrows raised as he spoke. "You are a tough woman, Miss—"

"Julian Mercado. Call me Julie. Just don't call me if you need marriage counseling." She held her hand out, shaking everyone's with a warm smile. Her superior, dry demeanor seemed to soften a bit.

"You're the first people that stopped to check on me—"

"We can help you get down *way* faster," Mike interjected, "if you want to come with—"

"I'm not certain, yet. You folks seem to be a bit... *blue-collar* for this place, so you're likely capable. More than I, anyhow. I suppose I could use a strong set of hands to assist." Becca could read her furrowed brow. *She doesn't trust us.* To be fair, Becca couldn't blame her; they were four *very* different people (two of whom looked like they'd fallen down a mountain) chasing a man covered with *blood*. Julie rubbed her nose, her eyes finding Becca's holstered pistol and refusing to leave it.

She smiled up at Jason first, before glancing at Mike and Q. "In return, I can pour you a cocktail when we get out of this place. God, I could use a drink..." Julie rubbed her nose before continuing.

"However, I *am* concerned... aren't the lot of you searching for that crazy guy you were just asking about? The one with all the blood on him?"

Becca flashed her FBI badge. "There's no point in hiding it; he's a suspect in a kidnapping case, and I'm pretty sure I just saw him kill two people. There's a third who's missing. I know this is a *lot,* but I think you should come with us. If he's around here, well... there's safety in numbers, right?" She extended her hand to Julie, unsure if she would accept—

A glance. A smile. A handshake. No words were necessary. And the party grew to five once more.

Upon resuming their descent, her ankle slowed them so drastically that Becca grew uneasy... but since they'd already offered their help, it would be *inhumane* to leave her behind. Julie was a member of her party, and she had to let Alset go, for now.

He was likely long gone, and with everything going on downstairs at this point... could she reasonably *expect* her backup to be there, still watching the exits? This situation was *unprecedented*... and Marissa wasn't the *only* one in danger.

Unless he's hunting me—and at this point, I'm counting on that—I've gotta focus on escaping. No more floors, no more searching. I'll keep my eyes and ears open, but I must get these people out of here—unless he comes to me.

As they descended, Julie leaned heavily on Mike, her painful foot causing her to *moan* and *groan* with every step. After a few floors, Mike practically *carried* Julie down the steps, Jason helping to balance her uninjured side as they descended deeper into the depths of the damned tower.

They came upon a man leaning in the corner of the landing, between floors forty-seven and forty-eight. He was on a cellular phone, but having zero luck connecting. Becca scolded herself again for forgetting her suit jacket on ninety-one... but she wasn't the *only* one reminded of their cell phone by the stranger.

"Oh!" Julie exclaimed suddenly, stealing her hand back from Jason as she did so. Mike halted in his tracks as she reached into her purse, the strap wrapped securely around her shoulder like a messenger's bag.

Q chimed in from behind the group. "What is wrong—?"

"My cell." She removed a small device from her clutch. "I wish to call my daughter back; she lives in Montréal—"

"You have *signal?*" Becca cried incredulously. "Please, I *need* to use your cell—"

"Oh, okay... I suppose a *quid pro quo* is in order, considering your assistance. Feel free to borrow—"

Becca nodded enthusiastically, eagerly snatching the device. Her heart skipped a beat when she looked at its front casing. The flip phone was an innocuous Motorola model, but silk-screened on the outer shell was the 'Nextel' logo. Her breath caught in her throat as she opened the device; the signal indicator showed nearly full bars.

"You're a *lifesaver!*" She dialed Bill's number into the phone and clicked the PTT button on the side of the phone.

BEEP BEEP! "Hello, Bill, are you there? This is Rebecca Taylor."

After a moment of silence, the phone emitted a *BEEP* in response.

"Rebecca? Where *are* you; are you *safe?*"

Hearing Bill's voice was very therapeutic for her. For the first time in a while, she felt confident again. The events of today had completely unraveled Becca's sanity; the kaleidoscope of images that played relentlessly in her head now included a pair of bodies with a slit throat, and a burning office—*lest we forget the red headband*. Becca was on the edge of *losing* it.

Now, she took a deep breath; she was rewriting her story. *I have a job to do.*

"I'm alright, but I'm still in the North Tower."

"Whose phone number is this? Can I contact you here?"

She glanced at Julie, whose eyes grew three times in size. Afraid of asking this woman for another favor, she shook her head.

"Negative... I-it's not important, but I lost my phone."

"Becca, I know you are probably already aware of this, but I don't *care* about the case anymore. I want you out of that tower."

"I'm working on it, Bill. But I think I've ID'd the perp." She paused for a moment to breathe. "I believe his name is *Al-seat Uh-hole-eh?*"

A few moments passed. "You're gonna have to write that one down." She shivered; that was almost what she had said to Alset verbatim earlier. Despite this, her voice regained its professionalism with each passing second; it was as if the conversation with her boss was *recharging* her.

"He's killing people, Bill. I'm pretty sure he's following us, trying to get rid of me so he can get away. I'm evacuating the tower with a small party, and Bill—he *murdered* two of my party. And another one is missing, presumed—" she stopped speaking to see Jason's steely glare, his eyes both stabbing, and simultaneously saddened.

BEEP! "...presumed to be dead, sir."

After a few tense seconds, Bill responded. "Is he with you now?"

"Negative. Are the exits still covered?"

The other line was silent as they began slowly resuming their journey. After an uncomfortable amount of time had elapsed, he finally responded.

"There's a command post in the lobby of the North Tower, next to the Fire Department," Bill informed his Agent. "When you get down, meet me there."

"Where are you, Bill? Are you here, now?"

She received her reply as they arrived at the landing on the 46th floor. "Don't worry about that, Becca. Just get out of there. *Now!*"

The tone of his words was meant to end their conversation, but Becca was far from finished. "How's Jimbo doing? You heard anything?"

"I can't chat right now. They're saying the South Tower is compromised. Serrano is going to be fine, but if you don't get your ass out of that building, he's going to need a new *partner*. Get out of there, now, Taylor—*that's a fuckin' order!*"

BEEP BEEP! "Copy that, sir."

"Well, now," Julie cracked. "Even *I* can't get undressed that quickly, dear."

Jason collapsed in a fit of coughing, nearly dropping Julie as he masked his laughter. Becca wasn't as amused as she handed the phone back to Julie, her expression defeated.

"He said the South Tower is compromised?" Q stated, his eyes wide as saucers. "But there must be thousands of people still in there!"

"If the other building collapses," Becca said, "it could collapse into ours. That's what they were trying to do in '93."

"Oh, yeah... I *remember* that!" Mike exclaimed. "I wasn't working at *Skydive* yet, I was still living in Chicago... but I remember seeing it all over the news. They talk about it all the *time* at work—wasn't it a Ryder truck or something like that?"

Jason nodded confirmingly. "Yes, and fortunately the building was too strong for that, but I mean... getting hit by a fuckin' Boeing tho... that's like getting hit by a *missile.*"

"More like a rocket," Mike scoffed.

"A *Boeing?*" Julie exclaimed, her voice shivering like a devil in an icebox. Becca watched her with mild amusement. Ever since they'd met Julie, she'd acted superior to them. This woman, obviously of a higher tax bracket than *any* of them, with a snooty air about her... she was simultaneously composed, but with an undertone of panic in every word she spoke. It was only in the last few moments, but her demeanor was changing rapidly. The lines she expertly hid with foundation; the gray hairs she adeptly colored, maintaining her roots, all in an effort to stay youthful and yet... she was *aging* before Becca's eyes.

Julie was on the verge of tears, and only Becca noticed it.

"You mean that enormous hole in the other building... that was a *different* plane?"

Mike nodded, hoisting her weight back up onto his shoulder. Jason was scrambling back beneath her other arm, enjoying his assignment *far* more than Becca was comfortable with.

"But there's no way this was an accident, then!"

The others comforted Julie as they told her what they knew about the attacks, and she realized that her newfound friends were dealing with a lot more than she'd bargained for... but with her ankle being injured, she hadn't much choice in who she traveled with.

In her mind, the fact that they were still willing to help her, despite knowing the danger they were in, made her very grateful.

As they continued through the stairway, Mike started to get excited, earning their attention.

"Oh, I just realized. We're close to my floor!"

"Your floor?" Becca echoed mindlessly before remembering.

"Oh, yes," Julie said, "you're the head chef of *Skydive*, aren't you? I *knew* I recognized you."

"*Executive* Chef, ma'am. Don't you forget it." He tapped his dusty Chef's tunic proudly, where his name was embroidered. "Y'all think we got time? I can whip you up something..."

"Are you *serious?*" Jason and Becca screamed in unison.

Mike's smirk betrayed his deadpan demeanor before he lost it, cracking up with Julie and Becca joining his infectious laughter. Before long, *all* of them were laughing—even Q (he had no idea *why* they were cracking up, but it was infectious). The levity was precisely what they needed.

*　　　*　　　*

As much as Becca was tempted to take Mike up on his offer for food, the magnitude of their situation forced her to ignore her hunger pains as they descended. When they reached Mike's floor, the party of five cheered upon reaching the landing. The sign proudly declared:

* * *

STAIRWAY C
FLOOR
44
SKY LOBBY

As they stepped onto the landing, Julie raised a hand. "All kidding aside, could I bother you folks for a couple minutes' break? My ankle is barking, and I am *dreadfully* thirsty."

The group let out a collective sigh as they entered another peaceful, undamaged elevator lobby. Mike pushed past Becca, his eyes wide. "Home, sweet home," he exclaimed, jogging into *Skydive* as he called aloud. "Hello? Anyone there?"

The restaurant was utterly deserted. Tables sat with freshly-served breakfast, but no soul around to enjoy it. The rows of salad bars and buffet-style dining bars were stocked with various fruits and breakfast foods, but the restaurant was entirely void of people. Dejected, he returned to his friends, who'd gathered around a security podium opposite the express elevators.

Meanwhile, Becca noticed tears welling up in Julie's eyes. Memories of the 78th Floor poured into her mind... when Q had embraced her. It had felt so unexpected—almost out of place—but it did a fantastic job of comforting her.

Without saying a word, she wrapped Julie up in a big hug.

She seemed taken aback at first, but eventually accepted the embrace. Becca had buried her issues for years at this point, and recognizing that these situations (even as relatively commonplace as they might be for an FBI Agent) were stressful *and* agonizing for anybody... sometimes addressing them was the right thing to do. When you bottle that sort of thing up, it becomes trapped in the human mind... and that's a scary place for things to fester. Sometimes, *all* it takes to beat those inner demons that bubble under the surface is to have someone who will be there for you in case you falter—that's what CeCe had done so adeptly for her.

Don't cry—don't you dare cry.

"We're gonna be okay," she told Julie, holding her closely as if they were sisters. *"All* of us are getting out of here. We just gotta stick together."

"That is right!" Q said behind Becca's shoulder. "We are a team!"

"Who's the head coach—Mr. *Rogers?"* Julie finally broke the hug after a few moments, her eyes darting away from Becca's own. "Please. Don't fret about *me* any more than you already have."

Becca hid a giggle. *She's acting tough, but her eyes were glossy...*

When Mike returned, Becca broke away to inspect the elevator lobby; it wasn't *nearly* as damaged as the previous Sky Lobby on seventy-eight. The lobby here had little to indicate that there'd been any explosion at all; some of the elevator doors were teasingly *pristine,* but when Q pressed the buttons on the ones going down, there was no indication of life. Becca guessed they'd been recalled to the ground floor.

I don't know if I would trust them anyway, but forty-four floors with an injured ankle... this is going to take us a while.

A swivel chair was positioned behind the security podium, and Jason guided Julie over to it, handing her a bottle of water after she sat, gingerly stretching her swollen ankle. As she sipped, the other four gathered around the podium, taking a moment to inventory their situation.

Becca glanced at her watch: it was 9:42.

"This is a long shot, Mike," Becca began, "But do you guys have any portable wheelchairs, so we can carry her down? Remember that lady up on, what was that, *sixty-eight* or so? With the two guys helping her down?"

Jason nodded. "True, and if there *is* one around here, this is likely the floor to find it on."

"Actually, we *might* have one of those up here," Mike suggested. "In the locker room, I think? It's *right* by my locker. I'm *pretty* sure I've seen it."

Becca took another cursory glance around the lobby, but to no avail. "I don't know if we should split up again, though. Alset could be *anywhere.*"

A dark curtain of doubt fell over Becca. The lobby was well-lit and clean, but it was *deathly* silent. Every shadowy corner, each closet or office—he could be in *any* of them. And now, here *she* was, in the middle of this lobby, constantly checking over her shoulder and expecting Alset to be standing there with a bloody knife in his hand, smiling...

Gee, that'll make for an exciting day of therapy.

"As long as we stay *together,*" she emphasized the final word, glancing at and making eye contact with each of the others as she spoke, "he can't get us... and if we see him, I'll handle him." Becca smirked, patting her holster. "But that means *no* more splitting up. We're in this *together,* and we're all getting out of here   "

"Aw, crap..."

The others flinched at the loud interruption. They wheeled towards Jason... and he was fortunate that looks cannot kill. His skin took on a hue even redder than his stubby hair.

"I, uh... I forgot to set up my fantasy football waivers on Yahoo." They stared at him in stunned silence, unsure if he was joking—or lost in space.

"Fool!" Mike exclaimed, smacking him upside the head. "We can talk about that shit once we're back on the stairs. I think I know where one of those wheelchair things is—Becca, you wanna go with me?"

"Okay. Mike, I'll stick with you. You three, stay put."

"But you just said..."

When Q objected to her proposal, she nearly laughed; she had expected this. "I know, I'm only a *girl*... but I can handle myself."

"Yes, Miss Rebecca, but—"

"I have a gun. I can protect two just fine, but I *need* you to stay with Julie and Jason. We're only looking for a wheelchair, we'll be right back."

Q nodded, frowning. "Whatever you say, Boss." He pulled his wooden dowel out of his pocket, holding it at the ready.

The two of them began their stroll down the T-intersection between the local elevators and towards the south-facing side of the tower. Becca's eyes darted along each hallway, her head craning to peek around every corner. Instinctively, she unholstered her Smith & Wesson, earning a glance from her comrade.

"There's a dishwashing room just over this way. It's our locker room," Mike whispered, nudging his head forward. "Follow me."

He pushed on a door, revealing a large office-type room with a linoleum floor and a dishwashing area on the other side. A hallway led towards the *Skydive* Restaurant, and as tempting as it was to investigate the smell of the baked goods that wafted through the corridor—she had eaten only a tiny bag of pretzels all day, and she was *starving*—they began their search.

The room was large, with basins full of dirty dishes and racks of plates and silverware. Silent, steel lockers stood like sentinels on one side of the room, with clean chef's tunics hanging invitingly on the wall next to them. A cursory sweep of the room indicated no signs of Alset; she holstered her weapon.

"It's around here somewhere." Mike began searching a row of lockers next to an industrial-sized steel desk. Becca wandered to the opposite side of the room, near the dishwashing basins, when a bellowing cry startled her, causing her to flinch.

"A-ha! We in there."

With one hand, Mike lifted it high in the air. It was a lightweight, aluminum-framed, bright-red nylon wheelchair, collapsed into a compact shape, with two foldable black plastic handles and two wheels. It had large, padded straps on the reverse of the backrest and could be worn like a backpack.

"Great job!" Becca beamed at him. "Do you need anything from your locker, Mike?" She nodded her head towards the locker in front of her.

"Nah, I have everything I need. I can get the rest later."

A placard proudly labeled this locker as 'Executive Chef Michael Manfred.' A small vinyl pocket was attached to the locker's door with several of Mike's business cards inside; she reached in and plucked one, shoving it in the front pocket of her slacks.

Mike picked the wheelchair up and shuffled towards the hallway, beckoning for Becca to follow. As they approached the others, they could hear a heated discussion about fantasy football taking place in full swing.

"But Jeff Garcia *ain't* Steve Young!"

Jason was complaining, emphatically gesturing at Julie and Quarren with his hands. "And this year he ain't got Rice, he went to Oakland, so... yeah. I dunno. I'm thinking about trading for

Drew Bledsoe."

"He's useless. I'd wager he gets injured the moment you acquire him, so you *must* get *his* backup, as well." Julie's suggestion earned a scoff from Jason; her fantasy football acumen amused Becca.

I should get CeCe to play fantasy football; she'd be killer at it.

"I tell my friends in my league, you always get *your* QB's backup as your own backup. It's basically *required*."

"What about the bye week?" Becca chimed in, hopeful she knew enough *not* to sound ignorant.

"Well," Julie considered, "you simply drop your backup for that week. Though I'm unaware who Bledsoe's backup is."

"Tim *Brody,* or maybe Brady—something like that," Jason sneered, "but he's probably a *bum,* though; I've never heard of—"

"Enough about football, man!" Mike plopped the chair in front of Q. "This will work, right?" *Ever since he found out about Donny, he's been all business.*

Q's reply was muted; his expression solemn. "We might wish to evacuate soon."

"What?" Becca followed his gaze. One of the local elevators had begun emitting smoke at a high rate, and on cue, the second elevator bank began belching out black clouds as well. One by one, fumes began leaking out from each elevator door, *oozing* through each gap, and the lights overhead became shrouded in the fog.

"Yeah, good call. Let's get moving."

The wheelchair was quite nifty, in Becca's opinion. It unfolded easily enough, and Mike offered to be the first mule, putting the wheelchair on like a backpack. Once Julie was strapped in, they assisted Mike in standing with her weight, awkwardly trying to pull him back to the ground.

"And don't you *dare* mention how heavy I am," Julie warned.

"If you need to stop, I implore you not to drop me."

Becca thought it looked hilarious. This muscular man now carried Julie like a toddler on his back, with Jason and Q on each side to help him balance. It was like Julie was the 'Queen of the North Tower,' and she giggled at the thought. *I wonder if that'll be in that new Lord of the Rings movie...*

"If you need a break, Michael, please let me know," Quarren instructed the muscular man, and Mike nodded back. "I am happy to take over if you need rest."

Becca shuffled back over towards the T-intersection. She opened the nearby door, which led into Stairwell B, and after a glance around, returned with a new smirk of excitement on her face.

"B looks pretty good, you guys. It's not as busy now. Under the circumstances, we should take B. Alset wouldn't *dare* attack us in there."

Jason and Mike nodded in agreement. "Let's roll."

XVII

"Ice Cream on a Warm Summer's Evening"

Becca couldn't determine if something was about to happen or if it was a renewed sense of urgency, but *something* was driving her instinct to hurry. As soon as they stepped into Stairway B, they were making excellent time, rhythmically gaining floors with increasing speed. Even with Mike carrying Julie on his back, they descended at a rate of about one floor every twenty seconds or so.

It was a synchronized effort, a steady beat they engineered. Jason and Q helped lift Julie's weight off Mike's back by pulling up on the wheelchair's handles as Mike moved forward, balancing his unusual load. Although it was awkward, they were moving as quickly as an unhindered person might, and at a consistent pace. Mike didn't *dare* slow down; gravity was the final factor pushing him downstairs. The fact that they didn't fall once while moving at this pace was incredible to Becca.

Julie was the antithesis to the others' urgency. She was having the time of her *life*, showcasing her peculiar wit with each passing floor. As they passed by folks in the stairwell, she made clever remarks and off-kilter greetings.

A woman was crying when they reached thirty-nine, and Julie laughed at the joke in her head before sharing it as they passed.

"Don't fret, honey, I cried when *I* passed forty, too!"

They passed a man soon after who was smoking a cigarette, and she tapped him on the shoulder.

"The smoking section was in Stairway *A*, sir. There's less jet fuel in that one!"

A younger woman barreled down, nearly bowling Mike over.

"Go ahead, young lady, we'll catch up!" she replied, holding her injured ankle out straight. Her sharp demeanor made Becca fall in love with her (despite her snooty attitude), and she quickly made friends with everyone in the group. Becca felt proud of the team they'd put together, working smoothly as a unit. As they hurried to escape, she realized their time together was slipping away, and that thought dimmed her mood a bit... but the light at the end of the tunnel—*Jim, food, a shower, and a long, long nap*—picked her up again.

As they moved along, she couldn't help but notice how this stairwell had grown less crowded in a surprisingly short period of time. It made perfect sense to Becca—the people upstairs were probably held up, naturally, by those further below, who also needed to evacuate. Now that everyone below was likely safe from danger, the crowd behind them was quickly closing in.

The numbers flew by in a blur. They passed the 40th Floor... then the 35th... and as the five of them reached the 30th floor, they stopped for a moment inside the lobby, which was silent as a church, and not terribly smoky.

"Let's swap, Q," Mike stammered, nearly, stumbling as he hurried through the doorway. Jason and Q helped Julie out of the chair without delay, already in the process of swapping the wheelchair onto Q's sturdy frame before Becca had a chance to ask. She glanced at her watch; the time was 9:50.

"Good *job,* you guys! We went down fourteen floors in about five minutes. Well done."

Mike was bent over and sheening with sweat, breathlessly mouthing the words "Thank you" and giving her a thumbs up.

Rest was a luxury they couldn't afford, however, and they were back underway quickly. For Q, Julie was a trivial load to carry, and he was moving so quickly he was outpacing the others. They weren't able to keep up with him to help him balance Julie, but he was so outrageously powerful that he didn't even want their help... much less *need* it.

They moved with purpose, and as they approached the 27th floor, they saw a sight they never thought they'd see again: a simple reminder of the outside world, and a sign that everything would eventually be alright.

On twenty-seven, Becca's party passed by a cluster of people in the stairwell... but they were going *up.*

"Holy crap!" When Jason caught sight of them, his voice cracked as he yelled. "We're *saved!* Thank God!"

As word spread backward through Stairway B, the sounds of clapping hands reverberated up the building, causing Becca's ears to hurt so badly she had to cup her hands over them; her eardrums threatened to pop.

The looks on the newcomers' faces made Becca's mouth dry. Unlike the numerous civilians evacuating the North Tower, whose faces were full of fear, anxiety, or determination... *these* faces were blank, focused... and *empty.* Whatever they'd seen downstairs had changed them.

One of the men coming up the stairs nodded at her on the other side of the handrail, and she stopped him. "Excuse me. What companies are responding to these fires?"

"What do you mean, 'what companies'?"

"Well, I know someone that—"

"Listen, lady. I know you've had a rough day." The fireman cut her off with a laugh, landing a heavy glove on her shoulder with a *thump*. "They're *all* here."

"What do you—?"

He looked dead in her eyes without moving a muscle.

"Every firefighter within fifty miles is either already here or on the way. Count on it." He lifted his duffel bag with a mighty grunt and continued.

"This is unprecedented," Jason exclaimed. "This is unbelievable!"

"No," he replied as he continued up, "this is *war.*"

*   *   *

Their progress in Stairwell B had been rapid, but the smoke was getting so thick that some folks were abandoning B. Becca was already considering changing stairwells, and was about to speak up when they approached the 21st floor. The door to the lobby was propped open:

"Well, we already ran into firefighters—maybe we'll find a food truck?"

"C'mon, Julie," Jason scoffed beside her. "You know perfectly well there aren't any—"

"It was a *joke,* numb nuts." Embarrassed by her mocking laughter, he looked away, blushing profusely... but when she placed a hand on his arm and smiled at him, he blushed *more.* Q was the first to enter, and Julie, still strapped into the chair, began waving her hands enthusiastically like C-3PO strapped to Chewbacca's back in Cloud City.

"You guys!" she waved emphatically, nearly knocking Q into the wall.

They stepped into what was essentially a field medical office. The lobby was filled with dozens of firefighters and civilians—some of whom were injured—as well as a few policemen as well. The fire department had begun mobilizing a temporary triage on this floor, and Becca entered the room scanning for one person, and one person *alone.*

"Excuse me!" Her voice boomed as she walked over towards a crowd of about thirty people, the vast majority of whom were FDNY—and not one gave Becca more than a customary glance. As she approached, tucking her badge into her waistband, the scene in the lobby was something she *wasn't* prepared for.

There were a few folks who had injuries lying on the carpet. A man with his face completely covered in blood; another with severe burns on his face to go along with a singed suit. Becca's eyes met his own; they seemed to tell her what she was already thinking.

I must look as bad to this guy as he does to me...

Standing near the man were a few men in clean suits speaking to the firefighters; one was holding a megaphone. She decided to approach them... if for no other reason than to warn them about Alset.

"What's going on...?"

Becca's speech trailed off completely. The words she'd intended to say abandoned her before she had a chance to mutter them. The tower, her group... even *Alset* abandoned her mind.

Something she saw transfixed her. Or rather, it trans-*ported* her... far, far away. Floating on her own two feet, she found herself swooning. Becca was a fan of hip-hop, and she loved West Coast style as well. A poem sprang to her mind, written by the late rapper Tupac Shakur: "The Rose That Grew From Concrete."

But even that fails to compare. Nothing could. Deliver me the first rose of spring—sweet, radiant, yet ringed with thorns—and it would pale in comparison with her. A prick by her beauty is worth twice as much in pain. In this thorn-choked wasteland, she is my rose.

Her jaw weighed a ton; her mind filled with helium. She was mesmerized by the most *beautiful* person in the world, her own little piece of heaven conjured up in the middle of this fear-inducing nightmare. Her heart seemed to stop beating in her chest. She neglected to breathe as she floated over to this person, forgetting entirely where she was and what she was doing here.

The woman she was transfixed on noticed her as well... and immediately wheeled towards her.

"Oh my God—*Babe?* What are you doing here?"

She dropped the hose she was unfolding and sprinted over to Becca, planting her hands on her hips and lifting her high into the air above her head.

When their lips locked, Becca swore she could see sparks flying around them.

"Oh, Cecilia!"

Becca laughed and hugged and kissed and cradled her head, caressed her face with her hands, this precious woman she'd longed to hold for *so* long; her hand knocked CeCe's firefighting helmet to the lobby floor, and CeCe held her while they spun in circles. Becca couldn't breathe in the tangle of her hair, but she didn't care.

As it stood now, dying like this wouldn't be so bad.

"I tried calling the house, but you weren't there!"

CeCe scoffed. "I told you that I was workin' today!" Becca was *totally* checking her out as she bent over to retrieve her helmet. She was in full firefighting ensemble, complete with the—*really, really fucking cool*—firefighter's helmet. Becca swooned, forgetting all about Alset; all about the burning tower.

"Why are you here, dummy? Don't you know—?"

"Listen, CeCe, I need to tell you something... remember everything I was telling you about at dinner? About Y2K and the 'Manhattan Mauler'?"

Cecilia nodded.

"I know who he is... and he's *here.*"

The fiery passion in her girlfriend's eyes morphed to frigid terror as they widened. "Are you *kidding?*"

Becca shook her head. "And he's killed three more people, all from our group."

"What do you mean, *killed?*"

"I mean, he took something really sharp and cut their throats. He *murdered* them."

CeCe *gasped.* Her eyes were filled with empathy... as well as rage.

"I know you're gonna be careful, but I need you to watch out for this guy..." Becca shared everything she knew about Alset with CeCe. As she finished her tale, a colleague of CeCe's overheard their conversation.

"Great, we're already dealing with all of *this*—and now we have to mess with a psycho killer, *too?*"

As she adjusted her helmet to fit back on her head, Cecilia's voice boomed with authority. "Where is this jackass? I *dare* him to try that shit with me, I'll bury this axe in his fuckin'—"

"I think he's following me. I'm kinda *hoping* he'll attack me again." Her finger flicked towards her holster, and a smug grin crossed her lips.

"Wait... attack *again?* What do you—?"

"It's a long story, Babe. For now, can we kiss one more time?"

Their lips melted together in a passionate lock. The intense environment around them melted away, replaced by a yearning to be together. When they finally came up for air, Cecilia held her girlfriend closely, which was fine with Becca—she didn't want to move, anyway.

"I don't like this, Babe."

"Neither do I," Becca said softly, staring longingly at CeCe. "But it's my job, right?"

"No," she shook her head. "Well, I mean, it *is* your job, that's not what I meant—I mean, I don't want you to stay in this *tower*. They're saying this is bad, ya know; both of these buildings might be compromised."

Her smile snapped in reverse. "In that case, you need to come with me, then."

CeCe's head subtly shook, and her eyes shut. "I *can't*. We're going up."

"What?" The upper floors held nothing except death and destruction, fire and smoke—*besides, Alset was still up there!*

"No!" Becca cried, pleading with her eyes. "Please, you—"

"Have a job to do... just like you, Babe."

CeCe gently pressed another wet, dramatic kiss on Becca's lips, right in front of a dozen firefighters. Unable to resist CeCe's enchanting magic, she gave in to her demands. She longed to ask Cecilia to join them and come down, but she understood deep down that it wasn't going to happen.

I mean, if the shoe were on the other foot...

"I can't stop you," Becca stated, tears streaking down her cheeks. "But I *can* love you."

"I can, I do, and I *will* love you, too."

She kissed her once more and pulled back to return to her party. "Please be safe?"

"Remember—clear your story, write your story, and then breathe... am I right?"

She snorted a short laugh. *Close enough...*

Becca turned to walk towards her party, and her girlfriend followed behind, curious about her group. When CeCe saw Julie limping back towards the wheelchair, she pointed at the injured woman. "Hey, lady! What happened to your ankle?"

Julie let out a scoff. "I broke a heel. *Worst* part of my day, lemme tell you..."

CeCe guffawed at her comeback. "Lady, if that's the worst part, you're doin' a whole lot better than some folks—"

This earned a rare guffaw from Julie. "No... the truth is, I was coming down the stairs back around, oh... fifty-five or so, and I sprained my ankle."

"Let me tape you up and give you some of the good stuff. You'll be good as *new*, and then we'll get you guys out of here—"

"Thank you," Julie replied sweetly, gingerly lying down and extending her swollen foot. She glanced back up at Becca, reaching into her purse as she did so. "I can get myself down from here with their assistance... so perhaps it's time to part ways?" She pulled out a handful of business cards, handing one of them to Becca:

Julian Mercado
International Sales Manager

C: (332) 555-0991
B: (332) 555-6612
F: (212) 555-1207

One World Trade Center
72nd Floor | Executive Offices
Manhattan, NY 11048

Arakawa Motor Company

"Julie," Becca began, shoving the card into her pocket, "please get out of here as soon as you—"

"I *intend* to, Mrs. Taylor." Her heavy makeup couldn't hide the crow's feet in the corners of her eyes, which had narrowed to pencil points. A *stranger* might assume she was annoyed, but they'd been together long enough that Becca could see the truth in those eyes. She leaned in for another hug, and *this* time, Julie happily returned it.

"Can we stay here with Julie?" Jason's high-pitched voice interrupted their embrace. As CeCe's glare shifted in his direction, his eyes flicked away, intimidated by her scowl.

"You... want to stay here, Jason?" Becca's brow furrowed. "You guys need to get out of here—"

"Um," Jason stammered, "I know we *should* evacuate, but we've been helping her get down this whole time; I think it'd be best to stay with Julie."

CeCe was replacing her helmet on her head, squeezing it past her tousled brunette locks. "All of you are welcome to stay here with her until she's ready to go. We'll make sure you get out— easy-peasy."

Becca *sighed*. As much as she felt responsible for her group, having to worry about them was stressing her out even more than Alset was. "I... think everyone should stay here and go with the firefighters. You'll be safer without Alset trying to mess with us."

Her companions' faces drooped with her statement... because they knew she was right. Holding up a business card, Mike approached them and handed it to Becca. "Call me after all this shit is over with. We can check in on each other, make sure everyone is safe."

She took the card, giving her one of her own from her wallet. Before shoving it into her slacks, she glanced at the card:

Jason H. Palmer

Senior Consultant
Toei Bank, LLC
(917) 555-2107

1 World Trade Center
New York, NY 11048

"I saw you grab one of mine, already," he winked. "When you get out of here, let's grab a beer or something." His smile was infectious as Becca latched onto Mike, barely able to fit her arms around the massive man.

"Thank you, Mike." Becca hated crying more than *anything*, so she bit her bottom lip.

"If you find that tall bastard, get him for me," he whispered in her ear.

"Well, *I* have decided I will stay with you, Rebecca. I trust you with my life." Q walked beside Becca and placed his hand on her shoulder. "We are in this *together.*"

"Are you sure?" CeCe's jaw clenched. "You're free to leave, of course, but you'll be safe with us."

"No way. Where she goes, *I* go." His smile shot through her like an X-ray. "We are *partners!*"

Thank you, Q. I wasn't that afraid to go alone... but having you with me helps.

Julie was openly weeping now as she lay on the carpet of the lobby, CeCe already working on her ankle. "Agent Taylor, you're a saint. I hope your boss doesn't fire you, but if he does, please call me?"

Becca's laughter shook her belly. "I don't think it'll come to that, Julie, but I'll keep it in mind."

"Thank you, Becca. And good luck."

"You're welcome, but..." she trailed off, her eyes bouncing off each of the people in the conversation... and finally, back to CeCe. "Can't I remain with everyone? We can all go down together, and —"

"No. *You* are going down, Rebecca Taylor!"

Becca could feel herself growing red. No longer concerned about Alset, or Marissa... or even *escaping*, she could only focus on Cecilia.

"Now hold on, that's not fair! I want to help people out here, too; I want—"

"I don't *care* what you want, Rebecca Taylor! You have a *job* to do, agent." CeCe's tone was one that Becca had never heard before. "And so do I."

"I—" Becca bit her lip, ending her rebuttal. *She's not wrong, but after all we've been through... I'm supposed to go down alone? How am I supposed to concentrate on anything else with her up here? If I lose her, I lose everything...*

CeCe's face went stern. "We have a son at home, too. Don't forget that, Babe. He needs his momma, more than I could *ever* need you... and you need him *too*, ya know?"

Her face went pale with the realization that her son hadn't crossed her mind in quite some time. It wasn't her fault; she'd been focused on finding the tall man, and on surviving in the *first* place. But in that moment, the horror of the worst-case scenario was dawning on her.

If neither of them made it out, *who* would raise her son?

But Cecilia was also right about another thing: Rebecca still had a job to do. It was a revelation of the obvious; it was nothing she didn't already know, but it had become a secondary thought to Becca's own desire to preserve her world, her life... her love.

But then... who will preserve Marissa's world? If I die here, today, Marissa dies with me... and I'm the only one that can stop that.

Becca rushed over to her girlfriend—no, her *hero*—and wrapped her arms tightly around her. And she held her. She didn't speak... she simply held her. To Becca, the moment passed far too quickly before CeCe broke the embrace. Her lips brushed past Becca's ears as she pulled away, her whisper an intoxicating spell.

"You're the *baddest* bitch I've ever met, Baby. I love you."

'Swooning' wasn't the right word for it; she was ice cream on a warm summer's evening in Cecilia's arms. Her whisper was almost involuntary. "I love you, too, Babe."

CeCe held onto her firmly. "And if you see this dude again, you know what to do. *End* this shit."

Finally, they broke the embrace, about to part ways, before CeCe stopped in her tracks.

"*Oh*, Becca! When you leave, don't go out on street level. Go through the mall."

"Really? Why is that?"

"Just trust me."

If CeCe was Becca's rose, she was wilting before her very eyes —as if she'd aged twenty years in twenty seconds. She wondered what she must've witnessed to warrant *that* reaction.

I've never seen her like this before; it kinda breaks my heart a little bit.

"I love you so much, Cecilia. Please call me when you're safe and sound."

"I love you *too,* and you do the same!"

$*$ $*$ $*$

The only two remaining survivors in Becca's group—once eight strong—walked side-by-side as they reentered the dank familiarity of Stairwell C, beginning their descent once more... though much calmer on this occasion. Not like an hour ago, when they'd fled from the chaos of the ninety-first floor. Becca shuddered thinking about it.

"You did a great job today, Boss." Q flashed his charismatic smile at Becca, forcing a simpered smirk in response.

"We aren't out of the woods yet, Q," she warned. "We need to watch out for each other, in case Alset is still watching us."

"Like I said, Rebecca—we are partners!" his voice rose an octave, and he clapped his hands loudly in the stairwell with an echo. "Just the two of us, Agent! *We can make it if we try!"*

He's so sweet, cheering me up like this.

Only an hour earlier, she had been chasing him through the tower, determined to catch him. Now, she was counting on him to help her escape the very same building. It was almost poetic how their relationship had changed since that first plane hit the tower. They had already rescued each other multiple times, forming a bond of trust that would have seemed unbelievable just an hour ago.

And when we get out of here, I have myself a new friend. That's priceless nowadays.

The good vibes only carried them so far, however, before a

meek-sounding *scream* stopped them dead in their tracks. The pair of them became statues in the stairwell, listening carefully... unsure if they were hearing things... until they heard the *shriek* once more.

"It came from *there?*" Q suggested. "Could it be Moira?"

"Doubtful," she sneered. Becca thought she'd imagined the sound, but when they glanced at each other, it was clear they'd *both* noticed it:

The door to the 19th floor was propped open with a rubber door stopper that looked *exactly* like the one on the 91st Floor... and a lot of smoke was sneaking through. Becca peered through the doorway and saw that the elevator lobby was burning... except these fires were suspicious. They were pitiful, tiny flames that were bound to extinguish themselves before too long, burning weakly in the center of the lobby.

"Strange," Becca noted, walking into the lobby. "None of the elevators here were on fire..."

Q stepped out after her. "You think this might be Alset again, trying to trick us?"

Absolutely. Becca could smell a rat.

"I'm not sure," she lied, opening the door to another Port Authority office. The office was silently lit by soft fluorescent lights from above, almost welcoming in its pristine state.

"But if it *is* Alset, I've gotta check it." Quarren nodded as Becca began to walk over to the open doorway.

"I'm gonna take a look, Q. You coming?"

They stepped through the door. As she did so, she glanced at her watch.

It was 9:58.

XVIII

"A Pervert's Game of Marco Polo"

A curtain of smoke promised carnage as Becca and Quarren stepped through the door, but that was betrayed when she found their source—two *pitiful* fires smoldered in the lobby. Her eyes flicked towards the elevators, expecting them to resemble the ones high above them... except these ones looked absolutely *normal*. In fact, the entire *floor* was pristine... aside from those fires.

It was enough to convince Becca—if Alset was trying to lure her into a confrontation, it was *working*. And, if that *was* his intent, she was *happy* to oblige.

The 19th floor felt unusually dark and foreboding. Compared to the last few floors they'd rested on, which had felt almost like a *sanctuary* to their group... Becca couldn't shake the sensation that something sinister was set to occur.

Something was not right here. Something was *evil*.

Becca was now on the east side of the building. The sun should've brilliantly illuminated the entire floor, but its rays were blocked by something *unnatural*. Thick, billowing smoke oozed from the gaping hole in the South Tower, high above their heads now, which the sun (now approaching its midday perch) failed to pierce through.

The artificial canopy acted as a filter, diffusing the sunlight into an almond-hued glow that painted the entire floor in a surreal, unholy palette. The shadowy smoke and supernatural shade unsettled Becca as she entered this alien world.

After a few quiet, tense steps, Becca drew her breath and her pistol as she entered the open office space. The only sounds came from Quarren's panicked gasps, who was right on her heels with his weapon held tightly. His wooden dowel was his *only* defense against what might lie ahead.

The tension was thicker than motor oil in an icebox, and there was no sound in the office.

Silent... and yet, *serene*. Deceptively peaceful.

Well, peaceful... if you don't account for the screaming they had heard earlier, which had since stopped. There was no sign of *anyone* on this floor—Alset included.

I won't fall for your tricks again, Alset. I'm not going into any room unless Q is watching the door.

As they crept along, she gripped her gun tightly. The clicking of the safety and the soft flow of her breathing were the *only* sounds pervading this sterile setting. At the end of the hallway was an open doorway leading to the south face of the tower.

She tiptoed into the office's open-style arrangement, similar to the 54th Floor. This time, however, Becca stopped after taking a single step inside. She glanced back at her friend, her eyebrows furrowed.

"Q, stay and watch the door, I'm gonna take a look."

"I will 'wistle' if I see him?" he asked, a contagious smile crossing his face... but Becca didn't catch it this time.

"Yes... but, Q," she turned back and put both hands on his shoulders, melting his smile away. Her gun was still in her hand, and Q was staring at it, as if it were a venomous snake about to *strike* him.

"If you see Alset... if he comes after you, I need you to defend yourself."

"You want me to... *fight?*" Q's face turned pale. "I—"

"I know, bud." She gave him a half-hug, squeezing his arms reassuringly. "Just stay close to me, okay?"

With a subtle nod in reply, Quarren gripped his dowel tightly as Becca entered the office. She held her pistol close to her chest as she peeked around cubicles, listening for *any* sign of life in the office. It wouldn't take long for her to find something if someone was actually in trouble, but as she pushed through the office with no sign of anyone... she felt like a *sucker*.

If it smells like a rat, it likely is one. This has got to be a trap.

One of the massive windows on the south face was broken out, and the breeze carried the sounds of the world below in. As she crept through the space, she looked over her left shoulder at Q, who watched with every ounce of attention he had.

I can't take this anymore! I'm so tired of tiptoeing around while this coward watches me.

"Come out and *face* me, you *pussy*... or ain't you got the guts to..."

She stopped. Something unexpected terrified her to the *core*.

That sound... I recognize that sound... No, not a sound. A *sensation*.

She recalled a documentary she had once watched with her father about decrepit hotel buildings that were once part of the Las Vegas skyline. Places like the Dunes, the Sands, or the Aladdin —classic hotels that had to be imploded to make way for newer mega-resorts. *The classic cycle of capitalism.* To clear that land for the new buildings, they implode the older structure, causing it to collapse *inward*. She'd watched the documentary of the implosion with both childlike fascination... and childlike *horror*.

And the sound... they made a whomp-whomp noise, like a—

She *felt* the sound before Becca actually *heard* it, but the combination drove her thoughts away once she did. The sound itself was a facsimile of a freight train... if one were on a downhill-sloping track, picking up speed as it rolled along faster and *faster*. And, as it picked up speed, it hit a brick wall.

And then another—

Then *another*—

All in rapid succession, growing terrifyingly *intense* as the air pressure increased, but she wasn't sure *what* was causing it.

Yet.

A thundering roar grew louder... and louder...

Whomp-whomp-whomp-WHOMP-WHOMP!

A sinister snowslide began barreling down upon them, an unstoppable avalanche God Himself was *powerless* to stop, and Becca screamed... yet she *never* heard it.

This can't be! Is this really happening?

"Rebecca!" Q shouted from the doorway, holding his dowel with a death grip. *"What is that?"*

She couldn't answer; she was *hypnotized* by it. Her jaw agape, she shuffled her feet towards the south windows, closer to the South Tower. She had to see for herself what on Earth could make that awful noise.

As she approached, large chunks of metal and concrete plummeted from the spaces above her, falling with terrifying speed past her window. It wasn't until she saw—with *vicious* velocity—a piece of the building's steel framing fall a few *feet* ahead of where she was standing, that it dawned on her *what* she was experiencing.

Is that from our building? I can't look away, even though one of these falling columns is probably meant for me.

The 19th Floor began to vibrate, harder and faster, until it became a rumble... then a shaking.

And then an *earthquake*.

And then an eye-rattling throttling that Becca fought against with *every* ounce of strength she had left, her knees threatening to buckle beneath her, though she wasn't sure if it was from the trembling or terror as she gripped onto a cubicle wall attempting to stay upright and stared, mouth agape, as the monstrous cloud of debris grew larger, thickening, darkening in color, deepening in volume, devouring everything in its path, crashing *upwards* around her, it must be the end of the world.

We took too long. I ran out of time. I'm sorry, Marissa...

A tidal wave of debris and dust, a pyroclastic cloud of death, rose from the earth and charged upwards, crashing upon the 19th Floor like a modern Pompeii. The world was a thundering waterfall, but this wasn't water—it was the *roar* of pulverized concrete; of twisting, screeching steel. Of a *billion* shards of glass raining a torrent of jagged death. Or freight train after freight train, *thundering* along on downhill-sloping tracks...

Yet, it was climbing upward.

And, as they picked up speed, each one smashing through millions of brick walls one, after another... and another... and yet *another,* all in rapid succession. The air pressure in the room seemed to get sucked out; she thought her skull might *explode.*

WHOMP-WHOMP-WHOMP—

She unsuccessfully attempted to scream when the windows surrounding Becca blew inwards into the tower in a shower of glass. But she couldn't... because the air had already been sucked from her lungs. Becca was flung backwards from the cubicle by a *tremendous* rebound of air pressure.

She landed on her butt, whiplashing *violently,* almost smacking her head on the corner of the cubicle, as she rolled backwards, tumbling along the floor. Her pistol went flying out of her hand, landing somewhere far behind her.

The air was lethal, filled with the poisonous dust of destruction that consumed her. She tried to open her eyes, but they were glued shut by it. Instead, she rolled into a fetal position, helpless, as the darkness blotted out the last bits of light in the world.

I smell metal, again.

The rumbling intensified. She could hear a second sound growing louder as the chaos continued: the squealing *scream* of twisting steel. It was unlike anything Becca had ever heard, the sound of Death himself rapping at a steel door with a *chainsaw*.

She remained on the ground, tucking herself behind the cubicle wall, waiting for a piece of steel to crash unceremoniously through the wall, waiting for the rest of the smoke and debris to choke her out, to extinguish her life force and put an end to their suffering.

Her eyes were seared tightly shut. She curled into a ball. And she screamed.

And Becca waited to die.

After a miserable fifteen seconds (which felt like *hours),* the shaking eased to a low rumble. Then a vibration. Finally, after an eternity of dread... the air fell silent, save for the constant *tinkle* of raindrops falling...

Except this was worse than even acid rain. A steady shower of concrete and metal debris, of pieces of glass and steel smacking against the side of her building. While the fury was winding down, the air whirled around her, as if the entire event was a category-five hurricane, and *this* was the eye of the storm. All was dark, all was silent... save for the screaming and sirens which now echoed from the streets below.

Becca's world was dark. No... this was pitch black. This was *beyond* that. She wasn't sure how long she'd waited before opening her eyes, because time moves differently in this darkness.

A minute? An hour? *If I'm dead, does time even matter?*

This time, she *was* dead; she was *certain* of it. Afraid to find out, she resigned herself to remaining still in this foreign world, this alternate dimension she found herself trapped in, for a lifetime or twenty... before finally determining that she *was* alive, and she should probably stand up and end this melodramatic posturing.

Daring to move was only half the battle—she found herself halfway buried in a pile of dust. Her entire body was caked from head to toe. She dug herself out, brushing herself off the best she could. Her eyelids might as well be made of *sandpaper,* and every blink was excruciating. She still couldn't see much; the room was a maroon hue of darkness, barely filtering enough light through to convince Becca that she was indeed still alive, and *not* dead…

Yet.

Tepidly, Becca rose to her feet, uncertain if she was still in the office (or even on the same *floor*). The air was sinister and dark, and everything disappeared a few inches in front of her. She tried using her tattered tie to breathe through, like a mask, but it was so saturated with dust that it only worsened things.

She noticed the fluorescent lights overhead weren't on anymore; *the power must be out—*

BEEP BEEP BEEP! BEEP BEEP BEEP!

Becca *yelped,* startled. She brushed off the top of her Pulsar, its alarm shattering the deafening silence. A frown etched into her dust-caked cheeks as she inspected her late husband's watch, pressing the little nubbin to silence it. *I can't believe it still works; it's scratched to shit.* The time was now 10:00.

Immediately after she silenced her watch, another sound announced its presence to Becca. She held still, listening through the silence. To Becca, this wasn't the same tower she'd been in for two hours, no… the experience she'd just survived brought her to the tipping point of sanity. *Was that a monster?* She was still in *danger!*

She heard the sound a second time, snapping her out of it. It resembled a man groaning, and it sounded like he was in pain.

"*Q?*" she coughed, struggling to speak with any volume. "Where are you?"

"Boss!"

The meager scream came from where Quarren was guarding the door. His voice sounded weak, and she rushed through the murky air, feeling with her hands for any point of reference.

"Where are you, Q?" The air was still so thick with dust that she couldn't keep her eyes open. "This is like playing a pervert's game of Marco Polo..." Something about this gave Becca the creeps. She couldn't quite place it, but she felt as if someone was in the room with her... *watching* her.

When she found the wall, she followed it to the hallway, making her way to the T-intersection where she found Quarren on the floor, lying in a pool of his own blood.

"Q! What happened?"

Quarren was lying inside the doorway, holding his chest with both hands. Rushing over, Becca gently moved them away from his chest to reveal a rapidly spreading crimson stain across his filthy shirt. She *gasped* upon seeing the size of his wound, extending diagonally across his abdomen.

It looks exactly like the wound that Jim suffered on January 1st!

"Boss... I'm sorry," he whispered, coughing weakly. "I... tried... to 'wistle'..."

"What happened?" The terror was threatening to take over. She wiped the tears from her friend's face in a panicked swipe. "Was it the explosion just now?"

"No... it was..."

Q muttered weakly, his face a twisted expression that Becca could barely make out in the darkness. Gasping for air, he pointed a finger in Becca's direction.

"It was me?" she asked, trying to follow his pointing finger in the darkness.

Q shook his finger weakly. "No."

He pointed behind her shoulder, and she turned slowly.

"It was me."

"*Wha*—?"

*   *   *

The blow hit Becca's face with *furious* force, just above her left temple with a sickening *thud*. The object was tough and dense, and she lost her balance, staggering over Q's body and through the open doorway, tumbling back into the office she'd just came from. It hurt like hell, and her vision was starry and black when she opened her eyes.

Rising to her feet as quickly as she could muster, she took a few wobbly steps back towards the elevator lobby, reaching for her pistol in its holster, but her hand grasped nothing but leather.

That's odd...

She was having trouble finding it in the dusty air, she was surprised she couldn't *feel* it—

The second blow hit her in the base of her neck, above her left shoulder blade.

Becca *yelped* in pain as she collapsed into a heap in the middle of the hallway, landing with a thud on the carpet. She began to crawl weakly towards the elevators. Her vision was blurry, and she swiped at her forehead, which was now streaked with her blood.

She was losing her grip on reality in spurts, and her neck now hurt with a sharp, stabbing pain that radiated through her spine when she turned her head.

"You are persistent, Agent Taylor. I like that in a woman."

She squinted through the fog and saw the blurred double-vision silhouette of a tall man. He was a bit taller than *Q* was, with a long, cylindrical shape in his right hand, and a bloody machete... or something resembling one in his other. She was revolted upon seeing his shirt, which was covered in blood—she guessed it was the Costas' blood.

And his eyes... his sunglasses were long-since discarded. His bottle-green eyes were bloodshot, wide—and filled with a carnal need to *kill*.

Alset shuffled towards her. Becca crawled backwards towards the west, desperate to escape this terrifying man. He dropped the bloody blade as he walked towards her, patting his free hand with the *other* weapon—a long oak dowel.

Q's weapon!

"All that destruction was a nice bonus," Alset said, encroaching closer. "I had *no* idea that was going to happen. I was going to push you out a *window.*" He took a step towards her, raising his brow.

"Perhaps I still will. But I want to take my *time* with you."

As he spoke, a random thought popped into Becca's mind. *His accent's gone... I knew it was fake.*

He licked his lips at her, and she shivered involuntarily as he shrieked, an animalistic sound which reminded her of a hyena. And, as she tried to push back further into the west hallway, Alset's laugh became a terrible screeching yell, a shrill of insanity that she recognized *instantly.*

It's the same sound from January 1st!

Horrified to the bone, Becca peed her pants.

The sudden shock caused every emotion in her to rise at once. She was running in the snow again, Jim bleeding out *exactly as Q was now*, as she approached the guesthouse with the two darkened windows that resembled a skull.

A symbolic building then; a grisly reminder, now.

It's the same sound it's the same sound it's the same sound—

"Why are you—?"

"Why am I *doing* this? It's simple, really. I screwed up."

Becca's face twisted into a confused scowl. *"What?"*

"I saw the cops this morning. I knew I was being followed. You think I *wanted* to run like this?"

He tapped the dowel in his hands as he spoke, threatening Becca with every smack of his stick. "I didn't count on *you* two getting involved with us again. I was gonna leave town with my new family, but you *just* couldn't leave it alone. So yeah, I'm just tidying up my... loose ends."

"You screwed up?"

She was incredulous. She wanted to rush at him, to claw the eyes out of his skull, but the pain in her neck was so biting, and every movement made her dizzy and nervous—

But she'd been chasing this man for *years!* This was no time to hold back; even *if* she was injured, he was right here—*I've been dreaming about this moment forever, and now it's here—*

"March 30, 1999. Kayla Spilka. Remember her?" Becca's vision was *finally* clarifying. *"That* was the moment you screwed up—when you started taking kids from *my* city!" Confidence poured back into her. Not wanting to give her strength away, she crawled closer towards the wall as she talked.

I need to buy some time until I can defend myself.

"Or would you like more reminders? Does Zach Kenner ring a bell?" She gritted her teeth painfully. "How 'bout Jeremey Young?"

"Shut up!" Alset stopped moving, pointing the dowel at her. "It's all *your* fault, Rebecca Taylor! You and your shithead partner, you *ruined* a good thing."

He took another step. Alset's shoes, now scuffed and filthy, reminded her of this morning when she was spying from underneath the lobster truck. They were as conspicuous to Becca as his golden tooth, which glinted in the dark with each spoken word.

"We just wanted a family, is that too much to ask?"

She was nauseous. Becca desperately wanted her gun in her hands right now. She had her flashlight, but against his dowel, it was as useless as fighting at Gettysburg with a pop gun.

How did I lose it? I must've dropped it when the debris started falling from the other tower.

"What do you know about family? You mean kidnapping and raping children?" She inhaled enough dust that she coughed, still trying to increase the space between them. "What about that constitutes a healthy family lifestyle, you demented prick?"

"You're wrong. I never raped them, *I never raped them!*"

Alset smacked the dowel against the marble that lined the lobby with a *thwack!*

"You don't understand, because you're just like the others. You're nothing but a clown, Rebecca Taylor; *just* like the others. I love the children, *love* them. I wouldn't *rape* them, no-no-no, they all loved me, it wasn't *rape!*"

The tone of Alset's voice rose and fell in both pitch and volume as he spoke. "I want a family, yes. *Love*, not rape. Don't I? *I do!* I didn't want to hurt them, but you... *you...*"

This was the most terrifying thing Rebecca ever experienced.

"I... what?"

Alset growled. *"You murdered my Shahla."*

Jim's words from the past shook Becca to her core. *"She fucking stabbed me, whaddya want me to do?"*

"So then, why kill the others?"

"Hah! You mean that French bitch?" He wiped his mouth with the bloody dowel. "Oh, that was just *perfect.* She was the last one in the lobby. All I had to do was call her over."

"What did you *do?*"

"What did I doooo? Oh, what did he *doooo,* oh *noooo...*" Mocking Becca, he giggled a sinister, rapid laugh. "You don't

expect me to kiss and *tell*, do you? Don't worry—it probably hurt a *lot.*"

Becca growled back at Alset with anger. "You're *sick,* man."

"Aren't you gonna ask about ol' Jersey Shore and her little 'Muffincakes'?" He mimed a little curtsy as his voice changed, from a terrible New Jersey accent to a *screeching* whine. It reminded Becca of Judge Doom from *Who Framed Roger Rabbit.*

Cackling, he whacked himself in the groin with the dowel, causing Alset to *wheeze* a bit. Becca considered rushing at him, and Alset noticed her body tense up. He grinned at her like an evil Cheshire Cat.

"Why'd you kill Donny and Janet, Alset?" Becca spat a little blood to the side. "They *weren't* gonna hurt you."

"It was so easy, Rebecca Taylor. I simply *called* to them. Don went first; he was dead before Janet even realized. She was tougher; she put up as much of a fight as little Jeremey did."

"Oh, you cruel *bastard...* " she growled.

"Oh, *you're* one to talk, *ain't* cha?" He stopped inching forward, and a fire lit in his eyes that made her nervous. "You took an innocent woman, she just wanted to be a mother and live happily with us, and you took her from us. You hurt *me,* Rebecca Taylor. So I had to hurt *you* back, even though it hurt me *more...* I *had* to take our son away from us."

Alset started crying as he took the dowel and smacked himself in the face with it a few times, actually rocking himself with his final blow.

"You can't play *God* like this, Alset!"

"Sure I can!" He flinched a charge at Becca, causing her body to tense again. "See? *I* have all the power here, silly clown."

He began to laugh again. "I took him away because..."

Alset dragged himself closer, hitting himself in the forehead with each step. His forehead was bleeding as badly as Becca's was, now; he closed the gap between the two of them with terrifying speed, and she prepared to make her move.

"Because..."

Shuffle-Shuffle. "Because..."

Shuffle-Shuffle. "Because..."

His voice reached a terrifying volume as he growled at her.

"Because-because-because-because—

"Because you murdered my Shahla!"

Alset swung the dowel down in a wide arc at Becca, and her instincts kicked in. Exactly how she'd done in the gym hundreds of times, she rolled to the side, easily dodging the blow. She scrambled back to her feet as she ran through the lobby, finally stumbling back to the floor after a few steps.

That was very telegraphed. He might be terrifying, but the dude can't fight.

She spat to the side. "Innocent my ass; you murdered *kids!*"

"No!" He whacked the dowel against a fire extinguisher box, the glass shattering all over the dusty hallway.

"It wasn't murder. They were *mercy killings*. We'd get to know them, to *love* them. But then I would hate them. When they told me they wanted to go home. But they can't go home. How could they say such a *hateful* thing when they were already home? *Our* home."

He smiled down at her. *Is he... drooling?*

"You're such a clown, Rebecca Taylor." Alset's smile twisted into a grotesque *scowl*. "I hate clowns." He growled like an animal. The tone of his voice was downright demonic.

"I cannot fucking abide by them!"

With incredible speed, he sprinted towards Becca, who ducked under the dowel as he threw it at her in another wide, hooking arc. She threw a sideways chop at his neck as she dodged, maneuvering behind him *exactly* as she'd practiced in the gym dozens of times.

As she moved, her head grew dizzy, forcing her to stumble. By the time she was behind him, she'd nearly *fainted*. She fell to the dusty carpet, crawling away as he began approaching once again—the blow to his neck had barely affected him.

Like some macabre zombie who only killed for sport, Alset slowly shuffled towards her, holding the dowel high above his head as he prepared to slam it onto Becca's skull. In a panic, Becca scampered backwards on her bottom, desperate to stay conscious.

"You're insane, Alset."

"I could've killed you on 106 when you started going downstairs," Alset bragged. "I've been following you since you found our group on seventy-six. I was minding my *own* business after the plane hit. I wanted to go home to my family, but even then, *you* had to show up and ruin everything."

His face transformed instantly as his voice dropped to a softer tone. *"They wewe so vewwy nice ta wittow ol' me.* Why did you have to make me *do* that to them, huh?"

His breath squeezed between seething teeth. The dust was settling, and the sunlight from the south created a diffusion effect. A white glow seemed to highlight the floor. His Cheshire Cat smile made her feel like screaming, glints of light flashing off his golden tooth through the foggy scene.

Attempting to sit up, Becca swallowed a lump of terror. "You're fuckin' crazy, man..."

"You have *no* idea." Alset smirked a simpered smirk. He stepped forward, his feet now straddling her right leg. "I have to teach you a lesson. *You* made me suffer first."

He took another step, smacking the dowel as he stalked her.

"Now, it's your turn. And once I get out of here, I think I'll get rid of your little sidekick Serrano too, so we can finally live in peace."

How does he know our names? How did he—

"Oh, I know *all* about you clowns, Agent Taylor." His clairvoyance added another layer of fear to Becca's anxiety. "You should thank me. I *was* planning on coming after you two before little Isabel showed up."

Her expression gave her thoughts away. "Heh. It was easy enough. Did you *know* that you can see all the active FBI agents online? I *never* forget a face, Rebecca Taylor... and your profile picture is *very* professional... yes..." He licked his teeth at her.

Becca leered back with a *growl*. "You really are an *Ay-hole.*"

"No! No! *No!*"

He whacked the marble with every word—*thunk, thunk; THUNK!* Alset's smile twisted into a horrid scowl, and his response was violent as he grew enraged.

"You got it all wrong. It's *Ah-hole-eh,* you *bitch!*"

He took a final step forward, straddling Becca's right leg.

She laughed confidently. "No, I meant Ay-hole. As in *asshole.*"

She brought her right foot up with every ounce of strength she had left, and her steel-toed boot connected squarely with Alset's scrotum. He dropped the dowel with a howl, doubling over in pain, his hands holding his tender groin as Becca scrambled back to her feet and ran.

Sprinting west and north, down the hallway, Becca ran until she reached a locked office door. Without hesitating, she kicked as hard as possible, sending the door flying with a *smack*.

This part of nineteen was completely isolated from the storm of dust that had pervaded the other side of the floor. It was now an alien world, a juxtaposition of darkened yet pristine office space —like finding an abandoned base on the surface of Mars.

Oh sure... especially now, with the power out.

"You'll never be safe, you hear me? *I'll hunt you to the ends of the Earth!"* His high-pitched scream sent shivers down her spine.

As she sprinted around the corner, her dirty boots slipped on the slick carpet, and she tumbled onto the floor, scraping the skin off her forearms. Unfazed by the carpet burn, she scrambled on her hands and knees, crawling towards the northeast side of the floor. Her vision blurred with blood as she tried to make her way to the door, which would allow her to reach the elevator lobby.

I need to find my gun... but I can't stay on my feet. I need to hide.

Despite being in the best shape of her life, Special Agent Rebecca Taylor was still human, and the *numerous* injuries she'd suffered today—not to mention *fatigue*—were starting to take their toll on her. The world wobbled in her view as she stumbled into a cubicle, collapsing once again. Her vision blurred as she lay on her back, staring up at the dormant fluorescent lights while she gasped for air.

But at least, she was *safe*... for the moment—

"Mar-cooo?"

Becca *gasped*.

*   *   *

The voice was so sudden, Becca wasn't sure she hadn't imagined it... or, perhaps, it was Quarren? She tried standing once more before giving up, crumbling to her hands and knees as she strained to catch her breath. Unable to slow her pounding heart's pace, she focused on her breathing instead. Despite her vision growing almost entirely black, she blindly searched the desktop with her hands, gasping for breath while looking for a makeshift weapon— *anything* she might use to defend—

"Mar-coooo..."

Absolutely not her imagination. *And definitely not Q.*

Reality hit her in the gut. Becca froze, horrified.

Choking on her breath, she peeked over the cubicle wall.

Only a silhouette stood silently in the doorway's darkened, dusty air. She lowered her head as soon as he began to turn towards her.

"Marco..."

And I'm not supposed to piss my pants at this?

Raising his tone, Alset's call was sing-songy.

Childlike, even. Like a horror movie villain.

Over the pounding of her heart, she heard a *smack... smack...* Alset slapped the dowel against his open palm.

"Maaaar... coooooo...."

A drawn-out call, almost hauntingly floaty.

Becca's vision was blurry, but she refused to move, terrified she'd give herself away. The dowel dragged over desktops and along cubicle walls, growing closer to Becca's hiding place. The sound got louder as he dug the dowel deeper and deeper into each surface it scraped along.

Clunk. Clunk. Brrrrrack.

"Marco!" This time, he screamed it.

If anyone can outsmart this Ay-hole, it's you, girl. This guy ruined your career; destroyed your life. You can't let him win; he's right there!

She knew she couldn't beat him in her condition... but what *if...*

There's gotta be something! Her hands fumbled around a fake potted plant and a filing cabinet, hoping for something she could fight with: an umbrella, a ruler... *anything*.

Clunk. Clunk. Brrrrrack. Clunk. Clunk. Brrrrrack. Growing closer... and *louder*. This time, his call was a growl—guttural and *evil*.

"...Marrr-co."

Clear your mind... write your story...

Becca shook the cobwebs off as best she could, as she fumbled around in the desk drawers, the contents knocking around, giving Alset audible clues as to where she was hiding, so she committed to it, silently whispering *"Fuck it..."*, she was now on her hands and knees, digging deep in the drawer of the desk in a desperate plunge, knowing Alset could hear her every move but she was committed to the play, hoping to find something, *anything*, and her hand brushed something promising in the pencil tray in the top drawer of the desk, so she closed her fingers on it, gripping it like a drowning man would grip a lifesaver as Alset's grinning face appeared in the cubicle entry, standing ominously above her— *never* has a smile driven her to *dread* as easily as Alset's, standing over his prey like a lioness on a hunt, the bastardly beast triumphantly raising the dowel high into the air with his right hand, his golden gnasher glistening as he grinned, Alset's bloodshot eyes were now entirely focused on Becca's, and if she didn't act now, she was as good as *dead*—

"Marco, clown."

She stared back into his own eyes, a cocky smile crossing her expression. She saw the surprise in his own. *And breathe*—

"Polo, bitch."

Her eyes focused on her target as her mind cleared. Becca drove the letter opener with *every* ounce of strength she had left, forcing it with her body weight using both hands, into the bottom of his left thigh, downwards behind his kneecap.

Alset howled in agony, dropping the dowel and collapsing backwards against the cubicle wall, trying to pull it out of his leg but unable to even *touch* it. She rolled to the side and crawled to her feet, dashing into the east-side hallway. Alset screamed in pain as she fled, but she had no time to look back.

"Where's my gun?"

Becca stumbled through the east side of the 19th Floor. She opened the access back into the southern area and re-entered the foreign landscape, this distant world which might as well be the Moon. Layers upon layers of dust covered every surface, and despite it being mostly settled inside, the skies were still ominous outside, with an enormous mass hanging in the air, still surprisingly *thick,* blotting out most of the sunlight.

I can't even see the South Tower through that cloud!

Echoes of Alset's bloodcurdling screams bounced back to Becca, adding an awful ambiance to the *already* alien-esque air in the area. She tripped and fell, bouncing against a chair and tumbling to the floor. She had permanent double-vision now, as she held her bleeding forehead, crawling as best as she could across the room. She scampered to the area where she had been standing earlier, when the great rumbling of the freight train had knocked her off her feet; she was hoping to find her Smith & Wesson, but nothing was recognizable in this moon dust.

Crawling desperately on the dirty carpet, hoping to find her pistol before it was too late, Becca wanted to cry as she struggled to stay conscious. Her bell was *rung.*

"Where *is* my gun?" she repeated, frantically crawling through the dust, back to the doorway where Quarren had been standing guard—

Becca froze in place, stunned. Q was gone.

"Q?" He'd been too injured to *move*; much less escape. "Where'd you go...?"

A trail of blood was streaked through the dust, just in front of her, through the door, and into the elevator lobby. Becca gasped.

She *knew* Alset had gotten him. She knew Q was *dead.*

"Oh, shit..."

When she glanced up from the streak of blood, she beheld Alset's figure, a shadowy silhouette standing at the other end of the lobby, holding the dowel high above his head. In the dusty air, she envisioned him as a horror movie villain, a poor impression of Jason Voorhees. Even in this dimly-lit hellscape, his gold tooth glistened, as did the letter opener sticking out of the man's thigh—

The letter opener! I can kick him right in that thing and drive it deeper into his leg.

Alset began to limp towards the woman, and Becca couldn't budge. She was like a deer in headlights, stuck on her hands and knees.

"You and James Serrano... you're both good as *dead,* you *idiot!*"

Alset licked the blood off the dowel; Becca was going to be sick.

She scoffed, spitting against the hallway wall. "You don't stand a *chance* against Jim."

"You are both in the way. You clowns know too much about us, already."

"Us?"

I knew it! I thought I heard him say 'us' earlier!

Becca couldn't shake the scene. January 1st. *"There's two of them, Rebecca."*

"What do you mean, *us?"* she inquired, cocking an eyebrow.

Alset limped closer, smacking the dowel in his hand. She had to buy time as she searched for *anything* to protect herself with.

His laughter was *inhuman,* and Becca felt a terror the likes of which she'd never experienced. Her skin crawled over her body, like it was made of ants. The charred carpet crunched under her as she crawled, adding depth in stereo to Becca's illusion of little tiny bugs invading her body.

"You have *nowhere* to run. I won't let you get to the stairs."

Alset was closer to Becca now than any route of escape. But she didn't *intend* to run; she was going to cripple this man for *life.*

"Once I've taken care of you clowns, we can be together with the little one... yes, just us."

"Who is this 'us', Alset?"

"Yes, *us,*" Alset cackled as he glared at her, growling through bared teeth. "Heh."

He rushed at Rebecca, and she kicked as hard as she could, driving her steel-toed boot at his thigh. This time, Alset stopped short and deflected her attack, smacking her leg with the wooden dowel in a mighty downward arc. The blow hit her in the shin so solidly with a *crack* that the dowel bounced off her shinbone, ricocheting backwards.

Becca's eyes went bloodshot.

"Oh, fuck!" She screamed at the top of her lungs in agony, *immediately* recoiling back as she scampered towards the end of the elevator lobby. The strike connected precisely in the spot where her leg had been trapped under the desk, back on ninety-one.

Instantaneous tears poured from her eyes as she moaned in pain, her shin busted open as a bleeding knot began pushing up from under her decimated slacks like some macabre volcano.

"I-I won't beg you..." she seethed through gritted teeth as she pushed back. "But you *won't* get away, you fucker!"

Alset cackled maniacally as he gripped the dented dowel. "I'm gonna take my time with you, Rebecca Taylor."

He dropped to his knees, seemingly unbothered by his injuries, and he crawled rapidly over the dusty carpet towards her, like she was a helpless fly, and Alset was a hungry spider.

Despite her pain, Becca fiercely smacked at his face with her left hand, but he caught the desperate blow. Once he had her hand, he grabbed it tightly and squeezed her fingers. She felt a knuckle dislocate, and then *pop.*

Her scream was involuntary, her voice cracking under the

pressure. She tried to headbutt Alset, but her injured neck shot sparks of pain down her spine instead, causing her vision to crackle with black-and-white spots.

He giggled. She squeezed her eyes shut as he mounted her, Alset's musky scent forcing her to *gag*. He held her hand tightly as he rolled the dowel up her legs, across her groin, and up her torso, brushing past her breasts and to her throat, stopping at her windpipe.

"Suppose I were to crush your throat, for a thrill..."

Becca *groaned*, clenching her right hand into a tightly-wound fist but biding her time, as Alset took her mangled left hand and directed it towards his crotch, placing it atop his private parts.

"I can think of only one better thrill, clown. Care to join me?"

Alset giggled like a little child, and Becca wondered if she still had the strength to crush his testicles with her broken hand. *They must be tender from that kick.*

Her eyes darted behind him, and about twenty feet away, lying next to the elevators, was the bloody machete he'd dropped earlier—the *same* one he'd slashed Q with.

If I can get away from him... even if only for a few seconds...

He licked her earlobe, whispering to her. "I'll wait to kill you until after you're satisfied."

Becca held her breath, ready to move if he assaulted her further, sexually or otherwise. She didn't want to telegraph her moves too soon. If only her leg weren't on fire, she'd have *no* problem pushing him off... but her eyes were filled with tears.

I've cried before, but from physical pain? Not since she was training in Quantico! But she was tough; if her leg was capable of moving, she was *gonna* use it.

Okay, then. That's the plan. I'll grab his balls and twist, then I'll punch his nose, and go for the blade. Grab, twist, strike, then move.

She clenched her fist, trying not to telegraph any of her movements—she wouldn't make a move until it was *perfect*. She might not get another chance to escape, and now, her right leg was *screaming* in agony, burning as if a hot coal were being held against her shin.

Biding her time, she wanted to fight now, *desperate* to attack.

Alset licked the blood from her cheek, causing her to wretch.

Not until she *had* to. Not. A. Move.

Girl, you only have one chance at this. Clear your mind—

"You *bore* me, clown," he whispered softly.

Only one chance to do this. She readied herself.

Unbelievably, Becca felt *calm* in that moment.

Write your story—

"I don't think I'll be bothered by you much longer."

Now was her chance. Her heart was *pounding;* her teeth clenched together. Her body trembled with adrenaline. She shut her eyes tightly as Alset loosened the dowel from her throat, rising above her leg.

And—

BANG!

Alset was forced backwards, the movement pulling him away from her, the stick freeing from Becca's throat. He was no longer paying *any* attention to Becca.

When she opened her eyes, Alset's expression had gone blank, staring down at himself in shock. A red hole in his shirt was rapidly spreading over the dried bloodstain, smoke rising from the fresh wound. He held a hand to his chest, and stared at it in disbelief; the entry wound was mere *inches* from his heart.

Becca's throat closed up. *Did the bullet go through his shoulder?*

Alset stood up. Laughing meekly, he pulled his hand away from his injury, *gingerly* gliding his bloody fingers together and watching them as he rubbed them, his eyes wide and unblinking as if his crimson-colored fingers fascinated him.

Finally, after a few agonizing moments where Becca thought he might continue attacking her... Alset collapsed backwards onto the dusty carpet, silent and still.

She blinked a few times, still attempting to process what had occurred right in front of her.

But... I-I still need to find Marissa!

Quarren fired the gun a second time, and a bullet screamed right above Alset's body, flying out a broken window and somewhere into New York City.

"Q!" she cried, exasperated that she had to stop him. "Don't kill him!"

Wobbling, Q stumbled from the elevator lobby towards Becca and Alset, his entire body covered in blood.

"I think I am going to lie down, Boss."

The gun fell from his hand with a metallic *clank* as Quarren collapsed in the hallway, a cloud of dust billowing around him. He was still. She turned to look at Alset, but he was not moving, either.

And the nineteenth floor fell silent.

*   *   *

Her first attempt to stand up did not go well, and she screamed before crumpling back into the dust. Becca gingerly touched her shin, unwilling to imagine what it looked like under her pants. Her hand recoiled instantly upon brushing the tender wound.

Standing up took everything she had. Between the spinning room, her awful migraine, her ringing ears and her bloody face, she barely even *felt* her injured leg... at least, until she tried to put weight on it again.

"Aahh!" She screamed in agony as she took a step on it. "Holy *shit* that fuckin' *hurts!"*

Groaning through pursed lips, she leaned against the wall of the lobby as she gingerly stood. Her eyes caught Q's motionless body; her pain was so intense she'd *forgotten* about him temporarily. Once she was on her feet, she limped over to Q's side, picking up her weapon as she did so.

"I'm right here, Quarren. Just relax now." She brushed his face as he moaned softly on the dusty carpet. "I'll be *right* back."

Becca checked the clip; there were six shots left. She fished her handcuffs out of her pocket and stumbled slowly towards Alset. Using the dowel as a crutch, she knelt and rolled her suspect over, holding his face down in the singed carpet with her boot, and finding *immense* satisfaction in how the tables had turned.

It's because this piece of shit deserves this.

For the first time, she seriously considered ending Alset's life, right here and now. It's not like anyone could *ever* find out. It would be *so* satisfying.... *Oh,* she wanted to, and *nobody* would question it. Hell—if this building ended up burning down or *collapsing,* he'd be erased with the evidence anyway!

The loaded gun, heavy in her right hand, argued *deafeningly* with the handcuffs in her crushed left.

It would be so easy. The self-defense angle practically wrote *itself.*

"Do the job!" Jim's voice echoed in her head, her only conscience in this cavalcade of evil.

I want to do it... I've never been so humiliated in my entire life. I've lost so much throughout my life, and yet, I've never felt this violated, this humiliated... and I admit it. I've never been this... scared.

I loathe this man so much, for the lifetime of pain he's gifted me over the last two years. All those nights when CeCe had to cradle me as I cried asleep after another nightmare. And now, he has personally hurt me, physically—and honestly, pretty emotionally, too—but you've already won, Rebecca. You can't let him beat you, now.

Don't ask what Jim would do. You already know what to do. Do the job.

Rubbing her scalp with the butt of her pistol, she glanced at Q, who was watching her silently. She saw innocence in his face at that moment, as if he were *begging* her not to.

When he had a chance to kill Alset, I made him stop. His face is telling me the same thing. C'mon, Becca, do what's right. Revenge is not the way to heal from trauma; you know this!

The rage boiled in her like a tea kettle, and she was about to boil over. But the words echoed loudly in her head. Constantly.

You clowns know too much about us.

Us... Us... Us...

"Marissa!" she exclaimed. Her senses swam back to her as the rage within her subsided. She would not make the same mistakes twice.

The battle was over. She was redeemed. She was victorious.

"I'm Rebecca Taylor, Special Agent with the FBI. Alset *Ay-hole*, I am placing you under arrest for the murder of Jeremey Young, the murder of Moira Desmarais, the murders of Donny and Janet Costas, for three *additional* counts of murder, dating back to 1999. For the murder of Isabel Esquivel, the kidnapping of Marissa Hernandez—oh, and because I can't wait to fucking see you in court... you sick fuck."

She locked the cuffs on his wrists.

He moaned in pain as she rolled him onto his back.

Even his shallow breathing sounded evil.

Dread filled her as she looked down at his helpless body.

Inside Becca, a battle between angst and duty was fought.

Didn't she still *fear* this man?

The truth was, she hadn't been afraid of him.

He was simply a symbol of her *own* demons.

Everything she defeated was inside *her,* festering and wicked.

Just like all of us, evil was inside Rebecca Taylor, as well.

Only unlike Alset, she hadn't let evil *or* fear win...

Becca had beaten them both.

*   *   *

"I apologize..." Q muttered softly as Becca knelt over Q's crumpled body. She ripped his tattered tie off his neck and unbuttoned his shirt, revealing a wound very similar to the one Jim had suffered on January 1st. It was a brutal injury; he'd been slashed downward, across his chest. This one, she worried, looked deeper than the injury Shahla had given to Jim on January 1st.

"For what, Q?" Becca was incredulous. "You have *nothing* to apologize for!"

"Yes, I do, Boss. I promised I would go to dinner with your family, but I do not think I will be able to keep that promise."

Alset was moaning in the corner. He had regained consciousness, but he wasn't moving, despite his wound not appearing to be fatal. After cuffing him, she'd looked him over quickly; the bullet had passed right through his shoulder, missing his lungs *and* heart.

Unfortunately, he'll live.

She joked to herself, but she *needed* him alive, and as luck had it, he would live long enough to escape. That's all that mattered to her.

Becca pressed Q's shirt into the stab wound, applying pressure, but she knew there wasn't going to be any hope of stopping the bleeding.

"Boss," he whispered weakly, "you have to get out of here."

She cried down at him. "You need to get up, Q. *C'mon,* stand up!"

His tears made streaks through the caked dust on his cheeks. His brilliant green eyes blazing through the darkness of the lobby, flashing brilliances of innocence she didn't know could exist in a man—not since *Ken* had passed, anyway. Such a handsome, kind man, and a loyal friend...

Some loyal friend he is... shaking his head instead of standing up—

Becca shook her head, panic rising in her chest. Her hands were slick with Q's blood, and no amount of pressure seemed to stop the bleeding. Unlike Jim's wounds (which were similar, but not as deep), the bleeding was only growing *worse* by the second.

I... I don't know what to do! I don't think I can do anything... Fuck!

The reality of the situation hit her like a ton of bricks. She stared at him; his handsome smile, however, offset the pain she knew he felt in that moment. As his body relaxed and his breathing slowed, she finally released the pressure.

"I am so sorry." Becca's head bowed. "About *everything.*"

"I am *not* sorry. I came here to get a job... and instead had an *adventure* I was proud to be a part of."

"Q..." she whispered, freely allowing her tears to fall.

"You gave me the best job in the world. I helped you *catch* that man. And now, you can save that kid from the napper."

Even through her tears, the levity broke Becca. "You're a *hero,* man." She giggled, kissing his nose. Her tears fell upon his cheeks, joining his own.

"You saved my life, in so many ways, friend." Becca found his hand with her own, gripping it tightly. "You saved Marissa's life, too. Now that I have Alset in custody, we *will* find her. We will save her life now, and it's thanks to *you*, Q."

Q's eyes glossed over; his hand grew clammy in her own. Even as life was leaving him, his smile never faltered.

"Thank you for being my friend, Rebecca," he mumbled softly. His eyelids slowly slid shut, but the corners of his mouth twitched upwards. She grinned in return—even in her *grief*, she couldn't resist that damned smile...

"I'm so grateful to you, Quarren Cambanda. Thank *you*."

"I..." Q trailed off as he ran out of breath; his chest did not rise again.

There was nothing she could do for him.

Becca glanced at her watch: it was now 10:10.

XIX

"Chaos"

"I swear to God," Becca gritted through her clenched teeth, with more than a hint of disdain staining her tongue, "if you don't shut up, I'm gonna *throw* you down these stairs!"

This generated loads of laughter from others in the stairwell, particularly those who'd heard Becca's story while descending together. Alset complained continuously as Becca escorted him through the newly pitch-black Stairwell A, with only her flashlight guiding them.

At this point, more firefighters were going *up* than civilians coming down. Becca displayed her badge on her belt, and they passed silent nods and salutes as they passed one another.

Despite their injuries, Becca had *little* choice but to rush. Gravity and dizziness weighed her down; at times, the only thing keeping her on her feet was her suspect in front of her, whom she pushed along.

Alset's hands were securely cuffed to his belt, and Becca twisted his wounded arm whenever he decided not to cooperate. The wound he'd inflicted on Quarren wasn't from a machete... rather, Alset had brandished the blade of a paper cutter to kill Q— likely, the same weapon he used on Don and Janet. Alset now accepted his fate; with his injuries, he wasn't about to escape. She'd removed the letter opener and patched his wounds the best she could, but he was severely injured as *well* as shot.

Becca thought it fortuitous, as it kept his mouth shut. *Mostly.*

There was a renewed sense of urgency driving her. She'd been knocked back into reality when she realized the other tower had collapsed. Now, she believed their *own* building might be in jeopardy. Regardless, she wasn't taking any chances, *especially* now that she had her man in custody.

No more breaks, no more stops. I'm getting the hell out of here.

A young man traveling just ahead of Becca and Alset tapped a pair of firefighters coming up on their shoulders. "I'm curious— you hear about the *other* plane?"

"The Pentagon?" One of them inquired.

"No—someone just told me that *another* plane just crashed outside of Pittsburgh or something like that."

"I don't want to think about that right now," his partner groaned, grunting with the weight of every step. They were tired and sweaty, but they kept on going. "I just wanna get *up* there."

They were now descending through the single-digit floors. Conversation in the stairway went one of two ways. The first was a rumor that the South Tower had collapsed, which some people argued was *impossible,* although others said they witnessed it first-hand. For what it's worth, Becca saw it happen *right* in front of her, and even *she* didn't know for sure if the entire building had gone down. Frankly, she didn't *want* to believe it.

The other was the flooding, and *everyone* was moaning about it. *This* was Alset's favorite subject to complain about, as if Becca could do *anything* about it... short of leaving him behind.

Tempting...

The river rushed down the stairs in a torrent, a chaotic mix of water, jet fuel, and *God* knows what else. Becca's shin throbbed, burning under her soaked slacks, as the mysterious liquid seeped into her wound, flooding halfway up her shin. But she wasn't alone; Alset's stab wound was *also* submerged in this toxic solution, and they *both* struggled to keep their footing in the surging water.

*The mall's gotta be impassable after Tower Two's collapse;
surely it must be flooded by now...*

When they reached the 5th Floor, two firefighters were
standing guard near the door that led back into the building.
Becca pushed Alset into a wall as one of the firefighters signaled
with their head towards the exit door.

"Exit's down in the Concourse," one man muttered in
monotone mumbles, as if he'd already read his line a *thousand*
times in the last hour. Becca's curiosity was piqued, and she had to
find out what they were doing here.

"Rebecca Taylor, FBI," she muttered, her voice weak and
strained, as she limped towards them. Their eyes roamed over her
body, visibly appalled by her condition.

"Holy *shit,* lady! You look like you've had one *hell* of a day—
no offense. You look like you two were in a *fight!*"

Alset opened his mouth to speak, and Becca elbowed him in
the ribs. *"Shut up!"* she cried in a sore, scratchy voice, before
pasting a simpered grin to her weathered face.

"You could say that."

"The South Tower completely collapsed, and we just got
word—we're *evacuating* this one."

"What about the fire department?" Becca's face went pale,
and she grabbed the firefighter's sleeve in her fists. "Are *they*
evacuating as well?"

"Yeah, uh... that's what I mean. We're evacuating the *whole*
building. *Everyone's* gotta go." The firefighter turned to peek
through the open doorway. "We're helping funnel folks from B
and C. The debris outside is pretty bad, so we're funneling
everyone down to the concourse level so that they can escape
through the mall. But you should be fine to take A to the lobby if
you want... it's just that..."

"What?" Becca asked, her brow furrowed.

"Take my advice—don't stop and look. Once you get out of the building... you *run*. Run across the Plaza and get outta here."

"I see," she muttered. "Wasn't there a command post set up in the lobby?"

"Yeah, I think so," he nodded with a frown. "But you aren't gonna like what you see, if you go there."

His face said a thousand words without a sound, and he shook his head as he passed her.

Is it really that bad out there? I mean, it's been pretty bad in here, too...

She decided it was best to rendezvous with any authorities in the lobby; she was utterly *exhausted,* fighting the urge to pass out. Every step made her feel like her boots were made of iron, and every shove of Alset forward was like pushing an elephant.

If Bill is here, I can give Alset to him. I need to find a doctor; my neck hurts, my head hurts, my forehead hurts, my broken fingers hurt, my ankle hurts, and I won't even look at my shin. My gut hurts, I'm thirsty, and—

Becca gasped as she looked up, cutting her thoughts off immediately; at long last...

When Becca stepped out into the sunlit lobby from the darkness of Stairwell A, she had only two things on her mind: William Bushnall and a ride to the hospital. However, as she limped into the world she once knew, she was an *outsider* stepping into some ancient civilization, long since eradicated, on some far-away planet with a questionably breathable atmosphere.

The lobby was abandoned, save for a few firefighters beckoning at Becca to keep moving. The sensation was like stepping out of the Eagle in July of 1969, and seeing Neil Armstrong's sterile, white boot leaving an everlasting footprint. While hers wasn't as important, she was stunned to find her *own* boot buried under almost an inch of powdery dust.

Becca observed the mezzanine, which was *unrecognizable* as she exited the stairwell, shoving Alset along as she walked. There was debris in here, too; most had fallen through the building from the other tower, and the southern and eastern exits were blocked entirely. Evidence of a few unlucky souls caught moments away from freedom caused her to grow lightheaded when she noticed.

Jesus, stop looking at them, Becca!

She directed Alset to the Command Posts, but there wasn't a living soul around. There was a desk with radios and a whiteboard, but nobody was standing post. Glancing around, Becca deduced they'd abandoned the station when the South Tower collapsed.

Unfazed, she pushed Alset past the dormant escalators, buried in concrete chunks and steel. That *wasn't* the way out anymore. Becca tried her best not to notice a few corpses who lay in front of the elevators, their charred bodies a terrible reminder of the morbid events that took place here not long ago.

"Hey, you!"

Becca jumped upon hearing this voice of authority boom out, and she squinted through the dusty lobby, searching for the source. Her eyes were still adjusting to the brighter light outside the stairwell. It was still difficult to see, and the light diffused throughout the particulates—the world seemed ghastly and uncanny. It reminded Becca of the nineteenth floor... which in turn, reminded her to elbow Alset in the ribs.

"Hey! Watch it, bi—"

A second jab cut him off. This time, he reserved his complaints. Becca turned her head towards a broken window, where a police officer stood in the frame, waving. As she looked around, it became clear that this was the best way out. The gap in the window was pretty wide; even Alset could easily fit through it.

As they approached, she uttered a muted "Thank you" to the man.

"You're Special Agent Taylor?"

"Yeah! How did you—?"

"I was down here watching the stairwells for you when the plane hit!"

Becca *gasped* dramatically. She couldn't help it, rushing over to hug the man, nearly knocking him off the windowsill. He laughed as he embraced her momentarily, before shrugging her off. Stepping back, Becca caught his name tag: Officer Earl Spilner.

Heh; sounds like a serial killer's name.

"I'm sorry, Officer Spilner. Are you alright?"

"I'm fine; Thank you, Agent Taylor..." he chuckled nervously. "I'm glad you got out safe... *ish.*" Earl scoffed at her condition. "Follow me; your boss is over with the fire chiefs."

She turned to usher her captive, but he was acting aloof and wandering away, like he wasn't planning on coming. She elbowed him again, although it was to get his attention this time.

"We're moving, Alset. You can either stay with me, or I can shoot you in your *fuckin'* kneecaps and leave you here to *die.* Your call."

She took her pistol out and loaded the chamber. "You wanna move, *right?*"

"Wait here a sec—" Earl stopped them, pausing a moment before dashing out towards the middle of the Austin J. Tobin Plaza. As her eyes followed him, they beheld things that burned deep into her retinas like a tattoo—evidence of evil that Satan *himself* would find appalling.

"Lord, have mercy!"

Becca forgot what was happening. Time seemed to decelerate. Debris surrounded them, as if the Plaza was transformed into a post-apocalyptic garbage dump. Papers, computer monitors, chairs, and other office supplies dotted the landscape, which no longer resembled the Austin J. Tobin Plaza at *all*.

This is another planet... there's no way this is still Earth.

"Okay, stick with me. We're gonna run northeast 'round 6 to Vesey, then east, okay?"

Becca nodded confidently. "Let's go!"

Ignoring the terrific agony radiating through her shinbone, she took off, dragging Alset along. As they moved, Becca was particularly struck by two other types of debris she noticed. The more prevalent variety consisted of various fragments she believed to be aircraft parts: sections of fuselage and wing, even a seat... all inexplicably littering the landscape that had been picturesque two hours earlier.

BANG!

Becca flinched.

The other debris was much more macabre, and she didn't want to look at it. She focused instead on the cop, who was returning towards her, waving at them to go.

Officer Spilner guided them through the Plaza. They hobbled east towards Church Street, which had transformed into something very different from their foot chase this morning. An ear-splitting alarm filled the air around her, a haunting screech she recognized... except, she'd only heard the sound of PASS devices at CeCe's firehouse. PASS devices, or "Personal Alert Safety Systems," are devices firefighters wear. If they are lost or downed, the alarm assists their comrades in locating them.

She'd *never* heard one in the field... but this wasn't only *one* she was hearing, now, no—there were *hundreds* of alarms, blaring their sirens desperately into the morning air. *One for each firefighter...* It *shattered* Becca's heart, and she nearly wheeled around to go back up the tower. Truthfully, if she wasn't injured, she might have... the thought that one of those PASS alarms might be sounding for Cecilia was...

Instead, she bit her lips and looked forward, only stopping once they passed the east side of 6 World Trade. As they reached the walkway to Vesey Street, she couldn't resist any longer, halting Alset so she could turn around. She *had* to see it for herself—

Becca's jaw hit the concrete. "I don't *believe* it... they were right..."

A mountain of steel and flame rose above the Plaza's southern area. It emitted a column of massive smoke that blotted out the rooftops of heaven. The South Tower of the World Trade Center, once one of the tallest buildings in the *world*... had vanished entirely, reduced to a burning, smoking volcano of mangled, twisted steel, broken glass, concrete... *and only God knows what else.*

Pieces of the outer structure remained upright where they'd been set decades ago, columns of steel tridents framing the debris in such a macabre way that it appeared to be the entrance to some ancient labyrinth. The mound of debris was massive, *towering* over her head and overwhelming her to the point of collapsing.

She fell to her knees. "How many people were still in there?" She moaned. "How *many? Oh, God!*"

"Are you alright? We gotta *move*, Agent Taylor!"

Officer Spilner yanked her to her feet effortlessly and shoved her forward. Her ears filled with a familiar *rumble* sound that convinced her; she shrugged her arm away from him, spinning towards the North Tower and expecting to see it falling—

The rumble escalated into a deafening roar as a squadron of

military fighter jets passed overhead in a blur.

What in the hell is happening?

Becca was suddenly struck with paranoia, expecting a missile to come crashing into them at any moment as they zipped past and over the Hudson. She turned to grab onto Alset, intending to resume their journey... except only the officer was still with her.

"What?"

She screamed this time. *"Where is Alset?"*

"Who?"

"The man I was with! Where—?"

The jets had passed by, and the rumble slowly dissipated. Blinking away her double-vision, Becca found Alset; he hadn't gone very far. Seemingly, he'd broken away, but escape was futile at his slow, limping pace. They were surrounded by mountains of steel and flame, lost in forests of death. Unholy events occurred here today, and as wicked as Alset truly was, even *he* was intimidated by what his eyes claimed they were witnessing. As Becca caught up to him, he'd already aborted his attempt, lost in observing the destruction encompassing them both.

"This is just... *chaos,*" Alset whispered scratchily. "The whole world is just... chaos."

BANG!

Becca flinched. She glanced at her watch; it was 10:20.

Officer Spilner stopped moving, and she noticed him turning back towards the tower. "Excuse me, officer?"

"Yes?"

"You said you knew where they were meeting up?"

The forlorn officer nodded and pointed his radio toward the intersection of Vesey and Church Streets, right in front of the Millennium Hotel. "Yeah, your director is with that group. That's the new rendezvous point." Earl turned back and looked up at the North Tower, almost staring *through* it, with glassy eyes. *It looks like the thousand-yard stare is creeping across his face.*

His unblinking stare focused on the top of the tower, which she followed; people were clearly visible on the upper floors, waving towels and hanging out the windows.

"Those poor people up there... I hope God has mercy on their souls."

Her *own* flirtation with death, back on fifty-nine, crept back into her mind. The feeling she felt in that moment crept back into her gut, and she felt the urge to flee madly. She *barely* resisted punching Alset in the back of the head, instead shoving her good hand in her tattered pocket, hoping to restrain her rage.

CeCe wasn't the only person on her mind. Thoughts of Quarren continued to invade her imagination, and she couldn't stop thinking about the young man who'd just saved her life... as well as *Marissa's.*

She still didn't have the girl's location, but had successfully caught her man.

It was worth it, Q. I'm so sorry you won't be here to—
BANG!

Becca flinched. "What is that noise?"

"If you don't know, then you don't wanna know, trust me." Officer Spilner waved her away. "Just get out of here, go to the hospital, or go home. Go *anywhere* but here... *please.*"

He's right. I need to finish the job. With a burst of energy, she pushed Alset along. "Let's go, asshole."

*   *   *

As they approached the intersection, Becca noticed a crowd of people huddling around St. Paul's Chapel, absolutely *caked* in dust; some looked *worse* than Becca. A similar cluster huddled inside the Millennium's lobby doors, and it dawned on her—those people had just run for their *lives*.

She shuffled onto Church Street at a *snail's* pace, her boots slipping on piles of dust and concrete debris because she couldn't stop staring at the scene. She saw row after row of NYPD squad cars and firetrucks to her right.

"There must be *dozens* of them!"

Some of the vehicles closer to the mountain of debris were crushed under massive steel beams or boulders of concrete; a few were on *fire*, burning in the middle of the street, with emergency crews walking around them like they were everyday sights for a typical New York afternoon.

Everything was covered in dust. Loose-leaf letters littered literally *every* surface, swirling around in air currents like a cyclone of spreadsheets, contracts, and forms fluttering freely in the acrid air.

Not far beyond the men Becca had observed, a large conglomerate of firefighters gathered around a Deputy Chief and a Battalion Chief, who were desperately trying to coordinate the evacuation of the North Tower. Becca had to swallow hard to resist the urge to run over and beg them to get Cecilia out of the building.

Directly beside them, Becca spotted a red-headed woman in an FBI windbreaker; she was also covered in dust... though compared to Becca, she looked like she was freshly starting her shift. Becca could spot that gorgeous auburn hair from a *mile* away... and when their eyes locked, she began waving excitedly.

"*Kelly?* Is that *you?*"

"*Becca!*" Kelly's smile was contagious to Becca as they embraced. Special Agent Kelly Willis attended Quantico alongside Becca. Class of '94. She was her classmate then... her best *friend* ever since. She worked out of Brooklyn-Queens, and was as competent an agent as anyone Becca knew. Kelly was a bachelorette... and Becca harbored an incredibly embarrassing crush on her, fully aware that she was only into men... *but that doesn't mean I can't look, does it? I haven't seen her in weeks! She's even prettier than the last time, somehow...*

When they pulled away, Kelly's grin contorted into a grimace, as if she'd been struck with a bad case of gas. Although it had been Becca checking Kelly out a moment prior... this time, it was *Kelly* doing the looking.

"Jesus Christ, Becca... were you, like... *in* the tower?"

"Yeah, we were in Tower One. I lost someone in there, but I found 'em." Becca squeezed Alset's arm firmly, causing him to *yelp* in pain again. She tried sounding excited to see her best friend, but she was cranky and everything was blurry—it was a struggle to simply stay upright.

"First things first," she yanked Alset in front of her, "where's the trashcan?"

"And who's *this* lovely fellow?" Kelly looked him up and down like a piece of meat, licking her lips in mock seduction. He snarled at her like a rabid dog, and she winked in reply.

"Kelly, I'd like to introduce you to Alset *Ay-hole.* Also known as the 'Y2Killer', or 'The Manhattan Mauler.'"

She rubbed her temples; ever since he'd struck her with the dowel, Becca had been suffering from a *terrible* headache, and she glared with rage at the tall man. This time, she gave in to it; she elbowed him in the upper thigh, inches from the wound in his knee, and he *howled* in pain.

"Did I mention he's also an asshole?"

"Oh, are *you* the lovely little piece of shit that's been snatching up our second graders?"

"This is police brutality!" Alset exclaimed, craning his head around, hoping for help.

"The only thing brutal here is your musky-ass *breath,* dude.

You brush your teeth with, like, cat shit or somethin'?"

She could always keep her sarcasm at the ready.

"I'll eat your *hearts* out, you clowns! Wait until—"

Kelly pushed Alset to the side, causing him to fall to the asphalt with a whimper.

"Yeah, he's *awesome.*" Becca's voice spat with vitriol as she rolled her eyes dramatically. "He beat the shit out of me before..." She trailed off, swallowing hard. "Before my friend saved my life."

Alset whined as Kelly yanked him back to his feet. Becca's following words came out very monotone and professional; Kelly felt her weariness through her tone, and she couldn't help but tear up empathetically.

"He's wounded. Gunshot to the right shoulder, stab wound to the left knee."

"You did really good, Becca. I've been reading up on this one; ya beat me to it."

She turned towards Alset with a flirtatious smile as she teased him. Becca knew the truth; she was fucking with him.

"She's a toughie, sir—looks like she got *you* pretty good, too. You got lucky, though, because I've seen her handle men *twice* your size. And, if it'd been me instead of her? I'd have hung your ass out the window of that fucking tower on a pole by your *dick* and watched you burn to death."

She spat in Alset's eye, and he didn't blink.

"How *dare* you hurt children in *my* district? You pathetic little scab of a man... I hope you fry in the electric chair and they broadcast it on TV, motherfuckin' *Pay-Per-View* that shit, I'll order some pizza and watch you fry like bacon! I hope they let Isabel's mom throw the *switch!* You sniveling, rotten, no-good piece of dog—"

"That's *enough*, Kelly!"

Becca reached out to her, pulling her away from Alset's face, and hugged her. It was a grab meant to shut her up, but it morphed into a clutch; Becca's neck injury caused her to nearly collapse into Kelly's arms.

While they held one another, Kelly could still make eye contact with Alset, and when he smiled that Cheshire Cat smile at Kelly, she again spat in his direction.

"Bitch."

Becca tried to laugh, but it came out a pathetic whimper as she looked down at her slacks. Her right leg was smeared in a sickening slurry of blood, dirt, and sprinkler water, creating a macabre cement of dust and... whatever the hell else might be in that stuff. *I don't want to know.*

She started to lift her pant leg to show Kelly, but the incredible stinging that came from the disturbance of her wound made her quickly wince—and she saw stars again.

"You need a doctor, Becca." Kelly frowned. "Come with me. Let's give this guy a place to think about things, while we catch up."

Becca recounted some of her ordeal as Kelly led the pair past the firefighters, towards a temporary triage area near some ambulances. One of them sat with its doors open, a dust-covered stretcher sitting ready for its first patient, and standing right beside it were three people in FBI jackets.

One of them, a familiar-shaped burly man, turned towards them, and it struck her that she'd never seen him this enthusiastic about anything in her entire career—*especially* Rebecca. He stepped away from the others, trotting towards the trio.

"Oh, Becca, you made it! *Thank God you made it!*"

Bill shoved Alset out of the way, and he was about to give her a bear hug before she hurriedly held her hand high to stop him. Her boss looked at his agent, and his eyes widened like an IMAX screen.

No more hugs, no more running, at least not until they pump some drugs into me.

"I called your line, but they said you went to see Jim?"

Kelly smiled sincerely. "I'll let you take it from here, Bill. I gotta get back to it." She leaned in, giving Becca a gentle kiss on her cheek. "Great job, Becca. Get some rest, okay?"

She nodded as Kelly turned to return to work, allowing her boss to catch up with his agent. Bill patted her on the shoulder gently.

"I'm so *glad* to see you. I was worried..." He glanced at her suspect. "Seems you have a guest?"

"I'd like to introduce you to Mr. *Ay-hole.*" She pinched gently in the area around Alset's gunshot wound, and he screamed out loud—a very high-pitched scream.

"Hey, watch it! Fucking clown."

She spat on his back, and Bill gingerly put his hands on her shoulders as she seethed. Alset glared at Becca scornfully, but it was a fiery gaze she no longer feared.

"Becca, Becca... take it *easy,* okay?"

"Can I hit him, Bill?"

She wasn't fazed, staring right into Alset's eyes. For all the tough talk he had in the Tower, to Becca he was a complete pussycat, now; after some time had passed, he averted his eyes away from her own.

She smirked to herself; *you're mine, now.* "Please?"

"No, you can't hit him in public."

Maybe later, then.

She sat on the back of the open ambulance, allowing herself to lie backward into the vehicle, her battered ribs exhaling along with her. *If I didn't have all this pain keeping me awake, I could pass out right now.* She hawked up another wad and considered spitting it in Alset's face, before she changed her mind and spat it into the gutter; Alset started screaming out to anyone who would listen.

"You see this bullshit? Police brutality! I'm like fucking Rodney King, man."

"Shut up!" Bill and Becca screamed in unison. Bill's eyes focused on his agent's busted brow. "You look like shit, Taylor. Did *he* do this to you?"

"Yeah," she said shamefully, but Bill didn't see shame in it. Instead, his eyes found the incredible mess that had solidified on her damp slacks, the lump in her shin protruding underneath.

"That's *gotta* be a record breaker. Did he use a nightstick on you or something?"

Becca laughed meekly as she undid the laces on her soaking-wet boots. "No! It was a half-inch wooden dowel."

"I can see why you want to hit him, now," Bill scoffed. "What happened?"

"It's a long story... I want to get to the hospital and see Jimbo." She looked up at the burning tower, which was emitting an alarming amount of smoke. "Thank you, by the way, for keeping people posted at the exit points."

"Becca," her boss replied sheepishly. "I..." She thought she understood—*it's not like both towers of the World Trade Center were on fire or anything.*

"How long have you been down here, Bill?"

"Since I left Presbyterian. So less than an hour... but I have a feeling I'll be here all day." He grumbled, lightly kicking the diamond-plate bumper of the ambulance with his heel. "Nina is gonna *kill* me."

Bill stared in thoughtful silence until Becca lost track of time, nearly falling asleep sitting on the back bumper. "Were you able to get the location of the girl?"

"No. I asked him, but he won't answer." She sighed, sitting

upright on the back of the ambulance. Her feet screamed, 'Thank you,' as she removed her boots. She ripped her wet socks off her swollen, aching feet, letting her pruned toes air in the breeze. Becca felt her nose scrunch. *My feet look and smell like a swamp.*

Bill took a seat beside her, not complaining about it one bit.

"Oh! That reminds me. We need to check out that address you staked this morning. PD sealed it off for us, but then *this* all started... we can look at it when you're up for it, okay?"

"Tonight," she stated, matter-of-factly.

Bill's mouth frowned, and Becca braced for the ass-chewing she was about to receive. She held up her hand. "He mentioned something odd, Bill. When we were fighting. He said, 'You clowns know'—"

"Ma'am, you're gonna have to lose the slacks," An EMT said, interrupting her as he collected gauze and supplies for Alset's wounds from the plastic drawers behind her. Squeezing between Jim and Becca, he turned to face her. "You're next."

She blushed a bit. "I hope you're not shy, Bill."

Becca unbuckled her belt and slowly lowered her shredded slacks with a painful *moan*—she was grateful she'd put boxer shorts back on last night. The day's stains and smells wafted away as she revealed her tender wounds. Her shin bone looked like a *volcano* had risen out of it, erupting down her right shin in a grotesque summarization of everything she'd gone through today.

"Holy *shit!*" Bill's face drained of color as he beheld Becca's wound. She scoffed.

"I know, right?" Despite trying to play it cool, the sight of her wound nearly caused Becca to vomit. The knot was more than a half-inch higher than her shinbone. She grew lightheaded as she lay back for a moment before continuing.

"Anyways, he had said, 'You clowns know too much about us.'" Sitting up, she reached to grab an alcohol wipe from a drawer behind her, and (with bated breath) carefully wiped dried rust and black grime away from the gash, taking extra care to avoid contacting her open wound.

Her boss had been watching her clean her leg in a daze when Bill's head suddenly shot up.

"Wait, he said '*us?*'"

"Yes, a few times."

"Jesus... yeah, that's *just* like the old Y2K MO, huh?" He scratched his scruffy chin in deep thought. "And we still don't know where the kid is. Okay. Do we have *anything?*"

Becca took a deep, exaggerated breath, and Bill swallowed hard. He'd broken the seal and sat back in defense, leaning back against the ambulance door.

"I have him confessing to the murders of Jeremey Young and Isabel Esquivel, as well as three additional murders that occurred *in the fucking tower*, although I only saw personally two bodies— Donny and Janet Costas. I also witnessed him murder another person..."

She trailed off as she glared at Alset, who was being strapped onto a stretcher. She felt as resentful as ever, and she struggled to stifle the sensation that she should've left him there to die. To rot alone in that tower until the damn thing burned down. Even *now*, the urge to jump down from the ambulance and throttle Alset to death was insatiable.

CeCe is still up there... get a grip, Becca! She fought to keep from breaking down into a blubbering mess as she struggled to continue.

"I saw him kill Quarren Cambanda. And he tried to kill *me* three times, the last one was right when Tower Two fell, and I—"

Bill's fingers gently found Becca's trembling chin. He looked at her, vulnerable, and he hugged her, and she hugged him back. Although their relationship had been tenuous since last January

1st, they were *still* close friends. Years of working under William Bushnall had nurtured a strong bond between them, and in this moment, neither focused on titles like 'boss' or 'agent'. They were *thrilled* to be in each other's company. Bill cradled her tremulant body, protected and safe now. His embrace helped; Becca swallowed the tears back just before she lost it.

No crying, girl. You made it this far. You can cry tonight, at home...

"You did good, Rebecca. Good job, you're safe now."

"Okay, Bill," one of the paramedics interrupted the embrace, tapping his shoulder, "we're gonna load them up. Headin' to Presbyterian. You ridin'?"

Bill nodded, moving out of the way so they could roll Alset's stretcher into the vehicle. "That's where they took Jimbo. He should be out of surgery soon."

"Okay, Agent Taylor, you're next," the EMT muttered as he gave her a shot of morphine. And Becca's pain melted away in an orgasmic wave of relief. At long last... after everything she'd gone through, Becca could *finally* relax.

As the ambulance drove away from the World Trade Center, the weary, wounded woman leaned against her boss in a drug-induced stupor; she was hopelessly trying not to lose the battle she now fought against sleep, her head resting on Bill's shoulder as they worked on her wounded leg.

She stared out the back window, a cloud of dust following the vehicle as they sped away, the sirens wailing and echoing through the city's canyon-esque streets. Becca glanced at her watch. It was 10:28.

She stole a peek at Alset, who was already asleep on heavy painkillers. Becca opted for the lighter approach; they'd temporarily patched up her shin and ankle, but her neck and face wounds would have to get stitched up at the hospital. She was still gonna get X-rays done, *just* in case.

But this morphine, though... wow! I can barely feel the pain.

Through half-closed eyes, Becca gazed out the rear doors of the ambulance as it rumbled away in a cloud of dust from the World Trade Center... a few blocks away from them now. Numbness wrapped around her like a second skin—as much from hours of maximum effort and an overload of emotions, as from the morphine. The skyline was muddled with smoke and dust, but she could see the gap where the South Tower had stood an hour ago... and had ever since she was a child.

And then, there was the North Tower, still ablaze... standing *alone*. Somewhere in that building was the love of her life, and she loved Cecilia more than she had ever loved *anyone*. And right now, that woman—Becca's hero—was inside, bravely doing her job, and having the proverbial balls to go up there knowing full well—

Becca saw the North Tower begin to collapse. She couldn't recall if she'd even screamed...

Everything went black.

XX

"Echoes"

"Well, it's about *time* you got here, Taylor!" Her partner was sitting in bed, eating a popsicle in silence, when the door to his room opened and Becca was wheeled into the hospital room. She tried to lift her head to glare at him, but when her sore neck shot pain down her spine, she settled for a sarcastic scoff.

"Please. You know I couldn't resist going on a solo job, so that I could make you *jealous* with my stories later."

"Tell me about it. Looks like you had yourself a day after all."

"I've had worse," she lied unconvincingly.

She glanced at her Pulsar watch, but it was no longer there; it had been removed as soon as she'd arrived at the hospital. The poor thing was scratched to hell; she'd have to get it restored at some point. *I owe Ken that much...*

Instead, Becca asked the nurse who was tending to her, "What time is it?"

"About twenty to four, madam." Becca stood from the wheelchair, groaning in tender pain as she did so.

"You know what, Jim? I lied. I don't think I've *ever* had a worse day."

"*Ha!* You and me both," he laughed as he rubbed his sore neck. "I gotta admit, the sponge bath was kinda nice."

"I wouldn't know; I only got my leg cleaned off."

She slapped her bed as she climbed into it. "I hope they can get something out of him," she said softly, looking at her bandaged hand.

Alset had broken her middle left knuckle, also known as a metacarpal break—she also suffered a hairline fracture on her right tibia *and* sprained her right ankle on top of that; her entire leg was in a walking boot—not to *mention* the possibility of infection from the lacerations on her shin and ankle.

For good measure, she'd also bruised several ribs, suffered a severe concussion from the crash with the Dodge, and she was suffering from whiplash (she was lucky he hadn't hit her neck directly with that dowel) *and* she'd hurt a disc in her back, as well.

The doctors told her that, with the walking boot, she could walk for short distances.

Joke's on you, doc, I just went down twenty floors on this bad boy.

"He got you pretty good, eh?" Jim was smirking at her.

Becca was incredulous. "You're one to talk, Serrano. *You're* the one who's gonna be in a wheelchair." She held her good hand up and used her injured left to count her fingers.

"Ruptured spleen, collapsed lung, and a little boo-boo on the leg. Dang, old man, is *that* what happens after you turn fifty?"

Jim rolled his head to glare at his partner, who was laughing and trying her hardest not to. "Well, if we're keepin' score, then I win," Jim said, tapping his cast with his hand.

His leg injury was *not* a 'little boo-boo', as Becca so eloquently put it. He had a spiral fracture of his left tibia, as well as bone spurs and a torn ACL in his left knee... not to mention, a *nasty* concussion of his own.

The leg break itself was nasty; it was one of the worst spiral fractures they'd ever seen. They'd operated on it earlier, and the prognosis was favorable, but he was going to be on crutches for a while. He'd also ruptured his spleen and damaged a kidney; fortunately, neither injury was life-threatening.

The two friends chatted for a long while. Becca was just glad to see him alive. She reflected on Jim's significant role in capturing Alset, but he didn't witness the events at Ground Zero (a term all the news channels were now calling the site). Jim had been watching CNN on the tiny hospital TV, though it was now muted; they were showing video of the alleged terrorists, and Becca read the captions:

> *SOURCES SAY THERE ARE GOOD INDICATIONS OSAMA BIN LADEN WAS INVOLVED IN THE ATTACKS*

"I didn't know you were actually *in* the building, Taylor, until you were already out. If I had known, I'd have been down there myself."

Becca imagined Mike carrying Jim down the stairs in a wheelchair, and she shuddered. "No... you did your part." Becca smiled at her partner (who was on his own concoction of drugs and painkillers) and gave him an empathetic nod.

"But I know you'd be there with me if you could've."

"This whole day is a blur for me, too, Taylor, but I was pretty fucked up... Bill told me after my surgery that you had been chasin' that... what's his face... *Al-set*, was it?"

"Al-*seat*," Becca corrected.

"Sorry, *Alset*, that fuckin' guy... Bill didn't tell me you'd gone *in*. That took some balls, Rebecca. Chasin' that guy down from the top of that thing, even *after* the plane had hit... I'm *impressed*."

Jim's compliment went right over her head. That was something Becca suspected hadn't settled in for her yet. She could have stayed on the upper floors a while longer—even ten minutes would've been long enough—and she would've been trapped as well.

If I hadn't chased Q down those stairs, I would've died... *another bullet point for Dr. Mitzel.*

But Q wasn't on her mind right now. Well, not nearly as much as her girlfriend.

Becca was worried sick about Cecilia, and they still hadn't heard a word.

She had tried in vain to reach CeCe ever since they'd arrived, but when they got to the hospital, Bill had ordered her to stay, to relax, and receive treatment. Becca was *exhausted,* in too much pain to argue. So she stayed.

The drugs they were both on made their agony seem *trivial,* and she was *amazed* at how strong she felt. They were *thrilled* to be roommates; it also worked out in their favor, allowing them to debrief one another.

Sighing, she opened her duffel bag. Bill had gone to her house to check on Chad, picking up a day bag for her while he was there. Inside were all her necessities: the most prevalent was a fresh outfit... although Bill's selection wasn't the most appropriate attire for an FBI Agent: her old, faded *Star Trek: The Next Generation* T-Shirt, and some cotton pants. Also in the bag were her personal toiletries, and a few items she *hadn't* requested— including her old pager.

"I'm *not* using a beeper in 2001, Bill," Becca had stated matter-of-factly. "Can you get me a new phone?" He said he'd take care of it. Still, she was very grateful for Bill, who once again showed his true colors.

He was not simply her boss; he was a true *friend*.

"Look," Jim continued. "I know you were hard on yourself for what happened on January 1st. But I want you to know something. That day, when I was lyin' in the snow, and you helped me, well... I didn't know how *bad* I was hurt, ya know? I was afraid."

Her jaw hit the floor. *"You?* Afraid?"

Jim had never admitted being afraid of *anything;* she teased him all the time about things that she *knew* he was fearful of—dogs, for instance. Jim refused to come over for dinner, all because of their 'vicious' four-month-old black lab. So she would always tease him about it in good faith, but deep down, she admired that aspect of his personality, because she knew how brave Jim *truly* was.

"I was, yeah. I thought I was gonna die."

Jim's confessional brought Becca out of her stupor as he shifted on his bed, his mangled leg hanging high in a sling above him.

"Even though Jeremey ended up... *you* know... havin' you *there* with me made me feel safe."

Becca's eyes welled with salty tears. She hated crying more than anything—*especially* in front of Jim. Even though the situation warranted it, she fought the tears back as hard as she could, opting instead to sip some of her water.

In the past, Becca was more apt to complain about her fears than try to address them. Her decisions on January 1st were wrong, even if they were made in good faith.

But *she* didn't cut Jeremey Young's throat (or shoot Shahla Sanderson, for that matter). And he was armed with a pistol, regardless... who *knows* how that night might've gone down?

I admit it: I was afraid, too.

She knew the risks, but she was still human. And seeing her oak of a partner bleeding in the snow brought terror to the forefront of duty, because she *was* afraid. Becca might've just as easily ended up in a body bag alongside them...

Today, I beat that fear. I can no longer use that as an excuse, because that beast has been slain.

"Jim, today was the most terrifying experience of my entire life. I was there in the *thick* of it, man. When he ran into the World Trade. I was *sure* he'd gonna get away, ya know... with all the subway stations down there..." She swallowed a lump and sniffed hard, steadying her voice.

"When he got in that elevator, every fiber in my being told me to go after him. But I couldn't get ahold of Bill because my cell had no signal. So I asked myself, 'What would Jim do?'"

"Oh, *really?*" Jim straightened up in bed, a smug grin on his weathered face. "And, may I ask, what pearls of *wisdom* did my handsome counterpart bestow upon you?"

She looked down at the cup of water in her hands as she spoke. "I acted on instincts. I asked security to call the PD and set a perimeter, and I went up that building."

"I'm proud of you, Becca."

"Like I said, I just thought about what you would do—"

"Don't give me that shit," he grumbled. "That was all *you*, Taylor. *You* did that." He gave her a subtle salute, causing her to blush slightly. "You did good, agent."

"Thanks, Jim."

She fought the urge to cry off again, wiping her nose with the sleeve of her hospital gown as she continued to stare at her water cup mindlessly.

"So after the perimeter was set, I followed Alset up the building."

"Jesus," he muttered softly. "Was it already on fire?"

"No."

"You didn't actually *see* it, did you?"

She didn't move her eyes, and Jim could see the trauma in her expressionless face; Becca only saw the red headband falling.

"I saw the *whole* thing, man." She sipped her water again, and the cool moisture was welcomed by her dry, cracked lips. "It's a long story."

"Well... I got time." Jim rolled over (as much as he could with his leg in a sling) and propped his head up on his hand. "If you wanna tell the story, I'm all ears."

"Oh!" Her outward cry startled Jim. "Thank you for telling Bill about his gold tooth."

Jim laughed bashfully; he'd forgotten about that entirely. "I figured it might help, since he was wearin' a mask."

"It did. *Big* time." She recalled the day's events to her partner —the chase, the ride up the tower... and when she met Quarren. When she got to the 91st Floor... her expression went blank.

"I saw the plane... heard its engines, and Jim... *they were wide-open,* full throttle. They rammed that fucking plane *right* into the building—*just* above us, maybe a couple floors. And there was a guy there, his name was, uh... Tim, if I remember... but anyways, he was just *crushed* by part of the ceiling; a beam nearly took his *head* off."

She swallowed hard. "I got lucky, I got knocked away by the blast before the ceiling collapsed."

Becca continued the tale for her injured partner, describing their struggle in great detail. How Q saved her life, and how they'd gone down together. When she reached the part about Alset and how they'd stumbled upon Donny's group, Jim's face twisted like he had a bad case of gas.

"I'm sorry, Taylor. If I had been there with you, you would've had the bastard right there."

"Perhaps," she shifted on the bed. She continued, telling Jim about Alset leading them away and taking Moira, and how Alset tried to kill her in the conference room.

She looked at Jim with compassion and trust. "I was alone, Jim. I was terrified."

"Jesus, that does sound bad, Taylor. How'd you escape?"

"Well, Q put the fire out and saved me, but before he did... I was trapped, and alone... I thought I was going to die. I really did. And he saved my life."

Jim must be as ashamed of my weakness as I am.

In fact, Jim had never been this proud of his partner in his life. He was incredibly enthralled with her tale. "When do you get the guy in cuffs?"

As Becca continued to fill Jim in on what had taken place, she realized that talking it out, recanting the tale in vivid details not seven hours later, while it was so fresh in her mind that she still saw a red headband every time she closed her eyes... despite making her upset, it made her feel better.

It was like ripping off a band-aid; it only hurt on the surface. She sensed it as she spoke; it was almost like *therapy*.

Group therapy...

"Cecilia!"

Her body shot upright as she tried to get out of bed, but was too drugged up and worn out to get far; she flopped back to the mattress. Breathing hard, she shook her head and attempted to roll over, but her body seemed to be asleep, despite her adrenaline.

Becca finally managed to reach over, straining until she pinged the nurse call button. Her nurse reappeared quickly enough to impress them both.

"Could you do me a favor, and call the Fire Department house for Ladder Company 84, please? I need to know if Cecilia Chapman got out of the Trade Center before the North Tower collapsed."

The nurse nodded, jotting CeCe's name down on a small notepad, and she quickly scampered off, but not before dropping her pencil where it bounced off the linoleum floor with a wooden *clink*.

Her head fell into her hands. "God, Jim... what am I gonna *do* without her?"

"So how did that scrawny old guy do *that* to you?" Jim laughed at her intentionally, hoping to redirect her anger at *him* and distract her from her missing girlfriend. She didn't realize it, but Jim was slicker than he looked—he had a knack for reading her emotions.

"You can kick *my* ass, Taylor; there's no way that guy could beat you, right?"

She recalled the entire fight from her perspective, and at first, she *was* upset with Jim; as she recounted the fight, she found herself missing Q... *and of course, missing CeCe.* She told him all the crazy things he'd said to her... leaving out the threats to kill Jim once he finished her off.

There's no reason to tell him that, now.

"But lemme tell you, he had me. He *had* me, man." She smacked her right fist into her lap, punctuating each syllable. "Dead. To. *Rights.* You remember me tellin' you how I lost my gun in the collapse? Well, it was *Q* that picked it up... and *he* shot Alset. He saved my *life.* "

She growled at her injured hand, remembering what Alset had threatened to do to her...

I think I'll save that part of the story for Dr. Mitzel...

She felt that irritating sting again, her eyeballs singed from the acidic tears they were marinating in. "He... might've saved Marissa's, too, if you think about it."

Becca couldn't shake the feeling that she could get the information she wanted out of that man. She wanted to be at the Javits building; she *needed* to focus on finding Marissa.

"Where's Bill? Is he still here?"

Jim shook his head slowly. "He met with Kelly to interrogate Alset. They're at the Javits building now."

As he spoke, the nurse returned with news. "Miss Taylor, I

called the number you requested, but nobody answered... I tried three times, but..."

She seemed distraught. Becca's heart broke for her as she left the room.

There's no way I can lay here, worrying about CeCe and wondering if Alset's gonna talk... I'm gonna go crazy!

She was on the teetering point. Becca was a steel ball bearing on a tabletop, and on each end, a powerful magnet pulled at her in opposite directions. One magnet was the Javits building... if she could somehow get in to talk to Alset, she might resist the more powerful pull of the other. And she had to choose soon, because once she started rolling in either direction...

Becca sat up again, this time a bit slower, and gave herself a chance to right the ship before she attempted to stand. Her booted ankle would be the issue... but the FBI office was only a ten-block walk or so.

"Where are you *going*, Taylor?" Jim might not have little ones any longer, but his 'dad voice' was very much in working order. Becca put on her clean clothes and replaced her shoulder holster under her windbreaker. She next snatched a brand-new crutch off the foot of her bed and hobbled to Jim.

"I've got a job to do." She bent over his bed and planted a kiss on his forehead.

"Taylor, *wait!* If Bill finds out you—"

"I'll try to come back tonight to see you, but first... Alset and I are gonna have a chat." She gave him a wink as she limped out the door to their room.

"If you hear from CeCe, please tell her I'm worried."

*　　　　　*　　　　　*

Manhattan was eerily quiet as Becca left the hospital. The staff was busy with the crowded triage in the emergency room, so nobody stopped her. When she walked back outside, dozens of people, *all* from the Trade Center, were still waiting for processing.

The weather was still nice; it had warmed into the seventies, and a gentle breeze helped force the smoke clouds out over the river. The sun was now to the west, shining through the smoky film, and the result was that familiar amber hue that cast a desolate shadow over everything around her.

The combination of the surreal landscape with the levels of drugs in her system made her feel like the last survivor in some apocalyptic movie—she expected to turn and see Bruce Willis and Ben Affleck standing there in spacesuits.

She was testing her injured leg's walking boot, and truthfully, it wasn't as bad as she thought it would be to walk on it, but she was still glad she had brought a crutch, just in case.

As she limped along the dusty streets of the city, there wasn't a soul around the hospital, except for the occasional emergency vehicle. It was *deathly* quiet where she was, with only the wind whistling wistfully between the high rises of Lower Manhattan. She could hear sirens and heavy machinery just a few blocks away. Becca could only *imagine* the scene now—numerous images lingered in her mind, and as she traversed this eerie moonscape that sharply contrasted with the powder-blue sky above, Becca felt uncertain whether she'd cry or go *insane*.

Perhaps both.

The entire time she'd been in the tower, she'd been so focused on getting out that she hadn't allowed herself to succumb to emotions. Even in the most terrifying moments, she had to keep her wits about her; now that she'd finally escaped, her *guard* was down; the tiniest trigger might send her.

Because, although she *had* cried today, she stopped herself whenever she could; she *definitely* hated crying more than *anything...*

But when she turned towards the west, she couldn't ignore it. There was a gap in the skyline now. Those ever-present sentinels of the city, loyal watchmen looking over the Big Apple... they were the city's guardian angels. As Becca crossed Centre Street, she finally spoke.

"I can't believe they're gone."

And something peculiar happened to Becca, something she would never experience again in her entire life, because the situation that allowed for it could have only occurred on this very day, at this exact time:

I can't believe they're gone—they're gone—they're gone...

Her own voice was the first sound she'd heard since leaving. For the first time all day, Becca was alone. She'd been *surrounded* by people ever since she left Jim's side this morning, and being amongst folks all working together and trying to survive had *energized* her.

Despite the terror, everything felt so *alive*. Now, she was surrounded by emptiness and *death*.

Despair won the battle as her trauma finally defeated her.

Becca fell to her knees, and she cried. She wailed. Like a baby, but harder. Like a widow grieving her fallen husband, except with no chance of solace or justice. Rebecca had won the day, yet she had lost everything, and she didn't care about anything anymore... not now.

So she wept, silently, lonely and disparate, on her knees in the middle of Centre Street, and Becca was completely isolated. She was utterly alone in the middle of one of the busiest streets, in the busiest neighborhood, of the busiest city in the world.

And so Rebecca finally allowed herself to cry... even though crying was her *least* favorite thing in the world.

*   *   *

By the time Becca stumbled through the door to the Jacob K. Javits Federal Building, she was flirting with fainting. She *barely* had the strength to press the elevator button for the 23rd floor. Her first trip in an elevator since that morning triggered extreme claustrophobia, and she held her breath in a desperate attempt to stave off panic.

When the doors opened, she stumbled into her office, gasping for air... and was *stunned* at what occurred when she walked into her workplace.

The office fell still. Approximately twenty people were working in the office, and everyone stopped what they were doing, staring at her in stunned disbelief. That was unusual; this was the busiest time of the day, and this was a skeleton crew at *best*. And now, they were staring at *her*.

She was anxious; were they judging her? *Do they know something I don't?*

Her aide, Jennifer, was still hard at work when Becca arrived, and she rushed to her, wrapping her in a hug. All around the office, people started to cheer for Becca, who was unprepared for any reception, let alone *this* one.

The scattered clapping became thunderous applause, and Becca blushed as it washed over her. She acknowledged her coworkers before limping across the floor to Bill's office. She was disappointed the office was dark, so she hobbled back to her aide's desk. By the time she returned, everyone had gone back to work.

"This place is a ghost town. What happened?"

Jennifer's mascara, usually *expertly* applied, had streaked down her face. Although they weren't exactly *friends,* she had a strong relationship with Becca and *many* of their co-workers. A lot of whom were not in the office...

"Well, like—there's a few people missing from our office, and you were *one* of them, and the towers fell, so we thought..." a hiccup interrupted her ramble, "and then Bill showed up with the good news, so we're all *super* excited to see you."

She looked away from Becca, sobbing into her hands; Becca rubbed her back before turning back towards her own cubicle. She shot an annoyed glance towards the abandoned director's office as she sat in her familiar chair. It felt foreign to her now; she almost *flinched* out of shock.

The angelic reflection she'd noticed yesterday again graced the framed photograph on her desk, and CeCe once more filled her thoughts before her gaze settled on the desk clock:

9 11 2001 TUE
5:32 PM

It was late. *They must be in interrogation by now?* The usual sounds and ambiance were absent as she sat quietly in the silent FBI office. She felt like she wasn't supposed to *be* there... back behind her desk, as she'd sat for countless months before today... She reclined in her familiar chair, a familiar pose to her when she was bored.

And bored, she *was*—as *soon* as she'd recovered her strength from her hike, she was going to find Bill and Kelly. But that familiar lump in her throat was returning; she was preparing herself for the undressing she was likely to receive when her boss saw her.

The lump was joined by another familiar sensation—a rumble in her tummy. The stack of file folders was still sitting on her crushed Ruffles from yesterday. Likely *stale* by now. In the hospital, she'd had some chicken noodle soup and some Jell-O, but she'd likely expended *thousands* of calories this morning. She needed *real* food... the sooner, the *better!*

However, *that* would have to wait. She put her hands behind her neck, leaning back—

And *that* was the first time she smelled her own body odor. Sure, her *feet* had stunk... but that was to be expected after *hours* of running, of dust and sweat, blood and urine, and... *whatever* that liquid in the stairwells had been. Only now did she realize... the smell was on *her,* in her hair, under her fingernails. Even her *skin* smelled like smoke and dankness. *Face it, girl—you stink!*

The nurses had cleaned her wounds, but her other parts were not as... attended to. Becca *needed* a shower—just another item on her growing to-do list.

Standing up with a *groan,* she limped towards the locker room to freshen up... when a familiar voice bellowed out over the office's ambiance, which had resumed its normal volume and activity. When she spun around, Bill was stepping out of the elevator. Kelly followed closely behind, a cup of coffee in her hand.

"Rebecca?" He was dumbfounded at the sight of her. "What the hell are you *doing* here? You should be in *bed!*"

"Nice outfit, Becca," Kelly smirked between sips, "Agent Picard would be *proud.*"

"Yeah, don't sue me; sue my *tailor,*" she replied, rolling her eyes at her boss. "I couldn't just lie there, Bill. I *needed* to know."

"Well, we're not getting anything out of him tonight," Bill admitted. "Doctor's orders. He's resting all night." He shook his head disgustingly... before smirking *mischievously.* "So, we paid him a visit *anyway.* But it's useless; he's on too many drugs. When he *does* talk, it's all gibberish and psychobabble."

Becca loudly rolled her eyes. "Tell me about it."

"Agent Willis is on loan to us. She's been working the case for her office, so she'll be with you once you're back to work, Taylor."

She nodded, smiling at her boss. "I copy that. I'm reporting to work, sir."

"*The hell you are!* You're *not* cleared, you *aren't* working. Willis, take her home."

"But—" Becca objected.

"No buts," Bill interrupted her objection, and Becca rolled her eyes at him.

"Sir, my car is here. Remember?"

Bill groaned in frustration. "Yeah, you're right... okay. Fine. You get in your car and go *straight* home." He waved to Jennifer, flagging her attention. "Are the bridges and tunnels still closed?"

"Yeah, Mr. Bushnall. The island is still on lockdown, unless we get permission from the PA."

At that moment, realization hit Bill like a brick.

"Wait a second—you're on meds right now, *and* you're hurt... and you want to *drive*? I can't believe you're even *walking* right now! Kelly, I want you to take her home. She can get her car tomorrow."

"Sir!" she objected. "I *can't* go home, sir."

"*That's an order!*"

Becca snapped. She grabbed his collar, bringing his face close to hers; she could smell his cinnamon chewing gum.

"You don't understand, Bill. My girlfriend is *missing!* She's probably *dying* right now, in that pile of rubble over there. And you want me to go *home?*"

Bill yanked her hands off his collar. "Rebecca, you have a son at home—"

"He's sixteen years old. He'll be *fine!*"

"Yeah, and he's probably *freaking* out because his family is missing and he has no way to get ahold of his mother!"

"I..."

She stopped, imagining Chad sitting at home right now, alone. She hadn't spoken to him since she was still in the tower.

Obviously, he *knew* his mother was alive; Bill had gone to her house while she was still in surgery. But still...

As usual, he's right... No matter what, I should at least call Chad and make sure he's okay.

"Bill... I sacrificed a *lot* today—nearly got myself killed. I didn't do it to prove myself to you. I did it to prove to myself that *I* could still do the job.

"But I still had to suffer through something that'll haunt me for the rest of my life, and I'm in an *insane* amount of pain. But I made it. I did it. I *finally* got my man." Becca shook her head incredulously. She got right in her boss's face once again.

"And you expect me to rest, *now?*"

He didn't blink, returning her gaze. "You're goddamned *right,* I expect you to rest."

"I've never been so ready to work in my goddamned *life,* sir!"

Without responding, Bill stepped away from her, turning his back to Becca as he walked towards Kelly, who was sipping coffee and watching the two of them argue. After a moment, Bill spun back towards her with a smile, and softly patted her shoulder.

"Rebecca, go home. I'll see you in the *morning,* okay?"

Becca's face lit up; this was a win in her book.

"You go home tonight and wait to hear from CeCe. Go take care of your boy, Becca."

Kelly stepped forward, putting a hand atop Bill's shoulder. "We'll get started early, tomorrow... okay?"

She knew she was not going to get her way tonight. "Fine. Where are you gonna book him?"

"We're just gonna hold him here tonight," Bill stated matter-of-factly. "With everything going on at the Trade Center, I don't feel like dealing with the logistics of it all."

He pointed at a large stainless steel Thermos sitting on an aide's desk. "I'm gonna stay the night here. We've got most of the

Field Office at the Trade Center, helping with the investigation and rescue efforts, so I'm already going crazy trying to balance everything."

Becca nodded compassionately. "I totally get it." She patted Kelly's hand, and she stopped as they turned to walk away. "Call me if that son of a bitch says anything that we can use."

"We've got him held as a 5150, just in case," Bill noted. "Alset will be supervised all night."

"He wasn't *acting* suicidal in the tower, but after I had him in cuffs, he was very..." She furrowed a brow. "Bill, if he says anything —"

"If he even breathes the name 'Marissa Hernandez,' I'll call you," he promised.

"I swear, if you don't—"

"Taylor! I said I'd fuckin' call you, alright? Now go home. *Now!*"

"I'll be right back, Kelly." They were stunned when she suddenly pushed them both aside, hobbling quickly into the break room. An exaggerated moan that almost sounded painful came growling from the area. They both heard her complaint from the main office.

"Becca?" Kelly was worried; Becca sounded like she was in a lot of pain as Kelly sprinted around the corner after her. Upon seeing her, Kelly *gasped*. Becca's face was redder than a ripened apple.

"What *is* it? What's the matter?"

"Somebody ate my fuckin' bagel!"

XXI

"An Old Can of Miller Lite"

"I'll take three—*three*, right? *Four?* Okay, four—yeah, I'll take *four* number three value meals, Super Sized, all four with cokes. And four apple pies."

Kelly winked at Becca. She was determined to get her pie, *regardless* of whether anyone else wanted one. When her passenger reached for her wallet, she playfully slapped her wrist. Nobody answered the phone when Becca called from work, but Kelly insisted on getting enough food for the whole family, just in case.

"I don't know if I'll be able to eat all that food, Kelly," Becca warned. "I'm on some pretty heavy-duty shit right now."

Kelly waved a hand at her friend, "Ah, so what, if you don't eat it, save it, toss it. Give it to your little doggy—what's his name, Pepper? Yeah, Pepper."

"Kelly?"

"Yeah, love?"

"Your Bronx is showing, love."

Kelly *huffed* at her remark. Becca always loved to tease Kelly for her accent, which was now *exceptionally* thick. Kelly was originally from San Diego; she only moved to the area after graduating from Quantico and quickly adapted.

Her accent's thicker than mine, now... and I've lived here since the second grade!

The plush leather of Kelly's car massaged Becca's sore muscles as she sank into it. Her Mercedes E 320 was an extravagant ride for an FBI Agent. It was more expensive than Becca could *ever* afford, but Kelly was still a single woman, without any kids to support—just herself and her two cats.

To each their own, I suppose...

The nostalgia-fueled fumes of freshly-fried McDonald's French fries filled the front of the Mercedes as the cashier handed them their bags. Becca was *ravenous* at this point; she instantly began drooling at that greasy, savory scent of fresh Mickey D's fries—she didn't stand a *chance*.

Kelly burst into laughter as Becca grabbed a handful before comically shoving them into her gaping maw. They hung halfway out, dangling like a little potato cigar.

"Uhm! Hmhm hmph!" Becca mumbled with her mouth full. By now, Kelly was cracking up as the fries inevitably tumbled all over Becca's lap.

"Too hot! I burned my tongue!"

They both laughed together. For the first time since yesterday, Becca smiled again as Kelly pulled back onto the roads of her deserted Belleville neighborhood. She'd expected more people to be out-and-about as usual, but couldn't *blame* anyone for wanting to be home with their families. Now that *they* were just a few blocks away from Becca's house, her *own* heart was bubbling with anticipation.

God, I hope they're home...

Even though no one was home when she called, she still expected Chad to be there. A voice in the back of her mind was telling her he was home *alone*, and *that* was making her anxious. She'd left them both a message, and it had been difficult for Becca not to break down and cry on the phone; ever since she'd cried after the hospital, she'd become an emotional mess... and understandably so.

I'm still struggling hard to process this entire thing, myself.

Becca's window was down. The gentle breeze felt amazing in

her freshly washed hair. As soon as Bill had dismissed them, they took a moment to hit the locker room. Becca couldn't believe how much cleaner she felt after getting all that rubble and concrete out of her scalp—even as it was a pain in the ass to shower with a bandaged hand and booted leg.

I had to ask Kelly to help soap me up! It feels so nice to laugh, though. After such a long, terrible day... I can't believe the sun hasn't set yet. Becca glanced at her watch; the time was 6:57.

"You wanna know what's *really* creepy? There's no service vehicles, like ambulances, or police cars... you'd think you'd at least see a *cruiser* on patrol, right, but no—not even a fire truck!"

"Yeah..." Becca mumbled, amused by her friend's clairvoyance, yet too exhausted to respond.

"It's so *lovely* tonight. Supposed to be pretty nice tomorrow, too. I can pick you up for work in the morning if you want—ya know, since your car's still downtown."

Becca nodded with an absent-minded "Uh-huh."

"We could take the train downtown, if you'd rather do that?"

"Uh-huh."

She was staring out quietly, the fast food bags steaming away on her lap.

"Penny for your thoughts?" Kelly offered with a friendly smile.

Becca had since tuned her out. She flailed her hand blindly across Becca's lap, mistakenly feeling past her crotch—this earned an *"Eek!"* from Becca—as her fingers fondled until they found the bag with the fries inside. She snagged a bigger handful before shoving them in her mouth as Becca had earlier.

"You *jerk!*"

She slugged Kelly in the arm playfully as they chuckled together, feigning embarrassment at her friend's goofy antics. After the laughter passed, Becca snagged and ate a stray fry that had fallen on her own lap.

"Oh, I know, it's just... I always tend to change my mind, or get distracted by little shit. Today, if I had done anything different, or doubted myself, like I had on January 1st... if a *single* event had gone differently, I might've died today. It's still sinking in."

Kelly smiled sincerely. "I second-guess myself all the time, love. It's part of the *game;* you gotta make tough choices. Sometimes, you don't have *time* to think, you just have to act."

"But I *never* did," Becca offered. "I *never* second-guessed myself after the first plane hit. I made up my mind, and I went for it."

Becca had a determination in her expression that Kelly found incredibly inspiring.

"I had a job to do."

As they approached Becca's house, two strange cars were parked in her driveway. She glanced around nervously as she limped up her driveway, Kelly following closely behind.

"You wanna come in and eat with us?" Becca offered.

"I thought you'd *never* ask."

The door swung open to reveal a small group gathered around the TV in the living room. As the pair of agents entered the house, they turned, *stunned* to see who was standing in the doorway. For her part, Becca was equally as shocked.

"Um... hi, everyone?"

Cheers erupted as they quickly rushed the two ladies—even Pepper bounded happily to the front door to greet them, his little puppy tail going bananas from excitement. Becca recognized everyone in her home: Cecilia's parents, Florence and Norman, were the first to hug her, followed closely by CeCe's brother Steven.

She was touched that anyone came at *all;* Becca's family was back in Minnesota, and most of her friends were in law enforcement. Although CeCe's family was there in support of their daughter, they were still very relieved when Becca came home. They all loved Becca as if *she* were family, anyway.

Besides, I'll likely have a million messages on the answering machine to listen to.

"I'm sorry, I didn't bring enough food for everyone!" she exclaimed, earning a burst of laughter from the guests. Cries of "Oh my God!" and "I'm so happy you're alright!" came pouring in as she gingerly limped through the crowd, setting the lukewarm food on the table (where it would remain untouched until it was downright *frigid*) as she pushed her way to the bathroom.

I love them all, but they've gotta wait...

When she returned, wiping her hands dry on her faded *Star Trek* T-shirt, she realized someone was missing.

"Chad?" Becca's throat twisted like a pretzel. "Son, are you home?"

Something was wrong; this wasn't *like* him. She'd *expected* him to be front and center, but he wasn't with her family. Becca turned back to her guests. "I tried to call a few times, but only got the answering machine..."

"We heard your message," Florence told her. "I'm pretty sure Chad knows you were safe. Have you heard anything from Cecilia yet, Rebecca?"

"I'm sorry, Flo." She shook her head. "Please excuse me; I need to go upstairs for a sec."

A lump stuck in her throat. "Chad?"

She screamed as she limped up the stairs, using the handrail as a crutch. *"Chad!"*

Her son's bedroom door was cracked. Sounds of a rock band screaming about being 'one step closer to the edge' bled into the hall—not Becca's taste in music. She nudged it open to reveal a pair of teenage boys playing *Tony Hawk's Pro Skater* on Chad's

PlayStation, the music so loud he wouldn't hear a *rocket* launch.

As soon as Becca entered his room, her teenage son dropped the controller and sprinted towards his mother.

"Mom? *Mom!*"

Not realizing her tender condition, he barreled into her, earning a loud *"Ouch!"* from Becca.

"Sorry," he laughed as he now gingerly hugged her, losing his grip as she held him. He didn't care that his younger cousin was in the room with him; he bawled into his mother's bosom as Becca gently stroked his hair.

"Oh *God,* Mom! I'm so glad you're home."

He cried harder than Becca had heard in *years...* but the following line *broke* her.

"Mommy, don't leave me again!"

She melted into her son, cradling her teenager as they cried together. When they finally pulled apart, her hair was matted entirely into his face, stuck to his tear-streaked cheeks. They shared a joyful laugh as Becca affectionately kissed her son on the cheek.

"I'm here, son. I missed you, too."

"Aunt Becca!" Fuller screamed, running over to join the bear hug (even as they both forgot he was there). Chad's younger cousin was less aware of his surroundings; he had been playing around with Chad's Power Glove (an old controller for the regular Nintendo), and the glove's cord was swinging wildly as he scurried over, nearly whipping Chad in the face.

"Why don't you two come downstairs? The whole family is here, and—"

"Have you heard from CeCe, Mom?"

Chad's voice cracked, so he loudly cleared his throat. His trembling body betrayed his emotions, foiling his attempts at trying not to look like a wimp again in front of his younger cousin.

Becca subtly shook her head before kissing him on his scalp, cradling him as he silently cried into her shirt. Her own eyes leaked silent tears she allowed, despite her disdain for them.

I am so glad to be home.

This was the first time since she'd left for work this morning that she felt relatively safe. Even in her melancholy state, she was happy to be alive.

Becca was home.

*   *   *

The rest of the evening of September 11, 2001, was a blur of love and support for Rebecca Taylor and her little family. Everyone stayed late, relaxing and reminiscing, and Becca was thrilled to have people there to keep her mind off of CeCe... who didn't come home that night.

They'd stayed up pretty late, and most of the TV programs Becca typically liked to watch were canceled. Every station was showing live pictures of Ground Zero or talking about the terrorist attacks. There was some discourse about the Taliban and replays of President Bush's Address to the Nation.

Becca was already sick of it all.

Instead, they turned the TV off and existed in the moment, loving each other and reminiscing about last Thanksgiving, when Uncle Steven had attempted to fry a turkey and accidentally started a fire.

"I was so *wasted,* that *Becca* had to put the damned thing out *for* me!" CeCe had exclaimed—that was the hot ticket joke around the holidays last year.

The stories poured in as they talked, and for Becca, it was more than comforting—this was chicken soup for her soul.

She found herself thankful that Bill had sent her home. She had thought earlier that the only escape from the images replaying in her head was to keep working, which might've worked... the problem was that damned movie replayed through Becca's mind *every* time it was silent.

Because Becca didn't need to watch the news to relive today, she could shut her eyes and receive her *own* exclusive scoop. And every single time she did, the events of the day played back in an endless loop:

The Dodge swerving into the tree, Jimbo spilling out on his leg.

Waiting for the elevator, thinking Marissa was good as dead.

Or her hubris when she caught Q, thinking she'd got her man.

BANG!

Odors of jet fuel, and the intense heat in the dry, dusty air.

Fluttering red headbands trailing after innocent victims.

BANG!

The smoky office, and feeling as if she was about to die.

Her short-lived jubilation at her reunion with CeCe...

Even Alset's terrifying golden tooth sparkling sinisterly.

Marissa, somewhere terrified, alone... likely starving to death.

BANG!

This was *torture*. Becca thought she was going to lose her mind. A never-ending horror film, but entirely based on real life, playing on repeat in glorious IMAX. She had no idea how she would sleep tonight, but she knew she had to try; the last person to leave was Kelly, who had gone home around 10 p.m. She'd promised she'd be by early to pick her up.

"How early?" Becca had asked, and Kelly laughed.

"Why don't *you* just call me when you're up and at 'em?"

After they'd left for the evening, with many promises to call one another if *anyone* heard from CeCe, she'd retired to her bedroom to try and rest. As Becca began undressing for bed, her battered, naked body stared pathetically back at her in the mirror.

Holy shit! Her mouth fell agape.

Becca froze. She was appalled; this was the first time she'd examined herself in a mirror. She was shocked by her condition; aside from the soft cast around her ankle and the large gauze bandage taped to her forehead, her body was covered in bruises, cuts, and scrapes. A particularly *nasty* bruise wrapped from under her left breast, all the way around to her back, where she couldn't see it anymore. She touched her armpit and *yelped* at how tender it was. Her entire body appeared to have been dragged foot-first by lasso behind some bandit's stallion.

This prompted a new scene in her mental movie marathon to make its mark.

It was Monday night, they were having a nice meal as a family, and then there was love, and it had all seemed so... perfect. Her lover was there, safe and sound, and life had felt... *simpler*. It had stood out to her in the moment—she was grateful to have appreciated it as much as she had. A simple meal with her family, which might've been taken for granted at the time... now felt like a bygone era she would *never* experience again.

And even being surrounded by friends and family tonight didn't change the fact that everybody was on edge. The sheer amount of rumors and speculation that trickled into their conversations betrayed the brave front they all plastered on their faces—everybody was *terrified*.

Something changed today. Not only with Becca herself... *everyone* was acting differently, now.

Now, reflecting on it alone, the slightest trigger might set her off. Finally tired of her battered body, she threw on CeCe's New York Jets extra-large T-shirt and turned to empty her day bag. As she removed her effects (the only clothing she kept was her belt and watch), she placed the crumpled business cards she'd collected during her ordeal on their dresser.

An object's reflection in the mirror caught her eye. Becca glanced back towards CeCe's nightstand... and sitting there was an old can of Miller Lite.

"Oh. Fuck..."

Her trauma was still vibrantly fresh in her mind; it was the only push she needed to fall off the edge.

Becca couldn't resist; she shuffled around the bed and took the warm can from where Cecilia had placed it last night. She looked into it; it was long since past its prime, flat and smelly. A smudge of lip gloss remained on the lip where she'd sipped it, and it reminded her of their last night together, and *oh God, what if she's trapped and—*

Becca broke down, crying once again. Perhaps not as intensely as she had earlier in Manhattan... But this was going to be a long night.

Although her tears were silent, Becca had forgotten to close her bedroom door. As she lay there in the fetal position, crying like a little child, releasing more pent-up emotions she'd bottled so feverishly in the tower... her teenage son and her puppy both wandered into the bedroom.

It didn't take long for them to all end up in a big bundle on the bed, cuddling each other.

It felt right to Becca; they could protect each other if they stuck *together*. She hadn't slept with her son since the night her husband had been killed, back in 1994; he was ten years old at the time. He had taken his father's death *way* harder than Becca, and that evening, he cried and cried, wailing like an infant. She had carried him into her bed, and they held each other and watched Nickelodeon all day, eating snacks in their pajamas.

This night, her son was able to repay the favor. Becca was *finally* able to calm down and get *some* sleep. This was the medicine the doctor should've ordered (Doctor Bill had tried his damnedest, for what it's worth), and tonight, her teenage son was ten again, and they were together, they were family... and they were going to get through this.

So long as my phone doesn't wake me up at four in the morning, again.

At two in the morning, the phone rang.

XXII

"That's the Trouble With Trauma"

The darkness blinded Rebecca as her bedside telephone's irritating ring brought her right back to reality. Her entire body screamed in agony as she rolled over, the bumps and bruises she'd accumulated yesterday waking up alongside her. Her exasperated moan woke Pepper as she blindly reached for the phone. However, she didn't get a chance to *speak* before someone spoke on the other end.

"Rebecca Taylor?" The voice on the other line was demanding. *Feminine yet monotone... perhaps even elderly?* Becca attempted to rub sleep from her eyes, to no avail.

"Hello? CeCe?" She glanced at her alarm clock; it was 2:01 AM.

"You have twenty-four hours to release Alset Aholé. We want one million dollars in unmarked bills and a helicopter. And if anyone follows us, the kid is dead. If you understand this, say yes."

Rebecca blinked stupidly. "I don't... who *is* this?"

"I'll give you one more chance. You have twenty-four hours to release Alset Aholé. We want a fully-fueled helicopter. We also require one million dollars, all unmarked bills. If you understand your instructions, say yes now."

"Yes. On one condition." Becca was quickly surfacing from sleep. Her face turned red with anger.

"You're not in a position to negotiate, Miss Taylor."

"If you touch that girl, so help me..." Becca's adrenaline fueled her body as she shot to attention, sitting up in bed with a jolt.

"I swear to God, if you hurt her, I'll hunt you to the ends of the fucking Earth. Say yes if you understand *that,* you demented bitch!"

The other line was silent, and this absolutely *sent* Becca.

"Say yes!"

She screamed at the top of her lungs, her voice scratchy from yesterday. Pepper flinched, recoiling into a tight ball under Chad's arms, who was also awake now, watching this unfold.

"You have twenty-four hours. Leave the helicopter on the Boardwalk in front of the old Asbury Park Casino."

"You're such an asshole, you know that? You think the FBI is going to simply *release* him after what he's done?" Becca wasn't kidding. She couldn't *wait* to hear Bill's reaction to this news; he was gonna have *kittens.*

"Well, Miss Taylor, that's *not* my problem. Do it, or the girl's dead by three. We will *not* be contacting you again. And if we think we're being followed, the deal is *off.*"

"Who *are* you?" Becca's voice dripped with fury. *"How* can we trust you? How can we let you know when it's ready?"

The other line clicked dead. She hung the phone up slowly, reaching up to click on her bedside lamp, before grabbing a notepad from her nightstand. Muscles in her body that she didn't even know *existed* seemed to hurt... she felt like she'd been hit by a *bus.*

Is a collapsing building close enough? Well, at least I didn't have another nightmare, again... must've been too tired.

"Mom?" Chad mumbled in the sudden onslaught of light, rolling over from CeCe's side of the bed. "What is it?"

"Give me a second—"

Becca scribbled everything down immediately. The numerous thoughts crowded her every lane of thought; her still-awakening mind had crashed into a traffic jam, which would remain bumper-to-bumper for a few moments longer.

"I have to go to work, son."

She turned towards him, a Mona Lisa smile crossing her lips, as he sat giving the puppy a belly rub. Becca stretched across the bed to kiss her son's forehead, and then stood, yawning a big yawn as she stretched a big stretch... or rather, *moaned* in agony as every joint in her body felt like it was filled with fiberglass.

Big smile, Rebecca. Don't let him see your pain. "Is your school open today?"

"I think so," he groaned, rolling back over to CeCe's side of the bed. "I might just stay home, though."

Becca's brow furrowed; he was a relatively popular straight-A student. He *loved* high school.

"Is it 'cause you're worried about CeCe?"

"Well, kinda, but also, um... ya know, just in case CeCe shows up and you're gone, *yeah!* I can fill her in."

The dog came up to Becca and licked her face, saying hello in Pepper's own little doggy way. She stroked his neck and smiled at her son reassuringly.

"If you want to go, then go, but you have my permission to stay home. You can even invite some of your friends over if *they* stay home."

"Welp, in that case, I'll see you when you get home, Mom."

Chad rolled back over and buried himself in pillows, earning a laugh as Becca peeled his pillow fort open like a banana, planting a kiss on his forehead and ruffling his bird's nest of a hairdo.

"I don't have my phone. If you need me, you can call Kelly. Her cell phone number is in the kitchen phone book." She snagged her wallet from the dresser. "Here's twenty bucks, you can order a pizza. Just... do me a favor—if anyone calls, don't answer unless it's me or CeCe."

"Sure, Momma..."

Her son was already falling back asleep as Becca stood,

proceeding to dress herself in a fresh suit, limping silently around the bedroom, and trying not to disturb them. Sneaking into the kitchen didn't work for Pepper, as the family dog followed her out of the bedroom, hoping for a midnight snack to find its way to the floor accidentally.

Well, here we go again, I suppose...

Becca called Kelly first, asking her to come pick her up, only telling her the important stuff for now. Her priority was getting to Alset, and squeezing him for *any* tidbit of information she might wring out of him. Her head pounded as she slammed an oxycodone down with instant black coffee (along with a few antibiotics she'd been prescribed).

Fortunately, Kelly lived a mile away from Becca's place, so she'd be there soon.

Immediately after speaking with Kelly, she phoned Bill and filled him in on what the strange woman's demands were. Surprisingly, he wasn't as angry as she'd expected.

"Oh, c'mon, Becca, that's *bullshit!* You *know* we can't do that."

She was limping back and forth in the kitchen, speaking into their cordless phone. She wasn't sure what Bill was more angry about: the idea that he'd have to let Alset go, or the fact that he would have to risk a chopper *and* a million bucks.

Maybe it's the fact the poor bastard is still at the office, from the sound of it.

"Oh, I know, Bill. I'm just saying, if we have to, we can make it *look* like we're cooperating."

"I said *no*, Rebecca!"

He'll come around.

An uncomfortably long silence followed, and Becca had to break the ice.

"I called Kelly, she's on the way to pick me up. We're heading down to the office. Are you still there?"

"Yes," said her boss, and he sounded cranky. "I'll see you both when you get here."

She had one more phone call to make. The voice on the other line sounded even crankier than Bill's.

Well... this was important...

"Taylor? *Jesus,* do you know what time—?"

"There's two of them. Again."

Silence filled the air, and it was deafening.

"The second person, a woman, just woke me up with a ransom demand."

The only sound Becca heard was an elongated *sigh.* "Are you going to be discharged today?" Even more silence. Becca was afraid the line had disconnected before he finally replied.

"I'll be ready when you get here, Taylor. Come get me as soon as you can."

And the line clicked dead.

*   *   *

September 12, 2001, felt *especially* eerie in downtown Manhattan, particularly during those early hours. Everything was remarkably still. Many buildings remained dark, with abandoned and forgotten structures quietly lining the dim, lonely roads.

Aside from a few homeless individuals wandering about, there wasn't a soul in sight. If it weren't for the street lights and traffic signals, you'd be forgiven for thinking that Manhattan was a ghost town. In the distance, the bright lights around Ground Zero served as a grim reminder of yesterday.

It made her very uneasy, and she wanted to get to work immediately.

Jim was a man of his word, waiting outside the emergency

room doors—on crutches, no less. His cast was quite impressive, requiring the ladies' assistance in climbing into Kelly's Mercedes. As they made their way towards the Javits building, Becca filled them in on what the mysterious woman told her; she was grateful that she'd jotted everything down while it was still fresh in her mind.

Their reactions were about as she'd expected.

"Becca, if you wanted to piss Bill off, ya know, we could've just told him they wanted his *wife,* too."

Jim guffawed at that one. "What'cha talkin' bout, Willis— *Nina?* I think ol' Bill would be *happy* to oblige in that case."

Despite the profound aura hanging over their heads, the levity of their banter eased Becca's anxiety. Cruising around together and joking brought her back to her rookie days, where Jim would bust her chops about every little mistake she made; he *always* brought it back in a way that made her laugh at it, rather than dwell on it.

He's always been good at that. It's one of the reasons I love that man.

Kelly parked her car in the Worth Street garage, right next to Becca's Eclipse (which was entirely covered in dust). This time, they met Bill inside the office.

A skeleton crew was working, but the office was deader than when she'd left. As they walked in, the graveyard receptionist was fighting gravity with her eyelids. Becca giggled when the woman startled herself awake by the sight of the three of them scuttling in from the elevator.

"Agent Taylor?"

"Yes?" She raised an eyebrow.

"Director Bushnall asked me to give you this." She handed her a manila envelope; Becca opened it to find a brand new Nokia phone, complete with all her contacts.

"He went back down to the Trade Center to debrief our agents out there; he told me to say he'd be back within the hour."

"Okay, thank you. Can you tell him we'll be in Jim Serrano's office?" Becca glanced at her watch; the time was 3:05.

The agents settled in Jim's office, where the notes about the Mauler were still laid out from Monday. There weren't any new tips awaiting them in his inbox. Jim slowly lowered himself into his chair, his broken leg protruding from under his desk like a giant plaster sausage, as he instinctively grabbed his mug of coffee... from *Monday*.

"Jim, you *might* wanna refresh that," Becca warned, and he grumbled as he stopped in the nick of time. She helped herself to his file closet; she removed a familiar, dusty cardboard box she'd not touched in ages (yet she was quite acquainted with the files it contained). The peeling tape adorning the lid had the letters "Y2K" scrawled in faded Sharpie.

"Okay," Becca began, blowing the lid gently before she opened the box, "let's think about this for a second." She pulled a file from the Y2K box and set it on Jim's desk, labeled 'J. YOUNG'.

"The Y2Killer case is directly connected to the Manhattan Mauler case, simply due to the fact that our main suspect of the latter case has openly admitted to being the former. However, we don't have it on the record, so we still need a confession, right?"

"Not necessarily," Kelly answered, "we don't need it if we can tie him to both cases." She thumbed through the files Becca had pulled, catching up on the details of the case.

"The Y2K killer... three kidnappings, all children, all deceased. All of them had their throats cut." Becca didn't even *need* to look in the file to remember the dates; she had these permanently etched into her mind.

"Jeremey Young died on 1-1-2000; Zachary Kenner's body

was found on 6-14-99, and Kayla Spilka's on 3-30-99. All three victims were found in different vacant houses in Jersey. This, despite the fact that they were all taken from different boroughs in New York City."

Now wearing his hilariously-cheap drugstore cheaters, Jim was reviewing the files from their current case, yawning and groaning as he shifted in his chair. His coffee maker began to bubble with a fresh pot, making Becca drool again. *I've had a combined eight hours' sleep since Monday night. Give me that liquid gold!*

"Marissa Hernandez went missin' two days ago; Isabel Esquivel was taken on August 16. Both taken from Queens; both taken from a bus stop. Isabel was found dead seven days later, in a Manhattan apartment not far from where we engaged with Alset yesterday. Found deceased, due to exsanguination and asphyxia..."

Kelly brushed her fingers through her perfectly straight auburn hair, still fabulous despite the hour. Becca's jealousy reminded her to put hers in a ponytail as Kelly spoke.

"Maybe Marissa would've ended up at that apartment if we hadn't spoiled the party?"

Becca's brow furrowed. "Perhaps. All three victims of Y2K were found with their throats cut, and their bodies were found at the scene of the crime."

She shut out the grisly ending of Jeremey's demise that flashed through her head. It was a sinister movie, but a classic Becca was *all* too familiar with; however, now it competed for space in Becca's head with all of the bullcrap she'd seen yesterday.

She felt sorry for herself... and was wholly justified in doing so.

"However," Becca continued, unfazed, "wasn't Isabel murdered somewhere else, *not* in the apartment where she was discovered?"

"That could mean anything, Taylor," Jim growled. "It's prolly a coincidence."

"Yeah, yeah... two is a coincidence, and three's a pattern..." She agreed with a silent roll of her eyes. "It still doesn't explain the ransom demands; Alset never once made any demands for money with his *other* victims, so that doesn't fit *his* MO."

Kelly shrugged. "This could be a desperate try to get us to let Alset go... yeah? Maybe it's just a distraction. Or like... maybe our boy's got some connections and needs money to get out?"

"I'm not so sure. Alset doesn't seem like the type that cares much for money *or* connections." Becca leaned forward, resting her head on her hands, her elbows on the desk. "I think we need to press him on this other person. Try to figure out their identity and where they might be living... which I believe is where we're gonna find Marissa."

She scratched her sleep-deprived eyes, which burned from irritation after all of yesterday's dust... *and crying.*

God, I can't stand crying...

"We can try investigating the areas surrounding Asbury Park's Boardwalk, but without any clue where to start searching, I don't think we should take the risk." She began to glance at her watch again before catching herself. "We just don't have that kind of time."

"You know, we *could* meet their demands and let it play out," Jim offered, leaning against his desk. "See what they plan on doin' once they get the money."

Kelly scoffed sarcastically. "No way, man. Bill would lose his shit. Besides, I don't think we can *actually* let that man go, even if we're tailing him." Her eyes flicked over to Jim's injured leg. "He's too dangerous to risk it."

"Now, *wait* a second," Jim objected. "If we somehow could keep track of him, maybe a tracking device or somethin', we can at least figure out where he's goin', right?"

Because that helped so much yesterday, eh? Becca could barely resist saying the quip aloud. "True, but if I were them, I'd have a second getaway vehicle hidden, ready to go."

"Nailed it, Taylor!" Jim banged his fist on his desk with a *thunk.* "Think about it; if *I* was them, I'd fly somewhere remote, ditch the chopper, and take an escape car." He took a massive swig of coffee, the caffeine fueling his train of thought. "We could have an agent pose as the pilot, and take 'em as soon as they land; easy-peasy."

"I dunno... that would be risky," Kelly had a hand on her forehead, as if the thought of releasing Alset gave her a headache. "If he gets away, the girl's as good as dead. Plus, his behavior in the tower tells me he's way too high risk to consider it. It's not just Marissa or us at risk; he's shown that he'll kill *anyone,* so what's stopping him from killing more innocent people?"

"Well, what other choice do we *got,* then, huh? You tell *me.*" Jim's face wore a frown which Becca understood without words; he was as desperate to find a lead as she was. "What did PD turn up in the apartment? I never went in, so I dunno what that guy had in there."

Becca shrugged. "I'm not sure, to be honest. Bill said the police barricaded it off and padlocked it. So if we wanted to look, we could."

"I'd love to go take a look in that shithole, but I have a feeling I won't be goin' out in the field today." He tapped his cast with the stack of photos before replacing them in the folder.

Becca got an idea. "You feeling like playing 'good cop, bad cop' with me today, Jimmy?"

"You think Alset will talk with ya?" He raised an eyebrow. "Gonna put the screws to 'em?"

"I dunno. Once he was in cuffs, he was very submissive. I *might* be able to crack him." After a few moments, she held a finger up.

"How about this? When Bill arrives, we'll wake our friend for a chat. We'll get some breakfast delivered, then we can bribe him with *real* food, over that jail slop. Even if he won't talk, he won't necessarily *walk*. *We'll* make that decision... *if and when* that time comes."

Becca cracked her good knuckles aggressively as she shifted her focus to Kelly. "In the meantime, we should go check the apartment. Photograph it, look for prints, or any sort of clues that might help us get a lead on the woman."

"Nah, we don't need prints," Jim scoffed. "Truthfully, we really don't need pictures, unless you find something like a *body* in there. I don't care about the case right now—I wanna find the girl. *Alive.*"

"Me, too," they said in unison. Kelly's expression was as empty as her response; Becca could tell she was as desperate for coffee and breakfast as *they* were. Becca closed the Y2K file.

"We have a decent starting point, but I still want to put the screws—as you so delicately put it, Jimbo—to our little friend in our holding cell. We can figure out our play afterwards." She cracked her knuckles on her good hand and sipped another drink of lukewarm coffee.

"What do we know about Marissa's location? Anything?"

"Nothing." Kelly looked concerned. "He wouldn't tell us *anything* last night, Becca. He was acting disturbed, and I wouldn't be surprised if a lot of that was the trauma of going through yesterday—you know, from his point of view, right? You know what I'm sayin'?"

Becca's brow furrowed. Kelly shifted in her chair, pausing momentarily so the others could consider her words.

"Well, remember—Alset saw everything *you* saw yesterday, right? He might be crazy, but he's probably still having trouble dealing with it, too, ya know? He's still human, even if he *is* psycho... and all that trauma y'all went through yesterday... trauma doesn't give a *damn* who you are underneath, because it'll just sit there on the surface, biding its time, until you get the *balls* to face it."

"Yeah," Jim muttered. "That's the trouble with trauma..."

"You're not wrong, Kelly, but forgive me if I couldn't give a *damn* about Alset's trauma. Fuck him. We have a kid to save."

"I'm just saying, he might need some special... *convincing*, is all, ya know?"

"Don't worry." A smug smile crept across Becca's face. "We'll get him today. I have a plan."

A knock at the office door caused the trio to flinch. As it swung open, William Bushnall entered the room carrying a tray of Starbucks coffee, his trademark red tie still askew on his neckline. His entire outfit was the same one he donned yesterday; streaks of dust stained his suit jacket.

"I see Agent Taylor got to *you* as well, Serrano. Early day today?"

Jim shrugged with a laugh. "C'mon, Bill, you know I can't eat that crappy hospital slop all day while *you* guys get all the fun!"

"As long as you don't fall out on me, man," he warned, setting the tray down on Jim's desk. "I see *one* moment where I think you should be in bed, and I'm sending you home—got that?"

Jim nodded reluctantly before quickly snatching one of the drinks. "Just ignore me if I make noises when I move; I feel like I got hit by a train. *You* guys try taking a dump with this thing on!"

You can call me Dino, 'cause I'm Dino-sore! Becca giggled. *I should tell that one to...* she trailed off, silently sulking.

"Have at it!" Bill's voice was joyful as he waved his hands at the drink caddy, but his scowl suggested otherwise. "The Starbucks downtown was giving out free coffees for first responders, and they gave me some extras to hand out!"

She sat for a short stint, silently sipping Starbucks as Bill filled them in about the first responders. Becca asked him if they'd heard anything from CeCe, but he'd forgotten to ask. Despite this news being frustrating, Becca understood; the FBI had plenty of its *own* missing agents, and the investigation into the terrorist attacks was stalling due to the search and rescue efforts. A *lot* of their friends were down there (many staying throughout the night).

He *did* mention that every firefighter in the Tri-State area was down there, so if she was alive, she was likely working as well.

"There's rumors of George Bush flying out here today or tomorrow," Kelly shrugged. *"That'll* be a shitshow..."

"Listen, Becca," Bill mentioned. "I'll keep asking until I find out about CeCe. If I hear anything, I'll call you."

"I appreciate that," she whispered.

"You sure you can work today?"

No, not really, Bill, if I'm being completely honest with you. Becca nodded.

Once the clock hit four, the sleep-deprived team slowly approached the holding cell block. Jim struggled with his crutches... *but I can't exactly brag; I'm not Tony Stewart in this walking boot.* By the time they arrived, they were both ready for a nap.

"We should let him sleep longer," the guard warned. "He was up until almost one. Kept complaining about his phone call, but I just kept lying—told him the phones were all down 'cause of the Trade Center."

Becca rolled her eyes. *That's illegal, dipshit.* "I think we should let him make it. We can monitor the call. See if he contacts the woman."

"I agree, Becca," Bill added, "but I also think we'll let him sleep in. I want you and Kelly to go to the apartment in the meantime."

Well, so much for doing the interview first. Becca cleared her throat.

"Sir, I *need* to be here for the interrogation."

"And you will be." Bill patted her on her bandaged hand, as if to remind her of her condition. "Jimbo and I'll stick around here. If he wakes up, we'll call you. You got your new phone?"

She nodded, pointing to her suit pocket.

"I'll drive, Becca," Kelly stated. "I know you're the better driver, but—"

"No argument here," she scoffed, patting her massive walking boot. "Alright, fellas; we'll try to get back before sunup."

As Becca and Kelly headed towards the elevator, their boss stood up, slurping the last drops of his coffee as he stretched.

"Jimmy, I'm going to take a nap."

"Wait, really?" Jim stared incredulously at Bill's empty cup; he had no clue how this man was functioning, let alone coherent. "Didn't you just drink—?"

"Serrano, I've been awake for twenty-seven hours straight. I haven't showered, I need to take a shit, and I've been *stressing* over two of my best agents nearly being KIA. The entire Bureau is digging around a mountain of burning debris, I got multiple missing agents—and I dunno if *any* of them are alive. I got an uncooperative suspect, a ransom demand, *and* I got a knot in my gut. *And the fuckin' kid is still missing!* So yeah, caffeine be damned; I'm gonna go sleep for twenty minutes on my *goddamn office chair!*"

His volume had climbed to ear-splitting levels as he threw the empty cup angrily; despite the speed and violence behind the toss, it found its way into Jim's trash can with a *clang* before he slammed the office door.

XXIII

"This Place Wasn't Meant to Be a Crime Scene..."

"Here we are," Becca announced as Kelly slid her Mercedes sedan to a smooth stop. "98 Madison Street." She took a moment to let the absurdity of their situation sink in. "It blows my mind I was right here, twenty-four hours ago." This time, it was a bit... *different*.

This was a mockery of lower Manhattan; the street looked like something out of Mad Max. The lobster truck from yesterday still sat where the Dodge van had smacked it, one of *dozens* of vehicles left sitting under a layer of particulate, which covered everything like macabre snow. The school zone sign Alset hit was still flopped over, broken and lying halfway in the street.

She approached the stairs where she had concealed herself the day before; her FBI jacket remained *exactly* where she'd left it, draped over the handrail and covered in that *dreadful* dust. It would've been *long* gone on any other 'normal' day.

"Well, whaddya know?" Becca always strove to find beauty in the little things. This morning, she wasn't wearing any top layers, so she shook the jacket out and put it on.

A little dust is worth it; I feel kinda chilly, and I don't think it's because it's cold out here.

The sleep-deprived sleuths strolled into the shadowy lobby of the building. The staircase beckoned to her, a foreboding corridor that gave Becca the chills. Goosebumps formed on her forearms, and she was already judging herself.

I suppose I can add staircases to the list of 'Places I need to *avoid for $400, Alex.'*

They climbed to the third floor, where the door was padlocked; yellow tape was plastered across the door:

CRIME SCENE - DO NOT CROSS

Naturally, Kelly ripped the tape down, opened the lock, and entered the apartment. The place was in *remarkably* bad shape, although Becca figured it was like this *long* before Alset began squatting there.

"This place should be *condemned!*"

Becca was incredulous upon walking into the apartment. Her boots made a *shlup* sound with every sticky step. She held a hand to her nose to plug it; the air in this wretched place smelled of stale cigarette smoke, old grease, and rat urine.

"Yeah," Kelly snarked, "and it's probably on the market for fifteen hundred a month." She glanced at Becca and winked. *"Not* counting trash and sewer."

"You sound like CeCe. She's always complaining about how expensive it is to live in New York these days." She scanned the wall with her flashlight until she found a light switch and flicked it on.

The ceiling-mounted chandelier, which Becca mused was made of plastic, illuminated everything, yet revealed nothing. The decrepit room, now cast in a dim, yellow glow, was devoid of all furniture except for a single chair in the center of the floor, with a conspicuous red telephone sitting atop it. The cord for the phone ran across the mangy carpet and into the disgusting kitchen, where it terminated in a wall jack.

That must be the phone Alset was talking on when Jim was here.

The cabinets were falling apart; several doors were missing.

The yellowed refrigerator was badly dented, and other than a few empty cans of vegetable soup on the counter, there was no sign of *anyone* living here now.

This is right out of Silent Hill! The conditions of Manhattan right now drove that comparison home even further, and Becca shuddered.

On the kitchen counter sat a cheap, plastic clock-radio; when she turned it on, it was tuned loudly to a local pop station. The grating sounds of Fred Durst singing about keepin' it "Rollin'" filled the derelict apartment.

"Shit!" Becca cried as she struggled to turn it down, earning her a glare from Kelly. They shared an awkward moment before they broke into laughter. The clock wasn't set, so Becca glanced at her watch: the time was 5:30.

"Thank you, *DJ;* I'll check the bedroom," Kelly scoffed, dancing as she shuffled through the broken doorframe.

A garbage bag was plopped carelessly in the corner of the room where something had chewed into it (a rodent was her best guess). The *smell* of a rat was thick in the bedroom—*and I'm not thinking about Alset.*

"I betcha this was where we would've found Marissa, had you not done your thing yesterday."

Putting on her work gloves, Kelly went to work ripping the damaged bag open, emptying its contents all over the carpet in the dingy bedroom.

Becca wandered in behind her. "I'm not convinced, yet."

The rest of the bedroom was abandoned and empty; besides the trash bag, nothing was left. She opened the closet door, checking the barren shelves, as Kelly carefully picked through the garbage with her gloved hands.

There was *nothing* inside the wardrobe. After striking out in the closet, Becca came back out of it to get dirty with her partner.

...Heh.

"Oh!" Kelly exclaimed, her sudden volume derailing Becca from her lewd train of thought. "Look what I found!" Becca limped over to her as she examined the paper she had plucked from the pile: a long strip of sales receipt.

"It's from Wal-Mart. Bunch of food and groceries, looks like they spent about $150." She uncurled the paper to its full length, stretching it over a foot as she examined it.

"Dated September 10th, 6:47 p.m. Neptune Township."

Becca knew *precisely* where that was; her jaw hit the floor. "No way!"

"Way. Check it out."

Becca observed the receipt. "Well, I'll be *dipped!*" She attempted to pull the strip of paper from Kelly, who held onto it with a vice grip, but stuck her tongue out as she released it.

"Another one," Kelly announced. She'd dove back into the pile and came right back out two seconds later. "This one's from Neptune Township as well." She handed it willingly to Becca this time; it was from The Home Depot.

"September 10th, 12:11 p.m." Becca's gaze narrowed as she observed it. *"Jeez,* Jim and I had been sitting down to eat lunch."

"Memorable one, I presume?"

She rolled her eyes. "It was Jim's birthday on Sunday. I heard about Marissa being kidnapped right before we went to lunch at the *Odeon*." As she stared at the receipt, Kelly watched her with a concerned gaze as her friend sighed.

"That's where we bought our water heater a few months ago." Becca *sighed,* playing with the receipt as she spoke. "CeCe *loves* going to hardware stores; she's like a kid in a candy—"

"Neptune City is, like, a mile from Asbury Park," Kelly noted, interrupting her pity party. "That's no coincidence." Kelly turned her attention back to the ripped garbage bag as Becca examined the new receipt. "It's about an hour and a half from Queens—we have to factor *that* in, right?

Becca was pacing as she studied the slips of paper. "So, if Marissa was taken around approximately 0700 on Monday, Alset and our mystery woman had five hours to take her someplace, to get her set up wherever they're holding her, and then one of them —I'll assume it was Alset—went shopping for... *oh wow!*" She held the receipt up in the dim lighting of the apartment. "Duct tape, nylon rope, garbage bags, double-A batteries, two keys, and a Red Bull."

A mischievous smirk crossed Kelly's face as Becca read the items to her. "Kinky."

Becca studied the bottom of both receipts in the hope of an additional lead, a golden ticket that would lead to cracking the case, but alas... "Damn. He paid with cash, both times."

"We could check the store security cameras; they usually have feeds at their registers."

Becca snapped her fingers. "Yes! *That's* how we can get an ID on him, or possibly even the woman. Might even see if there's a parking lot camera—we can find a car, maybe a license plate." *Unless he drove the Dodge van...*

Kelly was scooping the trash out of the bag in giant handfuls now, creating a mess on the disgusting carpet, but the remaining clutter was ambiguous. It consisted of some rags and towels, fast food trash, a *New York Times* paper from Sunday the 9th, and a crumpled, creased issue of TV Guide from a few weeks back, with the cast of *Star Trek: Enterprise* on the cover. Poor Scott Bakula had a crease going *right* through his face.

Becca folded both receipts and tucked them safely in her jacket pocket. As Kelly continued her romp through the trash, Becca searched around the dank, disgusting dwelling. Mold covered the ceiling and walls—*especially* near the windows, and the carpet was so matted and dirty in some places, it was as hard as linoleum. The place was rank, stinging Rebecca's nostrils with the mixed scents of dirt and grease, mold and mildew, trash and cigarette smoke.

Oh, and rats... lest we forget the fucking rats.

The window was cracked, letting in the breeze, and she welcomed *any* relief from this dense, dingy air. It was eerily quiet in the city this morning, but on any other day, you'd be serenaded by the sounds of Lower Manhattan.

For the first time in Becca's life, she missed that ambiance.

"Nothing else in the trash bag, Becca; I'll check the shitter."

While Kelly took a peek in the bathroom, Becca thoroughly searched the kitchen. The busted fridge didn't have any power; she quickly closed the door to trap the ghastly smells inside, where they couldn't hurt her any longer.

Inside the oven was a surprise, to be sure, and a welcome one: a box of matches... *and only the box?* It was *extremely* lightweight. However, when she lifted it, she felt something inside shifting around... and it *certainly* wasn't a matchstick; she dropped it back onto the oven's shelf with a *yelp*.

"What is...?" Becca bit her lip.

She cautiously snatched the box a second time, as if the oven was still warm, before opening it slowly as if she were Indiana Jones in some old tomb. Inside were two keys: one was for a vehicle (likely the Dodge van, which was probably still slammed into that tree).

The other was a freshly cut house key.

"I got something, Kelly!"

As her partner exited the 'office', she held up the larger key for her first. "This one's probably the van." Becca then handed Kelly the house key.

"Brand new?"

"Feels like it. I *doubt* it's for this place."

Kelly quickly jogged back to the front door; the key went halfway in but wouldn't fully seat. "If you ask me," Kelly stated, "I bet you *lunch* that unlocks the place where our victim is being stashed."

She tossed the key into the air towards Becca, like Michael Jackson flicking a quarter at a jukebox. Becca was about as smooth as sandpaper, so she criminally fumbled the key to the sticky ground with a *plop*, where she retrieved it awkwardly with a pained *grunt*.

"The Dodge van can be connected to Alset; this key connects them both here. We found it together with this other house key, which is *not* for this apartment." The key was pristine; she wondered if it had ever been *used* before. Becca nodded in concurrence.

"I can't take that bet, Kelly; I think you're *right*. It's probably for the place Marissa is stashed, if I go based on Y2K."

She paced back and forth nervously, her boots making sickening sounds on the linoleum of the kitchen's sticky floor, sounding like wet velcro.

"We found two receipts, one for Wal-Mart and one for The Home Depot—the *latter* of which had key cutting on the damned *receipt*, so we can probably connect Alset to that trip. Additionally, the time on the receipts suggests that they could have taken Marissa from the bus stop and driven back to Neptune Township, as they have no other alibi yet.

"I think you're right—Alset and his partner, they'll have the girl... *here.*" Becca put the key in the box and closed it, tapping the box for effect. "The only thing that doesn't make sense is... *here* here." She tapped her boot on the dirty linoleum. "But what is the point of bringing her here to kill her? It seems risky for *no* reason."

"If Alset is also Y2K," Kelly suggested, "then perhaps his MO hasn't really changed?"

Becca raised an eyebrow. "What do you mean?"

"Okay, so, remember, like *all* of Y2K's victims died where their bodies were eventually found, right? And Isabel, the Mauler's first victim, was moved *after* she was murdered, to where they found her body. Which was in the city. That, uh... that just seems *off*, doesn't it?" Kelly's goofy smile faded into a thoughtful smirk. "I'm just sayin', maybe something went wrong, you know, and they had to pivot?"

"Uh-huh; that's what Jim was saying, earlier." Becca began to understand what Kelly was hinting at all along. "You think Isabel was an outlier, and doesn't fit his MO?"

"Yeah." Kelly tapped the matchbox, still in Becca's bandaged hand. "You should play this one like Y2K, Becca."

"Perhaps something went awry, and they had to move her body?" Becca continued to talk it out, as she nodded in agreement. "We need to press Alset on that. We also need to try to find out who this mystery woman is—*any* lead helps. We could bring her up to Alset and try to get him riled up."

"If we strike out with Alset, we should ride out to Neptune City afterwards," Kelly suggested. Becca nodded in agreement.

"Good plan. We'll check the stores for clues."

"God, I want to watch this interrogation *so* bad." Kelly punched her fist into her open palm with a loud *smack*. "I can't wait!"

"Ha, ha," Becca mocked. "But, you're right. This place wasn't meant to be a crime scene."

Kelly took a step towards the front door, but Becca stayed put. She stared at the chair and the phone, which were set up similarly to the scene where Isabel's body was found. "It almost looks like they were gonna bring the girl here, but for what? Ransom?" She looked at the moldy walls with disdain. "This could also be some hideout he used while he was still scouting for a victim or something. What do you think, Kelly?"

Her brow furrowed. "When we get back, I'll search the database for Alset and check for any properties he owns or rents. I bet you there's nothing; he's, like, probably *squatting* here. Regardless, we need to pivot. This apartment is a dead end."

Becca tapped the matchbox once more. "Not a useless one, though. The keys, the receipts... we have a lead, now." She salivated about nailing Alset down. "We have a case brewing, too. If we can get him for a *single* kid, we can recommend capital punishment."

"Oh yeah, we're rollin' now." Kelly nodded confidently. "Let's get back to the office. It's time for our little chat."

XXIV

"Mother"

The evidence that Rebecca and Kelly retrieved from the vacant apartment now sat innocuously on the table outside the interrogation room, an evidence sticker haphazardly slapped on each item. Fighting her heavy eyelids the only way she knew how, Becca was having another cup of coffee before they decided to go in and have a chat with Alset. All Becca wanted to do was drive to Neptune City and check every single house out there.

Nervous, Becca glanced at her watch as she sipped; the time was now 6:26.

While impatiently waiting for Alset to awaken, she had been filling out a mountain of reports discussing her ordeal yesterday, leaving out the 'less flattering details' whilst keeping it professional and accurate.

While she typed away on her work laptop, a spot of curiosity took hold, and she decided to look up Quarren Cambanda. To her dismay, he didn't exist... at least, not in *their* system. There wasn't even a search result for his name, let *alone* a file; of the millions of people that lived in the New York City metropolitan area, there was precisely *one* Quarren—and he was nearly *seventy* years old. Despair invaded her senses as she tried various searches, *all* coming back empty-handed.

Now, I'm even more bummed about leaving my suit jacket upstairs yesterday.

Quarren's wallet was likely decimated in the collapse. The more she searched, the more she was convinced that Q was *actually* some apparition she'd conjured up, as if he were nothing more than a guardian angel sent to help her escape that tower.

I'm still so grateful to you, Q. I'll never forget you—even if history might.

Alset had declined to hire his own attorney, so Kelly was fishing for a public defender to take his case. However, today was not a typical day—they were having a lot of trouble finding *anyone* willing to help, so they were grateful he was cooperating to the extent he *was*. He could refuse to talk if he wanted, and they'd have no legal leg to stand on.

It's not the case I'm worried about, though. It's Marissa.

As Becca worked on her reports, Kelly was on her own laptop, searching for clues and reconnoitering the Boardwalk. Like Becca, her searches were mostly fruitless—there was no record of Alset Aholé *anywhere* in their system.

The Home Depot in Neptune Township was their next stop. Becca supposed they could check the VHS tapes from their security system, hoping they might identify someone using the time on the receipt. They could check Wal-Mart as a backup.

The door to the interrogation area swung open, and Jim Serrano limped in on his crutches, followed by Bill. Her boss was carrying bags of Burger King, and she could practically *taste* the hash browns from here. Becca felt like Bugs Bunny floating through the air to the other table, where Bill was setting their food out.

"You got food for *all* of us?" Kelly cried. "Yo! *Thanks,* Bill!"

"I didn't even have to pay; they wouldn't even *take* my money." He dug out a variety of Croissan'wiches, hash browns, and other various breakfast treats. "They're passing out food to everyone at Ground Zero."

"Seems like everybody's doing that," Becca admired. "It's very sweet of them."

Her boss set some of it aside. *"That's for Alset."*

"Should we wake him up?" Becca nodded towards the interrogation room, and Jim held up a finger.

"Nuh-uh. He can wait, Taylor. I'm *hungry*. I'm not doing nothin' till *we* eat!"

The four of them ate their breakfast, taking in the moment peacefully. This was the first time the four of them had worked together, and for Becca, this was the *perfect* reprieve. She now understood why Jim was adamant about eating before getting to work.

She smiled and glanced at the others, each a *friend* as much as a colleague, silently enjoying a meal together in a clean and quiet place, where they could all relax and not worry about work—

"Did they find anything in the van?" Jim said to Bill, his mouth full of food.

So much for eating first.

Bill handed him a napkin, a look of disgust on his face. "Besides the stretcher? Some nylon rope, a tiny portable black and white TV, a jerry can full of fuel, and various clothes. Nothing else stood out."

"We have the van in the impound now?"

"No, it's still in the park where he crashed it." Bill laughed between bites. "I forgot to get a wrecker out there; I bet it's *impossible* to hire one right now."

"Yeah," Becca mumbled through a mouthful of hash browns, "Jim's G-ride is probably still sitting in the middle of Pearl Street."

"I *noticed* that," Bill grumbled. He looked annoyed at her, but didn't elaborate further.

"I emailed a public defender who lives in Queens," Kelly announced. "He just emailed me back, he's heading downtown. I, um... I don't know the guy very well, but my partner told me he trusted him... so why not?"

She gave a half-hearted 'heh' before standing up to provide an exaggerated salute, comedically slapping herself in the forehead with her hand.

"Eddie Gonzales, *attorney at law.*"

"It takes a special kind of asshole to defend the undefendable," Becca muttered, wiping the grease from her hands. "After yesterday, I don't think Johnny Cochran would take this case."

As the spurt of laughter from her co-workers subsided, Becca took the opportunity to recall her story from yesterday, while the others finished eating. She figured, why *not?* They were all curious anyway and had time to kill while waiting for Alset's lawyer.

It was riveting storytelling to them, but it was as easy as closing her eyes to describe what she'd been through to Becca. Everything was vividly fresh in her memory; every detail crystal-clear to her, as if she was experiencing virtual reality simply by shutting her eyes.

But none of that got to her emotions quite as much as talking about Quarren.

As she finished telling the crew her tale, Becca stared at her half-eaten Croissan-wich, her appetite overruled by the knot in her gut.

"I would give *anything* to get CeCe back; to get Quarren back. But I can't sit here and feel sorry for myself; we still have a job to do."

The familiar afterimage of the red headband captured her attention for a split second, and she blinked it away rapidly, before taking a final, big bite of her sandwich.

"You ready, Jimbo?"

Her partner nodded. "Just remember what we learned from January 1st."

She glanced back at him, confused. "What was that?"

"Pay attention to details. Vocal inflections, pronouns. We *know* there's two of them. Let's try to look at every minuscule detail. Facial features, expressions, twiddlin' thumbs... *anything.*"

"Oh, I *got* this one."

*　　　　*　　　　*

"I changed my mind," Alset stated flatly as the two injured FBI Agents limped into the room. The jaded suspect sat reclining in his chair. His scuffed dress shoes were propped up on the table next to his jail meal, which sat untouched and unappetizing as ever. Jim shoved them off, and a small cloud of dust flew out of the laces as Jell-O and oatmeal crashed to the floor.

"I want a lawyer."

Even though he's a piece of dog crap, I still feel kinda bad for him. It's like Kelly was saying: he hasn't had anyone to help him process the entire experience with, except his own insane mind.

And that was the thought that chilled Becca to the core. If *she* was struggling to come to terms with everything, how bad was it going in Alset's mind? She shivered, realizing that she didn't *want* to know.

Alset made eye contact with Becca, and he grinned terribly. "You could be my lawyer, Rebecca Taylor. We had a good working relationship, did we *not?*"

He licked his lips sickeningly, and her breakfast began bubbling in her belly, threatening to join the meeting.

I take it back; I don't feel bad for him one bit.

"Hey, why don't you stop lickin' your lips at my *partner,* tough guy? Or *I'll* give you a bloody lip to lick." Jim wasn't about to let Alset harass Becca, not after what he'd been told.

"Well then, leave me *alone* until my lawyer gets here." He crossed his arms again, leaning back in his chair. Jim's expression didn't soften.

"We're waitin' for your defender to get here, but it's kinda tough to get one today. You know? Big thing happened yesterday —maybe you heard about it?"

"Well then, you need to let me go," Alset replied

Becca laughed. "That ain't happening, champ."

Alset unfolded his arms, slamming his palms against the table. "Then get me a lawyer, *clown!*" His voice reached that terrifying note again, and Becca felt a familiar lump in her throat. She was grateful for the long table separating them.

"This ain't like goin' through a drive-thru, Mr. Aholé," Jim grumbled, breathing heavily. "If you don't stop orderin' me around, I'm gonna stick your ass back in that cell for a week."

"No, you won't." Alset seethed through his Cheshire Cat grin, and Becca felt that familiar tingle in her belly. "You can't. And we *all* know it."

"Relax, Mr. Aholé. He'll be here soon." Becca's role was to calm Alset down, but she also wanted to restore Jim's composure. "Do you want to wait for him?"

"I don't care," he replied, crossing his arms in a pout.

After they'd left the Trade Center yesterday, Bill had stayed with Alset during his treatment before *personally* bringing him back to the Javits Building, where he'd been since. As he sat with his arms folded, his clean orange jumpsuit hung off his frame like a canvas tent. It hadn't been *easy* to get a size that fit his tall frame, and a size 3XL was all they had that *remotely* fit. It was a strange contrast to his scuffed dress shoes—size sixteen shoes were a tougher item to source quickly—but they were happy they got him out of his bloody, tattered suit.

"I don't care," he repeated, scratching his bandaged gunshot wound. "You clowns already got what you need from me. Fucking shoot me, blame me for killing a bunch of people with *no* evidence. I shouldn't even be *talking* to you without a lawyer, and you *still* want me to talk?"

Much to Becca's dismay, he spat on the floor, playing up his lies. "Dude... you confessed *everything* to me right before you tried to *kill* me!"

In defiance, he spat again, making an exaggerated hawking motion with his neck. He smiled at Becca, his gold tooth prominent in the spotlight shining directly in his face.

"Fuck you, Rebecca Taylor."

"No," Becca said softly, trying to remain calm and professional. "I'm not gonna play this game with you, Alset." The 'good cop' thing usually came naturally to her, and she wanted to entice Alset to spill the beans. As antagonistic as he was towards her, she was *determined* to stay calm.

"We simply want to find Marissa Hernandez and take her back to her family safe and sound."

Alset sat, his arms crossed and his lips pursed, without making a sound.

"You straight up *admitted* it yesterday, Alset; you *bragged* about it. Why so quiet today? Do you *really* think you're gonna get out of this?"

The man sat silently, his arms tightly folded.

"Is it because something went wrong the last time? With Isabel?"

The words echoed in her head, as clearly as they'd been spoken to her yesterday morning.

"Now that I've taken care of you and your partner, we—I, can be together with the little one... yes, just us."

The man refused to speak, whistling mockingly towards the back corner.

"I mean, you can play hardball if you want. We *do* have a case against you if you do that. Or, we can work with *you* if you're willing to work with *us.* "

Alset asked a million questions without saying one word. His eyebrow raised subtly.

Jim cleared his throat. "Look, big guy. I'll make it simple for you. We *are* gonna find the girl. And you *are* goin' to prison no matter what, I *assure* you. But lemme tell you, pal, you're lookin' at eight counts of murder. *Nine*, if we can't find the girl."

He didn't reply, but his gaze shifted downward. Despite his outward appearance and words saying otherwise, Becca could *bottle* the guilt pouring off his face in sweaty droves. The man was on edge, and it showed; he was sweating profusely now.

"You don't have anything on me, and you—"

"Kayla Spilka, eight years old, was found deceased on March 30th, 1999. Zack Kenner, five years old, found deceased June 14, 1999." Alset watched Jim speak now, his attention entirely on the older agent. The names he read seemed to pique his interest.

"Jeremey Young, seven years old, found deceased January 1, 2000. Isabel Esquivel, also seven, found deceased August 16, 2001."

Alset's eyes squinted as Jim read her name. It was as if he was upset about something, as if some *event* had gone awry. His eyes quickly darted over to Becca's, who was watching him closely.

She averted her gaze, almost by instinct.

Jim's voice grew louder, bellowing like his voice was a superpowered megaphone.

"And in the tower, we have eyewitnesses who paint you as the prime suspect in four more murders. Agent Taylor, can you repeat those names for our dense friend?"

She cleared her throat; she had thought this interrogation would be a blast—she was very good at this lost art—but the *reality* of everything was sinking in. Becca wasn't having fun anymore.

"Janet and Donny Costas, murdered in Tower One of the World Trade Center. Moira Desmarais, also murdered in the North Tower." Becca read the final name, her voice growing softer with each one.

"And finally, Quarren Cambanda, murdered in the North Tower."

"Yeah," Jim cried in a booming voice that caused Alset to flinch, as he dramatically slammed his own palms on the table. "And they're just the ones we *know* about!"

Alset sat there in silence, refusing to speak.

"Not to mention, the petty racket you've built up. Resistin' arrest, multiple counts of felony assault on *two* Federal Agents, that little pleasure cruise downtown did some damage—and *so* much more that won't even be *used* in court, since your ass is about to be nailed to the fence.

"Eight counts of murder, with multiple victims sharin' similar fates that all had similar circumstances. That makes you a serial killer, and a pretty bad one, too, *pal*." He scoffed.

"Heh... if we get these charges to stick, you'll be *beggin'* for the death penalty."

It was Becca's turn. She had been studying Alset's face as Jim spoke, and most of the names barely made him flinch—all *except* for Isabel's.

Very sociopathic behavior. Should Becca press him on her? *Or should I focus on finding out who the woman is?*

Ready or not, it was Becca's turn.

"Listen, Alset, like Agent Serrano said, you're in *such* deep shit, that we *can't* get your charges dropped altogether. We're not gonna make a *miracle* happen here.

"But if you scratch our back here, we can do you a solid. You can make your future a bit brighter, you know? Give the rest of your life some *purpose*. And you can help a family reunite, with just a *little* help."

Becca stared into Alset's face, and he refused to return her glare.

"I know you want a family, Alset, but you need to face it—you're *never* getting out of here, man. If you don't cooperate, she's dead... but if you *do,* we can make it worth your while."

She leaned in close, fighting the pain in her neck.

"We *just* want the girl, Alset."

"You can sit there quietly," Jim demanded, "but we already know your plan, buddy. Why not just—?"

Becca held a hand dramatically up as she shifted in her chair, noticing the man's gaze never met hers. *"Hold* up... can you *smell* that?" She snapped her fingers high above her head, and a few moments later, a guard came in with the bag of fast food.

"Agent Serrano, are you *hungry?* I brought some Burger King for us."

Alset's lip quivered, but he didn't speak.

"Oh, *thank* you, Agent Taylor, but I already ate." Jim rubbed his belly in dramatic, over-the-top circles, which made Becca giggle.

"Oh really? Well, I guess I can try to eat *both* of these meals..." She crumpled the top of the paper bag.

"What a waste of perfectly good food, unless..." She raised an eyebrow at Alset; the man hadn't moved. "You know, Alset, I could make this food disappear, or I could—"

"I'm not hungry."

Alset's arms were folded in front of his chest, and he was shaking his head no, despite tears forming in his eyes.

Jim groaned in frustration. *"Bullshit,* tough guy. You want it or not?"

Becca put the bag in front of him.

"Prison slop is for the birds. And I don't even *want* you to answer anything in return for it, unless you want to. You can eat and relax until your lawyer gets here."

Alset didn't budge, so Becca pushed the bag closer to the man with her fingers.

"You know, you might not get another chance to eat Burger King for a *long* time..." She knew Alset wouldn't talk, so she decided to play the long game. Earn his trust and make him comfortable; later, she could press him further.

"It's not *poison,* dude. Look—"

She reached over to demonstrate to Alset that the food was perfectly edible, but he snatched the bag greedily from the table. He demolished and ripped into the bag, leaving a trail of crumbs and paper all over the desk. It looked like the bag had been thrown into a propeller blade; food and trash were scattered *all* over and around Alset.

He must've been ravished! I've never seen anyone eat this fast. He's like a starving dog that knocked over the trash can!

Jim glanced over at Becca, who winked slyly in return. She rested her head on her bandaged left hand. "Listen. We *know* about your partner."

Alset kept eating.

"She called me last night. Why demand a ransom *now?* You've never wanted money before today, right?" She leaned forward in her chair. "Who is she? Is she your new girlfriend? Does she *know* where Miss Hernandez is?"

He rolled his eyes, but he kept eating.

"We searched the Dodge van *and* your apartment on Madison Street, too."

Ignoring her, he continued to eat.

"You used the apartment as a base of operations while you scouted for victims; is that right?"

His jaw continued to mash, with little care for Becca's claims.

"I promise you, Alset, you're gonna *want* to help us. Staying silent won't help anything."

He kept eating.

"Besides, we already know about the mansion in Asbury Park."

Alset froze. He stopped chewing.

Finally, I got you, ya son of a bitch.

It was subtle. Only a few seconds passed before he swallowed his bite, but she didn't even *need* a confession from Alset to pick up the pieces. He had given them valuable information even if he didn't say another word.

Yep, Kelly was right. Asbury Park is our huckleberry.

"If you're willing to work with us, if you can help us catch your partner and find Marissa alive, I'll talk to the DA about keeping the death penalty off the table. I might even get you some choices of where you'll end up after trial. But you *have* to play ball my way, because... lemme tell you, it's not looking good for you, Alset."

"We shouldn't be offerin' this *joker* a plea deal, Agent Taylor. He's a piece of *shit*, I mean, *look* at him!"

Alset barely flinched at Jim's words, which were overdramatic and bombastic. He played the bad cop well, but their suspect wasn't falling for it.

"He's still human," she retorted; the artificial empathy in her voice was nowhere near believable. But she was determined to stay in character. *But what I really wanna do is reach across the table and throttle the man to death.*

"Agent Serrano, we should give him a chance to help us. And if he does, we can scratch his back."

When the man finished his hash browns, he tossed the baggie to the floor and folded his arms.

"I don't know what that stupid woman's plan is. I told her I didn't want anything to do with it, I couldn't care *less* about money. *We* just wanted a child of our own, can't you see that? That's all I *ever* wanted!"

Becca couldn't help it; she scoffed at his words. She might've bought his story, perhaps a *smidge,* if she wasn't aware of Alset's sick tendencies—*not to mention the fact that he'd already murdered four innocent kids. Yeah, model father-type, right here...*

"She told us she wanted a chopper in Asbury Park, with a million bucks in it." Jim cleared his throat. "We know that you guys have the girl stashed out that way. We *know* you don't have an alibi for when she was taken. We know about the mansion, and we can tie *everything* together with the evidence we took from your apartment and the van. The only thing missin' is the motive for the money and the—"

"I don't know *why* she's doing that!" he screamed. "We *barely* get along. I told her this plan was foolish, it was gonna get us caught—"

"But now, you're under arrest, anyway," Becca cut him off. "What, is she *desperate?*"

"What for?" Alset countered. "They don't need *me* to get the money."

They? Becca was floored. *Was that a slip of the tongue, or...?*

Jim slapped the table, frustrated. "Of course they do. You're either leverage, or you're a distraction, dude, and you're tellin' me you ain't got no idea *why?*"

"Who is '*they*', Alset?" Becca leaned forward. "Is there more than just the other woman? If she's involved as well, she'd be on the hook for—"

He rose in his chair, cutting her off. "It's my *mother's* fault. She's the one that—"

It's his mother's fault? It all makes sense, now. He's protecting the other person.

Jim crawled to the edge of his seat, joining Becca. They weren't expecting a full-on confession. Without warning, Alset's face twisted into an expression she hadn't seen since the 19th Floor of the North Tower. His voice took on a sinister tone, and a familiar terror rose in her gut.

"Can... you say that again?"

"I said, it's all my *mother's* fault."

Jim and Becca both gasped audibly as the man looked down at the table, tears forming in his eyes. It was the first time Becca had seen any semblance of humanity in this monster.

"She didn't get involved until after last year. She wanted me to have kids, but I can't; that's why I was taking the kids."

Becca's mouth was as scratchy as sandpaper. "You can't have children?"

"No, I'm sterile. Shahla and I tried, but I *can't;* that's why we started taking kids; they wouldn't let us adopt. But we never *meant* to hurt *anyone.*"

"Sure, bud," Jim scoffed. "That's why you murdered those kids, ain't it?"

Alset didn't reply; he was crying, but his voice was steady. "When you took Shahla away from me, I was lost. Then I met Crystal, and my mother got excited again."

What? Who is Crystal? The story finally made sense to her—but who was this new woman? *There's three, now?*

"What, like, she wanted you to kidnap again?"

Jim broke in. "So your mother had nothing to do with any of the kids?"

"I..."

His face was a twisted mess of emotions and regrets. Becca almost felt sorry for him, again; his eyes were human now—it was the first time he'd acted this way.

"Mother had nothing to do with the others. Not until Isabel.

When she learned about little Isabel, she threatened to turn me in if we didn't help with her plan.

"*She* wanted money. *She* was the one who pressured me to find the girl, so I did, I didn't want to, I was done with that, but she made me do it."

"If she's the one who made you kidnap," Becca said, "then why not help us? Tell us where Marissa is, and we can save her."

"I can't," he cried, "because Mother is with her. If you clowns show up..."

Becca read between the lines. "Can't you at least give us the address?"

"No... I can't..." He was weeping openly now. "I could *never* betray Mother."

"But she betrayed you *first,* you see? Why are you *protecting* her?"

Alset slammed his fist hard on the table with a *bang.* "*She* was the one who wanted to move her to the apartment and ask for money. I told her no, that was *my* little Isabel, but mother would *punish* me, so I had to tell Crystal to hide her. To hide her. But Isabel tried to run away. So we had to punish her, too. I had to, I *had* to..."

The man broke down into histrionics, blubbering away as he cried uncontrollably in the middle of the interrogation room. Becca wanted to discard it as a shallow attempt at manipulating them, except Kelly's words echoed in her ears.

"*He might be evil, but he's probably still having trouble dealing with it. He's still human, even if he is psycho...*" Except this had *nothing* to do with yesterday.

No, girl... this guy is just sick.

"So, when you lost Isabel, that's when you started looking for Marissa?"

When he didn't reply, she nodded subtly, as if she were

accepting his tears as a confirmation.

"Was that your mother who called me, Alset?"

Alset crumpled the remnants of the bag and tossed it aside, where it smacked off the one-way mirror embedded in the wall, and he folded his arms once again. They had pushed *too* far, and his demeanor changed. The evil glow to his eyes, the one that she remembered from the nineteenth floor—the one that Becca imagined every time she stared into that man's soul—was back, and stronger than ever, amplified by the tears he'd been crying.

"I'm done talking to you. I no longer care about that confused woman or her greed." He looked at Becca, and to her dismay, his arms were folded as he began pouting again.

"I want my lawyer, clown."

*   *   *

They couldn't get anything else out of Alset; he refused to say another word. Kelly's public defender didn't show up. Later that evening, they would learn the NYPD had denied him clearance to cross the Brooklyn Bridge into Manhattan, *even* though the FBI had called in advance. They informed him they would attempt again later, and that was the end of it. Alset would remain in the holding cell while the team continued their work.

"Wait, are there *three* of them, now?" Becca was incredulous.

Kelly was trying to keep things straight. "Let's take it one step at a time, here..."

I wonder how old his mother must be; Alset himself has to be pushing fifty! "And the other girl was 'Crystal'? Who is *that*?" Her arms were flying wildly as she spoke

"Can we search all the Crystals in the area?"

"C'mon, Taylor," Jim scoffed. "There's probably fifty thousand in the Tri-State!"

He's not wrong, but I don't have to like it...

"I still say we use him as bait," Jim offered.

"That's risky, Jimbo. He's showing classic sociopathic serial killer behavior."

"You got a better idea, Taylor? If we don't release him, the girl's as good as *dead!*"

Unable to counter with a superior plan, she folded her arms. They were left with more questions than answers, and they shelved the conversation for now; it would only lead to another argument and more stress.

Becca decided to wait until the lawyer arrived to speculate further. For now, they needed to spend their time elsewhere. *And sitting around waiting for Bill isn't helping.*

After a few moments of silence, she couldn't stand it anymore. "I'm going to check the Home Depot out; you wanna come with me, Kelly?"

Her friend gave her a half-hearted grin. "Only if *I'm* driving."

Becca wasn't about to argue; her leg hurt something *terrible.* Besides, Wednesday was as gorgeous as yesterday had promised— albeit with the weight of the *world* hanging over their heads. She rolled the window down, allowing the morning air to flow through the car, blowing her ponytail against the headrest of Kelly's Mercedes.

Instead of friendly banter and music, the car ride was full of talk radio and news. Lots of discussion about Osama Bin Laden, and George W. Bush; rants about retaliation were running *rampant* throughout the Big Apple. The radio station was inundated with maddening monologues about World War Three, and that the people who attacked New York needed to be wiped off the face of the Earth... and she understood the animosity.

People were angry, and hurt, and shocked, and *scared*, and it was just—

She'd had *enough* of it. Craving a reprieve, she turned the radio off, staring out the side window to the south in silence. The smoke from Ground Zero rose high above the Hudson, and the light of sunrise cast an orange tint on everything, it seemed; the buildings in Brooklyn all had a golden glow this morning.

"Penny for your thoughts?"

"I... just wanna get there," Becca mumbled. Her mind was on a specific person... a firefighter. She glanced at her watch; the time was 7:27.

However, as they crossed the Brooklyn Bridge, a surge of optimism ran through Rebecca. She hadn't realized the extent of the eerie aura pervading Manhattan until they entered the bureau —Brooklyn was *bustling* with life. It might have been less busy than usual... but this *was* typical New York City...

And Becca felt so alive with the familiar sight of it all.

Pedestrians were walking, some of whom were on cell phones. An NYPD cruiser was on patrol. Buses, trucks, and cabs weaved through the busy streets, full of honking horns and jaywalkers *oblivious* to the vehicles zipping around them. Spirits seemed high and full of patriotism; there were American flags *everywhere*. It brought a smile to her face.

Maybe things are gonna be alright, after all.

Becca wasn't upset by the lack of discourse, but she wished she felt more like chatting; anything to take her mind off Cecilia was welcome.

I would be happier knowing her fate, even if the news is bad. I just... need to know the truth.

After over an hour of cruising, they arrived at the tiny town of Neptune Township, not a mile from the Jersey Shore. It was a quaint little town with some big-money houses in the area, a large suburban conglomerate of a community.

As they stepped out of her Mercedes, Becca began to look at

her Pulsar again before Kelly joined her side; she stopped herself in the nick of time.

"What time is it, Kelly?"

"Oh, 'bout a quarter to nine, I suppose," Kelly said, lifting her leather briefcase as she checked her watch. "Why, you hungry?"

"Nah, just curious."

They walked into the hardware store, where only a *few* customers were shopping despite it being open on a weekday. The lady at the customer service counter smiled politely at the two suited agents approaching her.

"Hello, madam," Becca greeted the woman. "Do you have a moment?"

"Sure! What can I help you with today?"

She flashed her badge. "I'm Rebecca Taylor, and this is my partner, Kelly Willis. We're Special Agents with the FBI. We're investigating a case, and our prime suspect might have shopped here recently. We need to check your security tapes and possibly your transactions from a few days ago."

Her friendly smile faded, and she looked nervous. "I'll... go get my manager."

A few moments later, she returned with a thin man who, Becca mused, was a *dead* ringer for Gilbert Gottfried. This lanky fellow walked up to them with an authoritarian gait, which made him look sillier in his tight-collar shirt. He smiled smugly as he approached the ladies.

"Charles Griffin," the man said, shaking their hands with a clammy, sweaty paw. He had a smug, sleazy grin and reminded Becca of a car salesman. "I'm the store manager. Come with me."

As Becca discreetly wiped her hand on her slacks, Charles led the women to a security office behind the customer service desk and plopped a shoebox on the desk in the room.

"Let's see... we usually use 'bout four tapes a day, so we'd needta narrow it down."

"The receipt says '12:11 p.m. on September 10th.'" Kelly pulled a photocopy of the receipt from her leather briefcase and slid it towards Charles.

"Well... we usually open at six in the mornin', so we start recordin' in-store 'round five a.m., but our outside cameras record twenty-four seven. Which ones you want?"

Becca examined the receipt for a register number and pointed at it once she found it.

"Ah, let me see..." Charles began shuffling the VHS cassettes until he saw the label he was looking for. "Here we go." He plucked the tape and inserted it into his security VCR. It whined and whirred alive as they all watched in anticipation.

"I wanna switch to those newfangled DVRs, but we ain't got a lot of crime out here, so corporate won't let us upgrade."

His drawl drilled into Becca's temples. *Ol' Chuck here sounds like he's from Appalachia.*

"I haven't had a felony theft since, oh, I dunno... it's been 'bout three years? Hell, I tell ya, it's 'cause we finally got a good guy in the White House. I thought Al Gore was *exactly* like Clinton, he'd have *pissed* his *pants* yesterday! Man, ever since Bill Clin—"

"Shut up!" Becca cut the man off with a glare in her eye. "Let's stick to business... *please!"*

"Jeez, lady, *sorry!"* Charles held his hands up innocently. "My apologies."

"Listen, don't mind her so much, Mr. Griffin," Kelly interjected, trying to take some of the heat off Becca as she patted Charles on the shoulder. "She's *cranky."*

That earned a glare back from Becca. Despite her annoyance, Kelly was right, and she knew it.

"I *am,"* she admitted with a sigh. She took a deep breath.

"I've had a long day, the past twenty-four hours."

"Tell me 'bout it... ain't we *all?* Man, yesterday was *brutal;* I tell you what, I got stuck on the bridge and I—"

That was it. It set her off. With an audible *growl,* Becca stormed right out of the security office with a *slam* of the door, stomping past the woman and over towards the lawn and garden section of the store.

She was pissed; she was trying her damnedest to stay focused on the job and to stay professional, all while trying to keep herself from being sidetracked by her internal fears and worries; the woman that she loved was missing—presumed *dead*—and Becca had *barely* survived an ordeal that, frankly, earned her a vacation. She was injured, tired, *and* stressed—

That is why Bill demanded that you take time off, idiot.

But she *couldn't* stay at home. Marissa was still out there. Besides, trauma doesn't take time off. It doesn't care if you have a case to solve or a tower to escape. It couldn't care less if you're five years old or *fifty.* It couldn't give a damn if you were late to work, or had a looming deadline—as Becca now was very well-aware she *had.*

She hadn't taken inventory of her mental health throughout the ordeal, even as she joked about returning to therapy. Lacking the time for reflection, she was responding to the trauma instead of addressing it directly. She had a lot to unpack—and would have to do it soon. She was *certainly* going back to therapy once this was all over and done with—*that* was set in stone the moment the first plane hit. *Or, perhaps the moment I saw Jim's mangled leg in the park.*

She wouldn't admit that it was the moment she saw the photo of the van on Monday. And now, it was only a matter of time; she was a ticking time bomb, stuck in a store talking to a smug, sleazy car salesman of a—

The stealth hug, coming from behind, surprised Becca. It reminded her of how Chad had hugged her last night. She felt safe in her arms, but didn't want to let her guard down—she was still pretty upset.

"Please, not right now."

"Yes, right *now.*" She hugged her tighter.

"Ouch!" Becca exclaimed. "Watch the *ribs,* Kelly!"

"Sorry," she whispered, loosening her hold. "But we go back too far just to ignore this."

"But... we don't have *time* for this."

Becca pulled away from her friend's embrace and limped away. After taking a few steps, she glanced back and beckoned for Kelly to follow her into the aisle with the outdoor power equipment, which was deathly silent and void of shoppers. Although Kelly wasn't sure why, she followed her... and once alone, Becca collapsed in her arms.

"I can't... I just can't..."

She wept, sobbed, and cried some more... but Kelly simply held her.

For five minutes, Rebecca wailed into her shirt, a giant stain of snot and tears forming around her face as she sobbed into her chest. Becca was unaccustomed to her partner expressing empathy; on the rare occasions she cried in front of Jimbo, he showed *zero* compassion for her. It's part of how she came to loathe crying— *especially* in front of Jim. It was tough love, but it *did* make her stronger... *right?*

Unlike *Jim,* Kelly didn't utter a *word;* she held Becca.

"I d-don't know if I can do this anymore!" she finally stammered between snot-filled sniffles. "I miss Cecilia *so* much, Kelly. Every time I close my eyes, I see her face in the tower, and I should've just grabbed her and taken her down with me; *she was right there!"*

Kelly didn't say a word; she held Becca.

"It took me *so* long to get over Ken—I'm *still* not over him—and now I have to get over CeCe, *too?* How? How can I do the job when my life keeps shattering all around me?"

Her questions remained lingering.

"What? Aren't you gonna say anything?"

Not right away, at least. Becca's tears had trailed off, giving way to concern. When Kelly remained silent, Becca broke the hold, wiping at her face with her suit sleeve.

"Listen," Kelly began, "I can't do this without you, but I can't do this *with* you if *you're* not up for it. You tell me you're good, and I'll believe you. But you've gotta pull yourself *together,* girl!"

She wiped a tear from Becca's nose. "If you need to vent, I'm here for you. But we have a job to do. A little girl needs our help. And I need *your* help to save her.

"You're the most bad-ass woman I've *ever* met, Rebecca Taylor. You can do this."

She's right. I need to stop acting like a victim.

Becca looked up, her eyes already dry. "I'm trying."

"I can't do this with you if you're just *trying,* Rebecca."

"I'll do my best, that's all I got."

"It's a *start,* " Kelly said with a shrug and a sigh. She stepped towards the office, her hand still outstretched in a warm gesture of reassurance, reminding Becca that she was *not* alone after all. Together, they returned to the manager's office.

With her free hand held up to her nostrils, Kelly turned and walked sideways, facing Becca and talking with her nose plugged.

"Like, oh my God; doesn't that guy, like, *totally* look like Gilbert Gottfried to you?"

Becca absolutely lost it. She snorted, collapsing onto Kelly's shoulder as they strolled together; Kelly felt grateful for the opportunity to bring some joy and positivity into Becca's thoughts...

Anything to push the darkness out.

XXV

"Aiming for the Bull's Horns"

The agents returned to the manager's office to review the VHS tapes together... and the footage *didn't* lie. Alset and an unidentified woman did their shopping together and paid with cash at 12:11 p.m. The woman in the video was *younger* than Becca expected, as well. It was tough to make out in the grainy footage, but Becca observed that she was blonde, with a wiry frame, and was tall, rivaling even *Alset* in height.

The most confusing part to them, however, was her age. She was not old enough to be his mother; in fact, she was at least *half* Alset's age.

"That's *gotta* be Crystal."

The parking lot footage was even more promising. It revealed Alset and Crystal getting into a small maroon pickup truck (which surprised Becca; she'd expected to see the white Dodge van). The video's resolution was too low to read the plate number... but at *least* they knew about the truck, now, in *addition* to Crystal's description.

It made the hours they spent worthwhile, but it also meant they were pressed to make their next move. Reminding herself of their time limit only made her angrier, and her entire body felt like she'd been hit by a *bus*. Becca didn't even *want* to hide it anymore; she was *beyond* grouchy.

"Becca, I'm gonna chat with Chuck a bit; do you mind going to the key duplication machine and getting two copies of that house key made?" Kelly smiled reassuringly as she spoke, and

Becca read between the lines.

The selection of keys she had to choose from was astonishing. There were sports team logos, cartoon characters like Mickey Mouse, and patterns like the American flag. She was feeling patriotic this morning—*I blame it on all the flags, everywhere*—so she grabbed two of the flag blanks and proceeded to make copies of the key. Kelly emerged from the office as Becca was about to check out; she was carrying two surveillance cassettes, holding them high above her head in both hands.

"Good job, Kelly." Becca held up the keys she'd just made, imitating her friend. Kelly rolled her eyes and took one of the copies, shoving it in her pocket. "What do we do now?"

The question hung as they checked out and left the hardware store. Kelly opened the trunk of the Cadillac, sliding the VHS tapes into her backpack.

"Well... we can start going door-to-door throughout Asbury Park and hope that someone answers the door like..." Kelly paused and smirked, her voice changing into a mockery of an elderly woman's.

"'*Oh hi there, Misses Agent ladies, come on in! Yes, my name is Crystal!' Or, 'Hi! I am the serial killer's charming old mom! And this is my kidnapped granddaughter! Say hi, Marissa!'*"

Becca wasn't amused. She turned and sat in the Cadillac, shutting the door without responding. She could hear her partner's muffled retort, but couldn't quite make it out, instead burying her head in her hands. She wasn't crying or emotional; she was simply *exhausted*.

Okay, fine. I'm lying to myself. I'm depressed because I miss CeCe.

Becca glanced at her watch; the time was 9:45. Almost a full day since she'd last seen her... *Might as well be a lifetime...* As Kelly climbed into the car, Becca continued staring at her Pulsar watch, almost willing it to travel back in time.

"We have seventeen hours," Kelly said. "When we go back, we need to squeeze Alset, but we don't have much to squeeze him with."

Becca itched her bandaged temple with her good hand as she pondered their predicament. "We won't return until close to eleven. We should call your lawyer 'friend' and convince him to meet us there."

"We go downtown, we interrogate Alset one more time... and *then?*"

Becca shrugged, out of ideas. "What do we tell him?"

"I dunno—*oh!* We could, like, tell him that we found his mother, and that we're gonna arrest her."

"And *then* what? We can't risk him finding out we're lying. He might not want to cooperate, or he might find out the truth..."

"Let's get Bill going on making some calls to get a helicopter fueled and ready, *just* in case, and we can start discussing Jim's idea of letting Alset 'go'." Kelly emphasized the quotes with her fingers. Becca almost protested the offer, but reconsidered when she started envisioning the scheme.

We don't have a choice. We just don't have the time, and the Trade Center will take priority for the PD... even for the Bureau.

"We have the start of a plan, but we need to go talk with Jim and Bill."

"Agreed." Kelly put the Cadillac's key in the ignition and fired the motor up. "Let's head downtown."

*   *   *

The phone call Alset had whined about had yet to be made. Instead, he complained about not having a lawyer, demanding representation before he'd talk again. Bill finally reached Kelly's lawyer friend; she'd given up after hours of frustrating phone tag. As the ladies returned to the Javits building, they were already prepping for another meeting. Unbeknownst to them, Bill got clearance for the lawyer who was already there when they returned.

"Mr. Aholé has no comment at this time, about the so-called 'whereabouts of Jane Doe' or whatever you *think* he is supposed to know."

Becca shook her head in frustration. "Listen, Mr. Gonzales, I'm not going to just let this girl die if this son of a... if *your client* knows anything. He's already *confessed*, and we're currently searching for both his mother and this Crystal. That's why we have a deal on the table. If he doesn't want to help, he can *rot* in a cell until his time is up, as far as I'm concerned."

She was playing the bad cop now, and it was coming very easily to Rebecca. She was method acting as an injured, sleep-deprived FBI Agent, with both a little girl's life *and* her job on the line—

Kelly was right. I am grumpy as hell.

Jim placed his folded hands on the table, addressing Alset's lawyer.

"Here's what our plan is, Mr. Gonzales. We are complyin' with the demands made by our Jane Doe: we're gonna have a chopper parked near the casino, and inside'll be one million bucks in 'unmarked bills'. We're gonna bury some bugs in the canvas, so we can track the helicopter until they land and swap the money over."

"That is," Becca interjected, "if your mom can even *fly.*"

"That is why we are insistin' on havin' a pilot. They'll be one of ours, briefed on the situation. But they'll be undercover, so they won't interact unless it's safe.

"Now, as far as your *client's* concerned, we need his

cooperation if he wants this deal. He cooperates with us *fully*—*and* we get the girl safe and sound. If everyone goes home happy, then the death penalty is off the table. Capiche?

"We're plannin' a supervised release—Alset'll be free of cuffs and at the scene. He'll make a phone call ahead of time lettin' his cohort know he'll be at Asbury Park."

His eyes shifted over to Alset's. "You *will* cooperate, and if you try to escape, Agent Willis will *personally* plant a bullet in your ear. You follow, big guy?"

"Sir—are you *threatening* my client?"

Oh God, Kelly, how did you find this dense mother—

"*Shut up,*" Becca spat. "Don't act like you have leverage here. *'Threatening my client'* like you didn't just meet this piece of shit ten minutes ago. *Please.*" She struck the table with a mighty *smack,* ignoring the seething pain shooting through her broken left hand. "This is about as much assholery as I can *take,* Mr. Gonzales. I watched a little boy bleed to death in my *arms.* I watched an innocent man bleed out in the fucking *World Trade Center* twenty minutes before the damned thing killed my... er, before it *collapsed!*

"I've dealt with some low-life scum in my career, but you're defending the most undefendable of them *all,* sir. *Eight* counts of murder. Four of which were *children."* She leaned in closer to Alset's lawyer. "You think I give a *damn* about this man? Or this *case?* I couldn't give *less* of a shit! The only reason I didn't leave him in the tower to die in the *first* place was the girl."

"Agent Taylor," his lawyer replied, "my job is *not* to analyze the 'morality' of the case; my job is to defend the defendant."

"Well then, listen closely. You payin' *attention,* defendant?" Her eyes bored into Alset's. "It's pretty basic, even for *you* simple-minded idiots. Help us out, and you live. If you don't, you *will* die. But I can promise you *this,* Alset—if your mother so much as harms a *hair* on that girl's head, so help me, you'll need a *bodyguard* to protect you from me, even on *death row."*

Jim watched his partner in stunned silence; it wasn't like her to get this angry.

"It's *your* decision, but don't waste our goddamn time if you aren't interested. We only have…" Becca glanced at her watch; the time was now 1:19. "We only have a little over twelve hours." She leaned back in her chair.

The other three people in the room sat in stunned silence; Jim's jaw was practically on the floor.

"So tick tock, bitch."

"Agent Taylor, putting my client in danger doesn't work for us. We'd be more comfortable if we—"

"I don't care *how* comfortable he is! He kidnapped a little girl —"

"Allegedly."

"He kidnapped a little girl, and someone told me this morning that if we don't cooperate with their asinine demands before two a.m. tomorrow, that this *little girl* will be cruelly murdered—"

"Allegedly!" Mr. Gonzales repeated, this time with his voice raised.

"Cruelly murdered, in cold blood—" her voice boomed even louder than the lawyers', "and you expect me to care how you *feel?* You should *be* so lucky.

"I could've left you in that tower to die, but I didn't. And I have that weight on my shoulders now. I couldn't give a *shit* if you live or die after this, but if *you* care, you have an opportunity to decide your fate.

"Most people who sit in that chair would sell their *mothers* to be so lucky. And *your* mother is trying to sell *you*, as a bargaining chip, using her son to make a quick buck, and you can stop that, *too!"*

Becca cracked her neck, ignoring the painful shock that shot through her body.

"The choice is yours, Alset. I don't care either way. I only want to save Marissa. And we're running out of time."

Mr. Gonzales whispered in Alset's ear, and he whispered back. After a few moments, Mr. Gonzales raised his eyebrows.

"We would like ten minutes to discuss this in a private, unmonitored room. Can we do that?"

"There's cameras," Jim replied, pointing to the corner, "but we can leave you. We'll let you out in ten minutes."

They left them in the interrogation room, and ten minutes took a lifetime for Becca as she nervously paced in her walking boot, ignoring the jolt of pain shooting through her shinbone with every single step.

"We absolutely *cannot* fumble this," she warned. "We need as many people as we can get."

Kelly was rocking back and forth in her chair, the back legs coming dangerously close to slipping and causing her to fall backwards. "How many people aren't at the Trade Center, Bill?"

Bill sipped coffee from his ceramic mug, making a 'zero' with his fingers. "All of them."

"Beg your pardon?"

"All of them. *Every* agent that isn't on a priority case is at the Trade Center."

"Like... you don't mean, *literally* all of them, do you?"

He cleared his throat and spoke in a booming, loud tone. "We're the *only* ones left, Willis."

The building was a ghost town. The Jacob K. Javits Federal Building housed numerous departments besides the FBI, which only utilized some of the upper floors for its purposes. And yet, the other floors in the building were *also* deathly quiet today.

Bill had been coming and going throughout the day, and he was feeling it as much as any of them were. As they anxiously waited for time to pass, he filled them in on the situation at Ground Zero and the lack of available agents. The area around Ground Zero was fully cordoned off, swarming with firefighters, police officers, FBI *and* CIA. Even the *Marines* were present, along with tradespeople from all over the Tri-State area, working to clear rubble and search for survivors.

"So yeah, that's almost everyone." He took another sip; his eyes were glazed over. Becca could only guess how exhausted that man was; even in her condition, she still felt a sense of pity. "It's likely just us five."

"Sir... you're going into the *field* with us?" Jim almost fell over.

"Do we have a *choice?* I can't get the Hostage Rescue Team involved on short notice with everything downtown, and the PD's tapped out. We'll need all the help we can get."

"Wait a sec—you don't think *Jim* is going in the field with us?" Becca's eyes were dinner plates. Jim was about to light her up when Bill held his hand up, cutting him off.

"Becca... we need *all* the help we can get."

Jim's face had already softened. "I'll stick to the perimeter. I doubt I'd be much help in the fray like this." He turned to Becca, who was a deer in headlights at his gaze. "So, Taylor, go over the plan? We have a chopper delivered, bring a bag of money with us, prep an undercover pilot, and wait for this woman to show up?"

Me? He wants me to take point?

Her mouth was as empty as the Sahara desert as her mind raced through its usual round of excuses—reasons why she wasn't ready to take the lead—

Clear your mind, write your story, and breathe. "Pretty much. With limited manpower, we'll need to be perfectly positioned before she arrives." Becca casually sipped coffee from her thermal cup, ignoring the burn on her tongue and her nerves.

Bill set his mug down. "I know it's been a while since I was in the field, but I'm a *hell* of a shot. I'll probably set up on a building rooftop nearby and lead our sniper team. I want multiple guns on Alset just in case he makes a break for it."

"If we can *get* multiple guns," Becca muttered.

"PD still has some ESU operatives we might be able to recruit, but again, the Trade Center is the priority for everyone right now." He stood, stretching his arms high above his head as he yawned. "We might be on our own, worst-case scenario."

"Okay, Bill. You see who you can get to help us. PD, FBI, Coast Guard—doesn't matter to me." Becca was sipping her coffee, unaware of her partner *staring* at her in astonishment. Jim was impressed with her ambition and wherewithal. She was stepping up without anyone's guidance—he hadn't seen this side of her in *years*.

"Jimbo, I'll have you on the perimeter. Give us a heads-up if *anyone* approaches. Obviously, we're looking for that maroon pickup truck." She spun in her chair. "Kelly, are you up for 'Alset duty'? I'm not at 100 percent, so I'll *need* your strength."

"You know it."

"Awesome. You'll lay low at the scene. If he tries to escape..." Becca used her finger to gesture across her throat, and Kelly nodded with a smirk.

Next, Becca pulled some packets of Sweet'N Low from a small ceramic container on the back edge of the circular table she was seated at. She positioned a few of the tiny pink packets around the table, like a football playbook.

"We put the chopper here, and park the car... *here*. Kelly will wait in the back, and her partner can be the person who'll fly the chopper, if it *gets* to that.

"Bill, you get your men and create a perimeter; if we see any activity, we move. Jim and I will be on the perimeter, searching for suspects.

"If they arrive by car, it's simple: find out where the girl is. If we get intel, then Jim and I will act—whether we believe them or *not*. By then, we'll be short on time, so we need to act *fast*. If we don't get the intel by then..." She trailed off, unsure what to say. "Then... I guess we just let them go and try to follow them."

Bill's brow furrowed. "I don't see how that's supposed to put me at ease, Becca."

"We don't have any options, Bill. The backup plan is the tracking bugs in the duffel bags. Jim and I agree; we don't think they'll fly very far. We think they'll ditch the 'copter and escape by car. But we have to be ready for *anything.*"

"When they get there, if it's the mother and this 'Crystal', do we grab 'em both?" Jim was rubbing his sore midsection. "What if it's only one of 'em? What if it's somebody new?"

Becca scratched her chin as she thought. "If it's only one of them, we should pay attention to the perimeter."

"You think they'll be watching for us?" Kelly scratched her chin. "She must know we're gonna *try—* "

She was interrupted by the door opening. Mr. Gonzales emerged with Alset behind him.

"My client accepts your offer. We'll cooperate in exchange for a plea deal."

XXVI

"The Fastest Police Chase of Becca's Career"

Becca clicked the button on the heavy walkie-talkie. "Radio check?" She was shuffling around in the driver's seat of her Eclipse, parked on the street in front of the Empress Hotel. The hotel's gigantic neon green sign flooded the roads with an olive tint; Becca looked like the Incredible Hulk in her rear view mirror.

She'd heard a ton about this place—especially from CeCe—but hadn't found the time to visit Asbury Park lately. Every time her eyes caught that neon sign, she kicked herself for missing the chance to take Cecilia there...

The address that Alset gave them while they were still downtown was a dead-end, *long* since abandoned. There was no sign of Alset's mother *or* Marissa. Alset *swore* he thought they were there, but Becca didn't buy it.

"I could never betray Mother." His words rang out in her mind, and they remained true, as far as she was concerned. Becca was suspicious of his willingness to cooperate *here,* as well... but they didn't have any other choice.

The clock on her dashboard read **11:45**. It was almost time. Rather than riding with Jimbo, Becca thought it best to use her own vehicle, in case things went awry. Usually, Bill wouldn't have even *considered* allowing it... but the last few days had been so incredibly unique, and besides, Becca made a good point; considering their lack of personnel, having another agent ready to move was *invaluable.*

Her boss took it well, only screaming at around *half* his

maximum volume. "I don't even think they *make* the waiver you need to sign for that!"

She could make out the helicopter blades in the faint moonlight of the waning moon, parked east of the Boardwalk near the abandoned Asbury Park Casino. This area of the Jersey Shore always depressed her when she'd driven to Atlantic City... it felt so *neglected*.

There were *few* people about, and the aura of emptiness that afflicted most of the world was just as prevalent here. Becca had to keep her eyes open—but at least they didn't need to worry much about collateral damage or innocent civilians.

"Radio's good, Taylor."

Bill was already setting up on the roof of the Empress, about four floors high; from there, he'd have a clear shot at the helicopter. He'd made some phone calls... but as he suspected, there wasn't *anyone* in the FBI available tonight, save for *one* person.

So he'd recruited a few detectives from the Asbury Park police, who were on the roof of the Empress with him, setting up snipers and monitoring the area.

That poor man is on his tenth pot of coffee since I've been with him. She felt so bad for him, but the man never complained *once*. He was right there with her, and she was *grateful* for it.

Jim was relegated to shotgun duty; shotgun *seat*, that is. He was riding with a plain-clothes Asbury Park police officer, stationed about a mile up the road in an unmarked Crown Victoria. If *any* vehicles were heading their way, his job was to call it out.

Alset sat next to Kelly in the back of a black GMC Yukon. The driver was the agent Bill *was* able to get—Special Agent Miles McLain, an old friend of Bill's, had arrived in the *nick* of time. On loan from the Newark FBI office, he was a former army pilot who volunteered to help.

Agent McLain returned from vacation that same morning.

He'd missed the 'excitement' of the Trade Center attacks, which is why he was available. A diehard football fan, he'd been in Denver for the Broncos versus Giants *Monday Night Football* game, and was in the air Tuesday morning when the attacks took place. When President Bush announced all commercial flights would be grounded, his flight was diverted to Philadelphia.

"Not only did my G-Men lose, but I got stuck in fuckin' *Philly?*" he'd complained.

The Asbury Park police provided the helicopter, as well as multiple units spread out over a quarter-mile perimeter, *all* of whom were undercover. They hoped the suspect would approach from the west down Asbury Avenue, and then park in the lot in front of the Carousel Building, across the street from the Empress and adjacent to the abandoned casino where the chopper was parked.

Once she arrived, Agent McLain would attempt to find out where they had hidden Marissa. If they did, the dragnet would close, and they'd have their suspect—and Alset would be in custody again.

Kelly was the contingency plan. If *either* of them tried to escape, she was prepared to arrest them both before they took off. She sat, ready to draw her Glock at a moment's notice.

Becca tapped her steering wheel nervously, waiting impatiently for *anything* to happen. Each second seemed to pass in slow motion, like a child counting down the days until Christmas. The seconds slowly melted into minutes, threatening to transform into hours. As midnight came and went, she fought the urge to turn the stereo on or to get out and check on Kelly, but Becca remained put. Similarly to yesterday morning, when Jim entered the apartments, she knew her role here.

That doesn't mean I like it.

The perimeter was set; the bait was planted. The only X-factor was Alset's mother. Becca did anything and *everything* she could to pass the time, but mostly lost herself in thoughts of CeCe. Eventually, a voice finally broke the everlasting silence, causing Becca to *scream* in a flinch. Her Pulsar showed 1:26 when she glanced down at it.

"Okay, team. We're stepping out."

The Yukon's driver's door swung open in the murky darkness. Agent McLain exited the car, opening the back door for Alset, with Kelly following closely behind. Alset was donning a bulletproof vest, and Kelly was fitting a black windbreaker over it.

"Inside your vest is a wire and a bug; we can hear you. If you need something and don't want to blow your cover, I want you to sneeze three times. Simple."

Alset nodded subtly, a frown on his face.

"If you *really* need to sneeze, and you sneeze three times, we're comin' in, so like, if you have to sneeze three times for *real*... you better fake a fourth one..."

Agent McLain was wearing a helicopter pilot's uniform. He was instructed to give this cover story: he was a helicopter pilot named Mack Miles, and the police had told him to fly the chopper; that's all he 'knows'. They all agreed; letting them take off was practically *out* of the question. If they couldn't get an answer, they'd be better off capturing the mother and finding the girl later. However, McLain was a veteran agent; he *wouldn't* blow his cover if he thought they had a lead.

Still, if the helicopter *did* fly, there were three tracking bugs in play—one in the bag of money, another in Detective McLain's pilot lapel pin, and one more hidden in the seat of the chopper.

Becca had a bad feeling about their plan, but there wasn't a good alternative. *It's because I'm on the perimeter; I should be in that car...* Except Becca knew better. Her beef with Alset was personal; if he gave them away, Marissa was as good as—

No... I'll stay back. I'll keep an eye out. Becca didn't like their odds much. It doesn't help that the gears of every clock in Jersey seemed to be greased with tar. She was nervous, but she *loved* the thrill of these moments... and the butterflies in her tummy were fluttering *madly.*

"Everyone, stay sharp."

One of the police officers on the perimeter radioed in. Becca's eyes immediately left the Yukon, scanning the horizon desperately.

"There's a Toyota sedan—looks like a gold Camry. Can't see the driver, tinted windows, but there's a single occupant, uh.... yep. Just a single driver, female."

Becca frowned. *A Toyota Camry?* Something was wrong. She pulled her Smith & Wesson, freshly cleaned of all the dust from the tower, and checked her load for the third time. She was ready to end this struggle. She holstered her gun and grabbed a pair of binoculars from the Eclipse's glovebox.

"Yeah, we confirm—we see the Camry." Jim's voice crackled through the speaker. "Headin' your way, Willis. Stay sharp."

Kelly climbed into the back seat of the Yukon, sliding onto the plastic bench seat and struggling to get comfortable. Detective McLain closed the door behind her and approached Alset.

"If he makes a *single* suspicious move," Becca said over the radio, "I'm moving in."

"Check your chatter, Taylor. They're *here.* "

Her heart seemed to stop beating as she stared out the windshield, unable to do anything except watch. The gold Camry pulled into the parking lot of the Carousel building, stopping behind the Yukon with a mighty *squeal* from the brakes. The windows were tinted as dark as Alset's Dodge van had been, and Becca could not see the driver.

"Stand by," Bill's voice came in, crackling over the radio. The Camry's engine shut off, but the car remained still. The air was deathly silent, save for the sounds of waves crashing into the Jersey Shore, and even *they* seemed to have toned down the volume in anticipation of what was to happen next.

Every second *rapidly* crawled by as Becca's mouth grew drier. She kept her good hand on the key, already seated *fully* into her Eclipse's ignition, ready to start the car's little motor *immediately*. She *barely* remembered to breathe as she watched the Camry, waiting at *long* last to see the face of the woman who controlled the fate of Marissa Hernandez—

"There's another car."

That was a different voice... Becca's heart skipped a beat.

"Another car?" she replied, dumbfounded.

It's the mother; it has to be! She shook her head, trying to keep it clear.

"Yep. Maroon Ford pickup. Looks like a Ranger." A moment passed. "'Bout a quarter-mile up Asbury Avenue, heading your way—*wait*... they pulled over next to a park."

"Who's in the *Camry,* then?" Becca strained through the binoculars. Was it Alset's mother? Or the tall, lanky woman from the surveillance video?

Jim quietly whispered on the radio. "Hold your horses. Wait for Willis' signal."

Alset and McLain stood beside the GMC as the Camry remained idling. It seemed as time stopped for *all* of them except Becca, who sat on pins and needles as she struggled to make sense of her options. She'd nearly convinced herself to stay put when a long, thin leg stepped out of the Camry, causing her to *gasp* involuntarily.

The blonde, fair-skinned woman stepped out of the car, and she could clearly see her face.

"It's Crystal!" she exclaimed into the radio. *"That's not the mother!"*

Crystal slowly approached Alset, a look of concern on her face. Becca couldn't read lips, but the woman appeared very tentative.

"The truck is turning around," the officer said over the radio. "About to head westbound on Asbury Avenue. Single occupant. Black female driver."

Becca couldn't explain it. But she *knew* it.

"Jim, I'm going after the truck."

"Wait, Becca!" It was *Bill* who silently screamed at her.

Am I sure about this? If the mother was here to ensure Alset *was* free, that meant the helicopter *had* to take off—and they would have to *land,* too. If they weren't willing to let them do that, the *only* way of getting Marissa alive was to catch Alset's mother. Anything *less* risked retaliation on the girl.

Becca gripped the steering wheel with all her might; her hands shook with adrenaline. She had no time to think. She had to act—*now.*

Clear your mind, write your story, and breathe.

"I'm doin' the job, Jimbo."

It wasn't until her headlights flickered on and she peeled around the corner that *anyone* moved. She earned a shit-eating grin from Alset, who stared into Becca's car as she drove by; Becca stared right back.

She next glared at the tall, slender woman she *thought* was Crystal, standing next to the Camry. As she passed them, Becca couldn't tell for sure—it was all happening so *quickly,* despite everything moving in slow-motion—but she *swore* that she saw the flash of a gun firing in her rear-view mirror.

"Becca—what on Earth are you *doing?*" Bill shouted as Becca sped away, zooming *well* past the speed limit while heading west on Asbury. She zipped past houses and buildings, shooting past Jim's parked Crown Victoria. The tiny convertible accelerated quickly, and Becca gripped the steering wheel so tightly that her knuckles turned as white as the bandages on her left hand.

After she passed a few intersections, she spotted the maroon Ranger. The driver couldn't see Becca approaching at first, but she floored the Ranger when the Eclipse began growing in her mirrors. Even though her truck was outmatched by Becca's little import car, she got up to speed before she caught up.

And the chase was *on*.

The pursuit began heating up as they sped through downtown Asbury Park, the pair of four-cylinder engines screaming through the little town. Buildings blurred by Becca as they bounded down the avenue.

The narrow street gave them *little* room to maneuver. Becca was grateful that traffic was as light as it was. They teased triple digits as the little truck barely stayed on the road, coming within inches of clipping a few parked cars as they screamed westward on the long two-lane road.

"I'm pursuing the suspect, maroon Ford Ranger, westbound on Asbury Avenue. I'm in an unmarked civilian vehicle, a green Mitsubishi Eclipse convertible." There was no reply on the radio, and she grew nervous.

Am I out of range already?

The chase had only been going for a minute or two, yet she was already a mile from the shoreline. They shot past State Route 18, dodging a spattering of early morning traffic as they continued speeding onward.

When they passed the Garden State Parkway, Becca's car was approaching the truck. Even in the darkness, she could see the driver's terrified expression in her mirror's reflection.

Soon enough, she was within a car's length of the woman.

This was too close for comfort. The Ranger slammed suddenly on its brakes and turned left, almost *flipping* the pickup truck as she turned. A flash of temptation struck Becca into considering a PIT maneuver, but she reconsidered, not wanting to cause a rollover.

"Suspect turned left, she is now turning southbound on Shafto Road."

Unlike on Asbury, there weren't any street lamps illuminating *this* road. The only things Becca could see now were the reflections of her headlights off the Ranger's chrome bumper and the starry night sky overhead.

I doubt she has the balls—

Her thoughts never concluded as the driver cut off the truck's headlights. She was invisible to Becca now, whenever the truck wasn't in the beam of her lights. "Suspect is ghosting. Driving without headlights."

She dropped the radio in the cupholder, realizing the situation's futility. *I'm on my own now.*

The pickup truck bounced back and forth, darting in and out of the Eclipse's headlight beam. The little red reflectors on the truck's taillights were the *only* indicator of the vehicle's heading. Becca's curiosity got the best of her as she flicked her eyes down to the speedometer; they were already pushing *sixty*.

The maroon Ford was practically invisible to Becca, but she could still see the erratic steering as the truck *barely* avoided a parked Volkswagen Beetle. Even with headlights on, the black Beetle was *barely* possible for Becca to make out. *How did she even see that?*

The question was forgotten as quickly as it was thought up. The truck swerved back and forth on the road for a few moments before it recovered; by that point, Becca was within inches of the chrome bumper. She backed off a few car lengths, and she reached for her pistol, considering shooting out the rear tires of the truck—

Becca never saw the parked trailer, but she'd already slowed enough that she had plenty of time to react. This good fortune did not befall the driver of the *Ford*, however.

The right side of the pickup drove up the back of the parked trailer like a ramp, flying through the air as if it were a Matchbox toy. It landed hard with a *crunch*, bouncing slightly before spinning back to the right; the top-heavy truck had *no* chance at their rate of speed. It flipped into the air, going end-over-end sideways on the asphalt.

To Becca, it looked like a crash from NASCAR. The Ford was shredding itself all over the street, tumbling end-over-end repeatedly in an *incredible* display of force. After yesterday, the screech of metal was very familiar to Becca; she heard a familiar cacophony as the truck flopped forward.

She screamed and stomped on her brake pedal. The Eclipse came to a screeching halt three whole *seconds* before the truck came to rest upright, in front of her. Becca ran out of the car, her pistol in her right hand and her flashlight in her bandaged left.

"FBI!" she screamed, approaching the smoldering wreckage carefully. Gas was pouring all over the road, and the truck was ominously ticking and clicking as she got closer. *"Let me see your hands!"*

With her breath short in her throat, Becca crept around the tailgate to the driver's side of the mangled vehicle. And that's when she saw her.

The driver's head was unrecognizably *obliterated*. Becca didn't *bother* checking her pulse; most of her skull and brain were missing. Her body was still convulsing in the driver's seat when Becca arrived, half hanging out of the truck.

Becca pulled her phone out of her pocket and hit the PTT button, dialing Bill's phone.

BEEP! BEEP! "Bill, I have the suspect in custody, code 55, we need EMTs out here *now*. I'm on Shafto Road, about a mile past

Garden State." The phone was silent... no reply.

What the hell? BEEP! BEEP! "Bill, do you copy?"

No response. She tried Jim's phone next, and then Kelly's. No reply. That was when an incoming call lit up the cell in her hands.

It was Jim.

"Hello?" she said, out of breath.

"Taylor! Where the *hell* are you?"

She wiped her face of sweat as the first witness was coming out from a nearby house, wondering what all the fuss was about.

"I'm on Shafto Road, I *have* her! I need EMTs out here—"

"We fumbled it."

"What?" She blinked stupidly. *Fumbled what? I got the bitch!*

"Alset got away. He's in the Yukon, and he has Willis with him. I'm in pursuit."

The road Becca was standing on zoomed away from her in a sudden rush, and she nearly fainted. Dropping the cell phone to the asphalt, Becca stood silently in the still September night as an elderly woman arrived. The witness emerged from a nearby house with a flashlight, slowing as her beam revealed the carnage.

"Are you okay—oh... oh my *God!*"

Becca didn't reply. She didn't even notice the woman talking to her.

"Do you need an ambulance? I-I'm gonna go call 911, alright?"

Becca could only stand there. She had killed her lead. She had put her best friend in danger.

And now, she was being *hunted* again.

XXVII

"The Mansion in Asbury Park"

"I heard the whole thing!" The elderly woman reappeared, scurrying across her dew-covered lawn in a muʻumuʻu and slippers. "I just called 911; they're sending out the ambulance. Are you alright? Do you *need* anything?"

"No," she muttered. *Nothing matters anymore. I blew it. Bill is going to have my head.*

The witness noticed her car still idling and undamaged. "Oh, were you *behind* the truck?"

"Yeah," she stammered as she acknowledged her. After moving like she was underwater for a few moments, her paralysis finally broke, and she turned to face her. "I'm Rebecca Taylor, I'm with the FBI." Becca thumbed towards the truck at the deceased driver, whose brains were slipping down the side of the truck's mangled door.

"She's under arrest."

"Oh, my..." the woman's voice cracked upon seeing the dead body; Becca assumed she'd likely *never* seen one before. "Is she...?"

"Yeah, I *don't* think she's gonna make it."

The woman looked uncomfortably at the corpse, still hanging out the shattered window of the mangled driver's door. "Um... alright, then. Are you *sure* you're okay?"

"Yeah. Give me a second."

Becca limped towards the truck, which was ticking ominously. She was worried the truck might burst into flames, so she needed to search it before it was too late. The woman in the muʻumuʻu was walking back to the house, shaking her head at the gruesome scene.

The driver was *clearly* deceased. The macabre scene inside the remnants of the crushed cab left *no* room for the imagination to pretend otherwise. She was elderly and dark-skinned, and what *remained* of her hair was as white as snow. When Becca attempted to open the door, it was jammed shut.

Immediately, a dark hallway full of smiling teeth flashed into her mind. The walls, bleeding to death around her, closing in as these monsters prepared to attack her and Q...

Nope-nope-nope, she complained, blinking rapidly. With every blink, the image was replaced by a floating, red headband. Shaking her head, she cleared the awful thoughts as she ran around the crash, attempting to open the passenger's side door... but it was *just* as damaged as the driver's.

Running out of options, she squeezed through the broken passenger's window. A conspicuous bulge in the woman's back pocket caught Becca's eye, and her instinct was correct; it was the woman's wallet.

Okay, now get out of this thing; you've had enough fire and smoke to last a lifetime!

The adrenaline filling her entire body meant she felt *none* of her injuries as she quickly squirmed out of the truck, sprinting away from the wrecked Ford like it was a bomb about to explode. By the time she returned to her Nokia, still sitting on the street where she'd dropped it earlier, she felt foolish for overreacting...

Especially now that her sore ribs and neck were screaming at her again.

Becca read the New Jersey driver's license information to herself before glancing at the woman's remains. "Nice to meet you, too, 'Mother'. Khari Shetty, huh? You're under arrest for being dead. *Blah blah blah.*"

She examined the license; the woman in the photo was *not* a young person. The license claimed she was seventy years old, and that pretty much confirmed she had to be Alset's—

Focus, Becca! Scanning the license only took Becca a moment before she found what she was looking for; her eyes quickly darted down the laminated card, and there it was.

"I knew it."

Sliding the wallet into her jacket pocket, she knelt to grab her Nokia (Jim had long ago disconnected the call) and found the SIOC in her phonebook.

I've gotta fix this; it's the only way to salvage this mess.

"Good morning—"

"Special Agent Rebecca Taylor, Manhattan. I'm in the field, I have a deceased suspect, a 10-33... but before we get to that, I need an address checked. *Immediately.*"

A moment of silence. "Go ahead, Agent Taylor."

"Khari Shetty. *Kilo-hotel-alpha-romeo-india,* last name *sierra-hotel-echo-tango-tango-yankee.* 667 Wonderfall Road, all one word; that's Wonder-*fall,* not Wonder-*full.* It's in Tinton Falls, New Jersey."

"I see the address now, Agent."

"How far away from the intersection of Asbury Avenue and —actually, can you text me the GPS coordinates? And then, relay to William Bushnall that I'm heading that direction, and *please* do so immediately."

"Director Bushnall? You mean, from—?"

"Yes, from the Manhattan office. He's in the field with us."

"Oh, goodness," the woman on the phone said. "I'll call him as soon as we disconnect."

"Thank you." She looked back at Khari's corpse, which was dripping various fluids all over the road.

"I'm at 2989 Shafto Road in, uh... Tinton Falls, might *still* be

Neptune City, but anyway, there's a single vehicle accident involving a maroon Ford Ranger. The driver's Code 55; she is the same woman whose address I just read to you, Khari Shetty. Send emergency services up here."

"'2989 Shafto Road', correct?"

"Yes. I'm leaving the scene."

"I copy, Agent Taylor. I'll call you back at this number with any updates."

The line clicked dead. She shoved the driver's license into her pocket and sprinted as fast as possible to her car, still idling in the dark street. After climbing into her car, she snagged the Garmin GPS from her center console. Her destination was only a mile or so away, but to Becca, she felt closer to Marissa than ever.

"Okay, let's do this. Clear your mind, write your story... and —"

BEEP! "Becca, can you hear me?"

It was Kelly. Her voice was extremely low, almost a whisper.

BEEP! BEEP!

"Kelly! Are you okay? Where *are* you?" She didn't bother waiting to finish the conversation; she was already gunning it back towards Asbury Avenue.

"I'm in the GMC. We're moving."

"What happened?" Becca's foot hit the floor; she hit the corner and downshifted, effortlessly bringing the Eclipse around at high speed.

"Well, when you took off, that lanky bitch gets out of the car and she just shoots McLain without saying a thing, and *all hell* broke loose! She's *probably* in custody now, but... Alset grabbed McLain's gun. Son of a bitch got the draw on me, popped me in the titty."

"You were *shot*? Are you okay? He hit your vest?"

"Yeah, knocked me out for a bit," she moaned. Her voice was

weaker than usual. "So he gets in the Yukon, and he's been driving like an asshole for a few minutes now."

"Where's Jim?" Becca sped down Asbury, her heart revving as high as her engine.

"I dunno; I didn't see their car when we drove up Asbury."

"You're in the Yukon?"

"Yes. I'm in the back, it's outfitted for suspect transport. It's barred. I can't get out." Becca was speechless. "He can't hear me, he's got the radio on. I have no clue *where* we're going."

"I caught the mother. She Code-55'd and I've got her ID. I'm going to the address on her license now." The car shifted into fourth gear as Rebecca pushed the little car upwards of ninety... and there was a *lot* of gear left in this girl.

"I copy, Becca. You did *good*. Your instincts were dead-on."

Thank you, Kelly.

*　　　　*　　　　*

Becca rolled down the windows and let the cool summer breeze cool the perspiration from her clammy forehead. She looked like Richard Petty behind the wheel... but she was barely breaking a sweat. Her muscles *twitched* with adrenaline, helping to numb the pain in *every* joint in her body. She hadn't felt this energetic since she'd met up with CeCe back—

No... stop thinking about CeCe. Focus!

That meant, of course, that she *was* thinking about CeCe. But she was also *so* ready for a fight... her girlfriend's death was only fuel for the machine.

She pushed the little convertible to *dangerous* speeds. She wanted to beat Alset there and thought she might have a chance; since Khari and Crystal were both out of the picture, *one* of them would be the first to get to Marissa.

She was determined *not* to be the second.

Becca turned the car onto Wonderfall Road. As she replaced the GPS in the cupholder, she dared a glance at the tiny plastic picture frame dangling from her keychain. The photo was of herself, CeCe, and Chad at the beach—the *same* photo she kept on her office desk.

"I did the job," she said, "and I did it for myself as much as *you*, Babe."

Becca felt the tears, but she didn't *fight* them this time.

Clear your mind, write your story... and breathe.

After what felt like an *hour* (but what was, in reality, closer to two minutes), she could see a dim light ahead on the left side of the road. Too far away to see the address numbers yet... yet close enough to cause her adrenaline to pump even *harder*.

She was confident. She was *ready*.

...she was too late.

The Eclipse pulled into the driveway of a dreary, rundown mansion, a three-story house with a detached garage. Lights were burning in both buildings—and a pair of bright lights shone brightly in the driveway.

It was the black GMC Yukon. The vehicle's headlights were still on. The engine was running. The driver's side door was still open, but Alset was long gone. There was no sign of Kelly, either. Since Alset didn't open the truck's back door, Rebecca assumed that Kelly was still back there.

If Alset is armed, I need to give myself a barricade. I'll let Kelly out, and we can make a plan together.

She parked the Eclipse *right* in front of the Yukon, allowing her to reach the back door safely. Scrambling over to the back door of the GMC, she yanked the door handle like the arm of a slot machine, and Kelly spilled out like a jackpot onto the gravel driveway. She was conscious, but it quickly dawned on Becca in horror—*She is in no position to help*. As soon as she was on the driveway, she belly-crawled towards Becca, *moaning* in pain.

"He's... in the house—"

"Stay *down*, Kelly!" She instructed her to crawl behind the front tires, lying prone in the grass beside the driveway. "Are you okay?" Becca's hand squirmed underneath Kelly's vest, and she checked the wound on the bottom of her left breast. There wasn't any blood... but she was *gasping* for air.

"I have my gun," she reassured Becca. "But I *can't* get up. Wind's knocked out of me."

"Where's everyone? I called the SIOC. They should *be* here by now!"

Kelly could only shrug weakly. Frustrated, Becca rolled her eyes as she rose to her feet. "I need to get in there," she exclaimed. "Can you cover me?"

"Ten-four. He's inside the house for sure. Go. I'll check the garage when I catch my breath." She put a hand on Becca's shoulder. "Watch your three. I've got your nine."

Becca nodded confidently. Wielding her pistol, she sprinted as quickly as her injured leg permitted, heading towards the overgrown hedges to the right of the forsaken front doorway. She slammed her hip hard into the stone exterior of the doorway as she took cover, shooting a breathless glance back at Kelly, who was lying prone beside the GMC.

"Go for it!"

Do the job, girl.

With a final, intense breath, Becca kicked the front door open, her Smith & Wesson *clinking* against her flashlight.

"Alset! Come out with your hands up!" she called into the darkened house. "Nobody else needs to *die* tonight."

Oh... but she *wanted* him to. Nothing would please her *more* than his refusal to surrender. She heard a familiar voice ringing through the cavernous house from deep in the distance upstairs, in one of the rooms on the second floor. A high-pitched, cartoony wail, *exactly* the same as the echoes that scarred Becca's memory.

"Fuck you, clown!"

"It's *over*, Alset, but if you hurt that girl, you'll *wish* you were dead, you hear me?"

Creeping through the mansion's entrance, the only sounds were the rustle of autumn leaves tumbling behind her in the driveway and the click of her boots stepping onto the hard checkerboard linoleum that lined the entrance. The house was *enormous*. Ornate wooden carvings adorned the plushly carpeted stairs, and the house was fully furnished.

If it didn't smell like a wet bucket of old cigarette butts in this place, I'd be pretty impressed with Alset's new digs.

She searched rapidly for *any* cover, fearing a potshot from upstairs, and found an ornate vase beside the central staircase. She slid behind it, leaning against the pillar it rested upon as she caught her breath.

"This is *my* mother's house, Rebecca Taylor!" She heard the sounds of glass shattering from wherever Alset was screaming. "You're not *welcome* here!"

Cautiously, she approached the grand stairs just inside the cavernous foyer, which split in two directions to the bedroom wing heading left... where Alset seemed to be.

"We were a *family*, finally a family, and you had to ruin it *again!* Clowns, *the lot of you!*"

"How long did mommy let you freeload, you *freak?*" Her foot landed on the first step with an annoying *creak;* she kept talking to cover the sound as she climbed. "Is that why she wanted to use you to make money? What's wrong, bills get too expensive? Maybe if her son actually, ya know, got a *real* job..."

The silence helped confirm to Becca that she *was* rewriting her story. She was determined not to let herself fear this man any longer. The benefit of the doubt had long since expired in Becca's eyes, and she'd already tried to do the right thing *multiple* times.

With a solidifying nod, she made up her mind. *This man needs to die.* Marissa's life wasn't the only one in the balance anymore... besides, she was *tired* of being afraid.

Tonight, this man would fear *her*.

Her foot prepared to land on another old, rotten wooden step. It echoed into the silent foyer with a *creak,* so she decided to disguise the noise. She knew *exactly* how to do it, too.

"Mar-cooooo..."

Becca sang as loudly as she could. It was *so* sweet being on this side of things.

"Aaaah!"

Alset screamed from somewhere beyond the landing. She heard glass shattering against furniture, the thudding of heavy objects smacking the floor, and she readied her pistol. He could appear at *any* moment, and she expected *anything* besides a peaceful surrender. She *expected* this lunatic to attack her. *And if he does...*

She did *not* bring a pair of handcuffs with her...

"We gave you a chance, dude. And you *blew* it. You ruined your girlfriend's life, *and* your momma's life... now it's *your* turn."

She was only one step onto the second staircase, but she could smell him from here. *Old, musty clothes, body odor... and fear.* She pivoted left and carefully waved the flashlight over the landing, scanning for Alset. As the next step began to *creak*, she sang out once again.

"Marco..."

"Shut up! Shut up-shut up-shut up!"

One foot on the first step, her foot barely on the second, Becca was standing still when Alset appeared at the railing. She took a step backward, planting her feet on the solid landing. He was unarmed, but he was acting very spastic and hysterical, teetering on the edge right in front of her. She was bearing witness to a man losing what was left of his mind—

A man who thrived on the fear of others, now wincing at the taste of his own medicine.

This is for you, Q. "I watched Khari die, Alset."

His green eyes grew as wide as saucers, *glaring* with evil intentions.

"You..."

"Yep. I watched that wretched old *bitch* die right in front of me. She ran. Like a *coward.*"

Alset growled, an animalistic and feral growl, a sound that at one point put the fear of God into Rebecca. She felt a tickle in her bladder, as if her instincts were screaming at her to cower.

But cower, she did *not.*

The man leaped in place like an angry kangaroo, stomping on the floor as if building up his kinetic energy. Without hesitation, he dashed down the staircase, his feet *barely* touching the steps as he lunged toward Becca, reaching out with his hands.

Alset had to have *known* how this would end—the woman was *clearly* armed, yet he *still* pounced. Desperate to attack, to shred, to *kill*... hopeful for one last chance to inflict damage on this FBI Agent who had been searching for him, unknowingly, for *two* years.

The amount of mental trauma she'd *suffered* through... the times she'd admitted to her therapist how she'd *fantasized* of killing the Y2Killer with her bare hands. When you think about it, January 1st was the least traumatizing to Becca in any *direct* way. She went home that day to her son, *and life goes on, you know?*

But it didn't. Something triggered in Becca's brain. The events of that day had redefined her. They had transformed her into a timid, meek shell of her former self.

It took a *truly* traumatizing experience to overwrite these deeply coded memories. Jeremey's death had affected Becca because she *was* a victim, as well. A victim of fear and self-doubt, of relying on others because of those fears and doubts. She became terrified that she might make another mistake, one that might cost another innocent life... and she vowed never to let that happen again.

It would take some situation where she had no choice... before she'd *ever* face that music.

September 11th changed the lives of *so* many people in many terrible ways. Even if the thought of CeCe's death might crush her spirit—

That wasn't something to be sad about, no.

Her memory was to be cherished... *celebrated*.

Every hero *deserves* that honor.

January 1st had turned Becca into a *victim*.

Only *this* time, she *wasn't* the victim... she was the *hero*.

Because it was her duty, there was a job to be done.

If she didn't do it, she only had *herself* to blame.

She planted her feet, preparing to move.

Deep in her mind, she saw Q's face appear before her.

Only this time, he was *smiling* that contagious smile again.

No longer haunted by a red headband, she smiled back.

"Everything is going to be alright, Rebecca." *I-I...* She took a deep breath, centering herself in her world despite the terrifying figure soaring towards her.

"It will be alright, Boss."

Will it, though? Will I be alright, Q?

"Just breathe... rewrite your book, clear your karma, and *breathe.*"

You almost had it, friend.

The moment Alset committed to his leap, Becca side-stepped to her left, down a single step. She aimed her weapon at the glint of flashlight that reflected off of Alset's golden tooth, and she squeezed the trigger.

Rebecca's aim was true.

*   *   *

As Becca breathlessly sprinted out of the dilapidated house, the driveway was abuzz with activity. An unmarked Police Cruiser pulled into the driveway, its bubble light illuminating the mansion's front yard. A second car was *right* behind them, another of the unmarked cars from the stakeout. Climbing out of the back seat was a familiar face.

"Bill!"

Her boss was not as excited to see his rogue agent. He threw an angry fist in Becca's direction.

"You're in deep shit, Taylor!"

Before she could take a step further, Bill caught her shoulder, yanking her back so hard her neck snapped a bit, shooting pain down her back.

"Ow!"

"Oh... I'm sorry," he retreated his hand, and blushed a little. "You get him, Becca?"

"Suspect is down, sir." She smiled smugly, still gasping for air before glancing at her watch; the time was 2:22.

"Good, I don't have to *fire* your ass. Where's Marissa?"

She shook her head before noticing Jim, climbing out of the first car and pumping his fist excitedly as the cavalry arrived. Multiple units could be heard approaching the scene; Becca was glad the fun was *finally* finished.

Alset was hers to dispose of, and the trash had been taken out.

She looked around, scared, as Bill helped Jim on his good leg; he was grinning excitedly as Becca rushed over towards him.

"*Taylor!* Did you get the bastard?"

"It's over, Jimbo," she muttered, holstering her gun. "Suspect is down. 10-55."

"He's *dead?* But then, where's the *girl—?*"

Jim was incredulous as Becca ran towards the driveway, ignoring him. She didn't care about Alset anymore. She only had one thing on her mind, rushing desperately towards the detached garage, the *only* place in the house she hadn't searched yet.

"*Marissa!*"

Becca was terrified of the unknown as she turned towards the driveway, imagining fresh snow with bloodstains lining the way towards the other building. Bill's outstretched hand went ignored as Becca hobbled towards the garage, a million thoughts racing through her mind.

Where is Marissa?
What if Alset already—?
Why isn't she here?
How did I lose control of this —?
Will this nightmare ever end?

One of the long garage doors began to rise slowly, right as Becca was mere steps from reaching it. The half-dozen police officers now huddled in the gravel driveway began drawing their weapons, spooked at this new threat... perhaps a *fourth* suspect— *or a terrible monster!*

Or with my luck, it's a portal back to the 91st Floor... and I can relive this nightmare all over again.

Instead of a terrifying creature, the silhouette of an hourglass-shaped agent contrasted sharply in the bright light pouring over Becca's face, forcing her to squint. Fiery locks wafted in the breeze as Becca's eyes adjusted to the light; the monster appeared to be...

waving at me?

"Becca, come here—have a look at this!" She struggled to identify the woman. Becca's mouth went dry again.

Now, what?

She stumbled into the garage, which was flooded with fluorescent light. Becca's head was dizzy from fatigue and adrenaline, so she allowed this woman to place her hand upon her chest, stopping her in her tracks beside a corner. She fished a key from her breast pocket and flipped it to Becca.

It was a freshly-made house key with American Flags all over it.

"Well, Taylor. The bad news is, the key was useless till *now*. It, like, opened the door to the garage."

"Okay—and what's the *good* news?"

Kelly lowered her hand and nodded to the side. Becca rounded the corner.

In the middle of the garage floor was a tiny little person.

"Hola!"

Her lovely yellow summer dress billowed in the artificial light, as if it were the midday sun. To Becca, the scene could only be described as a miracle. She'd gone through hell and back to save this little girl... but she could only *imagine* what this poor young lady had suffered through these last few days. Becca's pupils dilated so fast she could *feel* them adjusting to the light level... although it was *probably* the dopamine rush she was experiencing.

Heaven was *here* in an old garage, embodied by an angelic mirage. She wobbled gently on her feet before falling to her knees on the concrete with a *thud*. It couldn't *possibly* be Marissa Hernandez, could it? The girl who'd gone missing less than three days ago... *Might as well be a lifetime.*

"You..." she choked.

"I only know a little English," she said shyly, smiling with a

400

large gap in her front teeth. She had a small bruise on her chin and hadn't bathed in *days*. It shattered Becca's heart; she wondered if the girl had even *eaten* today...

"My name is Marissa Maria Hernández. It's nice to meet you, *señorita.*"

"I... I'm Rebecca Taylor, sweetheart. And... I'm here to take you home."

Marissa glanced away shyly.

Becca hadn't noticed the police crowding around Kelly, silently observing them. The sudden presence of so many people had Marissa nervous, even if Becca didn't understand *why* yet.

"C-can I have a hug?" Marissa stammered softly.

"Oh my God—yes, please!"

Becca welcomed the little girl with open arms as she barreled into her embrace, holding her just as tenderly as she cradled her own son on that fateful December day. She squeezed gently yet *firmly,* wrapping the child in warmth and safety as she wept into Becca's bosom, almost as if she were her own mother. At that moment, she found safety in the agent's loving, steadfast embrace.

The room erupted into applause as Becca held the little girl.

"You're safe, now."

She kissed the little girl's scalp and cradled her head before the roaring of officers celebrating behind her became apparent. As she glanced back, weight seemed to lift gently off her exhausted shoulders; she could barely *speak* through her quivering lips.

"It was all worth it."

It was all worth it. It was all worth it. It was all worth it.

Becca wanted to hug her *forever,* to *protect* her. In a way, she wasn't holding Marissa. Marissa meant *more* to Becca than that. It had been a *very* long time since she'd been on a successful mission with stakes this high, and she was *awash* with emotion.

This was the happiest she'd been in a very long time, so no...

it wasn't only *Marissa* she was holding.

She was holding *everything*.

Her tears dried as she released their embrace, and Becca stood slowly, silently cursing the terrific pain in both her knees. "Where's Jim? He deserves to meet her, too."

"He's outside," she motioned with her head behind her, towards the Yukon, which was still idling in the mansion's driveway. Becca wiped the tears from her flushed cheeks as she knelt beside Marissa.

"You wanna meet the nice man that helped us find you?"

"Si; por favor!"

A smile crept through Marissa's matted bangs. She pulled away from Becca's arms and ran excitedly, barefoot, through the crowd of bystanders. Her feet *plopped* along the asphalt as she sprinted out of the garage and into the cool morning air.

Becca followed her outside, where Jim Serrano was alone, leaning against the Yukon and grunting in pain at his leg. His arms were folded, staring at the front door of the mansion. He'd been the only official *not* to join the reunion in the garage and wasn't aware of what had taken place... *yet*.

Marissa stopped twenty feet from Jim, who had yet to notice the three women. Becca knelt next to Marissa once she caught up and softly spoke in her ear.

"Marissa, this is one of my *best* friends, and one of the *bravest* agents in the whole FBI! This is my partner, Jim Serrano."

When he *finally* noticed them, the last thing in the world he expected to see was Marissa and Becca, smiling mischievously at him. His usually stoic expression softened as he saw them.

"Es un placer conocerle, señor!" Marissa nervously glanced back at Becca, who was beaming with pride. "It is okay to hug, too?"

Becca cracked through her tears with a reassuring laugh. "I

think he'd like that *very* much."

Jim's face lit as the little girl ran towards him, leaping into his outstretched arms and nearly bowling the injured agent over. He lifted the child as if she were his own, laughing with a tone of unbridled joy that, in all their years of working together, she'd never quite made out in his voice.

I wonder if this was how he had been as a father. I suppose a parent never quite loses touch with those instincts.

Jim's laughter was endearing, with a tone she'd never quite heard before... but that wasn't the *only* first in that moment. *And I know he hates it as much as I do...*

Becca had never seen Jim Serrano cry.

XXVIII

Becca glanced at her watch; it was nearly six a.m.

"Mom's home," she flatly announced as she stumbled through the door, tossing her car keys nonchalantly onto the kitchen bar as she approached it. There was *no* party here to greet her this morning.

The house was silent and dark, but the telltale evidence of teenagers was abundant. Chad took his mother up on her offer to have friends over. It seemed he'd ordered a pizza, and the Nintendo 64 was hooked up to the living room set; controllers and cables *littered* the living room floor. Even though she was annoyed at the mess, Becca was *far* too exhausted to pick up the remnants of the party; she'd worry about it later. She was *so* exhausted that she didn't even bother plugging her cell phone into the charger; instead, she dropped it next to the cordless phone dock.

The silent house stood undisturbed as she shuffled towards the fridge. The only sounds were of thumping paws as Pepper came tumbling down the stairs, groggily greeting Becca.

"*Hey*, boy," she exclaimed, scratching him behind the ears before kicking her left boot off in the middle of the kitchen floor, where her dog opted to investigate it. Next was her bra; with a practiced maneuver, she released the undergarment from the outside of her dress shirt, dropping it haphazardly to the floor.

Ahh... glorious relief.

Her poor, aching feet had done *so* much over the last few days—she was grateful that Bill had dismissed them for the rest of the week.

"Yeah, Bill, but *you* need sleep more than *any* of us," she'd told him as he'd dropped her back off at the station, after taking Marissa home.

After a quick visit to the hospital for a checkup, Marissa's family celebrated a tearful—yet *joyous*—reunion. Becca had *never* been so happy to awaken a family at some ungodly hour. And, for those few moments of the happy family reuniting, she knew it, deep down inside, and was finally able to accept it.

It was all worth it.

Bill promised *he* would get some sleep, but she *knew* that wasn't going to happen. Despite their shared triumph, their victory was muted; what was happening downtown was on the forefront of *everyone's* mind, and for *none* of them as much as Becca, who tried desperately not to dwell on it.

For her part, Becca was *very* ready for bed, but after the excitement of the past few hours... *I might need some help in that department.* Limping towards the refrigerator, she glanced out the window into the backyard, where the first hints of sunrise were beginning to tease the horizon.

Twenty-six hours, she'd been awake. The day after she'd gone through hell and back. It was a miracle she was even *awake*... let alone lucid enough to feel *depressed*. It was *easy* for her to fall into that trap, but she had to keep reminding herself that CeCe wouldn't want to be a martyr—she was a *hero*.

Just like Becca was.

It was all worth it.

Even as Tuesday's events had fractured her *own* home, Becca believed it was *still* all worth it. When the little girl hugged her parents, she imagined her son returning from school with a backpack full of homework, a second grader with a mind stuffed with knowledge he couldn't *wait* to share. Marissa's parents had lost their self-control, babbling in broken chains of English and Spanish, holding their precious daughter as they *never* had before.

Even now, she couldn't kick the thought, the repetitive lyric she kept singing to herself, trying to distract from thinking about what she *herself* had lost.

It was all worth it. It was all worth it. It was all worth it.

Pepper eagerly awaited his turn for more attention, his tail wagging optimistically. Becca closed the fridge with her can of beer as she bent to scratch the little Labrador's ears again, and fished a biscuit from the box on the counter.

"Don't tell Momma," she whispered, before she stopped. Her face drained of color, and she nearly *fainted* in the kitchen, swaying on her feet as a wave of vertigo *smashed* her in the forehead.

Once she recovered, she left the kitchen, taking a seat at their breakfast bar. The flashing light on the answering machine caught her eye the moment she dropped her cell phone on the counter.

Brace yourself, girl. You're gonna need a lot more beer.

With a *groan*, Becca cracked the can of Miller Lite, taking a long swig and savoring the pleasant burn in her throat as she pressed the 'play' button. The tape player *clicked* and *whirred* with life.

"MESSAGE ONE—TUESDAY, SEPTEMBER ELEVEN— NINE OH NINE A.M.—

"Cecilia? Are you *there?* Rebecca? Hello? This is Flo; I *just* saw the news. I'm just calling because I'm worried about you two. *Please* call me back. I love you."

"END OF MESSAGE—TO DELETE PLEASE PRESS DELETE NOW. TO SAVE—"

A twinge of sadness came over Becca as she reached across the kitchen counter, where a bottle of wine they'd cracked open last night sat unfinished, most of its contents still inside. She couldn't have given less of a damn about the fresh beer still half full; she grabbed the bottle with her bandaged hand, and took a giant swig as the answering machine continued.

I'm probably gonna need more before this is over...

"MESSAGE DELETED. MESSAGE TWO—TUESDAY, SEPTEMBER ELEVEN..."

As the messages poured in and she grew more and more drunk, she was *touched* by how many people had reached out on Tuesday. Almost *everyone* in their immediate families had called the house—even Becca's cousin rang from St. Paul—as well as a few friends and co-workers. The messages were all similar in scope: people were worried sick and scared... yet *neither* of them was home to reassure them.

The prospect of *actually* calling everyone back made her queasy; it would take her *days*.

It made sense that people were worried, but after a while, hearing the constant perturbation in their voices started to drive Becca *bananas*. Once she reached message number thirty, if she didn't recognize the caller, she would delete the message— especially the awful, melodramatic one she'd left *herself* Tuesday night.

Nobody needs to hear that. Especially Chad.

That changed when she reached the messages from September 12th. The frequency of calls slowed to a reasonable trickle... and one in particular caught her ears, despite her tipsy attention span. As the message began, she returned to the fridge, grabbing her *third* can of beer.

"MESSAGE DELETED. MESSAGE SIXTY-TWO— WEDNESDAY, SEPTEMBER TWELVE—FOUR FIFTY FIVE P.M.—

"Rebecca! Cecilia! It's Michael Manfred, I work in the North Tower of the World Trade... well, I *used* to. You know... before...

anyways! I hope you don't mind. I tried the cell number on your card, but it didn't pick up, so I looked your number up in the phone book. I *really* wanted to give you a call."

Nicely loosened up by now, she leaned back on the barstool and rubbed her sore neck as she listened and grinned. Mike was a nice guy, and although they'd only spent a few moments together, his confident, calm demeanor was *refreshing* in the intense atmosphere of the North Tower. She was thrilled to hear his voice, since she'd not heard from *any* of her party, yet; she still had *all* of the crumpled business cards she'd collected sitting on her dresser upstairs, and likely would've reached out to him eventually.

"Anyways, I, uh... I just wanted to say thank you! Thanks to both of you, the whole fuckin' *group* got out! And Cecilia, you were on *point,* man... the fire department got us down quick as hell... haha. And, uh... we were able to get out through the Mall before the building came down.

"We hadn't heard anything about you, Becca, but we figured you were *way* ahead of us, but, uh... yeah, I just wanted to make sure you both made it out. Oh, and if Q made it out. Also, if you, uh... saw that Alset guy again?

"I didn't know if you'd want the news that we got out, but I just, uh... I figured I'd let you know. Because... well, you two are *heroes,* you know? Whether you want to admit it or not. Not only because you helped us get out of the building, but that Alset guy was with us that got Donny... you *probably* saved my life. You *both* did.

"I told my wife and kid about you and, well... *thank you.* I just wanted to say that, ya know?

"Anyways, call me when you have a moment to chat. I'd love to take you two to dinner, or *whatever!* I also got everyone in our group's numbers and stuff, if, uh... if you wanted to talk with them. Love you, Becca. Love you, CeCe. Much love you two, hope you're safe and sound. Have a blessed day!"

"END OF MESSAGE. TO DELETE—"

Becca hit the 'SAVE' button on the machine, and the miniature cassette tape whirred away. She took another chug straight from the bottle, swallowing the flat, warm drink, which earned a groan from Becca.

That groan intensified when the bottle dripped empty.

Annoyed, she shuffled over to the fridge and grabbed another cold Miller Lite from the door, cracking it open with an icy *pop*. It reminded her of CeCe and the beer she'd left on the nightstand. Her eyes started to water a bit as she slumped back onto the barstool.

"MESSAGE DELETED. MESSAGE SIXTY-THREE— WEDNESDAY, SEPTEMBER TWELVE—FIVE OH FIVE P.M.—

"Hello, Rebecca. This is Doctor Gail Mitzel."

Becca's eyes rolled audibly. *Oh, perfect...*

"I'm just calling to let you know that it's been a while since we've seen you, and with everything going on, I've just been reaching out to all of my clients, letting them know that I'm here for them if they need to meet up.

"I know you're probably pretty busy, but as you well know, dear, the trouble with trauma is that it doesn't *care* about all that. So, if you decide that you need to have a chat—"

Becca hit the delete button on the machine as she sipped her beer. The ice-cold brew felt so refreshing as it went down smoothly, and she drunkenly put her head in her hands as the tape whirred to life, playing the next message back to her in a robotic voice.

"MESSAGE DELETED. MESSAGE SIXTY-FOUR— WEDNESDAY, SEPTEMBER TWELVE—FIVE TWENTY THREE P.M.—

"Hi, Rebecca, this is... this is Captain Jack Jansen, from Ladder Company Eighty-Four. I tried your cell, but uh... yeah. Anyways, um... your aide at the office just called me, said you'd been trying to call down here all day asking about Cecilia—"

Becca gasped. She wasn't drunk enough for this... and the room was already *spinning*.

Here we go.

She leaned on the counter, on the edge of her stool, preparing herself to process the news she'd *known* she'd hear eventually.

"...and I wanted to call and let you know that she's alright. She's been down at the Trade Center with the First Response, and uh... she's a fuckin' *trooper*... and..."

She didn't even hear the rest of the message. The world zoomed in around her.

She's alive she's alive she's alive she's—

She danced on her injured leg like she was *floating*, as if the weight of the world had lifted from her shoulders. The kitchen transformed into a boundless blue sky, where she was a carefree sparrow delighting in a joyful spring day.

No... this wasn't joy. Not even relief. This was *freedom*.

Never in Becca's life was she more alive than *now*. Cecilia was *alright*. And the air tasted of life.

Sweet, glorious *life*.

Growing lightheaded, she stopped herself on the edge of the counter, balancing drunkenly on her good leg. A framed photograph of her family caught her eye. The snapshot captured a moment of *perfect* bliss—herself, Cecilia, and Chad at the Boardwalk weeks prior, dressed in their bathing suits, with sun-kissed smiles as they laughed to the camera.

"END OF MESSAGE. TO DELETE THIS MESSAGE—"

Suddenly lucid upon hearing the recorder's prompt, Becca scampered towards the machine and slapped the "Save" button, her fingers shaking so hard she could barely even work them.

"CeCe... you really *are* my hero."

The silent tears ran down her cheeks, still scratched from yesterday's ordeal in the tower, the scabs still red and tender. They were superficial wounds; they'd heal in a few days. A week at most.

The scars, however... they'll take some time to heal fully...

"*MESSAGE SIXTY-FIVE—WEDNESDAY, SEPTEMBER TWELVE—FIVE FIFTY SEVEN P.M.—*

"Hi, Babe... It's me."

Becca froze again.

"I'm *so* sorry I haven't called. I tried your cell, but anyway, I know you're worried sick. *I* was worried, *too*... just so you know. But I'm *relieved* you got out, Babe.

"I've been helping out down here at Ground Zero, it's been God-awful as you know, we've been searching for people out there in the rubble. It's been absolutely *chaotic*, but I'm just calling to tell you I'm heading home, I've been up for like thirty-five hours straight, so if you're out there working, I'm just telling you that I love you, I was *worried* about you and they told me you were calling, you were *so* worried about me... oh, *God*, I love you, and if I'm asleep when you get home *please* wake me up—"

Through the veil of tears, Becca saw Pepper's attention turning away. *Someone* was standing at the landing at the top of the stairs.

She slowly stood, stopping the slew of messages entirely.

"How long have you been standing there?"

"Oh... since about when you got *that* beer out the fridge."

She turned on the kitchen light to reveal Cecilia Chapman standing in the hallway at the top of the stairs, staring down the steps at her. She smiled behind her tousled curly brown hair, her hazel eyes, the faded New York Jets T-shirt hanging off one of her muscular shoulders, and Becca was running up the steps as fast as she could move, her injured leg be *damned*.

When she reached CeCe, she tackled her like a linebacker. They kissed forever and a day. They were *never* happier to see each other.

Like two teenagers finally alone for the first time, they could not stop, as Becca tried—hard as she might—to fuse their bodies together as they embraced each other in the middle of the stairs.

CeCe pulled away from the deluge of love, a breathless gasp as her eyes rolled back in her head. Upon recovering her composure, she squinted into Becca's eyes seductively.

"Chad spent the night at his friend's house."

That was all Becca needed to hear. They didn't even make it to the bedroom.

XXIX

"A Snowy Evening at the Odeon"

"It ain't a surprise if I know about it before we *get* there, Babe!" Becca pulled her knit hat tightly against her head as she trudged through the slushy snow, desperate to get indoors where the biting cold couldn't hurt her any longer. Before she could reach the *sidewalk*, however, CeCe grabbed her arm.

"Wait, Becca!" CeCe protested in a cloud of breathy steam, hurriedly pumping quarters into the meter. "I know 'bout it, too. But we still gotta *act* surprised!"

"Babe! I'm, like, going to *die* out here!"

"Relax, you're actin' like a *baby.*"

Cecilia glanced back as Chad rushed to catch up, the last one out of Becca's brand-new Acura MDX. He slammed the SUV's back door shut, nearly slipping on the slushy snow as he stomped across the sidewalk.

"Do we really need to live on *Hoth*, Mom?"

"Both of you; my *goodness!* I ain't seen 'whining' this good since the night your Mom got the *killer!*"

The family cracked up over CeCe's pun, their breath billowing like smog into the frigid Manhattan air. It rose high against the gently-falling snowflakes, past the bunting and tinsel hanging from the lampposts that lined Broadway.

Definitely 'tis the season. 'Twas the night after Christmas, and I get to have a nice dinner with loved ones. Fittingly, I'm feeling the spirit this year.

She rubbed her mittens together rapidly as she eyeballed the

413

doors. "I'm going in, CeCe. I can't *stand* it anymore."

"Okay," she nodded. "Play *nice*, Babe."

Becca cracked the door open. An invigorating blast of warm air rushed over her, inviting her into the restaurant. She barely noticed the familiar smells of French cuisine wafting into her nose; the seductive comfort of the heated restaurant was *all* she yearned for.

As they stomped snow off their boots, an usher in fancy garb opened the second set of doors, greeting the family with a friendly grin.

"Happy Holidays. Welcome to the Odeon, folks. We've been *expecting* you."

Although she hadn't eaten here since September 10th, she'd dined here frequently enough in the past to know what to expect. However, as Becca entered the cozy atmosphere of one of her favorite spots, she was taken *aback* by what she saw.

The tables were rearranged, as if the place had transformed into a banquet hall. Despite it being a Wednesday evening, the joint was jam-packed (not completely unheard of for this place; Becca knew *full* well how popular the Odeon was).

And every single person here was now standing and staring at her.

What is this? Who are these people?

However, she then began to notice *who* was in attendance. The crowd, nearly a *hundred* strong, began to applaud the family, even as Becca was still shaking snow off her shoulders. Chad stood in stunned silence, watching as *every* person in the room celebrated his parents. Even the servers, bartenders, and bussers participated in the applause surrounding them.

CeCe was already hiding her face, blushing bright red. "Babe... they're clapping for you."

Becca giggled before leaning in and planting a soft kiss on her lips. When she pulled back, it was *CeCe* who was tearing up.

"No, Cecilia. They're clapping for *us.*"

CeCe gawked at the thunderous throng with a mighty sniffle, *immediately* recognizing a large portion of them. Beside a small table which seated her parents and her brother's family, a row of firefighters stood dressed in their pressed uniforms, cheering louder than *anyone* else in the room. She grinned from ear to ear as she waved at her co-workers—no... her *brothers,* her *sisters*—and was overwhelmed nearly to the point of *fainting* before her station captain, Jack Jansen, escorted her to the family's reserved table.

Meanwhile, *Becca's* eyes landed first on the folks she recognized from the office. Her aide, Jennifer, looked as professionally *lovely* as she always did at the office. The table right behind theirs sat her closest friends in the FBI. Bill, Jim, and Kelly were huddled together, hooting like fans at a football game, with Agent McLain standing beside them. Just as CeCe was being escorted away, Becca began heading towards the FBI table. She hadn't seen them in *weeks,* and—

"Becca!"

She flinched at the volume of this new greeting and held a finger up towards their table, gesturing for them to hang on. A thin, red-haired man had spotted her and was rushing to wrap a bear hug around her, before another pulled him off of her with one muscular arm.

"Whoa, dawg— give the lady some *air,* bro!"

"I am so happy to see you, Becca, I'm sorry... I just really *missed* you—it's so *good* to see you again!"

"It's good to see you too, Jason," Becca laughed, pulling her hands from his excited grip as Mike dragged him back to their table. Julie Mercado was standing on two healthy legs, absolutely *stunning* in a snazzy plum dress with long, silver earrings.

As Becca and Jason pulled apart, another smiling face from

the table rose to hug her—one whom she didn't recognize at first... but he surely remembered *her*.

"Agent Taylor!" he waved excitedly. "I'm happy you made it out!"

"Um... oh... N-Nick, right?" She tilted her head, as a curious dog might do when he hears a bag of treats jostling about.

"Yeah, Nicky Rice!" He held out a massive paw to shake Becca's hand. "I met you up on, uh... ninety-one, remember? Boy... I'm so *glad* you made it out."

Becca couldn't help but laugh at his presence. "It's great to see you, Nick... but how did you find out—?"

"*Oh,* your girlfriend called me last week!" He nodded towards CeCe, who was now seated amongst her firefighting friends and laughing in a mob of her own admirers. "She found my business card, and asked me to come so... here I am!"

Nick's laughter was infectious; Becca could *hardly* recall the traumatized expression he wore that day. "Are you doin' alright, Nicky?"

"Not really, if I'm being honest..." His smile melted away as he leaned in close to Becca to whisper in her ear; the scent of Acqua di Giò cologne filled her nostrils, making her dizzy as he whispered into her ear.

"I've... been going to therapy ever since that day. I can't stop seeing the people falling, ya know... it's driving me *insane!*"

She embraced him in a light hug, patting his back softly. *I can relate, Nicky... I can relate.*

"Is that how you all knew to come out?" As she released her hug with Nick, Becca glanced back at Mike, who'd barely spoken so far. "I ended up keeping all of those cards..."

"Correct," Julie explained. "Cecilia was the darling who coordinated *most* of this shindig."

"Yeah," Mike added sheepishly, "I didn't expect a fancy soirée like *this*, though… I've never eaten here before." Mike's eyes darted around at all the bustling staff, and Becca wondered what he was thinking.

"Typical chef," Julie scoffed from behind Mike's shoulder. "Too high on your own supply to enjoy some fine dining, *eh?*"

"Please!" Mike let out a bellowing laugh. "I don't make enough on a chef's salary to afford this place like you *business* folks can."

"We can't afford it *either,* Mike." Julie held her clutch up; it matched her violet dress perfectly. "We just put it all on plastic. Indulge now—worry *later!*"

"Julie," Jason said awkwardly, lowering his voice and gesturing with his hand for her to do the same, "don't you think we *shouldn't* talk about our finances in public like this?"

"Spare me," Julie scoffed. "I gross more than *you* do, anyway."

"We heard about Quarren, Becca." Jason's glance shifted down. "I'm sorry that he didn't make it out; he was a good guy."

"He saved my *life,* Jason. *And* Marissa's…" Her eyes began to dart around the room, hoping to find the little girl's family in attendance.

Mike patted her on the back. "You're a hero, Agent. I read all about the Manhattan Mauler case on AOL. I'm so proud of you for finding that *Ay-hole* and saving the child."

"Excuse me," a woman seated beside Mike's spot offered. She stood up, muttering something to Mike that caused his face to *droop,* before turning towards Becca with a friendly smile, offering her hand. "We haven't met yet—I'm Michael's wife. Sheila Manfred."

"Oh!" Becca's smile stretched wide. "It's great to meet you, Sheila! Mike's told me *so* much about you!"

"I'm sorry I didn't introduce you *sooner,*" Mike scoffed, glancing at his wife. "I wanted you to meet our daughter, Ariana, but she stayed home..."

Becca could barely hear him speaking. Something caught her eye, and she'd completely forgotten about Mike's daughter. Not far from her own table sat another table at which three people sat. A middle-aged Latino couple... and *their* young daughter.

"Marissa!" she cried, momentarily forgetting the folks she'd escaped the tower with. "Mr. and Mrs. Hernandez! I'm so *happy* you guys made it!"

"Hola, Agent Taylor!"

Mr. Hernandez stood proudly next to his lovely little daughter; the entire family was dressed sharply in their best. When Marissa performed a cute little curtsy in her purple wool coat, Becca's heart *melted.*

She embraced the girl. And everything *was* alright.

*   *   *

"Ken?" Becca called softly, her voice trembling as she stood on the 107th floor of the North Tower, alone amid the quiet grandeur of *Windows on the World.* She gazed out through the glass, her eyes flickering quickly, as if searching the still city below. Gentle snowflakes drifted down in delicate, slow motion. The cityscape was *eerily* silent, deserted, presenting a chilling silence that gave her the *creeps.* The snow seemed to seep inside, settling like a white, whispering web over everything—including *herself.*

"Ken!" Becca put her face to the glass as she stared down at New York. She was scanning the roads for a taxicab, *desperate* to stop the impending crash, but the streets were absolutely empty—

"I'm here, Rebecca."

She whirled around to see her late husband, although, to her eyes, he looked *younger* than she remembered. Standing there, he was an aberration of ghastly origins that she was *terrified* of... yet, she was simultaneously *mesmerized* by his presence.

After a moment of hesitation, Rebecca rushed to embrace Ken, but upon reaching him, she fell right *through* his body, almost as if...

"Are you dead?" she muttered, her back to him.

"Nothing has changed."

"Then *why* are you here?"

Her words were an accusation, bellowed from her core; she wasn't mad at Ken... she was angry with herself. "Is this a dream? Where is CeCe?"

"Yes. When you wake up, you'll be with CeCe again."

She shook the cobwebs off, trying to gain some sort of lucidity; although she *was* aware this wasn't real, she had no control of her body—*or* her emotions.

Only her *words* seemed to be hers.

If that's all I have, I'll use the only weapon at my disposal...

"You know," she giggled, "tomorrow is our anniversary, Darling. Our *fourteenth.*" She reached for his face, her trembling fingers falling through his neatly-trimmed goatee. "Ken... I had to let you *go*. I—"

"I know. You're *healing,* Dear."

His body seemed real enough as he approached her. Ken lifted his cold hand to her cheek as she stood there, unable to move, cry, or even blink. She *thought* she could feel his touch; she decided to convince herself that she *could*.

"*Am* I? I still miss you dearly. Every time I look at Chad, I miss you." Rebecca glanced at her watch... but her Pulsar wasn't there. It was on Ken's wrist. "Chad misses you *so* much."

"You're doing a great job without me, Rebecca. He's turning into a *fine* young man."

With a surge of self-control, she stepped away from him, backpedaling until her rear end bumped into an empty dining chair.

"I'm moving on... I can tell... yet, I still *love* you, Ken. We both miss you dearly."

"I love you, *too,* Darling, and I miss you both so much."

He turned back towards the window Rebecca had been staring out of, floating towards it until he passed right through it. His body hovered outside in the mid-air snowfall as Rebecca approached the glass, intending to follow him until her nose smacked into the pane.

"Will I *ever* be alright?"

Ken's body flew backwards, further from Rebecca, as she helplessly watched Ken leave her yet again. His body faded into the snow before it vanished entirely.

"Yes, Dear. You're going to be alright. Just clear your mind, and write your story—"

And breathe...

Ken was gone. She spun around, hoping Cecilia would be there... but instead, she was now standing in a snowy driveway. The white Dodge van was still parked in its place, and lying in red snow, surrounded by mounds of fresh powder... was *not* Jim Serrano.

"Q?" Becca exclaimed, rushing over to his side. "Are you *alright?"*

Quarren's body was buried halfway in the snow; the gaping laceration across his chest was no longer bleeding, but the cut still appeared fresh. As she approached him, she noticed something strange—despite his mortal wound, he smiled up at her.

That damned smile... She involuntarily grinned back at him.

"No, Boss," he shook his head. "I must know—are *you* alright?"

Becca flinched at Q's words; she didn't expect them to *sting* quite as hard as they did. She glanced over at the van, knowing that Jeremey Young was about to—

"You *need* to move on, Rebecca."

Q stood up suddenly, and effortlessly, as if his wounds no longer concerned him. Still grinning, he casually brushed the snow from his clean, pressed business suit, and walked towards the van.

"I did! I'm *much* better now, Q." She tried to grab him, but he was out of range; she wanted to follow him but couldn't move her legs.

"Then answer the question. Babe, are you alright?"

"I—wait, *what?*"

"Babe?"

*   *   *

"Babe, are you alright? You've *barely* touched your omelette!" The Odeon rushed back into Becca's senses, snapping her back into reality. She didn't respond to her girlfriend's question, opting instead to poke her fork around on her plate, twirling the mass of eggs and filling around haphazardly.

"Rebecca? Are you alright?"

She finally returned to her senses (albeit momentarily), her eyes still transfixed on her artistic endeavors with the melty cheddar. "Oh, yes, CeCe; I'm fine," she lied.

"Don't *bullshit* me, Babe. What's the matter?" It wasn't a request for information; it was a *demand*. "Is it because tomorrow's your...?"

Becca shook her head, dropping her fork on her plate with a subtle *clank*. "No, it's not that," she muttered. "I just feel *empty.*"

"Whaddya mean?"

"I don't mean to sound *ungrateful,*" she began, a familiar lump forming in her throat, "but I don't feel right celebrating without Q. He *deserves* to be here; without him—"

CeCe placed her arm around Becca's shoulders and kissed her on the scalp. "Babe..." she interrupted Becca's melancholic monologue, "he *is* here. Look *around* you."

Typically, Becca was immune to the type of manipulation CeCe was attempting; she *knew* what she was trying to do. Nevertheless, she obliged, scanning the restaurant once again.

"He is here... inside of *everyone* that you saved, Babe. He is here with that little girl, and those folks you led down the tower to me. And, he's here with *you* as well." CeCe lightly planted a finger upon Becca's breastbone, pointing towards her heart.

"You might not have made it out if he hadn't been there. I only met Q briefly, but I am forever *grateful* to the man."

Becca knew CeCe was right: things would likely've gone *very* differently without Q. If she hadn't met him, she would've been trapped on the higher floors, searching for Alset when the plane hit. Not a *single* person above the ninety-first floor in the North Tower survived on September 11th. She was *that* close to being one of over *fourteen hundred souls* that were doomed the moment the first plane struck.

Not to mention, he was the one who saved her from Alset...

It wasn't the *first* time she'd considered that, but at this moment, CeCe's words hit differently for Becca. She proudly scanned the group, recognizing many faces whose lives Becca had touched that day—and if not for Quarren, this night would have felt *very* different.

"I *am* alright, Cecilia." Becca couldn't defeat the smile creeping across her cheeks, thwarting her plans to feel sorry for herself. "I promise."

She felt that familiar urge to tear up, but she swallowed it away. Instead, she leaned forward with a smile, nearly knocking her omelette to the floor as they lost themselves in each other's lips—

"Oh my *God,* you two—get a *room.*" Chad rolled his eyes at his mother's public display of affection. "Seriously, it's *embarrassing.*"

The two women pulled apart, Becca blushing profusely, as she sat up to tackle her dinner once again. Truthfully, her appetite was *long* gone, and she was trying to convince herself to take another bite when a presence over her other shoulder caused her to flinch—she jumped in her chair and nearly *screamed*.

"Hey, Taylor," came a familiar, masculine voice.

"Jim! Don't sneak up on me like that."

She wiped her hands on her napkin as she pulled a chair out for her partner, but he waved his hand, nearly dropping his crutch on Becca's head as he did so.

"I'm sorry; I was going to make my way to your table, but then dinner was—"

"It's fine, don't be so *dramatic.*" Jim seemed to be in his usual, cranky mood tonight, but she saw through it—he was actually having a *blast*. His expression was one of comfort and relaxation... *And judging by his red complexion, a few beers, no doubt.*

"Come to our table when you're ready."

"Oh?" Becca wiped her eyes with her napkin and turned to face him. "I'll probably head over there in a few—"

"Bill's about to do his speech. Me and Kelly'll clue you in."

A sudden surge of anxiety shot through every nerve in her body; she looked over her shoulder at Cecilia, who was smiling ear-to-ear.

"Go, Babe. And remember what I said."

Becca stood slowly (her newly healed leg still giving her phantom pains) and shuffled with Jim over to his table. On his way through the crowd, Jim waved at another table. When Becca saw the young adults at the table, her mouth dropped.

"Michael? Jessie? Oh, my *goodness;* I haven't seen you two

since you were in *high school!* Wow—and who are *these* little ones?"

Jim introduced Becca to his infant grandchildren, and Becca's heart absolutely *melted* as she caught up with them. It reminded her that she wasn't the *only* one with precious things to lose in life...

He'd become so distant after Stacey left him. She was even *more* surprised to discover that Jim and Stacey had rekindled their friendship. *Good... he needs someone to keep him grounded.* Becca certainly was sick of doing *that* job.

After the pleasant detour, Jim led Becca to his table, where Kelly and Bill sat. Jim and Kelly had been passing around a super-sized bowl of dinner salad, but Bill wasn't a salad guy. Instead, he was choking down a tiny cocktail of *giant* red-skinned shrimp.

Not exactly a cowboy-sized portion there, eh, Boss?

"*Becca!* You look lovely," Kelly beamed, greeting Becca with a peck on the cheek as she joined their table. "Are you excited to get back into the field?"

Her breath escaped in a massive *sigh.* "You have *no* idea, Kelly. I'm so damned *bored!*"

"Don't worry. We've got work waiting for you on Monday, so don't party *too* hard this weekend." Bill patted Becca's shoulder as he stood, before he produced an envelope from his jacket pocket. "This is for you, Rebecca. I'm sorry I didn't get it to you before Christmas."

Becca tore the envelope open and pulled a paper check out of it. It was made out to her name. Her eyes found the amount on the check and—

"*Bill!* I can't accept this."

"I told you I was giving you and Jim a Christmas bonus if you caught the 'Mauler'. And you *did.*" He guffawed loudly when she glanced up at him, tears forming in her eyes. "Don't worry; Kelly's office also gave her a nice bonus."

Becca was dumbfounded. "But *sir,* this is more than I make in three *months!*"

"Yeah, well, when I get done embarrassing you on stage, you'll probably think I didn't give you enough!" Bill guffawed as her eyes kept darting back and forth *on* the check.

"Thank you, sir." Her eyes were glossy, but she managed a smile. She felt vindicated. For the first time since last January 1st, she felt like she *deserved* the honor.

Bill's eyes flicked towards the bar, where his wife was slamming a cocktail. "I'm going to go make sure Nina isn't gonna start singin' karaoke; then I'm heading to the 'office' to 'fill out some paperwork.' When I return, I'll go up." As he walked away, Becca stood there, watching her boss squirm through the crowd towards the bar...

And Rebecca Taylor *was* alright.

"He's gonna mention *everyone* involved in the case," Jim warned. "I just wanted you to be ready; he's gonna lay it on *thick.*"

"Oh, I'll be *fine,*" Becca laughed nervously, waving it off despite knowing full well she was *already* struggling with her emotions, which felt like they were dancing on the cutting edge of a knife. "I've been through the worst—I can handle Bill *fluffing* me up a bit."

"We know you can," Kelly offered. "You might not see it, but you've changed a *lot,* Becca. And I mean for the better. You've *earned* the right to soak this in."

She held up her glass of beer and tipped it to her before finishing her drink. With a shit-eating grin, Becca exaggeratedly tipped her *own* glass (filled with Coca-Cola... she *was* driving, after all) before scanning the crowd again.

Her eyes found Agent Miles McLain at the bar—he was oblivious to the evening's darling now sitting in his chair. He, too, would receive awards for his work that night, but the gunshot he took had barely bruised him through his vest... *unlike Kelly's wound.*

Kelly had *also* been shot on September 12th. Her vest had *mostly* stopped the bullet, but Agent McLain had his pistol loaded with target rounds. Full metal jacket. Luckily, it didn't pass *through,* but the damage to her torso was palpable; the shot would've penetrated just below her left breast. Becca was one of the lucky *few* that Kelly showed her wound to. By the time a week had passed, her *entire* chest was purple, and she couldn't lift her *arm!*

Their plan was doomed the moment Crystal stepped out of the Camry that night. She'd intended on shooting *everyone* and escaping with Alset—the mother, Khari, was out of the loop *entirely!* It turned out that *Crystal* was the person Alset called, *not* his mother. They *had* monitored his phone call, but he never said *anything* that raised any alarms.

Alas, as soon as 'Mack Miles' began asking questions, Becca's Eclipse swung around the corner to pursue the pickup—and that was all the distraction Crystal needed.

It had been Alset who'd broken the tension. He'd called out McLain as FBI, so Crystal drew her pistol and fired without hesitation. Her shot was nearly point-blank, but it hit McLain directly in the vest. Alset then took McLain's pistol, and while Kelly was focused on Crystal, Alset fired. She'd been knocked out by the shot momentarily, collapsing in the back of the Yukon.

Bill was the only other person on-site who discharged their weapon, shooting Crystal in the leg. They took her into custody once Alset fled the scene... leaving *her* to answer for *his* crimes. She was the only suspect that survived, and she was still facing trial.

I wonder if I hadn't caught Alset's mother, Khari, how the situation might've unfolded? Kelly might've been able to save

Marissa without me, but—

No, Becca, stop. I don't want to dwell on that anymore. That's all theoretical nonsense; I did catch up with Khari. I did stop Alset. 'What ifs' are only survivor's guilt, or perhaps impostor syndrome, trying to get me to feel like I was simply lucky... but even if I'm completely wrong, the reality of what happened is all that matters.

Kelly pulled a small box out of her purse and offered it to Becca, who was lost in thought. "We were given this a few days ago; I figured it was the *perfect* Christmas present."

She turned the ornately wrapped box in her hands, wrapped in shiny foil wrapping paper with purple ornaments. *And little Vikings logos on them.* Her eyes stung as they beheld her gift.

"If you open this *now,* it might make you upset. I just wanted to warn you."

"I'll open it when we get home, then." Becca leaned in, planting a friendly kiss on her as she accepted the present. "Thank you, Kelly." As she placed the box in her jacket pocket, she glanced back at Mike's table, where she heard a... grown man crying?

"What in the *world*—excuse me a moment, you guys," she politely excused herself, as she squeezed between tables. Her heavy wool jacket brushed against everything; she regretted not taking it off and leaving it with CeCe as she bumbled towards the table of survivors. When she arrived, it was *Julie* who spoke up first.

"Oh, greetings, Rebecca; everything is fine." Julie's eyes flicked away, and Becca followed them to Jason. He was weeping uncontrollably into his clenched hands.

"I can *see* that." She stifled a giggle as she sat next to Jason. "What's the matter, dude?"

"No," he whined, sniffing hard as he lifted his head. *"Nothing's* the matter—I'm just very *happy."*

Jason revealed what was hiding in his hands: a jewelry box.

"Wha—?" was all that Becca had time to mutter before Julie

lightly grabbed her chin, directing her face towards Julie's upheld left hand. A brilliant, glistening diamond sat buried amongst many smaller gems, set in a *gorgeous* rose gold ring.

Jesus, that had to have cost a fortune. What is the old saying... three months' salary? She tried to recall what Ken told her he'd paid for *her* ring, but that was long ago...

A lifetime ago.

"I *just* proposed to this guy, and he hasn't bothered accepting yet. He's been *weeping* the entire time." She shook her head, smiling slyly as she did so. "I know this guy; he cried at the ending of *Twister.*"

So Julie paid for her own ring? How does that even work?

"*You* two? I didn't even know!" She hugged Jason from behind, then embraced Julie. "Congratulations! That's *amazing,* you guys!"

"We shouldn't even be *alive,* but thanks to you, I get to marry the woman of my dreams!" Jason stood up, blotting snot and tears away from his face with a napkin as he did so. "We wouldn't have met without you, Becca; I-I can't even *begin* to thank you enough —"

"*Please,* you're so melodramatic," Julie scoffed, playfully slugging him in the shoulder. She smiled her drop-dead gorgeous smile at Becca, causing her to blush profusely. Julie *was* truly a lovely-looking woman for her age.

"So... *you* two..." Becca smirked. "When did you start *dating*? After—"

"I assisted him with his fantasy football league. He's in first place, now, by the by. He asked me out... and I suppose I fell in *love* with the guy." She flashed her ring again, and Becca swooned. It wasn't the first time she'd considered asking Cecilia to marry her, but now that this was behind her—

"You know, Becca," Mike interjected, smiling down at his

wife, "you touched all of our lives. My marriage is stronger than ever now, thanks to you. Ever since September 11th, I've—"

"*Whoa...* Wait a second, now," Becca backed up, holding her hands high. "Look, you guys; I am *beyond* grateful for all the nice things you're saying, I want that to be clear. But, all I did was endanger the group... *You* guys got out of that building without me.

"I was a broken woman before 9/11. I was depressed and *beaten*. In that tower, I had no choice but to suck it up and do the job. Quarren was the first person in that building to help me, but *that* was after I'd already put *him* in danger to *begin* with."

"Well... if you hadn't chased Q down that stairwell, wouldn't he have been trapped above the impact?" Mike's arms were folded tightly against his chest, his polo shirt stretched to the seams.

They might split like a banana peel if he flexes any further.

"Possibly... but *anyway,* I had to find my mark. I had to stop Alset. I wasn't focused on helping Q escape—"

"True, but your leadership pointed Q in the correct direction," Julie interjected. "Not to *mention,* perhaps your disinterring of Jason's party doesn't occur."

"Yeah! And, you found *us* because of that, *too.*" Jason was finally under control of his slobbery blubbering, and was facing the others, still seated at the table.

Becca blushed again. "Well, sure, but it was by accident. We *literally* stumbled on you guys—"

"Yeah," Jason nodded. "And you directed us up a floor. Donny was a *hard-ass;* he wasn't gonna listen to me, or even *Mike.* We might've been stuck in that room for an hour if you hadn't come by."

"But that was pure *luck,* right? I stumbled across everyone that I helped; I was—"

"Incorrect, Agent Taylor... *I* stumbled on *you,* if you recall?"

Julie laughed as she reached for her glass of champagne. "If you hadn't been searching for the others, if you'd continued downward, I would've been left abandoned in that stairwell, like *countless* others did—and I don't blame them. Someone else might've helped, certainly... but nobody *had* to that point. Perhaps I'd still have been there, forsaken in that stairwell, hobbling down the stairs when the building inevitably *collapsed,* if you hadn't assisted me. Who can truly say?"

Mike unfolded his arms, patting Becca on the shoulder. "In a way, it almost sounds like you were already beating your demons before you *ever* entered that building. You think it was pure luck, and perhaps some of it *was*. But don't fool yourself—you *led* us to Cecilia. You got us away from that serial killer. Cecilia might've gotten us down the rest of the way, but you saved our *lives."*

Mike leaned in, giving Becca a hug. "So yeah, you *did* save my marriage, you *did* save our lives, and thanks to you, these two found each other. I don't give a fuck what the other people think you did, or even what *you* think... I just know *I* think you're a damn hero. You should be *proud* of yourself, Agent Taylor."

"I am, but if it weren't for CeCe, then—"

"No." Mike released the hug, but gripped her hands tightly. "I mean, be proud of *you."*

Surprisingly, Becca's eyes remained dry as she playfully fought his persuasive grasp. "I am. And I'm proud of you guys, as well. We did well, didn't we?"

Mike's own eyes didn't move. He continued holding her hands in a vice grip. "Rebecca..."

"Okay, *fine!"* she exclaimed, forcefully shrugging Mike's hands away. "I *am."*

"Becca?" came a voice from behind her chair. She turned to see Kelly standing beside them. "Bill's coming back; do you want to sit with us?"

She turned back to Mike once more, his eyes still screaming at Becca to take some credit for her actions. Yielding, she nodded silently at him.

"I *am* proud, Mike. I *swear* to you."

That would have to suffice. He waved his hand towards Kelly's table, nodding subtly before focusing on his half-eaten steak. She quickly hugged the others before returning to the other table with Kelly, walking arm-in-arm as they navigated the tight maze of dinner tables and waiters.

"This is either going to be completely business-like," Becca began as she held onto Kelly's arm for dear life, "...or overwhelmingly *cheesy.*"

"Actually, it *ain't* bad. I've read his speech. You're gonna *like* it."

Bill emerged from the restroom with a few sheets of notebook paper in his hand. His face was covered in perspiration; Becca suspected he hadn't *actually* used the bathroom.

He looks nervous... I've never seen him sweat like this before.

Bill swallowed his own lump as he climbed the steps to the portable stage they'd erected beside the bar and tapped the microphone. A loud series of *thumps* emanated from its speakers, accompanied by a brief *squeal* of feedback, which announced his presence to the restaurant.

It was effective; within a few seconds, the dining room's constant ambiance of chatter and the *clink* of dishes fell silent. Other than a few stray coughs and shuffling feet, their attention belonged to William Bushnall.

*　　　　*　　　　*

"Good evening, ladies and gentlemen, and Merry Christmas and Happy Holidays to all. Thank you all for coming. Before I discuss the main reason we're all gathered here tonight, I wanted to give a quick update on a few things.

"Father Bradley Jackson from St. Francis hosted a midnight mass at Ground Zero on Christmas Eve, this past Monday, and the turnout was *fantastic*. He's collecting donations to raise money for the families of first responders, so if anyone here's interested in helping out, *please* speak with him. Stand up, Father, and let everyone know who led that *beautiful* mass for us."

Becca took her seat at the FBI table as they applauded. She wasn't the most religious woman in the world, but she *was* the only person not applauding, so Becca joined them.

I don't know why he was nervous; he's a natural at this!

"Next, I'm happy to announce that we have an agent returning from her leave..." Bill's eyes landed on Becca's, and her mouth went dry.

Here we go... Clear your mind... write your story... and breathe, Rebecca. You got this.

"...and I cannot be thrilled enough for her return. *This* Special Agent was the driving force behind stopping the 'Manhattan Mauler', but she suffered injuries in the field during that mission that kept her sidelined until she recovered. You all know who I'm talking about—we'll get back to *you* in a minute, Agent Taylor..." The crowd let out a murmuring laugh as Becca's face went the shade of a ripened tomato.

"We have a few cases where I need my *best* agent in the field, so I'm thrilled to announce that she'll be reactivated this Monday." He smiled brightly at Becca, this time addressing her directly as his eyes met hers.

"Welcome back to the Bureau, Taylor. It's great to have you on the team."

The crowd erupted into a raucous round of applause, and rather than feeling embarrassed, Becca felt a different emotion—

pride. She slowly stood up and took a moment to look around. The entire room was cheering enthusiastically for her, just as they had when she'd walked in almost an hour ago.

Truly. I am proud of myself.

She spun slowly in place, staring unbelievably at the cheering people, unable to process the amount of support that was lovingly presented to her... yet grateful for every clap she got. As the applause washed over her in waves, she gave the diners a gracious bow, and the cheering grew temporarily in volume and density before *finally* winding down.

Bill cleared his throat before continuing. "We're here to celebrate the successful resolution of a case, but we're *not* here to forget about 9/11. I know we've all heard this to death, but we will *never* forget," a spattering of applause cut Bill off, and he paused momentarily. "We will never forget what happened, or the sacrifices our friends and family made that day."

He pointed towards a table in the back where four uniformed NYPD officers sat with their wives. Becca thought she saw Officer Spilner at the table. He was the officer in the tower who'd been watching the elevators when the plane hit.

But she recognized no others. Bill later told her that one of them was Officer Rumph—the policeman who tailed Alset the morning of September 11th, along with his partner.

"Whether it was our allies in blue, our partners at the Bureau-" Bill's hand waved across the room towards the rows of tables where *dozens* of FBI employees were seated. "Or, the countless firefighters that climbed those towers, both the ones that are with us tonight..."

He motioned towards the table behind Becca's, where CeCe was still seated. The dozens of firefighters and captains, lieutenants and chiefs, stood and applauded as if they were giving Bill a standing ovation. The fever-pitched clapping combined with a few whistles and hollers as they clapped for each other, and the air *vibrated* from the roar.

Bill cleared his throat and continued. "As well as the ones who are *not.*"

The room fell silent; the firefighters returned to their seats. Becca stared in awe as the men and women who, moments ago, were cheering like they were at a Yankees World Series game... now sat silent, somber, and still.

"So many of our loved ones are not with us today... and *all* of them would've been welcome. They aren't here because they sacrificed *everything* to protect the people of New York.

"Some of those we lost were not *soldiers* in this battle. Innocent civilians, minding their own business as they prepared for their workdays, or those unlucky souls who needed to catch a flight that day. Folks simply trying to live their *best* lives. That day, those evildoers who decided to invade that peaceful existence brought darkness into their brightly burning lives.

"But to those of us that took it upon ourselves to bring light back into their world; to restore hope where *all* hope was lost... the first responders... they had a choice. They knew that going into that building most likely meant meeting their God... and yet, they chose to do the job."

Jeez, that was really good. I wonder who helped him write this...

"For those of us who lost everything, or know someone who performed that ultimate sacrifice, we honor you now, in this short moment of silence."

Bill lowered the microphone and bowed his head. The room fell silent; servers halted in their tracks, and the only sounds were a few coughs as Becca slowly closed her eyes. She was bracing herself for that everlasting image of a red headband falling past a window on the 91st floor... but this time, she didn't see the headband.

This time, I see Quarren.

After thirty seconds or so had passed, the crowd erupted again, standing up as if Bill had finished his speech, but he held a hand up as he cleared his throat.

"Thank you, folks, thank you... If you'll please bear with me, I have a few more things to say.

"As we know, a lot of us did *not* return home. But some of us did. We all knew the stakes that September day, but we *all* had a job to do. And two of my bravest agents did just that. Jim Serrano and Rebecca Taylor are two of my best, serving my branch with the utmost courage, honor, and integrity that any FBI Agent worth their salt would be *lucky* to showcase... or any Director would feel lucky to have on their team. I trust these two with my *life,* and that's why I entrusted *this* young lady's life with them."

He motioned to Marissa's family, where a spattering of applause interrupted Bill's speech.

They don't speak much English, but there's no mistaking the vibe in the room; I hope they realize how everyone loves them. I know how happy they make me, seeing them sitting there as a family...

"Agent Serrano was *severely* injured just before Ground Zero was attacked, and Agent Taylor had a choice to make: stay behind and tend to her partner, or go after her suspect. It's hard to understand if you're not in the business, but our partners are some of our *best* friends. Serrano and Taylor have been working together for years, and when you've worked alongside a partner for that long, they become *more* than just a friend. Your partner is your *brother...* your *sister*.

"When Agent Taylor saw her partner injured, she had to make that choice, as impossible as it might have seemed. And she went with her instincts, prioritizing the job over her fears. Despite his injuries, Serrano, along with Agent Kelly Willis, were all integral pieces of this puzzle-solving team, and Taylor knew they were more than capable of handling themselves, so she did the job.

"When she pursued her suspect into that tower, it was *not* yet under attack. She diligently climbed to the very top of the North Tower and began going down floor by floor, searching for the Manhattan Mauler. So, when American Airlines Flight 11 struck the tower at 8:46 a.m. that Tuesday morning, she was a *victim*, along with countless innocent people."

Becca peeked at her perfectly-polished Pulsar; the time was 6:48.

"She could've dropped the job and focused on her *own* escape, and who could *blame* her? She has a wonderful family at home—same as *most* of us first responders. Unlike most of you who went up after that first plane, however, she was there from the *absolute* first moments of terror.

"And yet, she triumphed. Moments after the plane struck Tower One, Agent Taylor had made friends with a survivor, and together, they began to escape the hellscape that I can't even *begin* to imagine. Unfathomable horrors were in that building, and yet, Taylor and her new friend braved them *all*, helping others down the stairwells while keeping an eye out for her suspect. Thanks to both of them, several civilians evacuated the tower before time ran out, and they are here with us today, as well."

Bill motioned his hand towards Mike's table. It was Julie who first stood, acknowledging him. Becca giggled; she was a *very* odd duck, but she enjoyed that aspect about her.

"That's where Cecilia Chapman comes in. CeCe, I am so grateful for the support you've given to my friend, Rebecca. It's refreshing and *inspiring* to see someone so willing to support the ones they care for, even in such a *terrible* situation. When Agent Taylor ran into Cecilia during her escape, her partner was doing *her* job, and yet, she understood the seriousness of *Becca's* job.

"She knew, more than anyone not seated at that table, how *important* it was personally, for Agent Taylor to capture the suspect, and save the girl from her tormentors. So Miss Chapman took it upon herself to help this group of civilians, allowing Agent Taylor to focus on her job. This brave firefighter helped many civilians evacuate, *including* Agent Taylor's group. Knowing their time was short, she was capable, and she led a small team down the stairs, getting them out with *minutes* to spare."

Becca looked over at CeCe, who was beaming proudly back at her. CeCe's hazel eyes were glazed with adrenaline; she looked like she might burst at any moment.

"Meanwhile, Agent Taylor and her friend—who survived the initial plane attack alongside her, by the way—continued their escape, intercepting the suspect on their way down. An *awful* struggle between her and the suspect took place, which would've been terrifying for *any* agent to confront, but she was able to capture the perpetrator thanks to her friend. I want to take a moment to shout him out.

"Quarren Cambanda. He was an immigrant from Africa who came to the United States in pursuit of the American dream. He was minding his own business and looking for a job. He had the right *idea;* he picked the wrong place... the wrong *time.* After surviving the attacks, this man not only saved Agent Taylor's life... he helped in evacuating others as well."

Bill paused a moment, and Becca swallowed hard. "Unfortunately, Mr. Cambanda did not survive the day."

"However, he *was* directly involved in the arrest of Alset Aholé, and if he were alive today... I'd give the man a job *anywhere* in the Bureau he liked. He sounded like a great man, Becca." Cracking, she looked down at her lap, unable to meet Bill's gaze any longer.

"I am so grateful to Q for assisting you that day. Thank you, Quarren. God bless you."

I am, as well, boss. I miss him more than you could ever know.

Kelly glanced at Jim, who hid a subtle smile. Becca didn't notice it.

"In a moment, I'll be giving the microphone over to our outstanding FBI Director, who has some... goodies he wants to pass out to some folks. But before I step off the stage... Thank you, Cecilia Chapman. Thank you to my wonderful agents for doing a great job.

"So in closing, tonight is a celebration of bravery, in the face of danger. We celebrate those who went into those towers and those who were already inside. We honor those who weren't able to come home to their families that night. And, we *strive* to be as brave as those who ignored that little voice we all have in the back of our heads, and put their personal goals and dreams aside, sacrificing *everything* for the sake of doing the job.

"To those of you, I salute *you,* and I *thank* you." His grin stretched so far that Becca couldn't help but match it.

"And God bless America."

The crowded restaurant rose to its feet once again; the place was *rocking.* Kelly turned towards Becca without looking in her direction, muttering to her. "Stand up, Becca. Give the people a bow—"

She cut herself off as she turned her head and saw her oldest friend *standing* on her feet, waving to the folks throughout the Odeon. Becca's eyes were dry, and she had a huge smile plastered to her face.

It seemed that she would have trouble with trauma no longer.

XXX

"An Ornately-Wrapped Box"

"That was so *nice* of her!" CeCe exclaimed as they hung their coats in the entryway closet, looking excitedly at the small box Becca had removed from her jacket. She'd nearly forgotten about it; the night had gone on longer than expected. The food was excellent; the company was *outstanding*.

But the award ceremony *completely* threw her off. Even Kelly hadn't seen *that* one coming. Twirling the ribbon in her fingers the entire drive home, she now held the medal in her hand, admiring the glossy golden finish on its five points.

A few months ago, I was worried about getting fired... and now I've been awarded one of the highest awards in the Bureau? She nearly laughed at the thought.

Becca received the FBI Star tonight.

It was awarded for her bravery despite her injuries. Jim was *also* awarded the FBI Star, while Kelly received the FBI Medal for Meritorious Achievement. Director Robert Mueller had flown from Washington *solely* for the ceremony.

An excited Labrador began smacking his tail against the wall with a *thump-thump-thump*. She replaced the medal in her hands with Kelly's gift, deciding to open the present right away instead of waiting. Her anticipation was at a fever pitch; Kelly always knew the *perfect* present to get Becca.

CeCe watched in tipsy fascination as Becca admired the present. *"Really,* Babe? The *Vikings?* Can we *burn* it instead?"

"Yeah... and we can use your Jets jacket as kindling."

She carefully removed the wrap and opened the box to reveal... a tattered old wallet.

Becca's *gasp* woke Pepper up. *"What in the...?"*

Instantly, Becca closed her eyes, and instead of their home, full of Christmas decorations and warmth... she found herself on the 91st Floor of the North Tower of the World Trade Center.

CeCe rested her dizzy head against Becca's shoulder as she watched on. Becca, however, felt a familiar lump in her throat. She inspected the wallet as her girlfriend watched on.

The wallet's navy blue canvas was severely damaged, yet Becca recognized it immediately. Despite its *atrocious* condition—stains from several dried fluids, dirt, and shreds rendered it nearly unrecognizable—there was a telltale giveaway: a dirty, faded photo of 'Mega Man' adorning its front cover.

Even in *this* condition, it was still held closed by its Velcro clasp. The smells that wafted from the canvas *instantaneously* transported Becca back to the North Tower... and her heart skipped a beat.

Of course, Kelly knew... She always knows...

"Is this *your* wallet, Becca?" Although drunk, CeCe knew full well that Becca used a brown leather wallet. "No... whose wallet *is* this?"

It must've survived the collapse, somehow? I know they've been finding items at Ground Zero like this, but never thought in my wildest dreams I would see this again...

"What's wrong, Babe?" Cecilia withdrew her face from Becca's shoulder, her demeanor shifting rapidly from flirtatious to solemn. "Why are you *trembling?*"

"It's Quarren's wallet."

With a *gasp*, Cecilia flew backwards against the wall as Becca slowly ripped open the Velcro. *Barely* able to hold itself together, the wallet opened to reveal a fake ID card—a slightly melted driver's license claiming he was "Quarren Michaels" from Los Angeles, California. Becca chuckled to herself, remembering Q's face when she'd pulled his wallet from his slacks back on the 91st floor...

A lifetime ago.

Becca searched the wallet, finding three scorched dollars in cash, a crusty, expired condom *(oh, Q...)*, and a few business cards, including a handful from some of the offices in the North Tower. She found his green card—the *same* one that had revealed a few truths about Q in the Tower. The *real* find, however, was his Senegalese driver's license... which was *thankfully* laminated. Printed on the back was his home address.

"What are you going to do with it, Becca?"

She replaced the cards, closing the Velcro tightly.

"I'm going to mail the wallet to his family."

"Oh, *Babe!*" CeCe gave her a kiss that tasted like whiskey and wine. It turned Becca off, but she didn't care; Cecilia's desire to go upstairs was the *last* thing on her mind.

She snagged the fake ID from the wallet. "I'm gonna steal this for myself to keep a picture of him; I'll send them some cash in exchange." She glanced back at her girlfriend, who was still watching with widened eyes. "I'll be a while, CeCe. I want to write them a letter."

"I'll be in bed, Babe," CeCe muttered as she leaned in for a kiss before stumbling up the stairs, Pepper bounding behind her.

When CeCe left the room, Becca dug into a kitchen drawer, fishing out a fake Holy Bible. Inside was a white envelope filled with cash. Quickly, she rushed towards her computer desk, snagged the photo paper from her fancy new printer, and plopped copy paper into the tray. Her iMac booted up while she stuffed $1000 into the flimsy wallet; it nearly *burst* at its weakened seams.

Finally, Becca sat down to write. Her word processing program stared back at her, its judgmental little cursor blinking rapidly, mocking her. Eventually, Pepper returned to her side as she contemplated what to type...

Becca cleared her mind, took a deep breath... and began writing.

To the loved ones of Quarren Cambanda,

I wanted to tell you all a short story about the most wonderful friend I've ever met. My name is Rebecca Taylor, and I work for the FBI. I was inside the Twin Towers on September 11.

I was in pursuit of a kidnapper, who was in the North Tower with me. After the attack, I befriended Quarren, and we teamed up to escape the building. As we evacuated, my suspect attacked me, and I was nearly killed. Your son sacrificed his life to stop a serial killer, and not only saved my life, but saved a little girl's, as well.

I only knew Quarren for a short time, but he touched my life in so many ways. It breaks my heart that I will never see him again. But I have his memory, which I'll cherish for the rest of my life. When his wallet was recovered from Ground Zero, I knew it belonged to his family and friends. I wasn't sure if there was supposed to be any money inside, so I've included a few bucks. Hopefully, you can exchange it to your local currency.

To anyone who knew Quarren, to ANYONE who
LOVED him, thank you so much for loving
him. He loved me in the short time he
knew me, and I know he loved each and
every one of you, as well. He deserved so
much love, so I hope you will love him
for the rest of your lives. Because I
certainly will.

With eternal love and appreciation,

Rebecca Taylor

FBI; Manhattan, New York; United States
of America

In her entire *life,* she'd never been this excited to show up for work on a Monday, but today, Becca happily waltzed into the office. However, her spirit was broken almost *immediately* as she reached her cubicle. The basket where incoming files went was completely empty; she glanced over the cubicle walls towards her boss's office, which sat dark and abandoned.

With a groan that started somewhere near her *shoes,* she looked at the clock atop her desk, loyally ticking away the seconds of Becca's life.

**12 31 2001 TUE
8:56 AM**

Two years to the day since the night that changed her life forever. She hadn't thought about January 1st since the dinner at the Odeon. In fact, it was beginning to feel more like a *footnote* in her past, rather than a ghost that continued to haunt her.

This *desk,* on the other hand... it would bring her no small amount of *joy* if she could burn the thing to the ground.

Becca glanced over her cubicle wall at Bill's office a second time. The lights flicked on. *He must've just arrived to work.* She considered greeting him, but thought better of it.

"Yeah... I'm not in the mood to get *screamed* at, first thing in the morning."

Well... that meant she had *nothing* to do... and without a case to start on or *any* idea where to begin, she did the only thing she could *think* to do: she went into Jim Serrano's office.

"Jim!" she exclaimed as she burst through his door. He was seated at his desk with a cold cup of coffee and a stack of files; she wasn't sure *which* he was more disgusted with.

"It's about *time* you got here, Taylor. It's almost nine."

"It's my first day back, Jim—cut me a *little* slack." She walked

444

around his desk to peek over his shoulders. "Whatcha got?"

"Another anthrax scare," he grumbled, looking at a photocopy of an envelope; the genuine article *long* since regulated to the evidence room. Becca groaned as she slinked around the desk and plopped into an open chair opposite her partner.

"Oh, great... I get reactivated just in time to go back to paperwork."

Jim scoffed as he reached for his cold cup of coffee, before remembering its awful taste and reconsidering. "What, is regular agent work too low-brow for you, Miss Hotshot?"

"Please," she guffawed as she plopped her hands on his desktop with a *smack*. "I just think it's strange to put two agents so accustomed to working with action that—"

Becca stopped talking, hoping too late that Jim wouldn't have a rebuttal; some teasingly mean thing to make fun of her with.

"You miss the thrill of the chase... don't cha?"

Becca was caught off-guard; it wasn't the response she'd expected. She rocked backwards in her chair, scratching her chin softly as she spun around.

"Yeah... I think I *do.*"

"Good, because this isn't *our* case. This is mine."

"Oh?" She wheeled back, nervous anticipation building in her gut. "What do you mean?"

Jim took his cheater glasses off and glanced up at Becca.

"What, Taylor, you think that because *you're* on leave, I can't work a case *without* you?" He rubbed his temples and grimaced down at the desktop, before he tapped his cast with his pen.

"Taylor... my doctors haven't cleared me for field work yet; I'm stuck doing detective bullshit." He rubbed his temples, his eyes closed from exhaustion. Although his leg was coming along, he was *still* using crutches. "We're *not* working together on this one."

Becca nodded slowly, despite the anxiety threatening to bubble up in her tummy. Jim had returned to work *much* sooner than Becca had, by his *own* choice. It made sense; he didn't have a family at home to spend time with. Despite the news that she wasn't working with Jim... it was nothing she couldn't handle.

After all... she was *alright,* now.

"What is *our* case, then?"

Jim shrugged his shoulders without looking up again. "I dunno. Go ask Bill."

With a grimace, she rose back to her feet, and she started whistling, playfully messing up Jim's paperwork.

"*Watch* it, Taylor!" Jim grumbled as she did so, before she left his office. Jim was still a hard-ass... but he *was* still her friend, and she found his stone-faced demeanor refreshing... *when I'm not with him twenty-four-seven.*

As she closed the door behind her, she was preparing to turn —

"Taylor! Why aren't you working?"

A woman's voice, from a few cubicles away, closer to Becca's. Her heart skipped a beat...

I know that voice...

"Kelly?" Becca exclaimed as she sprinted away from Jim's office. She stood and saluted dramatically as Becca embraced her, nearly bowling Kelly over. "What are *you* doing here?"

"Well, I knew Jim was on assignment already, and I had the chance to transfer, so I made some calls..."

She transferred! She transferred! Becca was terrible at poker; Kelly could read her excitement on her face. *This is too good to be true!*

"Are you saying...?" Becca was practically bouncing on her toes.

"Yes, I am... *partner.*"

She leaped into the air with a holler, earning spiteful gazes from the other agents and aides working in the office. She lifted her from the floor, twirling her around.

"Easy, Becca!" she wheezed; Becca hadn't realized she was squeezing her so tightly. She placed Kelly back on the floor just as Bill's office door opened.

"Where's *your* cubicle, Kelly?"

Kelly giggled before pointing to Becca's cubicle. She didn't need to ask; Becca's eyes lit up like a Christmas tree. She'd been asking Bill for her own office for *years* now, but because Jim already had *his* own, she was always told no. Glancing around the office, she wondered where her new office might be—

"Taylor! Willis! In my office, *pronto!"*

"Yes, sir!" they screamed in unison. Becca began to glance at her Pulsar, but she stopped herself before she pressed the nubbin. The images of Becca's future office faded quickly away as she bounded around the cubicles with a familiar surge of adrenaline; she *always* used to feel like this going into her boss's office. It only occurred to her *briefly,* however; once Kelly shut the door, she sat in that familiar leather chair as her boss circled the desk like a *shark.*

"What's the scoop?"

"Come in, agents. I have a hot one for you two..."

About the author:

JSR is a Twitch streamer, known for performing over 400 speedruns—as well as his speedrunning Shiba Inu, Peanut Butter. Together, they've set over seventy world records and raised over $200,000 for charity. He lives in the Midwest and enjoys making music, improv comedy, and helping his community (in addition to reading, writing, and enjoying movies). His follow-up novel, "Raising Judy Kata", is being penned, with a targeted release in 2026.

Please visit thedoge-o.com for updates, links to social media and Twitch, PB&J content, and more!

Credits:
James "JSR" S: Author, editor, concept.
Nathan "OnlyLevelOne" W.: Cover and logo design
Kelly "Threach" M.: Beta Reader
Thywren: Beta Reader
Fred Coughlin: Beta Reader

Special thanks to:
Stephen "StormRider" C.
cmykFlutterby
Glasseyy
James & Christie O'Brien
Chris Perkins
Rob "Mea__Culpa" R.
Cesar Antonio Garcia Salinas